I0658746

The Prague Plot

The Cold War
Meets
the Jihad

James E. Mosimann

Brightview Press
Gainesville, Virginia

i

For Miloš Pacak
who left in 1948 and never returned,
and Jiři Pochobradsky,
who left in 1968 and did.

This book is a work of fiction. Names, characters, events and places are the product of the author's imagination or are used fictitiously. Any resemblance to persons, living or dead, or to actual events and places is coincidental.

Contents

Prologue
Early September

Like many a successful European entrepreneur, he wore an expensive dark suit with a double-vented jacket, black shoes of Italian leather, and a conservative tie. But Abdul Rahman, "the Servant of the Merciful," hated Western businessmen. He did not like their ways, he did not trust them.

Still more did he detest those godless unbelievers, the atheists. At least the infidels who were "People of the Book" (Jews and Christians) admitted Allah's existence in some fashion, although to Mr. Rahman, the Christians with their Trinitarian God were not monotheists.

There is one God and Muhammad is his messenger.

Rahman took his seat at the table and studied the three men across from him.

These men were distasteful. They were truly godless. They were former communists, and whatever ideals they may have had before, now their only god was money. The three were ruthless and without human conscience. They were "trustworthy" only because they would receive most of their payment *after* completion of the task.

Rahman, the "Servant of the Merciful," concluded his evaluation of the men before him. He knew only one by name, a Czech, a Mr. Moravec who had arranged this meeting.

Moravec stood to talk. He wasted no time. He finished his proposal in ten minutes.

Five minutes into the presentation, the normally unflappable Rahman was excited, after ten, he was stunned. *Is this truly possible?* He swallowed hard.

He studied the eyes of the other two men. There was no doubt. They believed Moravec. The proposal was genuine.

Incredible. It was a one-time opportunity! And Moravec's plan could work!

Rahman put his briefcase under the table.

He clenched his fist and exhaled a silent, *Allahu akbar!* *"God is great!"*

If these infidels could deliver what they promised, the United States, the Great Satan, would suffer a blow infinitely more deadly than the destruction of the twin towers!

The room was quiet. All eyes were on Rahman.

He peered out the window.

It was evening. The streets of the *staré město*, Prague's Old Town, were aglow with spotlights that hid the soot and decay of once-splendid buildings. Rahman cringed at the thought of decadent old structures and godless neighborhoods.

The West was dissolute. The time was indeed ripe for action. The worldwide Caliphate *would* be a reality, perhaps in his own lifetime.

Rahman drew in a deep breath. He paused to straighten his tie, then he made his decision.

He agreed to the infidel's terms, millions upon millions of Euros. His backers were true believers, flush with petrodollars. Thanks to the recent upswing in oil prices, money was no object.

Amid their smiles, Rahman stood to leave.

He did not shake the proffered hands. He would not soil his own. He managed a slight smile.

He strode from the room. The meeting was over.

Out on the street, a light rain fell as Abdul Rahman walked to his hotel. He did not notice. He mouthed over and over to himself,

"Allahu akbar! ... Allahu akbar! ... Allahu akbar!"

***

******

Chapter 1
Wednesday, November 17

Anne Simek did not like insects, not any of them, but mostly she detested roaches. It seemed that every time she rented a beach house on the Outer Banks of North Carolina, the roaches of coastal Carolina scheduled a convention at that spot. But today was to prove her fears unfounded. Her realtor cousin, Mila Patekova, had found a rental for her in the town of Corolla. The brand-new house was absurdly huge for one person, but Mila had obtained an off-season rate that was too good to pass up.

Moreover Mila had assured her that the house was completely pest-free. Anne wanted to believe her.

Anyway here she was, in Corolla, unpacking her bag in a bedroom whose high ceilings were bright with sunlight that streamed through wide glass doors. These latter opened on a railed deck two stories above the ground. Visible from the deck was a gray wooden walkway that stretched through the brown marsh grass to a tidal creek of the Currituck Sound.

The late afternoon sun shone on the pristine walls of the west-facing bedroom. Anne scanned the surfaces carefully, looking for dark specks that might move. There were none. She unfolded her bed linens. She had carefully washed them before her departure. They were free of six-legged invaders.

Gingerly, she pulled back the bed cover, fully expecting to see a brown form scuttle away from the light. Nothing. She sighed with relief, and attached the corners of her fitted sheet to the mattress. She tucked in the top sheet, and spread a light blanket, also from home, over it. A shake of the pillow into her clean case, and she was done.

Good old Mila, I thought I could trust you. You said this place was spotless, and it is!

Anne was tired, the drive to the island from Norfolk International Airport had been tedious, and the last part had been over a rough unpaved road.

She stretched out on the bed. *Why not grab a quick nap?* She shut her eyes.

***

Born in Chicago, Anne Simek was all American. Her birth certificate confirmed this. Thanks to her mother, (and to the Registrar of Births) it read "Anne Simek" not "Anna Simekova" as her Czech father might have preferred.

Anne's grandfather, Marek, was born near Prague in the town of Kladno. There, as a young man in June, 1942, he had watched columns of smoke spiral upward from Lidice, a village across the valley. Those dark spirals signaled the death of that village and its male inhabitants as Hitler avenged the assassination of his friend, Reinhard Heydrich, the deputy Reichsprotektor. Due to those columns of smoke, and the wanton slaughter they signaled at the hands of the Nazis, Marek became a dedicated communist, a true *Soudruh*, a true "Comrade." He stood with the Red youths in Prague's Wenceslas Square to celebrate the Party's ascent to power in 1948.

Twenty years later, in August, 1968, Marek's disillusioned son, Havel, (Anne's father to be) stood in that same Wenceslas Square as Warsaw-Pact armor brought all hope of the "Prague Spring" to a violent end. Later, and not far from that square, a puzzled Havel watched as Soviet-made tanks blasted the façade of the defenseless building that housed Rudé Právo, the newspaper of the Czechoslovak Communist Party. Only with the arrival of film crews from the Soviet news agency, Tass, did he understand that the event was staged for propaganda.

The next day Havel's good friend Johan or "Jan" stood with him in protest, but when troops fired above (and into) the crowd, Johan fled. Havel cried out.

"*Jane, kam jdeš?* 'Jan, where are you going?'"

To no avail. Johan disappeared down a side street.

Two days later, Havel was arrested as an anti-socialist agitator after an informant gave Havel's name to State Security, the *Státní bezpečnost*.

Anne's father spent over a year in prison. It was there that he learned that the informant was none other than his former friend, Johan.

After his "rehabilitation," Havel was released. He escaped the Czechoslovak Socialist Republic for Austria. There, he met Anne's mother, an American studying Physics in Vienna. After a rapid courtship, and the less rapid completion of her doctorate, the young couple returned to Chicago, where some years later, Anne was born.

***

Throughout his life, Havel Simek nurtured the bitterness of Johan's betrayal. Havel was by no means a Christian, but riding the "L" in Chicago to accompany his young daughter to school, he had repeatedly told Anne the story of Saint Peter fleeing from Nero's Rome.

As Anne understood it, Peter was fleeing persecution when he met the Christ heading towards Rome and asked him.

"*Quo vadis? Pane, kam jdete?* 'Where are you going, Lord?'"

To this, Christ had answered.

"To Rome to be crucified again."

At that reply Peter, convicted of cowardice and lack of faith was shamed into changing his mind. He went back to Rome to, himself, be crucified.

To young Anne, this story was at best a garbled version of her father's experience in Wenceslas Square. True, like the fleeing Peter, her father had posed the question, but he had not fled. It was Johan, the one questioned, who had run away.

Accurate analogy or not, these discrepancies were unimportant to her father. To him the connection was vivid.

Johan's answer to "Quo vadis?" was for Havel to be "crucified" instead of him!

***

To Anne, now nearly thirty, the story might have remained just that, a story, but for the fact that Johan's son Peter Zeleny, a young M. D., recently had immigrated to Chicago to take a position in a local Mental Health Clinic. Anne had spotted Peter's photograph in a newspaper article announcing his appointment. She once had met Peter during her (aborted) study of Medicine at Charles University in Prague.

When she showed the picture to her father, his eyes had bulged while his face turned purplish gray. Slumping into his chair, he had signaled weakly for a glass of water.

The contrast between her father's ashen face and Peter's smile in the photo impacted Anne. In those two expressions, Anne saw how bitterness destroyed its bearer, not its target. She resolved to the best of her ability to live in the present, and never to dwell on past hurts.

After that newspaper article, Anne thought no more of Peter Zeleny or his father, Johan. She separated herself from old family issues, and happily immersed herself in her own doctoral studies in Philosophy and Religion. Her work filled her life, and the Outer Banks became her favorite locale to think and write.

***

Anne awoke with a start. The room was deep in shadows. *How long did I sleep?* She sat up. To the west, the sun was only a red glow on a horizon interrupted by dark clouds. She shook her head clear, stood up, and reached for the light switch.

She hesitated. The thought of brown forms with six spiky legs flashed before her. She steeled herself and flipped the switch.

The room flooded with light, but there was no movement, no scuttling. No roaches, nothing! She exhaled with relief. *Score two for Mila!*

Anne first met her cousin Mila in Prague when Anne had been a student at Charles University. Since that time, Mila had emigrated from the Czech Republic. She now had her "Green Card," and was on the way to U. S. Citizenship. Mila worked as a realtor on the Outer Banks and neighboring mainland. Her residence and Realty Office were in Nags Head.

Anne's trust in Mila, was not limited to roaches. Mila had forwarded to her an unsigned letter from Prague. The anonymous writer, a man, knew of Anne's scheduled vacation from Chicago to the Outer Banks and wanted to meet her there. Mila knew and vouched for him. She had assured Anne that the visitor was trustworthy with good intentions. With some trepidation Anne had agreed to meet him during her visit to Corolla. *I have to trust Mila!*

Anne stared out over the dark deck. Out on the sound, red and green pin points of light marked the movements of distant boats.

In close, barely discernible among the moonlit shadows, an old man rowed a small skiff past the end of her dock. Anne was not worried. Mila had told her of the harmless "local graybeard" who occupied a drab shack on the sound. Still, she was fully exposed in the illuminated room. She pulled the heavy curtains shut across the sliding glass doors and wedged a heavy stick in the slide's runway.

Besides that shack, no other houses were nearby. Mila had found an isolated location near Corolla.

Anne left the bedroom for the living area where an expansive glass front faced towards the ocean. The drapes were drawn, but even when open, no waves were visible. The view of the beach was blocked by extensive dunes topped with wavering Sea Oats backed by clumps of brush whose evergreen branches were rounded by salt-spray.

She sank into the padded sofa and clicked on the TV.

American football. *No thanks!*

She thought to change the channel, but hit the off button instead. She reached for her laptop and opened the cover. Moments later she was typing vigorously.

***

It was midnight when the first gust of wind rattled the wide glass doors. Rain quickly followed. Sheets of water hurled themselves at the sliding panels and flowed downwards in continuous waves. From the ceiling above, a flapping sound signaled distressed shingles, while lights flickered on and off as some distant power station tried to adjust to storm-lost lines and blown transformers.

Anne left her computer on the sofa and went to pull back the drapes. She could see nothing until a flash of lightning revealed clusters of sea oats pressed to the dunes in submission to the wind.

She started. Had she imagined a shadowy form heading her way, struggling through the dunes against the gusts? *Stop it Anne. Don't be a wimp! The meeting shouldn't be today.* (Anne had arrived early.)

Distracted, she looked at her feet. They were damp. Water had seeped under the doors and dripped off the window sills to merge into a pool that edged towards the expensive rug. Anne reacted. She stuffed towels from her suitcase under the openings. The towels soaked quickly. She found a bucket, wrung out the soaked items and replaced them. The seepage was contained. She returned to the sofa.

The lights flicked off and on again, then off for good. Outside, wind and rain continued unabated. Inside, the only light was from the pale screen of her laptop, now on battery power. Anne returned to the sofa, reassured by that dim glow.

The house was built on stilt-like wooden pilings that lifted the rooms on the first level well above the sand. The great room was higher still, on the top level, and Anne felt the floor and walls vibrate in the violent wind.

She shivered and pressed her arms against her body, prepared to wait out the storm.

After a while, the gusts lessened and came at more regular intervals. The rhythmic cadence of the shaking siding provided relative calm, hardly soothing but not as scary. The regular beat resonated with her thoughts.

Who wants to meet me and why?

Mila had vouched for this person! Mila trusted him.

She settled the computer on her lap and studied the words on the screen, a PDF of Thomas Aquinas' *Summa Theologica*. She concentrated on the text. Did Dietrich von Hildebrand agree with Thomas? She tried to focus, but her thoughts faded.

Her eyelids drooped. Moments later, she was asleep.

***

Also in Corolla, and not far away, the driver of a minivan squinted to keep the rutted roadway in his headlights, but without success. Sheets of water slid beneath and around the struggling wipers to coat the glass in an unbroken murky film. The driver cursed and pressed hard on the brake pedal. The wheels splashed and slid sideways to stop in a water-filled depression. He could drive no further, and he was nearly a mile from his target.

Damn this storm! The Northeaster had risen quickly and unexpectedly. No one had expected it this far south. It could spoil his plans. He cared little that from Delaware to North Carolina, the beaches were being gouged and scooped into the waters of the Atlantic by a surging Labrador Current. Those capitalist vacation-home owners would pass their losses onto others, but he could not let the weather delay him. He had a task to perform, for a large amount of money. He would continue on foot.

On the passenger seat were two semiautomatic pistols. The closest was a Makarov. He started to pick it up, but hesitated. The other pistol was a CZ-52, made in the Czech Republic. Its 7.62 mm (.30 caliber) ammo could penetrate a Kevlar helmet. It offered more penetration but less stopping power than the 9 mm Makarov. His grimace became a smile. The Czech weapon was appropriate for this task, and it certainly would suffice. He would not need much stopping power.

He stashed the Makarov under his seat and fondled the CZ-52. It had good features to protect against accidental discharge. He tucked it into his belt. Twisting, he donned a dark jersey and raised a gray poncho over his head. Then he opened the door and stepped out into the cold wind.

A gust tore the door from his hand and lifted the hood of the poncho upwards. The rain pelted his cheeks. He found that stimulating. He seized the door and slammed it shut.

The unpaved roadway was puddled with ankle-deep stretches of water. Shoes sloshing, he stepped onto dryer sand. Face to the wind, he trudged north behind the dunes. There was no beach. Instead, foaming waters, cut and coursed through a foot-deep channel along the edge of the dunes, well above the usual high-water line. The flow paralleled the roiling Labrador Current offshore.

He had walked only a few minutes when a flash of lightning revealed a large house ahead, standing high on a stilt-like foundation. The form disappeared instantly, but that momentary illumination sufficed. He smiled for a second time. The target was closer than he had imagined.

He trudged onwards. The wind exhilarated him. This storm was not bad. Thanks to it there would be no witnesses to what he had to do.

***

******

Chapter 2
Thursday, November 18

After last night's storm, the morning sun was bright. Jim Harrigan of the Duck, North Carolina, Police Department was not on duty, at least not officially. He was moonlighting in Corolla, to check the empty vacation home of a Norfolk resident who paid Jim to provide security for the property during the off-season.

Though not on police duty, Jim's police instincts were always active. At the moment those instincts were telling him that something was wrong. Ahead, to his right, a lone minivan appeared to be abandoned. It was "parked" off-road just behind the storm-washed dunes that fronted what had been a wide beach only the day before.

Harrigan carefully kept his wheels in the ruts of the narrow lane and guided his Ford F250 toward the stranded vehicle. He stopped his pickup facing the van, and immediately saw the problem. The two wheels on the passenger side had strayed from their rut and sunk up to the hubcaps in the sand. The driver-side wheels were still on the lane, but in the "wrong" rut to Jim's left.

Clearly, the ground in front of the minivan had been inundated during last night's storm. Evidently, the driver had swerved to avoid the pooled water and dug the wheels into loose sand.

The van was locked and unoccupied. Jim peered through the driver-side window. His worst worries were confirmed.

The window was splotched red with blood and the passenger seat was smeared with dark stains!

***

Harrigan circled the van to look for tracks, but if there had been any, the rain and floods had obliterated all traces. He climbed a dune. To the east, a path wove around and between impenetrable thickets whose tops had a salt-spray trimmed look. He followed it and, after climbing a final dune, the ocean came into view.

The waves were low, and the water looked cold. The beach, what was left of it, was littered with a stranded brown seaweed whose air bladders gave the dark washed-up clumps the look of leafy bubble wrap. Jim was no marine biologist, but a friend of his once had told him that the ugly seaweed was "bladderwrack."

Jim stepped onto the beach. He kicked at one of the clumps of wrack in frustration, but his foot met something more than seaweed. He stooped down. There entangled in the brown mass was a man's jacket. He pulled it free from the wet sand.

There was little wear on the cloth. It had not been in the water long, perhaps no more than a few hours.

There was a hole in the left front of the jacket matched by a similar hole in the back. Worse, the back of the jacket had a wide dark stain, clearly visible despite being soaked in the sea.

The stain surely was blood. The owner of the jacket had been shot once, from the front. The bullet had penetrated cleanly and exited almost as cleanly.

Jim felt certain that the passenger in the minivan and the wearer of this garment were one and the same. He looked ocean-ward. Had the body been swept away? He scanned the beach. At a distance, the accumulated drifts of bladderwrack could easily be mistaken for a body.

He took out his cell phone to inform the Duck Police Department of his find, but the battery was dead.

He pocketed the useless instrument and headed north along the cluttered beach.

***

In Nags Head, Mila Patekova awakened early. She was troubled. She had not revealed the identity of the visitor to her cousin, because Anne might not have agreed to meet him. Now Mila was filled with self-doubt. The visitor had arrived earlier than expected, and the meeting should have taken place last night.

Anne was not answering her phone. How had the meeting gone?

Either Anne's cell-phone was turned off, or last night's Northeaster had disrupted service from the cell tower. The latter possibility was not likely. Mila's phone service was working perfectly, and her call to the North Banks Restaurant & Raw Bar in Corolla had gone through perfectly.

She left a message.

"Anne, it's Mila. Call me!"

She decided to drive to Corolla. She picked her way through the water-filled depressions left in the parking lot by last night's storm. Her feet were dry when she reached her four-wheel-drive Ford Escape. At least she had the proper wheels to reach the remote location of Anne's rental in Corolla.

Mila headed north *Damn it, Anne return my calls. Don't you know that I worry?*

She pressed hard on the accelerator.

***

When she arrived in Corolla, Mila Patekova still had not heard from Anne Simek. The long lane to the beach house was covered with debris, and badly puddled. Even with four-wheel drive, there was the real possibility of getting stuck.

A broken branch of a scrubby pine blocked her passage. Mila hopped out and dragged it to the side of the driveway. She continued on foot. The beach house was in view, and she could see the rear deck clearly. At this distance, it appeared that the deck and its walkway over the marsh were unscathed by the storm. She saw no movement.

Mila continued her trek to the house. Several gulls sat on the rail of the side deck. They shifted feet and fluffed their feathers as Mila approached, but did not take flight. Last night's winds had rendered them wing-weary.

There were no cars parked under the elevated house, and there was no evidence of damage to the wooden supports. Mila

13

rounded the ocean side of the house and climbed the stairs to the top-level deck. She peered through the expansive glass front. She saw no one, but someone, doubtless Anne, had piled towels against the base of the sliding panels to stem incoming water. Mila nodded to herself. Anne was always responsible, even for property that was not hers.

Mila called through the door. There was no answer.

She dialed Anne's cell one more time. It switched immediately to message mode. She frowned and stuffed the unresponsive instrument into her handbag.

Mila studied the expanse of dunes to the east of the house. Again, no sign of Anne.

Damn it, Anne, where are you?

From the front deck, Mila descended steps to a gray wooden walkway that led through the dunes to the ocean. She stopped halfway. At her feet, projecting vertically from a crack between the weathered planks was a small object. She pushed it with the toe of her shoe. It flipped free of the crack and landed flat on the gray boards.

Mila recognized the item. It was a passport. It lay face down on its cover.

She picked it up. Before turning it over, she guessed what was on its cover. The reddish color, standard for the European Union, bore the words "ČESKÁ REPUBLIKA." It was a Czech passport whose pages were soaked from last night's storm and stuck together.

Mila's hands shook as she separated the cover from the first wet page. She hoped she was wrong, she was not. She saw the name,

Vaclav Pokorny.

She shuddered. It was Vaclav Pokorny who was supposed to meet her cousin, Anne.

Mila had arranged the meeting when Magdalena, a close childhood friend, had begged her to set it up. She had hesitated. Vaclav's father, Dr. Pokorny, had been Anne's professor in medical school. He had resigned from Charles University, when

Anne revealed that he wanted sexual favors in exchange for grades. Shortly thereafter, Anne had quit her studies in Prague to return to the U.S.

Still, Mila knew Vaclav a bit, and Magdalena had spoken well of him.

"Vaclav is trustworthy. He understands his father's weaknesses. He only wants to make things right for Anne. He's truly honest, ... etc. etc. And he'll be in the U. S. only for a short while. ... He has urgent business."

Finally, Mila had succumbed to Magdalena's pleas. She had arranged the meeting. But now?

Anne are you all right? What went wrong? What happened here?

***

Mila's realty agency handled the home that Anne had rented for the weekend, and she had a key to the rear door that faced the Currituck Sound. She followed the walkway on the side of the house towards the rear.

She looked down. Below the walkway was a dark object, half buried in the sand. Mila peered over the railing.

It was a gun.

***

Jim Harrigan stood on the beach before the wooden walkway. A contorted mass of brown bladderwrack lay on the sand that buried the first step. He kicked the seaweed aside. A small mottled crab scuttled sideways and disappeared.

This was the first house he had encountered since finding the blood-stained jacket. Jim left the beach and headed up the wooden planks.

A female voice stopped his progress.

"Excuse me. Can I help you?"

In a reflex action, Jim hid the blood-stained jacket behind his back. With his other hand he held out his badge.

"Sorry, I didn't mean to disturb you. My name is Harrigan. I'm with the Duck Police Department. Are you the owner of this house?

"I'm Mila Patekova. My realty handles this rental, but no, I'm not the owner. My cousin is renting here this weekend. What are you looking for?"

Jim hesitated. He decided to be forthright, but did not mention the bloodstains in the van or the bullet-holed jacket.

"There's an abandoned vehicle stuck in the dunes a half-mile south of here. This is the nearest house. I thought someone here might know something about it."

Mila turned sideways so that Harrigan did not see her slip Vaclav's passport into her handbag. She spoke.

"My cousin, Anne, was supposed to stay here last night. I thought she would be here. I don't know where she is."

Mila cast a furtive glance at the gun protruding from the sand. Harrigan did not notice. He handed her his card.

"Miss Patekova, when you see your cousin, please have her call me at the Duck Police Department. It could be important."

His tone scared Mila.

"Was someone hurt?"

"It would seem so, but whoever it was is gone."

"My God. It might be my cousin."

Jim Harrigan had not meant to alarm her. He thought of the jacket, and spoke.

"It wasn't your cousin. It was a man."

Mila was more disturbed than before. She felt the passport in her bag and glanced furtively at the gun in the sand.

She blanched. *My God, Anne, what have you done?*"

***

******

16

Chapter 3
Thursday, November 18

In Bethesda, Maryland, Jeannine Ryan lifted her head from her pillow and groaned. She pushed auburn strands of hair from her eyes as diagonal rays of sunshine lit the bedroom. The room faced southeast, onto a backyard bordered by a mature stand of tall tulip poplars and white oaks with a lower stratum of dogwoods. Thanks to the trees, privacy was not an issue. Her windows had no curtains, only blinds that were permanently up. One result of the unfettered windows was her habit of rising early. When there was no cloud cover, the early sun was bright.

Last night, Jeannine had worked on her laptop until two in the morning when, finally, the incessant swish of disturbed branches and the sound of rain pecking the window had lulled her senses. She had slept only a few hours.

She sat up, bare feet on the cold floor. She shivered, grasped her arms, and looked out the window. The storm had left a clear sky, but the back lawn was strewn with fallen branches amid a carpet of stripped leaves. Nothing moved. A lone squirrel huddled high on a branch, its fur fluffed against the cold.

Jeannine shook her head awake just as, dictated by the timer, the aroma of freshly brewed coffee filled the bedroom.

All right Jeannine, it's time to face the day.

Jeannine Ryan headed her own firm, Ryan Associates, that specialized in statistical consulting. She was a Ph. D. statistician, a specialist in statistical forensics, the exposure of fraudulent data. Aileen Harris, a Ph.D. in Bioengineering, was a minority owner of the company. Previously, she and Jeannine had found suspicious data in a medical research project. Their discovery uncovered terrorist plans to use a novel medical device to assassinate an Israeli official. Jeannine and Aileen, together with Bill Hamm their friend, had thwarted the plot.

Jeannine and Bill were close, but their romance was on hold. At the moment, work came first. Bill had returned to the CIA and was overseas, based in Vienna, Austria. Jeannine was occupied with building Ryan Associates into a first-class consulting firm for the detection of fabricated research.

Thanks to a contract with the Israeli government, Ryan Associates was financially solid. However, Jeannine was keenly aware of the dangers of over-expansion that depended on "future" contracts. Her last employer, the consulting firm StatFind, was now defunct partly due to such expansion. Because of that experience, Jeannine kept expenses to a minimum. Ryan Associates worked from a modest office in the refurbished basement of her home in Bethesda.

The basement was at ground level. The most expensive part of the office design had been the construction of an outside rear entrance along with a driveway and rear parking area. Those features had been installed after dickering with the local home owner's association and city officials. Approval had come at a potentially irritating cost; informally, Jeannine had agreed to help the home association when statistical assistance was needed.

After a quick shower, she slipped into her jeans and a gray pullover. She noted that they were the same size as when she had attended graduate school at Fairland University some years previously. Closer to thirty than twenty, Jeannine still drew second looks when she walked by.

Before going downstairs to the office, she stopped in the kitchen and poured a large cup of dark, French Roast coffee, black. She savored the rich aroma and sipped. Her head cleared.

Time to work.

***

Jeannine was in the basement office and on her second cup of coffee when the phone rang. She picked up.

18

"Jeannine, this is Larry Hodges at the Food and Drug Administration. What's happening with Hus-Kinetika's report defending its anticonvulsive drug, Xolak?"

"Dr. Hodges, it's on my desk. I started it last night."

"Jeannine, please. It's Larry, remember. But when can I see your comments? An advisory committee has been formed to see if Xolak should be removed from the U. S. market. Two of the members will be in town next week for the American Pharmaceutical Society meeting. I need to give them the FDA's evaluation."

"OK, Larry, You'll have my comments in 48 hours. All right?"

"Thanks. That's great. The Commissioner is pressing me to act. Hus-Kinetika is a Czech company and the State Department is on our back. There's a lot at stake. There's some sort of defense deal with the Czech Republic in the works and they don't want any glitches. There are a lot of users of Xolak in this country."

"I'll do what I can, OK?"

Larry hesitated and then added.

"Jeannine, maybe we could do lunch to go over your comments? How about it?"

"Thanks Larry, but I'm busy."

"All right. I'll send a messenger over for your comments whenever they're ready."

Dr. Hodges hung up.

Jeannine frowned. *When will he get the message I'm not interested?* She opened the report and started to read.

***

Jeannine was still reading when her partner, Aileen Harris, entered the office.

"Jeannine, I'm sorry I'm late. Mary Catherine isn't feeling well. She didn't go to school. My mother is taking care of her."

Aileen Harris was a divorcee. Her mother lived with Aileen and her daughter, Mary Catherine. Aileen's ex was not part of her life.

"No problem. You remember that drug Xolak, from that Czech Pharmaceutical House?"

"You mean Hus-Kinetika?"

"Yes. Their headquarters are in Prague. A Doctor Zeleny at a Clinic in Chicago, reported an increase in the number of patients exhibiting adverse allergic effects to Xolak. The clinic reported the cases to the Food and Drug Administration. The FDA told Hus-Kinetika to monitor the allergic side effects of Xolak.

Jeannine placed a graph in front of Aileen.

"This graph is from Hus-Kinetika's response. They recorded severe reactions to Xolak in five states, Maryland, Virginia, Michigan, Illinois, and Wisconsin, almost half a million current users."

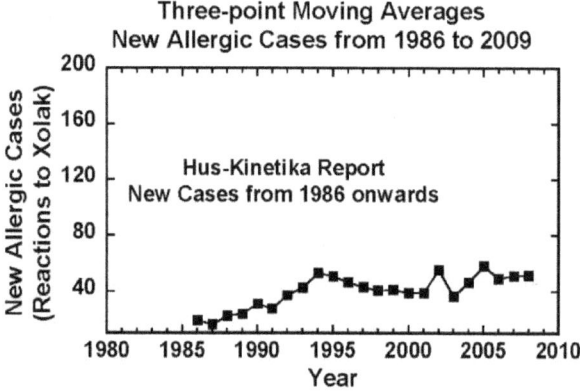

"Why does the graph start in 1986?"

"The FDA only approved Xolak for use in the United States in 1985."

Aileen nodded and studied the graph. After 1993 there was a stable level of subjects with adverse allergic reactions. There was no increase in the numbers of new allergic cases.

"But Jeannine, I can't interpret this graph without knowing the total number of cases. If the number of users decreased, then a stable number of new cases would mean an increase in the per cent of adverse reactions."

"You're right, of course, but the report gave the total cases too. They don't change much since 1995. The graph shows no increase in new cases as numbers or per cents."

"So there's no problem. What's worrying you?"

"I have a bad feeling about this graph, that's all!"

Aileen was surprised. Normally Jeannine was driven by logic, math and analysis, not intuition.

"OK, why does the graph worry you? Is it because of Dr. Zeleny? That guy is a jerk."

Dr. Zeleny, the neurologist who was the original complainant to the FDA about Xolak, had called Ryan Associates several times yesterday to schedule a visit. Aileen had taken the calls. He had treated her as a secretary.

Jeannine started to speak, but the phone rang and Aileen picked up.

"Ryan Associates, Dr. Harris speaking."

She covered the mouthpiece and held the phone to Jeannine.

"It's him! It's Zeleny."

Jeannine took the instrument. Aileen heard only Jeannine's side of the conversation.

"Yes, this is Dr. Ryan. … … Yes, Dr. Zeleny, I'm consulting with the FDA on the Hus-Kinetika report. … … No, I didn't know they had given you my name."

She motioned with her hand for the report in question. Aileen lifted a spiral-bound volume from the desk and handed it to her. Jeannine flipped the pages while keeping her ear to the phone. Finally she spoke.

"Dr. Zeleny, I'm looking at the report right now. According to Hus-Kinetika the rise in adverse reactions at your clinic isn't repeated elsewhere. Doesn't that concern you?"

Aileen did not hear his reply. She only heard Jeannine.

"Dr. Zeleny, I didn't realize you were in the area. I thought you were in Chicago. Of course I'll meet with you. If you're on Bradley Boulevard you're only minutes away."

Jeannine hung up. Aileen spoke.

"What was that all about?"

"Dr. Zeleny is coming here. He was in Rockville at the Parklawn Building to see Larry Hodges. Zeleny says the number of reactions to Xolak is increasing at his clinic. He doesn't believe the Hus-Kinetika report."

"So?"

"So, Hodges warned me that Zeleny's clinic is small. The increase in reactions there may not be typical. Maybe they're doing something wrong. And too, Zeleny may be biased. Larry says Zeleny is a Czech who has no love for Hus-Kinetika."

"Why is that?"

"Zeleny was a resident at the Motol Teaching Hospital in Prague when his mentor, a Dr. Pokorny, found fake data in one of the company's clinical trials. Hus-Kinetika objected and complained to the medical school. There was some sort of scandal with a female student named Simek and Zeleny's professor was canned. Zeleny hasn't forgiven or forgotten."

Aileen frowned.

"OK, so he doesn't like Hus-Kinetika, and I don't like him. What does he want from us?"

Before Jeannine could answer, Aileen sniffed.

"This jerk is biased against women."

A loud knock on the office door stopped further comment.

Dr. Zeleny had arrived.

***

Dr. Zeleny was not as Aileen had imagined. First he was young, trim and tall, the sort of man who turns eyes when he enters a room. He wore a loose gray sweater and fitted jeans. He turned towards Aileen. He spoke with a slight accent.

"Dr. Ryan?"

Jeannine stepped forward.

"I'm Dr. Ryan, and this is Dr. Harris. She's my associate. You must be Dr. Zeleny."

Dr. Zeleny scanned the wall of the office. He took in the framed doctoral diplomas on the wall, and the two certificates of appreciation from the Israeli government, one each for Dr. Harris and Dr. Ryan. *Impressive.* His eyes bounced from

Aileen to Jeannine and back. As a blonde, Aileen matched Jeannine's auburn good looks. His smile grew.

"I'm Peter. Larry, Dr. Hodges, at the FDA referred me to you. Do your husbands work here too?"

Jeannine laughed. *Kind of obvious, but I'll play along.*

"No husbands. We're both single, although I have a friend. His name is 'Bill,' and you?"

"Sorry. I forget myself. I do not try to pry. I'm *svobodný*, that's Czech for 'free' or 'single,' however you prefer to interpret it."

He glanced sideways at Aileen.

"Now we're introduced, maybe I can know your first name?"

"I'm 'Aileen' and Dr. Ryan is 'Jeannine,' but do you treat all women as secretaries? Are you always so rude?"

Peter fell silent. Aileen continued.

"Dr. Zeleny, we all know this isn't a social visit, so why, precisely, are you here?"

Peter Zeleny's brow furrowed. He sighed.

"I think that Xolak has dangerous side effects. Some of my patients have been seriously hurt by it. Hodges, at the FDA, thinks I'm biased against Hus-Kinetika, but I can explain that."

He took a breath.

"My problems with the company started after I completed my studies at the First Faculty of Medicine at Charles University in Prague. I took a position in the Motol Teaching Hospital of the Faculty. My mentor, Dr. Pokorny, had a dispute with Hus-Kinetika over one of their clinical trials."

Jeannine interrupted.

"A dispute?"

"Actually, he found faked data in one of their reports. They weren't happy. They located a student of his, a woman named Simek. Her father had been an anti-socialist agitator, and everyone knew that my mentor, Dr. Pokorny, was a communist. It was a set up. This Simek woman was quite attractive."

He paused and looked at Aileen.

"She looked like you, actually."

He turned back to Jeannine.

"Simek claimed that Pokorny had offered her grades for sex. He denied it, but Hus-Kinetika pressured the university to fire him. Rather than be fired, my mentor resigned in disgrace."

"Did you believe the Simek woman?"

"I don't know. My mentor had a reputation among women. Simek was American. After testifying she quit her studies in medicine and went back to the States. She studies philosophy in Chicago. All I really know is that her testimony was damned convenient for Hus-Kinetika. Maybe the rats paid her."

Jeannine fell silent. Aileen took over.

"You don't have any evidence that they did, do you? And why did you come to the U. S, and why pick Chicago?"

"I wanted to do clinical research in neurology. I applied for several positions at home, but Hus-Kinetika is powerful there. I did not survive the interviews. I had a friend in Chicago's Czech community. He told me about the Mental Health clinic that needed a neurologist. It was my only offer."

"So you come here and after a year you find problems with Hus-Kinetika's premium drug, Xolak. You know that many people, including me, might think you are biased against them."

"What can I say? Anaphylactic shock is serious."

Aileen grew silent. Once again Jeannine stepped in.

"All right, why don't you tell us about the patients at your clinic, and what raised your first concerns about Xolak."

Peter Zeleny was troubled. His English lost its fluidity and his accent became more pronounced. He searched for words as he described a patient's seizure and how he had tried to help her.

Aileen softened.

"Peter, with the EEG you describe, you did the right thing. Any competent neurologist would have read that the same way."

He flashed her a look of thanks. The remaining conversation revealed little that Jeannine and Aileen did not already know.

After a muted exchange of goodbyes, Dr. Zeleny left.

***

******

Chapter 4
Thursday, November 18

In Corolla, North Carolina, Jim Harrigan drove slowly back to Duck. His thoughts were of a jacket with a bullet hole, and a blood-stained van. Soon, he would have nothing to do with the abandoned van, or the jacket. The Duck Police Department had no jurisdiction. The Currituck County Sheriff's Office served Corolla.

He parked his F250 next to the door. Just inside, the secretary, Terri, intercepted him.

"Jim, what's going on, you're not supposed to be on duty today."

"I'm not. I'm moonlighting, security work in Corolla, but I found this abandoned van with blood stains and that jacket. It's got a bullet hole front and back."

He put the bloodstained jacket into a plastic bag and handed it to her.

"Log this and put it in the evidence room. And there's a minivan being towed here. Call Johnson in the Currituck Sheriff's office to arrange to pick it up. They have a secure lot on the mainland, and it's their case, not ours. They'll need that jacket too."

At the sight of the jacket, the secretary's eyes opened wide. Jim did not notice. He continued.

"Terri, do you know a realtor named Mila Patekova? She handles the rental for the house near where I found the van."

"Of course. She's a good friend of the family and she's a sharp realtor. She handles the rentals for my mother's beach house. She's from the Czech Republic. I like her. She has a neat accent."

"Anything else?"

"She's single if that's what you mean, and she's darn good looking for over thirty. But you talked to her, so you know that. Why do you ask? Are you interested?"

"Come on Terri. It's only a case. I have a hunch that she knows a lot more about that van than what she told me. I don't trust her. She knows something."

Terri shrugged. *Big deal, you cops never trust anybody!*

She turned back to her work.

***

After the policeman from Duck left, Mila retrieved the weapon from the sand under the walkway. She handled it with a paper towel, mounted the stairs to the top level, and stuffed the weapon under a cushion. Mila knew nothing of guns, and this handgun was heavy and felt unwieldy. Its mere presence distressed her.

She. left the great room and went to the deck outside Anne's bedroom. There she sat with her head down.

The sun disappeared below the horizon to leave a blazing red sky interlaced with streaks of gray clouds. She scarcely noticed.

Her thoughts raced. Whatever had gone wrong, she was to blame. She never should have arranged the meeting with Vaclav. And she should have told Anne who it was that wanted to see her. If she had, then perhaps Anne would have refused to meet him, and no one would have been hurt.

Mila shuddered. *Anne, have you been stupid? Did you shoot Vaclav? And where did you get that gun? I don't think Vaclav had one.*

She stood up and looked out over the marsh, towards the sound. After a moment she decided. She would sleep here tonight. She stepped back into the bedroom. Clearly, Anne had been in the bed. The coverlet was off and the sheets rumpled.

She returned to the great room. Anne had left her laptop open on the table. The screen was dark.

At the base of the sliding panels were the towels and cloths that Anne had pushed against the sill to absorb the storm water. Ever the realtor, Mila collected the soggy clumps and took them to the dryer below. She returned upstairs and wiped the remaining moisture off the floor.

Mila lay on the couch, eyes wide open. *Should I call the police? Not yet.* She shuddered. *Damn it Anne, where are you? What did you do to Vaclav? Damn it, call me. I'll help you.*

Finally, her eyes closed.

***

At Ryan Associates in Bethesda, Jeannine sat at her desk. Aileen came over.

"Jeannine, what are you doing? What are you staring at?"

"It's this Xolak graph that I don't like."

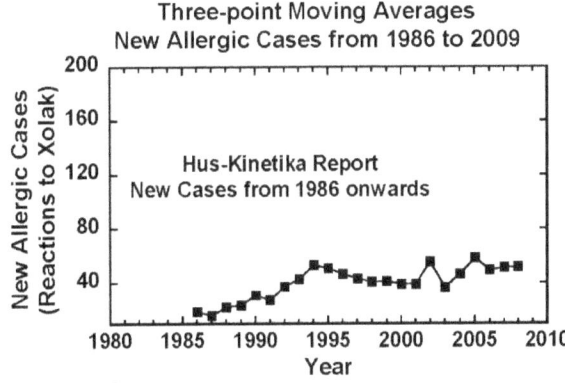

Aileen looked.

"It says that the points are 'Three-point Moving Averages.' What does that mean?"

"It's not a problem. The numbers are smoothed to show the general trend. Each year is the average of three consecutive years. The number of reactions for 1996, say, is the average of those for 1995, 1996 and 1997. Here's the equation."

$$\frac{n_{1995} + n_{1996} + n_{1997}}{3} = \text{Moving Average 1996}.$$

She turned to Aileen.

"The numbers for the graph are in Table A in the Appendix. Here it is."

Year	3-Year Average	Year	3-Year Average

New Cases of Allergic Reactions to Xolak by Year. Maryland, Virginia, Michigan, Illinois, and Wisconsin. (3-Year Moving Averages.)			
Year	3-Year Average	Year	3-Year Average
1985	xxxx	1997	43.33
1986	19.00	1998	40.67
1987	16.33	1999	41.67
1988	22.67	2000	39.00
1989	24.00	2001	40.00
1990	31.33	2002	57.33
1991	27.67	2003	37.11
1992	37.33	2004	46.89
1993	42.67	2005	58.44
1993	42.67	2006	49.56
1994	53.33	2007	51.22
1995	51.00	2008	51.78
1996	46.67	2009	xxxx

Together Jeannine and Aileen studied the Table. There was no increase in cases after 2004.

"But Jeannine, Peter saw an increase in allergic reactions in his clinic in 2004."

"That's what he says, but the numbers in the report don't agree with him."

"That's why Peter doesn't believe the report. He observed an increase so these numbers must be wrong. They must be faked. Can you show that?"

"I don't see how. The numbers in Table A are only summary data."

"What do you mean?"

"They're summarized. Without the original records we can't do much."

"Damn it, Jeannine, that's not fair. Peter deserves a hearing. Get the FDA to make Hus-Kinetika give us the original data?"

"The FDA tried that. Hus-Kinetika said that they had trouble with one of their servers and the original data files were lost.

Since the summary data show no trend, the FDA wants to accept the report as is."

"Make Hus-Kinetika re-enter the numbers from the original data sheets."

"Because of privacy issues, the original written records were purposely destroyed after the data were coded and in the computer. The data in Table A are all that are available. Do you have any ideas?"

"No, but you're the one troubled by this graph."

"That's true, but we're stuck. This report exonerates Hus-Kinetika and we've got no way to show that it's wrong. Besides, maybe there's no problem with Xolak. Maybe Peter's clinic is at fault. Maybe their protocols and dosages are bad. Hus-Kinetika can't be blamed for their incompetence."

Aileen slammed her fist on the desk.

"No they can't, but I believe Peter."

"I thought you didn't like him."

"He's a sexist, but maybe not a complete jerk."

"I don't think he's a sexist. He's from a different culture. In spite of everything, I think you like Dr. Zeleny."

Aileen frowned.

***

At his room in the American Inn in Bethesda, Peter Zeleny was confused. He had just met two intelligent professional women, and had failed to convince them of Hus-Kinetika's duplicity.

Worse, for the first time, he doubted his own arguments. *Maybe they're right. Maybe I'm not objective?* He went over his clinic's regimens for Xolak.

What am I missing? No! Our procedures are fine! And damn it, Mrs. Morgan's anaphylactic shock nearly killed her! I can't be that wrong!

But Peter's confusion was not simply because of Xolak.

Aileen Harris had left him dazed. Peter was no stranger to women. Generally, they sought him, but Aileen was different. He wanted her to like him.

Get hold of yourself.

Damn it!   Why was I rude on that phone?   Despite his "democratic" life in Chicago, he had treated Aileen as an underling.   "Old world" class distinctions had reasserted themselves at the worst moment. His boorish behavior had been inexcusable.

Oddly, Aileen bore a strong resemblance to Anne Simek, the instrument Hus-Kinetika had wielded to cause Dr. Pokorny's downfall. He had seen Anne at the Motol Hospital, but had paid little attention to her. He had been too busy launching his career.

He lay on the bed, arms folded under his head, eyes open wide, and stared at the ceiling. *What's the matter with me?*

Thoughts of Hus-Kinetika faded as a pleasing image appeared in his mind, that intriguing blond, Aileen Harris. Then unexpectedly, the image morphed into one from years past, another blond, that troublemaker student, Anne Simek.

She was smiling.

***

In a room in North Carolina, Vaclav Pokorny awoke. Half conscious, eyes glazed in pain, he struggled to focus.

Where?

He tried to remember. The storm, the cold wind pushing sheets of rain into his eyes, his nose. A fall. The raging waters on the beach.

His thoughts cleared enough to know that he was in a bed. He tried to turn, but his muscles shrieked and froze in pain.

The gun!

Through half-open lids he saw a face, a woman frowning.

He fell back unconscious.

***

At the office of Ryan Associates, Jeannine continued to study the Xolak report. She reached for her coffee cup, but the report fell on the floor. The pages flipped and exposed Table A.

She stared a moment and cried out.

"Aileen, It's the decimals! They're wrong!"

"What do you mean?"

"Hang on."

Jeannine clicked rapidly and brought up Table A but with only the decimal endings.

Decimal Endings of 3-Year Moving Averages from Table A			
Year	Decimals	Year	Decimals
1985	xxxx	1997	.33
1986	.00	1998	.67
1987	.33	1999	.67
1988	.67	2000	.00
1989	.00	2001	.00
1990	.33	2002	.33
1991	.67	2003	.11
1992	.33	2004	.89
1993	.67	2005	.44
1993	.67	2006	.56
1994	.33	2007	.22
1995	.00	2008	.78
1996	.67	2009	xx

"Aileen, look. From 2003 on the decimals are wrong. See the decimal for 2003 is 0.11, and for 2004 it's 0.89. That can't happen."

"Why not?"

"Because when you divide a whole number by 3, to get the moving average, the remainder must be 0, 1, or 2, so that the decimal must be 0.00, 0.33 or 0.67. It can't be 0.11 or 0.89."

Jeannine was on a roll.

"Hus-Kinetika used raw counts to compute the moving averages, so the number of cases in any given year is a whole number, and the sum over three years is a whole number too."

Aileen understood.

"Before 2003 the decimals are .00, .33 or .67. They can occur with whole numbers divided by 3, but none of the decimals after 2002 are OK. Those results must be faked."

Aileen fell silent. *Maybe Peter is for real after all?*

Jeannine stood up and waved an empty cup.

"That's it. I'm going up to the kitchen. I need to make more coffee."

But her mind refused to slow down. *Those decimals after 2002 are curious. Wait!*

She was halfway up the stairs when she raced back down

"Aileen, I know how they did it. They saw that the averages after 2003 were high, so they divided them again by three."

"Why do you say that?"

"Because dividing twice by three is the same as dividing the original number by nine, and when you divide a whole number by nine, the remainder must be 0, 1, 2, 3, 4, 5, 6, 7, or 8, and the fractions range from 0/9 to 8/9."

Aileen quickly jotted down a table with the decimals.

Decimals for a Whole Number divided by Nine								
0	1	2	3	4	5	6	7	8
.00	.11	.22	.33	.44	.56	.67	.78	.89

After the year 2002, all of the decimals could occur after division by nine! She turned to see Jeannine typing vigorously on her laptop. Jeannine looked up and pointed. to the screen.

"If I'm right, this graph has the 'real' averages and there's a big increase after 2002. Xolak has gone wrong like Peter said."

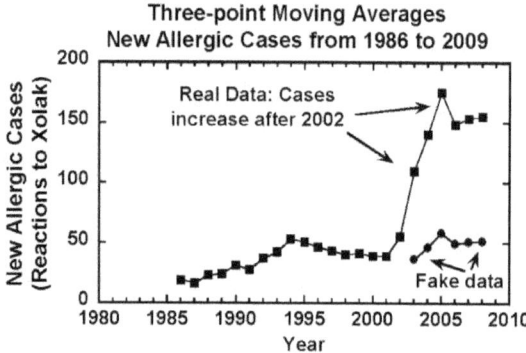

Jeannine summarized.

"Here's what we know so far. From 2003 onwards, none of the years are correct because they have *impossible* decimals. Moreover, these numbers *could* have been produced by division by nine. I think that when they saw the averages were too high, they divided them again by three. That's the same as dividing by nine."

"I get it, but Peter should know about this. I'll call him."

Aileen picked up the phone.

***

But two calls later, Aileen turned to Jeannine.

"Peter's not at the hotel. He's disappeared. He didn't check out. No one saw him leave, but he's gone. A woman in a nearby room thought she heard a commotion. The staff found his room empty. His keycard was on the dresser."

"Did the hotel call the police?"

"What for? The woman wasn't sure, and they have the imprint of his credit card. It's no problem for them."

"Well it's a problem for us! Call his clinic in Chicago."

"I did. They thought he was still at the hotel."

Aileen took a breath and added.

"Peter's in trouble."

***

******

Chapter 5
Friday, November 19

In North Carolina, Jim Harrigan woke up early. He called the Duck Police Department.

"Terri, I'm not feeling well today. I asked Lou to take my shift. He'll be there at eight."

"All right Jim, I'll tell the Chief. How bad is it? Will we see you tomorrow?

"Just a cough. I'll probably be in tomorrow."

Jim hung up.

There was no cough. Jim was fine, despite a restless sleep in which he had been disturbed by dreams featuring bloody car windows, jackets with bullet holes, and the evasions of a deceptive realtor.

Jim had done his duty. The van and jacket were in the hands of the Currituck County Sheriff. It was their case, but he could not let go.

Somewhere was a severely injured man, or a dead body.

He took a last sip of coffee, donned his jacket, and drove north to Corolla. He was sure that woman realtor knew more than she had let on.

***

Stretched on the couch in Anne's rental in Corolla, Mila opened her eyes. The room was bright with light from the East. She stretched but felt a twinge in her back. The couch was not soft like her bed.

She sat up and looked about. All was quiet.

She went to the kitchen module and turned on the coffee maker. She looked across the counter to the dining table. Something was missing. Then she understood.

Anne's laptop was not there. It had been on the table last night, open, its display dark. Now it was gone.

Mila went to Anne's bedroom.

She stared in amazement. The bed was stripped. Anne's linens were nowhere in sight. She slid back the folding door of the closet. Anne's suitcases were gone!

Mila examined the bedroom doors where they opened onto the rear deck. There was no sign the catch had been forced. A stick was wedged in the slide to prevent its opening.

The stick was in the same spot Mila had lodged it the evening before.

Mila returned to the great room and stood in thought.

Someone had been in the house while she slept and removed Anne's possessions. Mila shuddered at the thought of her own vulnerability.

Anne had a key. The thought that Anne might have removed her own things reassured her, but only for a moment.

Why are you sneaking around, Anne? It's me, Mila! You can trust me.

But Anne had trusted her once, and things had gone horribly wrong.

A banging on the entrance door interrupted Mila's thoughts.

***

Mila went down the stairs. The entrance was on the mid level facing the sound and had its own set of wooden stairs with no access to any of the decks that lined the house. The solid door had a peep hole. Through it Mila saw the distorted image of a man. He looked like that policeman from Duck.

A second later this was confirmed. A badge filled the circular field of vision. The holder knew her name.

"Miss Patekova, may I come in? I'm Jim Harrigan. I spoke with you yesterday."

Mila pulled the door ajar. She frowned.

"What do you want?"

"I'd like to ask you a few questions. It's unofficial. You don't have to answer if you don't want to."

"What kind of questions?"

"First, why did you stay here last night? And where is your cousin? Has she contacted you?"

Mila did not like his tone.

"You're from the Duck Police Department?"

"That's right."

"You can come in, but I have to call them first."

He shrugged and stepped inside. He followed Mila up the stairs to the top level. His eyes swept the room while she spoke on the phone.

"Terri, this is Mila. One of your deputies is here with me. His name is Harrigan. He wants to ask me some questions. What can you tell me about him."

Jim waited. Mila listened for almost a minute.

Finally, Mila spoke.

"Thanks, Terri. Thanks very much."

She hung up and looked at Jim Harrigan with a wry smile.

"Apparently, you've had a quick recovery from your cold. No matter, Terri Miller says you are OK."

"Thanks."

Mila paused and stood still. Finally, she spoke.

"All right, Mr. Harrigan, Terri's word is enough for me. I'm worried. I need help, and I think my cousin does too."

Her decision taken, she reached into her purse, and handed him Vaclav's passport.

Jim saw the reddish cover, and noted its provenance, the Czech Republic.

Mila pointed across the room.

"And there's a gun under that cushion. I found it in the sand by the side of the house. I don't know what to think. Anne never had a gun."

Jim retrieved the weapon. It was Czech, a CZ-52. He knew it from his work overseas with the "Agency." He had seen one also when he was with the Raleigh Police Department. The CZ-52 was a fairly common import.

The barrel was clogged with wet sand. He could not say if it had been fired.

Mila sat frozen. There was no turning back now.

Jim stared. *A Czech realtor, a Czech passport, a Czech handgun? What the hell is going on here?*

Mila's brow furrowed. She pointed to a comfortable chair across from her.

"Maybe you'd better sit down. This is going to take a while. I'll tell you what I can."

***

Mila recounted how she had set up the meeting with Vaclav Pokorny whom Anne had known when she was a medical student of his father in Prague. How Vaclav felt guilty about his father's sexual advances to Anne while she was his student, and even more so because Vaclav himself had tried to stop Anne from testifying before the university panel about the harassment.

At that point, Jim Harrigan broke into the narrative.

"Look Miss Patkoh ..."

She interrupted him in turn.

"Call me 'Mila,' it's easier to say."

"All right Mila, call me 'Jim,' but I must warn you. I'm a cop. I don't know what Terri Miller told you about me, but I'm here to find out what happened. I can see you're worried that your cousin did something bad to this Vaclav guy. You're afraid for her, but you have to know that if she did something wrong, I won't stop until I find her. I'm a cop, not a counselor."

"I understand. But Jim, Anne doesn't have a gun. That gun is someone else's. She's a grad student in philosophy and theology. She couldn't harm anyone."

"OK, I see you believe that. Tell me about Vaclav's father."

"He was a communist before the Velvet Revolution. Doubtless still is."

"And Vaclav?"

"He's a capitalist, like me. He and his father don't agree on anything, but Vaclav loves his father even though his father won't speak to him. Vaclav works for a pharmaceutical company, Hus-Kinetika, that his father despises: his father lost his appointment at Charles University because of that company."

38

She started to add *"and because of my cousin's testimony,"* but thought better of it.

At this point Jim's cell phone vibrated. It was Terri Miller in the office.

"Jim, I just got a call from Irv at Dominion Power in Corolla. The night of the storm he was on the road to replace a blown transformer. He told me another van passed him near the spot where you found that Safari minivan. It was a Honda."

Terri added.

"I thought you should know there were two vans, not one."

A pause. Jim sensed Terri smiling at the phone.

"Jim, how do you like Mila now? Isn't she neat!"

Jim coughed as Terri hung up. He turned towards Mila.

"What kind of car does your cousin drive? Is it a van?"

"Hardly, she has a Ford Focus."

"Mila, I have some news that could help your cousin."

Mila's eyes brightened. For the first time, Jim realized they were lustrous brown.

***

In the Parklawn Building in Rockville, Maryland, Dr. Larry Hodges sat at his desk. Across from him was a desirable woman who routinely rebuffed his attempts to get personal.

Larry was conflicted. Jeannine Ryan had delivered her Xolak comments to him on time and in person. Ever hopeful, he was grateful for that, but the substance of her comments upset him. He could feel the rise of acid in his stomach. *Damn!*

"Look, Jeannine. You don't know that the increase in adverse reactions is the way you graphed it. It's your guess that someone divided the numbers by nine. Give me a break. I've got a lot of pressure to approve this damned Xolak report."

"No, Larry, you look. The guess that they divided the real numbers by nine is a good one. All the decimals are consistent with that possibility."

She pressed on.

"But it does not matter. It's not a guess that the numbers Hus-Kinetika presented *are* false. The decimals cannot occur after division of a whole number by three which is what they say they did. That alone is cause to reject their report. If I also have an explanation of *how* they faked the data by dividing by nine, that's just a bonus.

The color rose in her cheeks.

"You wanted my comments and now you have them. If Hus-Kinetika is so great how come they 'lost' the data on that server. Wasn't that too convenient? Didn't that raise a red flag to you."

Dr. Hodges shifted in his seat.

"I'm sorry. You're right, of course. And I see your arguments. It's just that this case is a major headache. The State Department is pushing the FDA to decide quickly."

"Quickly? They want you to decide in favor of Hus-Kinetika!"

"That's about it. There's a political deal with the Czech Republic in the works. If they think that we are treating Hus-Kinetika unfairly, they could scratch the whole thing."

"Spare me the politics, Larry. The FDA is supposed to protect Americans, and to make sure that medicines like Xolak are OK. Are you going to wait until people die before you act?"

Larry looked down at his desk. After a few moments, he picked up the folder with Jeannine's critique.

"All right. I'll delay the approval of the Xolak report, but you could help your case with more evidence, like personal testimony. What about that Dr. Zeleny?"

"I don't know where he is, but I'll try to find him."

Larry stood up, unsmiling.

"I guess I'd better pass your comments on. Call me if you locate Zeleny."

He nodded and left the office. Minutes later, Jeannine squeezed into a "down" elevator crowded with workers headed to the Parklawn Building's main cafeteria.

She reflected. This meeting marked a "first."

Larry had not asked her to lunch with him!

***

******

Chapter 6
Friday, November 19

It was late afternoon in Elizabeth City, North Carolina. Half the tables of the Albemarle Diner were filled with early dinner arrivals. Peter Zeleny waited in a corner booth. He was uncomfortable. He was a long way from Chicago, his bowl of chili was cold, and a second cup of coffee was lukewarm.

The moment she entered the diner he recognized her. She was still attractive. She had not changed since those years in Prague at the Motol Teaching Hospital where she had ruined the career of his mentor.

He signaled. Anne Simek came to the booth and sat opposite.

"Dr. Zeleny, Vaclav thanks you for coming. He wasn't sure you would."

"Miss Simek, I came but I'm not sure why. It's a long way here. Why did Vaclav tell you to call me?"

"He needs to see you. There's no other doctor he can turn to."

"Why me? He works for Hus-Kinetika. I'm the enemy."

"You worked under his father at Motol Hospital. Vaclav thinks you are honorable and he knows that you respect his father."

"Miss Simek, did you respect his father when you testified against him at the Motol?"

Anne stared down at the cold chili. She spoke softly.

"That's none of your business. Vaclav respects me. He knows his father used women, but he loves his father anyway."

"Vaclav works for Hus-Kinetika. His father can't like that!"

Anne's eyes flashed.

"Look, are you going to help us or not? I told him this wouldn't work."

It was Peter's turn to look down. He collected his thoughts.

"All right. Where is he?"

"He's safe, not far away, but he's hurt. He's been shot."

"Shot! Why didn't he go to a hospital, and to the police?"

"He couldn't. You can guess why. He doesn't want 'them' to know where he is. You of all people must understand that."

"'I thought Vaclav was on 'their' side, you too. Am I wrong?"

"It appears that you are, but we're wasting time. He's hurt. He needs help."

"I'm no surgeon and I haven't treated a gunshot wound since Prague."

"It's a clean wound, through the shoulder. No vital organ was touched. The bullet passed right through. The exit wound is not that large."

"Then why do you need me? You studied medicine."

"Not enough, and I can't write prescriptions. You can. We need something to fight the infection in his wound, but mostly, Vaclav wants to talk to you about some papers he took from Hus-Kinetika. He trusts you. I don't know why."

"I don't know about any papers."

"He sent something to you in Maryland."

"Why Maryland? I never got anything."

"So you say."

She looked at him in disbelief and rose from the booth.

"I'm going to the bathroom. When I come out, I'm walking straight to my car. Will you come?"

"But why are they after Vaclav?"

"He'll have to tell you that. He trusts you. I don't."

Anne frowned and continued.

"My car is the red Focus. If you are coming, follow me in yours."

Nearby a couple stood waiting for their booth to be cleaned. Anne pushed by them and went to the rest room.

Frowning, Peter fingered his cell phone. He had not charged it since Chicago and the battery was low. He tossed several bills on the table and went to a phone hanging on the wall. He made a quick call to Maryland before Anne appeared from the rest room. She left the diner without looking back.

He rushed outside to follow her. Her red Focus was parked across the lot. She was already behind the wheel.

***

As Peter Zeleny left the diner, Gustav Slavik took a last sip of coffee and slipped off the counter stool. He stepped to the door of the diner and watched Peter run to his car. Nearby, Anne waited in her Focus. Gustav ground his teeth.

So Pokorny survived. Damn you Simek!

Gustav hurried to his minivan. Seated behind the wheel, he reached down and felt the cold metal of the Makarov pistol under the seat. He was comfortable with this weapon, a "GDR" Makarov, made in the cold war German Democratic Republic. It was in excellent condition due to his constant care.

The round went straight through Pokorny. I should have used the Makarov instead of the CZ-52. He would be dead now.

He put the Makarov on the seat and drove out of the lot. He took his place in line behind Peter, but far back. Gustav was in no hurry. His "work" was best done under cover of darkness. He drove slowly, staying well behind Anne's two-car caravan.

At the junction of Route 158 with Route 168, the caravan turned south.. Gustav smiled. His task was simple now. This road was bordered by the Currituck Sound to the East, and a branch of the Albemarle Sound to the West. Anne Simek's destination was the Outer Banks.

He fumbled in his shirt pocket for his Petra cigarettes. He lit a king-sized, inhaled deeply, and glanced at the Makarov on the seat.

This time Pokorny, you will die.

Gustav grimaced.

And you two, Simek and Zeleny, if you get in my way!

***

In Bethesda, Aileen Harris sat in the office of Ryan Associates. The phone rang and she answered.

"Ryan Associates."

43

"Aileen, it's me, Jeannine. I saw Larry Hodges this morning at the FDA. Then I went to the Israeli Embassy. I'm on my way back. Did you find Dr. Zeleny?"

"The Chicago Clinic still hasn't heard from him. What did Hodges say? Will he recommend that the FDA reject the report?"

"He wants to approve Hus-Kinetika's report, but the fake data have slowed him down. He's stalling. He says he wants to talk to Zeleny again. We can't depend on Hodges."

Aileen hung up.

Damn it, Hodges, what will it take to make you listen?

She started. Someone was at the office door.

Who is it this late?

Aileen looked through the peephole. It was a man, unshaven with a grizzled beard. He spoke with an accent.

"Please, Dr. Harris, open the door. I need to talk to you. My son trusts you."

"Who are you? What do you mean your son?"

"My son, Peter, ... Dr. Zeleny. I'm his father. My name is Johan. I know no one in your country. I just arrived, please."

"All right, come in. But what does Peter want? He barely knows me."

Johan entered. He smiled at Aileen.

"Peter thinks you are a smart, attractive, honest woman. I can confirm the 'attractive' part. Very nice."

Aileen glared, but Johan continued.

"Peter called me. He wants to know if someone named 'Pokorny' called you, maybe talked about some papers he had?"

Aileen gauged the man before her. He was old and posed no physical threat. She could handle him.

"I've never heard of a Mr. Pokorny and I don't know why Peter would think he would call me. Now you tell me how I can reach Peter. He needs to know that we can prove the Xolak data from Hus-Kinetika are fake."

"Hus-Kinetika! Warped Capitalists. They ruin my country. And now they ruin my son!"

He took a seat, his left leg vibrating.

"They are fools, traitors, lackeys of Washington."

He ranted on. Aileen stopped listening.

Mercifully, minutes later Jeannine returned to the office.

Together, they convinced Mr. Zeleny to go back to his motel. Aileen agreed to drive him.

***

The sun had disappeared in the West as Peter Zeleny drove after Anne Simek's Ford Focus. He was confused. He was alone in North Carolina, a state new to him, and on a strange road following a woman he barely knew, a woman who had ruined his mentor's career.

Why does Vaclav want to see me? Who shot him? Why? He works for Hus-Kinetika. What am I doing?

Peter's father had always disparaged Anne's father, Havel: He was a weakling, a traitor to socialism, an ingrate who had refused to accept correct ideas while detained by the State for his own good, a sneak who had fled his homeland.

His father's views did not disturb Peter. They were archaic, and boring. The past was the past.

What disturbed Peter was not his father, but Anne. During their shared time at the Motol Teaching Hospital in Prague, he had seen her only on formal occasions. But at the diner in Elizabeth City, something changed. Sitting with Anne in the booth, he had found her most appealing, like Aileen Harris.

And like Aileen Harris, she had shown a marked distaste for Peter! He was used to being pursued, not disdained. And both these women had the upper hand on his feelings. Upset by two women in two days! And now blindly following one of them.

He shook himself.

Do I want to impress Anne Simek? Is that why I follow her?

Ahead of him, the red Focus grew smaller. Peter pressed the accelerator to catch up.

***

Dusk fell and Anne Simek turned on her headlights. Behind her, Peter Zeleny switched on the lights of his rental Accord.

45

Anne memorized their spacing. Once in traffic she would need to know if the car behind her was Peter's. In the distance, behind Peter, she spied a minivan. Its lights were on. They were more widely spaced than Peter's. Anne mentally recorded that difference.

Once across the bridge to the Outer Banks, Route 158 runs into Route 12 at a right angle. To the north, Route 12 leads to Southern Shores, Duck and Corolla, to the south, Kitty Hawk and Nags Head. Anne turned south towards Nags Head. She had sequestered Vaclav at a bed and breakfast in Wanchese on the southern portion of Roanoke Island. To reach Vaclav she needed to go to Route 64 and cross the bridge to that island.

She looked in her mirror. The familiar lights of Peter's Accord had turned after her. Minutes later, as she drove through Kitty Hawk, another set of lights appeared behind Peter's.

Anne gasped. The pattern and spacing of the lights were those of the minivan that she had noted before.

Now Anne was truly disturbed. She wished she was back in Corolla, at peace, lost in her studies.

But her world had changed.

She relived that stormy night two days ago.

***

She awoke. A gun shot? Out on the deck.

She stepped outside. A hooded figure grappled with a man. Vaclav! He fell. The hooded man raised a gun.

No time! She rushed and shoved the shooter.

The gun flew away. The man toppled over the railing and landed head first. Stunned, he lay still.

She turned to Vaclav. All that blood. Help!

They stumbled down to his van.

She pushed him in and ran to the driver's side.

The keys? There, in the ignition.

She drove on the flooded roadway. Sheets of water flowed down the windshield.

The van slid sideways into the sand. Stuck!

She grabbed Vaclav and pulled. He slid from the vehicle. She helped him to stand. They abandoned the van and, feet wet, splashed away on foot.

The rain and wind-borne sand stung and blinded them. They moved forward and stopped. Where? A gully, the beach!

Vaclav tripped into the channel that churned at the foot of the dunes.

She grabbed his jacket, but it ripped off. She stepped into the knee-deep water and pulled him out.

She led him through the dunes back to the road.

His weakened limbs gave out. He slumped to the ground. She could not lift him.

Her car was at the house. She ran back through the dunes. She stopped to scan the side of the house.

The attacker was gone.

She drove her Focus back, somehow not getting stuck.

Vaclav was as she had left him.

He sat up and she got him into the car. She headed for the hospital in Elizabeth City.

He protested, eyes filled with fear.

"No, no hospital, hide me."

"But Vaclav?"

"No!"

She gave in and drove him to a place near Wanchese where they knew her. She hid him in the car and took the room.

He was incoherent as she guided him up the stairs and onto the bed. She bandaged him as best she could.

Finally his fever broke and he asked for Peter Zeleny.

***

A nightmare? No, it was real.

Anne shook her thoughts back to the ever-following minivan with widely spaced lights.

I'll be at the intersection with Highway 64 soon. I have to get rid of that van before then.

She could not let it see her turn towards Roanoke Island and Wanchese.

She shook with fear.
What am I doing?

***

******

Chapter 7
Friday, November 19

In Prague, the elaborate high-walled office featured an almond-colored stucco ceiling edged by stylized flowers across which plaster cherubim romped and cavorted. The decorative angels looked down on a ponderous walnut desk that made the man behind it appear powerful. That individual was ensconced in a stiffly padded chair. A well-tailored suit tightly configured a muscular frame. He had hair that was partially gray, but his torso exhibited a youthful vigor. An alert demeanor signaled a readiness to trade the chair's cushioned comfort for action at a moment's notice.

The man looked up as an attractive woman entered the room. Stylishly dressed in a trim suit, her spike heels accentuated her shapely bearing. She approached the desk.

"Sir, Gustav called. Vaclav survived. He is still alive."

Karel Moravec frowned and peered over his reading glasses. "And?"

"And Gustav says he will finish the matter within 24 hours."

"And our documents?"

"Gustav is sure that Vaclav still has them."

"If Gustav fails, Ivana, What then?"

Ivana stood slightly to the side to present her distinctively feminine profile to her superior. Straight blond hair, falling just off her shoulders, added to her classic good looks and well-formed figure. She had struck this pose before. Karel enjoyed this view.

"Sir, I did as you said. The backup team you wanted is in North Carolina. They will act should Gustav fail."

"Good. They will be needed. Your Gustav failed once, and he will again. Ivana, I want you to learn from his failure."

"Sir, you seem sure about Gustav. Why?"

"My life is to know people. You must learn from me. When I let you choose Gustav, I hoped he would succeed for your sake, but I had my doubts. You will learn from this episode. There are costs to unwise choices."

"But if Gustav should succeed?"

Karel's lips widened, almost a smile.

"He won't, but either way we have no further use for him."

Ivana stared out the window. Across the river, lights illuminated Prague's landmark, the resplendent Hradčany Castle while the lamps on the Charles Bridge sent glowing streaks that shimmered in rippling reflections across the dark waters of the Vltava River. Ivana's brow furrowed.

"Ivana, dear, do not be concerned. Trust me. I anticipated Gustav's failure. That is why I had you arrange the backup team."

He switched his address to the diminutive.

"Ivanka, we have nothing to fear. My backups will take care of Vaclav and the stolen records. They will eliminate Gustav too."

Ivana's eyes widened.

"But why kill Gustav?"

"Don't you worry about that. I have decided. Now go, there is another matter I must attend to."

He opened a folder on his desk. She turned for the door.

Karel looked up and smiled. Ivana from the rear was as pleasing as from the front. He called after her. "Ivanka, tonight you and I shall dine *ve starém městě*, in the Old Town, at the Hotel Leonardo's Platina Restaurant. Wear that outfit with the red silk scarf. It is quite appealing."

Ivana did not respond. She opened the heavy door and left.

Karel watched her go. Then he scribbled notes on the pad in front of him.

***

It was not tourist season in coastal Carolina, so Jim Harrigan and Mila did not need reservations for the restaurant in Duck.

In fact, they had their choice of tables. Mila chose a booth with a view of Currituck Sound. The late afternoon sun, suspended well above the horizon, imparted a golden sheen to the marsh grass, while a gentle wind rippled the open stretches of water.

Mila studied the menu and ordered.

"The 'crispy cornmeal-fried Carolina catfish' please."

She turned to Jim.

"What would you like?"

"I'll just have coffee, thanks. I'm not hungry."

"Jim, thanks for babysitting me. I don't want to be alone. I don't know what to think, about Anne or Vaclav. Anne must be OK since she came back for her computer."

"Maybe, but if it was her why didn't she wake you, and let you know she was all right."

"She knows I deceived her about the meeting. If she had known it was Vaclav, she might have refused to meet him."

"You know your cousin better than I do, but suppose she is with this Vaclav character, and suppose he was shot. Why not go to the hospital? There have been no reports of gunshot wounds locally. Where would she hide him?"

Mila's eyes lit.

"Jim, that's it!. There is a bed and breakfast that Anne uses. It's in an isolated spot, near Wanchese."

The waiter arrived with her catfish, but Mila had already jumped up.

"Can you box that for me. I'm sorry, but I have to leave."

The waiter frowned. Jim Harrigan protested.

"But Mila?"

"No, Jim. Anne may be in Wanchese. I have to go now!"

"Then I'm coming with you."

"Thanks, I hoped you'd say that."

They took Mila's Ford Escape. She drove south.

***

On Roanoke Island near Wanchese, Bordens' bed and breakfast was a simple frame house isolated from its neighbors by mixed woods of pines, evergreen oaks, and other hardwoods. The dated structure sat at the end of a shaded lane whose surface was topped by layers of pine needles and dry live oak leaves.

The first level of the two-story house had a screened porch that projected out from the main structure. The branches of a nearby live oak tree provided easy access to the porch roof.

Vaclav Pokorny's room was on the second floor. It was furnished in quaint "country" style with an old-fashioned bed whose deep mattress accommodated awkwardly, but comfortably, any and all human forms. The room's windows faced onto the porch roof. The attached private bathroom was modern. It was there that Anne Simek had dressed the wound in Vaclav's shoulder. Various hues of red streaked the white marble of the sink and there was blood splatter on the floor tiles.

Vaclav lay on the bed, his forehead beaded by moisture. The room was hot and stuffy. He stared at the ceiling.

Anno, kde jste? 'Anne, where are you?' Why aren't you back? Did you find Peter? I must tell him about the plan!

Exhausted, his eyes closed.

***

The gray Ford Excursion stopped at the end of the lane to the bed and breakfast. The driver sipped his coffee while the passenger slipped quietly out of the car.

Minutes passed. The driver looked up as his partner returned.

"He's there all right. He's stretched out on the bed, passed out. He's in a bad way. The room is bare except for the bed and a dresser. I looked in the drawers. There's no other place to hide the files. Pokorny is out cold and the owners are in the kitchen downstairs in the rear extension. They're old. They won't hear a thing. I could finish him now."

"No. Our job is to get the files back to Mr. Moravec. Pokorny is helpless, so Simek would not have left them with him. She has them, and she'll come back to help Vaclav."

"So what now?"

"We wait."

***

Their wait was not long. A white SUV, a Ford Escape, its interior lights on, turned down the lane to the bed and breakfast. The passenger appeared to study a map. The SUV disappeared around a bend maked by the low branches of a Live Oak tree.

The driver of the Ford Excursion spoke first.

"Damn! Did you see that?"

"The SUV? Simek drives a red Focus."

"No, damn it! The people in the SUV. That woman is Simek's cousin. Her name is Mila Patekova. She arranged Pokorny's trip. The guy with her is that local cop who found Pokorny's minivan."

"He doesn't know anything."

The driver's knuckles whitened on the steering wheel. He turned to his partner.

"Idiot, if he doesn't know anything why is he here? Damn!"

***

Mila parked near the kitchen door of the bed and breakfast and knocked. A white-haired woman appeared.

"Mrs. Borden, I'm Mila Patekova, a realtor from Nags Head, May we come in?"

Mrs. Borden frowned and turned to Jim Harrigan.

"And who might you be?"

"I'm with the Duck Police Department. I know your son Tony. We worked together on a case last year."

Mrs. Borden's son was with the Manteo Police Department. She peered into Jim's eyes.

"Have I met you?"

"No Ma'am, but I know his wife Louise, and little Anthony. He told me about his 'Granny Katie.'"

At the mention of her grandson, Mrs. Borden unlatched the storm door, turned down the TV, and pointed to her coffee pot.

"Would you like some coffee? At my age, I have to be careful. My husband is asleep in the den. Have a seat."

Jim took a cup. He and Mrs. Borden chatted while Mila sat silent. *Hurry up, Jim. Get to the point. Ask her about Anne.*

Finally. Mila was done waiting.

"Mrs. Borden, I'm sorry. I need to know if my cousin, Anne Simek, is staying here. She's stayed with you before."

Mrs. Borden did not like Mila's accent, and she did not like her attitude. She turned to Jim. He spoke.

"Anne's a blond. Has she been here? It's important."

Mrs. Borden knew Anne was a blond. In fact, she knew Anne well. Anne spent most of her visits in her room, reading and typing on her laptop. This morning, Anne had sworn Mrs. Borden to secrecy about the male visitor upstairs. Mrs. Borden had not seen him, but Anne had implied that he was a boyfriend whose presence she needed to conceal.

She ignored Mila and spoke to Jim Harrigan.

"I know the girl you mean. She's very sweet. She hasn't been here recently. Today, none of our rooms is occupied."

Jim nodded. Only one car had been outside when they arrived. He turned to Mila.

"It was worth a shot, but Anne's not here. We'd better go."

Mrs. Borden shrugged and clicked on the TV.

Mila and Jim left.

***

The driver of the Ford Excursion watched the white SUV turn out the lane and leave. He looked at his partner.

"They didn't find Pokorny."

"The old woman must not have told them about him. But why not?"

"I have no idea. But if Patekova doesn't know he's here, she's clueless. She must not know that Vaclav stole the files."

"If Patekova doesn't, then Simek must. She hid Vaclav."

"Damn right. If we find her, we find the records."

"But where is she?"

"She'll be back. Vaclav is here. Trust me, she'll be back."

The driver knew stakeouts. He handed his cup to his partner.

"Pour me more coffee. The next visitor will be Simek."

***

******

54

Chapter 8
Friday, November 19

In Old Town Prague, it was two a.m. and Karel Moravec was snoring. Ivana eased his limp arm from her waist and slipped out of the bed. She stood up and tied her negligee about her.

Karel stirred and reached his hand for her vacated pillow.

Ivana stared and waited, frozen.

The sonorous breathing resumed. Ivana stepped to a chair and retrieved her purse from under her red scarf. Three steps more and she was in her spacious bathroom. She shut the double doors and switched on the lights. The mirrored wall reflected the outline of her shapely breasts and hips.

Ivana could still feel Karel's hands pawing at her. *How much longer can I endure this animal?*

She shuddered. *Ivana, get hold of yourself.*

Karel provided well for her. She wore designer clothes, enjoyed the haute cuisine at upscale restaurants, skied on vacations at Val Thorens in France and Graz in Austria, and drove a beige Mercedes registered to Karel Moravec. Not least, she lived in this upscale apartment in Old Town with a splendid view of the Charles Bridge and the Prague Castle.

Yet she was unhappy. She abhorred her body, though it had brought her Karel's rewards.

She dropped the negligee to the floor and gazed, full length, in the mirror. Her breasts were round and gracefully tilted, but what good were they? They had not nurtured life as her own mother's had.

Mine are good only to nourish his lusts, the needs of a beast.

She remained staring at her breasts.

Were her breasts to swell with milk, due to a new life in her womb, Karel's rejection would be immediate and final. How many times had he threatened her to be careful.

She thought of her own mother and cringed. Ivana had been young when her mother died, but she had seen her pray and heard her sing of heaven. She had loved her mother. Thank God, her mother could not see what had become of her daughter.

Or maybe her mother could see her? See what she had become, a possession, a commodity, bought, paid for, and without love.

She continued to stare at her reflection. A hot flash coursed over her. Sweat beaded her forehead. She wanted a shower, desperately. She needed pure water to cover her, to cleanse her.

She sat on the edge of the Jacuzzi, head in her hands. She murmured.

"*Není to dobré.* 'It's no good.' It won't work. Think, Ivana, think."

She resolved to break with Karel. *But how? He was dangerous.*

She needed to take a step, a single step, any step. *But where to start?*

Ivana thought of Gustav. Her father, Ivan, had deserted her mother when Ivana was born, but Gustav had befriended them. He had bounced her on his knee. And now Karel was going to kill him. For no reason.

I cannot let that happen. I will not!

She must alert Gustav. It would be a small step but one towards freedom nonetheless. Then Gustav would owe her.

Ivana picked up her cell phone.

Deftly and rapidly her fingers touched the desired sequence of letters. Soon, an encrypted text was on its way across the Atlantic to North Carolina.

Done! Relieved, she sat on the edge of the Jacuzzi.

She switched off the lights before opening the bathroom doors.

Quietly she drew a bathrobe about her and went to the padded lounge. She sat, eyes open, wide awake.

She shivered. No way would she get back in bed with the "beast" this night.

Finally, her chin lowered and touched her throat. She dozed.

***

In North Carolina, Gustav Slavik followed Anne Simek's twisted route. He could not afford to lose her.

Gustav was a native-born Czech, although his mother was German from the "GDR," the East Germany of Cold War days. She had named "Gustav" after her father. Fortunately for Gustav's mother, the name "Gustav" was admissibly Czech. His Name Day was August 2. (A child's name had to come from an official "Name Day" list.)

Thanks to his mother, Gustav could speak "familiar" German, but his educated language was Czech, with some Russian added due to his early schooling. In the eighties he had added French while working as a liaison to a French terrorist based in Liège, Belgium. There too, he had picked up his English from the Sky channel on TV.

He was an old-school Communist, a man of the people. In the name of the people he was willing to undertake many tasks. In particular, and for a fee, the assassination of a capitalist like Pokorny. He smiled. A blatant capitalist like Karel Moravec was paying him good money to eliminate enemies of the people. Capitalism would always defeat itself!

He hated Americans! A corrupt capitalist named Reagan, together with a Polak Pope, had brought an end to Gustav's preferred way of life!

***

After her diverting maneuvers, Anne slowed down, causing Peter to slow also. Anne waited for the third car to pass. It did not. The lights stayed discretely to the rear.

She sped up. Peter did likewise. She looked in the rearview mirror hoping to see nothing behind Peter. That hope was dashed. The third set of lights had kept pace. They remained as before.

***

Gustav did not think that Anne was aware of his presence, but nevertheless decided not to follow closely. He was a safe distance back when his cell phone signaled the arrival of a message.

He checked the sender. It was Ivana, his contact with Karel.

Gustav had known her mother before her marriage. Her husband, Ivan, had been a true worker, a *Soudruh*, who had supported Gustav through several struggles with traitors to the Party. And he had known Ivana as a little girl.

Too, Gustav knew Karel Moravec and detested him. He hoped that Ivana's relation with Karel was only business. But he knew the man.

Gustav read the text message. Ivana's warning was clear. He owed her, big time!

Děkuji moje děvčatko. 'Thank you, my girl.'

The message changed his plans. Gustav pulled the minivan off the road and parked.

***

Anne Simek was elated when the lights of the minivan disappeared. Relieved, mouthing a silent thanks, she turned onto Highway 64, and drove across the bridge to Roanoke Island.

Shortly thereafter, she turned south on Route 345. Peter Zeleny followed.

Anne turned on her CD player. The dulcet tones of Dennis Brain's French Horn reverberated from speakers back and front, Mozart's horn concertos. She smiled. Mozart had loved Prague, as had Anne. She turned up the sound. For the first time since Elizabeth City, she relaxed.

She took the unpaved road to her left. Not far ahead was the lane to the Bordens.' All was peaceful.

Calmly she drove down the lane to the bed and breakfast. The evergreen oaks and pines, once cheerful in the sunlight, now were dark and somber. They blocked the little available moonlight from the roadway. From a far-removed perch, a screech owl provided its eerie call.

Anne was glad the lights of Peter's car were close behind her.

Her headlights swept around the bend and illuminated the porch of the bed and breakfast. Peter's headlights followed. Vaclav's room was dark. Only a lone yellow bulb glimmered above the kitchen door.

The Bordens' car was parked in the rear.

Anne stepped out. She turned to Peter and whispered.

"The Bordens are asleep."

"Where are we?"

"Never mind. Vaclav is on the second floor. Follow me. I have the key."

She entered through the front porch. Peter followed.

They took the stairs to the second floor. The wood creaked under Peter's weight. They reached the upstairs hallway.

No sound came from Vaclav's room.

She turned the key.

"Vaclav, It's me. I'm back."

She opened the door.

The bed was empty, its mattress upended and slit. The drawers of the dresser lay upside down, empty. The closet door was open, hanging by a single hinge. In the bathroom, the lid of the commode lay on the floor.

A piece of paper was taped to the bedpost.

Simek, We have your friend. You have the papers. We'll trade. Stand outside chapel at Whalebone Junction, tomorrow noon. Alone, No cops or else.

Anne handed the note to Peter. He stared at her.

"What do they mean? What papers? What are they talking about?"

She shook her head.

"I have no idea about any papers or records, but Vaclav wanted to discuss some documents with you. You must know what about."

"They must be records or reports from Hus-Kinetika's files. That's probably what he wanted to show me. He knows that I think Hus-Kinetika's drug, Xolak, is dangerous, and that their inaccurate report conceals that fact."

"But I don't have any papers. And when I brought Vaclav here there was nothing with him."

"OK, let's back up. It was Mila that arranged your meeting with Vaclav, right?"

She nodded affirmatively. He started to speak, but she continued.

"Look, I'm studying religious Philosophy. My thesis contrasts von Hildebrand with Kant and Thomas Aquinas, and emphasizes von Hildebrand's stand against the Nazis. I'm no longer in medicine. I never heard of Xolak or fraud or any of this."

She kept on.

"All I know is that after Vaclav was shot, I brought him here to the bed and breakfast. He was sure Hus-Kinetika was behind the shooting, but to me he wanted to talk about his father, to know if his father really had tried to have sex with me in exchange for grades in medical school. I told him yes. He understood, I mean we understood each other. He knows how his father was with women."

She looked straight at Peter. Her face reddened.

But his focus was now.

"So the only people who saw Vaclav were you and your cousin, Mila."

"That's right, who else is there?"

"And you don't have the papers."

"I told you that!"

"Exactly. That means you have to talk to Mila."

***

******

Chapter 9
Friday, November 19

Neither Anne Simek or Peter wanted to be near Vaclav's blood-stained room. Without waking the Bordens, they slipped out of the bed and breakfast and headed for the Outer Banks. They decided to stay at a Comfort Inn in Nags Head. It was close to Whalebone Junction, where Anne was to meet Vaclav's captors at noon the next day.

Anne drove in silence. *Mila, you got me into this mess. Now you have to get me out of it. Whatever papers you have, for God's sake let me have them or Vaclav will die.*

She looked in the mirror. Peter's car was right behind her.

She turned into the motel parking. Peter followed.

They took two rooms, but the desk clerk eyed them with a grin. Anne wanted none of that. She spoke loudly for his benefit.

"Good night, Doctor. I'll see you at breakfast."

Once in her room, she called her cousin, Mila.

There was no answer.

***

In Nag's Head, Gustav Slavik had a new mission. He parked his minivan under a beach house whose shuttered windows showed that it was closed for the winter. He cut the motor and extinguished his headlights.

Wooden posts lifted the house a full floor above the ground, so that his car was completely sheltered from above. The location of the posts provided Gustav with clear views of two buildings across the way, the Patek Realty office and the adjacent house.

Patek Realty occupied a frame building comprised of a single floor at ground level, To either side, wheelchair accessible ramps flanked a small central entrance directly attainable by three steps.

Next door, Mila's house was set on posts, so that her first-floor windows looked down on the roof of her office building some yards away. Her home's main level was attained by a single wooden stairway that mounted from the driveway. There was no deck on that level, so that other than climbing one of the splintery posts, access to her house was only by the stairway.

Gustav's thoughts were all of Mila.

This woman knew about Pokorny, what he's is doing. She's no innocent. She's involved and she knows.

You're slipping, Gustav. You should have seen this earlier. Simek's only in this because of Pokorny's father. She knows nothing. Patekova either has the papers or knows where they are!

And thanks to Ivana, I know Karel's plans!

He lit another Petra and puffed. His thoughts returned to Ivana. She had risked her life to help him. If Karel found out that she had warned Gustav, she would die, and painfully.

Damn you Karel. If you dare hurt her!

He knew the man.

Gustav rapidly tapped a message to Ivana on his phone. After sending it, he studied Mila's house once more.

Karel's goons could not be far.

He needed to act. He slipped out of the van.

***

In Prague, Ivana could not sleep. She went to the window and gazed outwards. The lights still shone on the Prague Castle, although to the East the horizon had lightened in anticipation of the sun.

The dark waters of the Vltava coursed under the arches of the Charles Bridge among whose glowing lampposts, shadowy saintly statues stood staring, awaiting daylight and the arrival of the vendors and artists whose booths served the ever-present tourists, even in a cold November.

For its glow at night, *Zlata Praha*, 'Golden Prague,' depended as much on artificial spotlights as gilded facades. In unforgiving daylight, the latter could appear marred and gray.

No matter, the ancient architecture and narrow streets of Old Town charmed visitors and residents alike, including Ivana.

She shivered and pulled her robe tight about her. Below, she smiled to see the first burst of activity in the graying light as artists and artisans claimed sites on the bridge for their kiosks and wares.

Her phone vibrated through the pocket of her robe and tingled her thigh. She reached for it. A message from Gustav!

She heard a sound behind her. It was Karel.

"Ivanka, little one, what is the matter? Why are you not in bed? I need you. You know that."

"Karel, I ..."

He saw the phone in her hand and reached for it.

"With whom do you speak?"

She drew away, the phone behind her back.

"With no one. It is a message from your backup team. It is only midnight in America."

Karel frowned and looked out the window. The sky to the east was light. After a moment, the furrows on his forehead smoothed out. He smiled.

"Then we shall pretend that the night is just starting here also. Come back to bed Ivanka. you work much too hard, little one. You need to relax."

He gripped her arm and pulled her to the bed.

She could not resist. He was strong.

As Karel rolled on top of her, she glanced back.

The phone with Gustav's message lay open and exposed on the padded lounge.

Terrified, she held her breath.

Would Karel see it?

She twisted to distract him.

***

Mila turned her SUV north on Route 158 towards Kitty Hawk and Duck where Jim Harrigan's F250 pickup was still parked at the restaurant.

He sat silent.

"Jim, what are you thinking?"

Ever the trained interrogator, Jim asked questions, he did not answer them. He looked sideways at Mila and broke the rule.

"I think Mrs. Borden was not straight with us. I watched her eyes. She was evasive. She has seen your cousin Anne, and recently."

"That woman doesn't like me."

"She's uncomfortable with foreigners. She probably doesn't like your accent."

"What's wrong with my accent?"

"Nothing, believe me, nothing at all. I like it. You sound like a movie star."

Mila laughed.

"It's OK, Jim. I like you too, and I'm grateful for today. Thanks."

They arrived at Jim's truck sooner than either of them liked. As he got out of the SUV, Mila called through the door.

"It's agreed then, we'll visit the bed and breakfast tomorrow morning, first thing."

Jim nodded.

Mila backed up and left for Nags Head.

***

Still dark on the Carolina coast, it was light now in Prague. Sexually spent, Karel was again asleep.

Ivana slipped out of bed once more. She retrieved her phone and read Gustav's text.

Karel is no good.

I will get Vaclav's papers and trade them to Karel for you.

I remember your mother. G.

She erased the message.

She went to the window and looked out. In spite of the cold morning, pedestrians in coats thronged the Charles Bridge. She yearned to join them, to be normal again.

And thanks to Gustav, there was hope!

Ivana stepped into the shower.

***

After leaving Jim Harrigan in Duck, Mila returned home in Nags Head. She guided the white SUV into the dark driveway, turned off the lights and cut the engine.

She sat silent for a moment. Jim Harrigan had been a big help to her. *Thank God for him. I know he likes me.*

She noticed a van, lights out, parked under the Martins' house across the street.

That's odd? The Martins' house is shut down for the winter.

She peered into the darkness. She could see no movement. She could not tell whether someone was in the van.

She turned and scanned the dark Oleander bushes that lined her own driveway. No movement was discernible.

Mila took a deep breath. She located her house key, and held it ready to insert in the door should she need to act fast. After that precaution, she stepped out of the car. With a single motion she shut the door and compressed the padlock symbol on the car's remote.

She heard the reassuring simultaneous "clicks." The SUV was secure.

Without looking back, she hurried to the stairway. She heard sounds (footsteps?) from the direction of the Martin house, but a sudden gust of wind rustled through her Oleanders, simultaneously rotating the creaking wings of the Martin's wooden "Mallard" weather vane.

She looked back but saw nothing.

She ran up the stairs. At the landing, she thrust the key into the lock. It turned smoothly.

She pushed the door open with her shoulder and stepped in.

Breathing heavily, she shut the door and twisted the lock handle. The dead bolt slid smoothly home. She heard the sound of security.

"Click!"

She was safe.

***

Mila stood panting from her dash up the steep steps.

She peered back through the peephole. There was no one on the landing. Had she imagined those footsteps?

Get a hold of yourself, Mila. Now!

She opened the fridge and drew out a bottle of beer, Pilsner Urquell. She stood numbly, then tipped the bottle and swallowed.

Her thoughts drifted to her rentals, from the demands of her cousin Anne for a "roach-free" house, to those of recent tenants for "smoke-free," houses.

Mila did not smoke. Her home *was* smoke-free.

Damn it, Mila. Stop the daydreaming. Concentrate! Something is wrong here. What is it?

Then she realized. A faint odor emanated from under the bedroom door.

Tobacco! The acrid smell of an East European cigarette.

She turned to see a man in the doorway.

His left hand held the offensive cigarette.

His right hand held a gun.

***

******

Chapter 10
Saturday, November 20

At the inn in Nags Head, Anne Simek ate a self-serve breakfast. She swallowed her coffee and flipped the rotating waffle iron.

Peter Zeleny was late. Their rooms offered a free breakfast, but only until nine. If he did not hurry he would miss it.

Anne wanted to like Peter, but she did not trust him. Vaclav Pokorny was in danger, and Peter seemed not to care. She took her waffle out and covered it with butter and syrup. Some people lost their appetite when nervous, but not Anne, she ate. Her mouth was stuffed with carbs when Peter Zeleny finally appeared.

"Peter. Where have you been? I have to be at Whalebone Junction at noon.

"Was Mila any help? What about Vaclav's papers? What did she say?"

"Mila! She doesn't answer her phone or call me back. She's useless. We need to do something."

That "We" worried Peter. He did not want to be part of this operation. He barely knew Anne, and he knew that her father hated his.

"What will you do? You don't have the papers. You can't go."

"I have to try to save Vaclav. I'm going anyway."

She snorted.

"And you can't stop me."

***

In Duck, North Carolina, Jim Harrigan rolled over in bed as the morning sun shone through his bedroom window. He rubbed his eyes against the glare and read the digits on his alarm clock.

Damn! Mila is waiting.

He kicked the sheets off, jumped up, and pulled on his pants.

He splashed water under his arms and rubbed on fresh deodorant. He shaved quickly, There was no time to shower. Still buttoning his shirt, he left his apartment.

Jim was off-duty today. Nonetheless, he settled into the driver's seat of his Duck Police Department vehicle. The Chief encouraged its use when off-duty, in the belief that the increased police presence deterred potential wrongdoers.

As he drove south towards Kitty Hawk and Nags Head, he punched Mila's number on his cell phone. There was no answer, only an automated message request. His eyes turned back to the road. Crews were at work clearing debris from the shoulders of the road where it had been pushed the morning after the Northeaster. There was little traffic and the drive was peaceful.

He slowed as he passed the doughnut store on his left. Whenever duty took him south to Nags Head, Jim stopped for free doughnuts and coffee. Jim was desperate for both food and coffee, but Mila was waiting. He drove by.

He parked in front of Mila's realty office. It was closed.

Jim turned towards her house. He trudged up the wooden stairway and stopped at the landing.

He froze. His stomach muscles tightened.

Her door was ajar. Through the crack he saw an overturned shelf, its books and papers strewn over the floor.

He unsnapped his holster and grasped his Glock nine millimeter.

✱✱✱

Jim held the Glock in both hands and pointed the gun at the doorway. He kicked the door wide.

No one there!

The kitchen was a shambles, the contents of cabinets strewn about, the table upended. The fridge door hung wide while frozen cartons, smashed and dripping with moisture, lay on the floor amidst bruised vegetables.

Glock ready, he moved to the living area.

Again no one.

This area was worse. Shelves were emptied, drawers overturned. The sofa's frame was turned on its side. Its cushions, ripped and torn, lay on the floor. The end table was upside down, its lamp sideways. Beside it were two pieces of a shattered phone.

The bedroom door was closed. He moved towards it, but stopped at the sound of footsteps.

Someone had entered the house.

***

Jim listened. Then he turned back, and pointing his weapon before him, stepped towards the kitchen. He gaped.

There stood Mila in fashionable jeans, her hair neatly arranged.

"Jim? How did you get in? Who did this? Who wrecked my house?"

Jim holstered his Glock.

"I think you should tell me."

He turned and righted the sofa frame onto its legs.

"Mila, what happened here? Where did you go?"

"How did you get in? I locked the door."

"The door was open. The place was a wreck. Someone searched for something. And they weren't looking for money."

A tilted drawer protruded from the end table. Five- and twenty-dollar bills had spilled onto the rug.

"I couldn't sleep. I was out of coffee. I left at seven to get some. I thought I'd be back before you got here."

Jim's eyes flicked to the half-empty can of Maxwell House Coffee spilled onto the kitchen counter.

She read that thought.

"I forgot it was in the cupboard. I mostly keep it in the fridge."

His next question caught her off guard. He pointed to a plate on the counter. On it were ashes and a spent cigarette.

"Mila, You don't smoke and that's not an American cigarette."

"No, It's a 'Petra,' a Czech cigarette."

"All right, who smoked it? Did he do this?"

He waved his hand at the wreckage. She spoke.

"A man *was* here. His name is Gustav. He's Czech. He's older. He had a gun. I never saw him before, but he knew someone I had befriended in Prague, a girl named Ivana. He was trying to help her escape from someone named Karel Moravec. He wanted to know where Vaclav was and what he had given me."

She waved at the room.

"But he did not do this."

"So the house was in order when you left? But you didn't go out for coffee, did you? You met someone, right?"

"No, I met no one. I went out for coffee like I told you. The house was fine when I left. What's more, I locked the door."

"I have to accept that, but this Czech guy, he didn't hurt you?"

"I was scared, but no, he didn't touch me. He knew I was Ivana's friend."

"What did he want?"

"He said Ivana was desperate, and I could help. He said if I gave him Vaclav's papers, he could save her. He had a cell phone, a pre-pay. He gave me the number and told me to call him if Vaclav contacted me. I told him I would. He told me not to tell anyone. Then he left."

"How did he get in the house?"

"He must have picked the lock. All the windows were locked."

Jim looked at the clutter on the floor.

"And you don't think he did this?"

"No, Gustav would not trash my house."

"All right, call that number. I want to talk to him."

Mila punched the number. There was no answer. The line shifted to "Message."

Jim took the phone from her and punched "Stop."

He stared at the mess on the floor.

"Mila, whoever searched your house wants what Vaclav brought, and they think you have it. Did Vaclav leave anything with you, a package, a computer CD, a thumb drive, a letter, anything?"

"Jim, there was nothing."

"All right, let's step back. When did you first see Vaclav?"

"It was last Tuesday. I was in Washington on business. I picked him up at Dulles Airport in Virginia. He had just come through customs. He had a carryon, nothing else."

"No packages, no other luggage?"

"Nothing."

"All right, what then?"

"My car was in short-term parking. We walked to it together. He was not out of my sight."

"Not even for the bathroom?"

"He did stop, but I stood outside with the carryon. It was only a few minutes and I was right by the door. Then we went to the lot to find my car. We got in and drove straight to Nags Head, to my house. It took six hours. We only stopped for gas."

"What time did you get here."

"Let's see. His flight arrived at Dulles at two, say an hour for customs, and then the drive here. It must have been about nine or ten in the evening."

"You didn't go out to eat. And he gave you nothing?"

"That's right, nothing. I heated a frozen pizza. Then we went to bed."

Jim raised his eyebrows.

Mila huffed.

"Relax, he was in the spare bedroom."

"All right. Did you or Vaclav go to your office that night?"

"No, and as far as I know Vaclav never was there."

"How did he get the minivan?"

"Wednesday morning, I took him to the Enterprise Rental in Kill Devil Hills. But you're a cop, I'm sure you already checked that it was their minivan."

Jim nodded.

"You're right. I am a cop. Look at this mess around you. Someone wants something Vaclav had, and they think you have it."

"But he didn't give me anything."

Jim surveyed the torn papers, ripped cushions and open books strewn about the floor. He kicked at the rubble.

He thought back to his days as a detective in Raleigh. Investigations mostly dealt with the obvious. *Of course!*

"Mila, the carryon. Where is it?"

"Maybe he took it with him in the van."

"It was not in the abandoned minivan. Your cousin could have it, or whoever shot Vaclav, or maybe it's in the dunes, near where I found the van?"

Mila froze. Silent, she stared out the window.

"Damn it, Mila, you know more than you let on. Don't hold out on me. Tell me."

He took her hand.

"You're in danger. You need to trust someone. Try me."

Mila's shoulders shook and her lips quivered. Jim put his arm around her.

"Mila, please, let me help you. Tell me what you know."

Her body went slack. She rested her head on his shoulder.

"I want to, but I'm afraid. Jim, can I trust you?"

She did not wait for a response.

"I'll tell you everything. The man who was here last night, Gustav, is the one who shot Vaclav. His last name is Slavik. He was a true communist, probably still wants to be, but now does jobs for money, what you call 'wet work.' He's an assassin, but because Ivana is my friend, he never would hurt me."

She saw his look of incredulity.

"Look, the eighties were all mixed up. In the same family some were communists, some were not, and many that were communists were liberal and against the Soviets. Our old folks had proved that too in 1968. It was *liberal* communists that gave us the Prague Spring before the Soviets crushed it."

She slipped her head off his shoulder and looked into his eyes.

"You have to understand that we Czechs are not barbarians. We are cultured. Mozart loved Prague. And we are Westerners, Western Slavs. Prague is west of Vienna!"

Jim Harrigan stared. *Where is she going with this?*

"Anyway, Gustav had a job to do for Karel, a bigwig with Hus-Kinetika. Because of Ivana, Gustav has turned against Karel. He wanted Vaclav's papers to trade with Karel for Ivana's safety, for her freedom. Gustav knew her mother and father."

"Mila, you are talking about a cold-blooded killer. What have you done?"

"I believed Gustav. I gave him what I had, Vaclav's carryon."

"You what!"

"Don't be angry. It might not be that important."

"What the hell do you mean by that?"

"There was nothing in the carryon but a change of clothes. But there is something else I didn't share with you."

Jim Harrigan shook his head in disbelief. *What now?*

"I told you the truth when I said Vaclav didn't give me anything. He didn't. But it wasn't the whole truth. When he arrived at the airport he had some newspapers under his arm. When I drove him to the Enterprise Rental, we stopped first at a UPS store. The newspapers were with him when he went in, but when he came out they were gone. He must have used them as packing. The point is he mailed something."

"And?"

"I saw the address on the receipt. It was to Dr. Peter Zeleny, care of some company called 'Ryan Associates' in Bethesda Maryland."

Jim stared in stunned silence.

***

In Maryland, at Ryan Associates in Bethesda, Jeannine Ryan looked up from her desk as Aileen arrived at the office.

"Aileen, where is Peter's father staying?"

"He's in Rockville, at a Motel on Shady Grove. That's where I took him last night."

"That's far away from us, at least a half hour."

"Not far enough. He's a womanizer. He's dangerous. I'd feel safer if Johan Zeleny was gone. How did he have a son like Peter?"

"He told you that Peter sent him to ask about someone named Vaclav Pokorny?"

"Yes, but I don't know if Peter did or not. I don't trust the old goat. He was all over me! He told me that he could see why his son liked me. I shoved him away and he started talking drivel about greedy capitalists and keeping up the 'People's' struggle, whoever the 'People' are, surely not me and you."

Aileen folded her arms and grimaced.

"What's more, I don't believe he knows where Peter is."

At that point there was a knock on the door. It was a UPS delivery for "Doctor Peter Zeleny" care of Ryan Associates.

No sender was indicated.

Jeannine Ryan studied the package.

"Strange, why us? But Peter's missing, I'm opening this now."

She tore open the wrapping.

"There's nothing here but packing, crumpled newspapers."

Aileen took several papers and flattened them on the desk.

"These papers are not the same. This one must be Russian, it's Cyrillic. And these are Czech, at least the alphabet is Latin. Wait, here's one in English, 'The Prague Post.'"

Jeannine pointed at a small crumpled mass.

"That's not a newspaper."

Aileen smoothed the wrinkles flat. It was a memo on Hus-Kinetika Letterhead from a "Vaclav Pokorny." She started. Peter's father had asked about "Pokorny." The text was in

Czech, but the subject clearly was Xolak. The memo featured a table of numbers.

Rok	2002	2003	2004	2005
Průměr	57.33	111.33	140.67	175.33
Rok	2006	2007	2008	2009
Průměr	148.67	153.67	155.33	xxxx

Jeannine looked at the numbers and turned to Aileen.

"Clearly 'Rok' means 'year,' so 'Průměr' must mean average."

She did some quick calculations.

"Aileen, these are the real 3-point averages for Xolak. From 2003 on if I divide them by three, I get the fake values in the report. The increase in allergic reactions to Xolak is large and real!"

She grinned.

"And look. 'Vaclav Pokorny' is cited in the Appendix of the report. This memo is the proof we need for Larry Hodges and the FDA."

She pumped her fist.

"This is proof that Hus-Kinetika faked the data!"

***

******

Chapter 11
Saturday, November 20

In Nags Head, the gray Ford Excursion had been parked on a street behind the Patek Realty all morning. Both the driver and his passenger wore earphones. The driver stopped listening and lifted the headset from his ears. He turned to his partner.

"I told you that local cop Harrigan wouldn't know to check for bugs. What do you think of Mila spilling her guts like that?"

"Why don't we kill Gustav and grab Pokorny's carryon for Karel? Then we can go to Bethesda and visit these 'Ryan Associates' or whoever and find that damn package."

"Sounds right."

"What about the Simek woman and meeting her at Whalebone Junction?"

"Forget Simek. She knows nothing. We know that now. It's the Patek woman who knows more than she lets on. She's clever. She tells only what she has to."

"Pokorny is dead anyway. What do we do with his body? It can't stay in the trunk."

"Hell, we'll dump him in Currituck Sound. The idiot never should have betrayed Karel."

"He may have been an idiot, but he got the papers out of the country and into the USA and we don't have them yet."

The driver fell silent for a moment. The passenger picked up his cell phone.

"I must text Karel right away. He needs to know that Ivana is betraying him."

"Don't be stupid. Karel won't believe you. He'll believe her before you. You accuse her and one of you will be in trouble, and it won't be Ivana!"

"You mean wait?"

"No choice. She'll slip up soon enough."

***

In Nags Head, Jim Harrigan looked down from the window of Mila's house. The Ford Excursion on the roadway behind Mila's realty had not moved.

"Mila, that car is still there. Where are your binoculars?"

Every Nags Head home had binoculars to watch birds and boats offshore.

She pointed to an overturned end table.

"They were in the drawer. There they are, on the floor."

Jim took them and focused on the Excursion. He turned back to Mila, a finger on his lips for silence. He penciled a note and held it before her.

The guy in the passenger seat has earphones.
He's listening to us.

Mila stood quietly while Jim scanned the room. Only one end table was upright. He ran his fingers under it.

When he stood erect, he held a small circular device between thumb and forefinger. He went to the window and put the device on the floor. He focused the binoculars on the Ford Excursion and smashed the listening device with his heel.

"Crache!"

The passenger in the Ford Excursion tore his earphones off and threw them against the windshield.

Moments later, the Ford Excursion drove away.

Jim turned to Mila.

"They must have planted that bug when they trashed your house."

"Aren't you worried there might be another bug, that they're still listening to us?"

"I don't think so. They didn't have a lot of time, and most of it was for searching. Besides they took off. One of them has a headache right now. His ears are ringing."

He added.

"But, you're right. We should check for more bugs. I have a tech friend who will sweep your place after we clean up, and that will take a while."

He frowned and took her hand.

"Mila, the damage is done. They know about your Gustav character as well as Vaclav's package and those Ryan Associates, whoever they are."

***

The passenger in the Ford Excursion held his hand over his ear.

"That guy broke my ear drum. How did he find the bug? You told me he was a dumb local."

The driver replied without taking his eyes off the road.

"That's what I thought. I'd better check on him. His name is Harrigan."

Keeping one hand on the wheel, the driver deftly thumbed a message on his phone. In seconds, the text was on its way.

They drove north towards Kitty Hawk. Minutes later, as the massive Nags Head dunes came into view on the left, the phone vibrated with a reply.

With one eye on the road, he scrolled the text and read. He hit the brakes and pulled onto the shoulder.

"Damn!"

"What?"

"Harrigan isn't a yokel after all. He was four years as a homicide detective upstate in Raleigh, North Carolina. He semi-retired to come to the Outer Banks."

"So what?"

"So before that, until his thirties he was with the CIA, and he wasn't a paper pusher. He was in covert ops in Austria, in Vienna."

"He can't know about Karel."

"The hell he can't. You heard what Mila told him. And he'll have contacts at the Agency. He can get information, and help too.

"What do we do?"

"For now, we dump Vaclav's body. Then we think."

He started the engine.

"Damn it, first Gustav, and now this Harrigan guy! We may have to kill them both, but we'll need help. I'll call Karel."

79

They continued north, the Nags Heads dunes disappeared. Some minutes later, the Wright Brothers' Memorial came into view.

***

In Nags Head, Jim Harrigan and Mila finished straightening the wreckage of her rooms. Now it was noon and they were hungry. They opted to eat out at the Tortugas' Lie Restaurant.

Mila ordered for Jim, a grilled yellowfin tuna sandwich with Teriyaki glaze, Swiss Cheese, and Portabella relish. Jim left it largely uneaten. *I wonder if she likes doughnuts?*

Still he smiled.

"It's been a while since I had lunch with an appealing woman."

Mila's lips thinned.

"Thanks a lot. You just ate with me at the Blue Point yesterday, remember?"

"I didn't eat, I only had coffee, and you boxed your catfish to take with you."

He smiled again.

"Besides, Mila, you *are* attractive. Trust me."

Mila cringed at the word "Trust," but touched his arm.

"Jim, don't you like the sandwich?"

He shrugged and reverted to 'cop' mode.

"Mila, if Gustav didn't wreck your house, then who did? Who were those guys in the Ford Excursion. I couldn't see the license plate. Damn it, who are these people?"

She looked away. He added.

"Mila, let me help you."

"Jim, try to understand. When I was little we could never trust the police. My mother was Catholic and people knew it. We were on a list. The *Pražské jaro*, the Prague Spring, was in 1968, before I was born. After it was crushed, Husak took over. His Communist thugs had a free hand to enforce their holy Marxism on everyone, especially my mother, but my father too, and he wasn't even religious."

"I was born in 1974. My mother died in 1979. Ten years later we had the *sametová revoluce*, the 'Velvet Revolution.' Everything changed, but hard-liners still hate that."

She swallowed.

"I do want your help. I liked you right away, but I was afraid too. Not just for Anne, but for myself. You carried a gun, and when I grew up, men with guns were *the policie*, never our friends. I know that may not make sense. Anyway, now that I know you, I see my fear wasn't justified. Forgive me."

Her eyes moistened. She looked into his.

"There *is* something I wanted to tell you before, but couldn't."

Jim winced. *Not again.*

She noticed but kept on.

"At the airport, when I picked up Vaclav, he made a phone call. I don't know to whom, but he spoke Russian. My Russian is weak, I read better than I speak, but he repeated one word several times."

She paused and wrote on a napkin, first in Cyrillic and then in the Latin alphabet.

новичок *novichok.*

Jim gaped. Mila explained.

"'Novichok' means 'newcomer' or 'new guy' in English. In Czech we say 'nováček,' it's close to the Russian."

"Mila, I know the word. What else did you hear."

"I recognized a man's name, 'Mirzayanov.'"

She looked down and separated the grains of rice on her plate with her fork while she resumed.

"I asked Vaclav about 'Mirzayanov.' Vaclav wouldn't talk about him. Instead Vaclav told me he had evidence that Hus-Kinetika was involved in a horrible plan, something bigger than Pharmaceuticals. That's why he came to America. He could prove it."

She looked up. Jim had half-risen in his seat. The intensity of his stare frightened her. She drew back.

Jim's shoulders slumped. He lowered himself down onto his chair. His knuckles paled as he gripped the table.

"Mila, in 1992, three years after the Berlin Wall came down, a former Soviet chemist, Vil Mirzayanov, revealed that the Russians had developed a new chemical weapon, a Weapon of Mass Destruction. It was a new class of nerve agents, said to be the deadliest yet. It's public knowledge. You can read about it in Mirzayanov's book, *State Secrets*."

He set his teeth.

"They had a name for the new agents. You just wrote it on that napkin."

"It's 'Novichok.' It's the 'newcomer agent,' the 'new guy' on the block."

"Mila, Vaclav must know that Hus-Kinetika is producing chemical weapons."

She gasped. Her eyes moistened.

"My God, Jim. Vaclav must have found out that Hus-Kinetika was involved with these nerve agents, That means the men who wrecked my house are Hus-Kinetika's goons, descendants of Husak's communist thugs. They will stop at nothing to destroy Vaclav and his evidence. They are killers."

She picked up the napkin and wiped her eyes.

"Damn it, Jim. They heard you in my house. You're in danger too!"

***

In the early afternoon, Anne Simek returned to the Comfort Inn in Nags Head. She left Peter Zeleny at the door to his room, and went down the hall to hers.

She slid the key card into the slot, but her hand faltered and the indicator light stayed red. She pushed again. The LED shone a faint green and the lock gave a welcome click. She stepped in, paused to throw the deadbolt, and fastened the chain.

For a moment she stood motionless. Then the sobs started, long and deep with shallow, intermittent breaths that could not furnish sufficient oxygen to her lungs. She threw herself on the bed, gasping and sighing out of control. By the time her breathing returned to normal, her pillowcase was wet with tears.

I did what they said. I was there at the Junction. Why didn't they call?" At those thoughts, she knew.

He's dead!

She rolled on her back and focused through wet eyes on the ceiling. In the shadows on the textured paint she imagined Vaclav's face.

Why did I leave you alone? But you told me to go. I had too. You insisted. I should have said "No!" I should have stayed.

Anne had arranged to meet Peter Zeleny in Elizabeth City when she and Vaclav were near the hospital there. But he had refused to go, so she had taken him to the Bordens' near Wanchese, far in the opposite direction. Now she regretted not changing the meeting with Peter to some place closer to the bed and breakfast.

Vaclav, I'm sorry, for everything.

Through the door she heard a voice.

"Anne, it's me, Peter. Open up."

"What do you want?"

"We need to talk. Open the door, please."

Anne arose, twisted the dead bolt and released the chain.

"Peter, they didn't come."

Her red eyes, swollen cheeks, and disheveled hair softened him.

"Anne, you did everything that they asked. You waited over an hour, alone, no cops."

She grabbed his arm.

"Don't you see. That means Vaclav is dead!"

As a physician, Peter had often borne bad news He did not believe in dissimulation.

"Anne, it's not good, but it's not your fault."

"How would you know? I'm the one who left him alone."

"If you'd been there when they took him, you'd be dead too. Hus-Kinetika's enforcers used to be Communist thugs from the *Státní bezpečnost*. That means 'State Security.'"

"I know what it means. I'm not stupid. I studied in Prague, remember. In the same hospital as you. Or didn't you notice?"

Peter may not have noticed Anne at the Motol Hospital, but here, in Nags Head he "noticed" her a lot.

"Sorry, that was dumb, forgive me."

She blinked. *An apology from a 'Zeleny?'*

"Peter, I left Vaclav alone. I have to live with that."

"Anne, there's nothing more we can do here. I have to go back to Maryland. You should come too."

Anne looked away.

"Peter, go! Whatever Vaclav wanted to tell you, it's too late."

"But what will you do?"

"I need to be alone. I have decisions to make."

"At least call Mila. Let her know you are all right."

"Mila! Forget her! Good bye, Peter."

She pushed him out the door.

This conversation was over.

***

******

Chapter 12
Sunday, November 21

Early morning, and Aileen Harris sat, lost in thought, in the office of Ryan Associates.

She looked up as Jeannine, coffee in hand, came down the stairs.

"Aileen, you're early. Where's Mary Catherine?"

"At church with my mother. I couldn't stop thinking about that package from Vaclav Pokorny. It worries me."

Aileen spread the newspapers from Vaclav's package on her desk.

"There's something about these newspapers I didn't notice yesterday. Some of them are marked up. Look."

Aileen picked up the English-language paper, the Prague Post.

"Someone underlined parts of this article about chemical weapons, organophosphate chemicals that block Cholinesterase from breaking down Acetylcholine. They're called 'Novichok Agents.'"

Jeannine looked. Various words in the articles were underlined, some were circled.

"What about the other newspapers?"

"They're marked up too, but they're either in Russian or Czech. I have no idea what they are about. If Peter were here, he could help, at least with the Czech."

"But he's not. What are these 'Novichok Agents?'"

"They're nerve gas agents, the so-called 'newcomers.' The Russians developed them to be undetectable by the tests that NATO had then, and to be effective against NATO's gas masks."

She took a breath and continued.

"We only found about them after the Wall went down. A Soviet chemist, Vil Mirzayanov, revealed their existence. He had worked on the agents and was concerned about environmental contamination. For that, the Russians put him in Lefortovo Prison, but they had to release him since he had only reported publicly available information. Mirzayanov published his experiences in a book with Outskirts Press in 2009. It's title is *State Secrets*. I read it."

"Aileen, how did you get into this?"

"I'm an electrophysiologist, remember. I did a lot of work with nerve cells, cholinergic receptors, acetylcholine, etc. Nerve agents block the esteric site on cholinesterase where acetylcholine normally attaches to be broken down. Consequently the acetylcholine doesn't break down, but accumulates and remains attached to receptors in the wall of the nerve cell, receptors that admit positive Sodium ions. That causes the Sodium channels to stay open, and keep the nerve cell in a refractory state. No more excitation is possible. Bang, you're dead, or at least very sick."

Jeannine gaped at her partner.

"Slow down. I'm not a biologist."

"But I am going slow. I didn't tell you about the two types of cholinergic receptors, nicotinic and muscarinic and their different effects. They ... ."

Jeannine grimaced and held up her hands.

"I surrender."

"OK, OK. Novichok compounds work the same way. They block cholinesterase from breaking down acetylcholine. There are many of them, but Novichok-5 and -7 are said to be really deadly, maybe eight times more so than VX, the gas Saddam Hussein probably used on the Kurds in Iraq."

Aileen frowned and continued.

"There's disagreement about the formulas for both Novichok-5 and Novichok-7."

Jeannine broke in.

"Enough. We don't know who marked these papers, but what could Novichok agents have to do with Xolak?"

"It beats me. Maybe something or maybe nothing at all."

Aileen shook herself.

"But if Hus-Kinetika is producing nerve agents, we have a lot more to worry about than Xolak."

***

In Wanchese, Anne Simek knocked on the kitchen door of Bordens' bed and breakfast. Kate Borden let her in.

"Annie, where is your gentleman friend?"

"Miss Katie, that didn't work out."

"I'm sorry honey, truly I am. Here sit with me and have some coffee. I'll turn down the TV."

"Miss Katie, you didn't go into my room to clean did you."

"You told me not to and I didn't. It's however you left it."

Anne thought of the bloody sink. She had to scrub the bathroom and clean the stained sheets. She wanted to eliminate all traces of blood. She finished her coffee and stood up.

"Miss Katie, I'd like to stay a few days longer."

"Of course, honey. I'll get you fresh towels and linens."

"Don't bother, I have my own. And don't worry about the room. I'll make do for today."

She moved to go upstairs. Mrs. Borden upped the volume on the TV. The announcer's voice stopped Anne in her tracks.

Breaking News. This just in. Police recovered the body of an unidentified man from the Currituck Sound near Duck this morning following an earlier report by a local fisherman that he had snagged what looked like a human body before his line broke. No further details are available.

Anne paled.

"Honey, what's the matter? Are you all right?"

"I'm fine, Miss Katie. I'm just tired. I think I'll go rest."

Anne went up to Vaclav's room. She was tired, but rest was impossible on "that" bed. She stripped the sheets off. Then she reattached the door hinge. Finally, with rubber gloves and cleaner in hand, she scrubbed the bathroom sink and floor.

She worked hard all afternoon. Her knees were sore after scrubbing floor tiles for an hour. The skin of her hands had red blotches that matched, in part, the holes worn in her rubber gloves from strenuous rubbing. As far as she could tell, Vaclav's bathroom was spotless.

She had achieved her goal. The bathroom sink and tiles were free of visual traces of blood. She poured the last bucket of dirty water down the toilet. Then she sat on the edge of the tub and wept.

***

In the Red Roof Motel on Shady Grove Road in Rockville, Maryland, a disheveled Johan Zeleny finished lunch in his room. On the end table, a near-empty vodka bottle lay on its side dribbling its remains onto the wood.

His phone rang. It was his son, Peter.

"The clinic in Chicago gave me your message. I'm still in North Carolina. Did you talk to Dr. Harris?"

"I talked to her. She knew nothing. Your cell phone wasn't working, so I called Chicago."

"It's charged now. What do you want?"

"My friend, Gustav, wants you to meet him in Maryland."

"Father, Gustav is an assassin. He killed Vaclav!"

"Don't you want to see your father?"

"Yes, but why are you with Gustav?"

"We represent a Czech company."

"Not Hus-Kinetika? You hate capitalists."

"These are changed times. We cannot always choose the company we keep. Even Hus-Kinetika has good projects. Some of my old comrades work there."

"Like Karel Moravec?"

"Moravec is a swine. He was in the Party, but never believed. His grandfather was a Nazi, a friend of Reinhard Heydrich."

"But Gustav?"

"You are wrong about Gustav. He did not kill Vaclav, Karel's men did that."

Johan continued.

88

"Peter, do not forget how Gustav helped us when you were a boy. He believes you can help him against Moravec. You must meet him here, tomorrow."

"But what can I do?"

"He thinks Simek will tell you where Vaclav's papers are."

"Anne doesn't know about the papers. Besides, she won't see me."

"She is a liar, like her father. Simeks are not capable of the truth. But she is our only possibility. Patekova gave Vaclav's carryon bag to Gustav. Gustav tore it apart. It had nothing."

Johan swept the vodka bottle off the table. It bounced on the soft carpet with a dull thump. His voice rose.

"Simek has the documents. Find out where. Don't anger Gustav. We are old comrades, but I can't control him."

"What of my complaint against Hus-Kinetika and Xolak. I cannot drop that."

"That is no concern to Gustav or me."

"All right father. I'll be there tomorrow."

Johan took a breath.

"And Peter, do not get attached to the Simek woman. She is Havel Simek's daughter."

Peter hung up.

***

Minutes later, Gustav Slavik entered Johan's room. He noticed the empty bottle of vodka on the floor and frowned.

Johan Zeleny waved him to sit. Gustav remained standing.

"Well Jan, you and I again. It is like old times, is it not? Tell me, will Peter help us?"

"Of course. He is my son."

"Good. But Jan, Karel's men once were our comrades. They are ruthless. Does Peter know how to use this?"

Gustav held out a 9 mm Makarov.

"He stopped practicing with me after his second year of Medical School. I doubt he's shot a weapon since."

"All right, I won't count on him."

Gustav put the Makarov away and went to the door.

"Make sure Peter is here tomorrow. And Jan, that company, Ryan Associates, the one with the Harris woman that you met, what is Peter's connection with them?"

"Peter wanted their help to prove that Hus-Kinetika lied about Xolak. Harris told me they can prove that the Xolak data are faked. Harris and Ryan only know about Xolak."

"You'd better be right. But you didn't tell Peter they had proof that Hus-Kinetika fabricated the Xolak data. Why not?"

"Aileen Harris didn't like me, so I didn't help her."

Gustav frowned. *Jan, you're too old for women now.*

"It's set then. I'll be back tomorrow to see Peter."

Johan nodded in acquiescence. Gustav grinned.

"Jan, better go easy on the ladies."

But his real concern was the bottle on the floor. Johan's vodka could be a real problem.

***

Gustav went to his own room. The door was labeled "non smoking." *Stupid Americans.* He improvised an ashtray using a plastic cup from the bathroom. Then he shut off the lights and sat motionless in the dark. After a minute, the tip of his cigarette shone orange, the only bright spot in the shadows.

Vodka made Johan weak and Karel Moravec was formidable. To face him, Gustav needed strong allies. He inhaled. The tip of his cigarette crinkled brighter orange. Then he made his decision. His enemies, the money-grubbing Americans, would bring Moravec down!

In the days of the Iron Curtain, Gustav had worked diligently against the corrupt capitalists, but he knew which Americans could defeat Karel. And he knew where to find them, at that Cold War CIA stronghold, the American Embassy in Vienna.

Gustav would made them an offer they could not refuse.

He sat and texted a message to Vienna.

Done!

***

******

Chapter 13
Monday, November 22

Jeannine Ryan stood in the office of Ryan Associates. Her face was as red as her hair.

"Damn it, Aileen, Larry Hodges won't return my messages. That's my third call to the FDA."

"It's Monday morning, he's probably in meetings."

"Sure, that must be the reason, right? The fact that he's a wimp doesn't enter the equation? Look, it's simple. He's afraid of his boss at FDA. He wanted proof about Xolak, and now that we have it, he's afraid to see it. He might have to act."

Aileen nodded.

"Unfortunately, you're one hundred per cent correct."

The phone rang. Jeannine's eyes lit with hope. She picked up.

"Ryan Associates."

Jeannine listened a moment and hung up."

"It wasn't Larry, only a salesman."

"Jeannine, you can't count on Larry to return your call. You just have to keep calling. The FDA has to know about Xolak."

***

Mila pulled her SUV up to the Currituck County Medical Examiner's office. She sat in silence. She did not want to look at any dead body, especially one that had been in the water, but she would perform her duty. *Is it Vaclav?*

At that thought, guilt overwhelmed her. *Why did I arrange the meeting with Anne?* Her shoulders slumped and her eyes filled with tears. A tap on the car window brought her to the present.

It was Jim Harrigan.

"Aren't you coming in? The attendant is waiting."

Mila swallowed and clicked the lock open. Jim opened the door.

"It won't take long. We're grateful to you for doing this."

Mila choked. She did not risk speaking. Jim took her arm.

Inside, the morgue attendant led them into a restricted area. The room was cold and bare. Mila shivered.

Next to the wall was a metal table. On it was a dark bag, whose contours matched the form of a human body. Jim took Mila's arm and guided her to it.

She stood rigid, eyes fixed on the silent plastic.

The attendant unzipped the top to reveal a gray, disfigured face. Something, perhaps crabs, had plucked the eyes. She knew those features, bloated as they were.

Mila gagged. She covered her mouth with her hands and backed away.

Her eyes turned to Jim. Her voice was a whisper.

"Jim, it's Vaclav. That's Vaclav Pokorny."

She broke into tears.

***

After Mila recovered her composure, Jim led her outside the Medical Examiner's Office. He pointed to the F250.

"You're in no shape to drive. Ride in my truck. We can pick up your SUV later."

"No Jim, I'm fine now, really. Besides, it's too far to come back here. Don't you have to work?"

"Not until tonight. If you must drive your car, let me follow you to Nags Head. We can grab some coffee together, and maybe a doughnut."

At that, Mila paused. *A doughnut?*

"Not this time, Jim. I have to get back to the realty office, and I still haven't talked to Anne. She left a message to call. I did, but she hasn't called again."

Jim's brow furrowed.

"You know the police will be looking for Anne now. They need to question her about Vaclav's shooting."

"She's not a suspect, is she?"

"At the moment she is a person of interest. Beyond that, I can't say."

"But Jim, Gustav shot Vaclav, Anne tried to save him."

"I believe you, but they need proof. Gustav isn't available. You should get Anne to come in. They want answers."

"She doesn't return my calls. Don't you trust me?"

"I do, but the police don't. She should call them."

"Jim, you're a cop. Anne is my cousin. I know her. I know she did not shoot Vaclav. And I know Gustav was not lying. I know he shot him."

Jim Harrigan looked at his feet.

"Mila, I don't know about Anne and Vaclav, but I do know you. And I saw the men who wrecked your rooms. They're professionals. I'm afraid for you."

"For me? How about Anne. The next body I identify may be hers."

***

Before meeting with his father and Gustav, Peter Zeleny took a room at a Rockville hotel. Once settled, he went straight to the lounge where he ordered a Scotch on the Rocks, and sipped slowly. He needed to think.

Two gulps later, he took out his phone and called Ryan Associates.

There was no answer. He left no message.

For a moment, he studied the ice cubes that remained in his glass. Then he ordered another Scotch.

He downed it immediately. His decision made, he punched the number of Anne Simek's cell phone.

"Peter, why are you calling? I thought you went back to Maryland?"

"I'm in Maryland now, but something has come up. I need to meet you. It's about Vaclav."

"They found his body in Currituck Sound."

"Anne, I saw the TV. They haven't identified the body. You don't know it was Vaclav."

"It was him. I know it. Those killers finished him, or they would have called me at the Junction. Anyway, what do you want? You know I don't want your help."

"Anne, I have to see you. Where are you?"

"I'm in North Carolina. That's all you need to know."

"Fine, but how can we meet?"

"Why?"

"Anne, you're in danger. I want to help."

"Oh come on Peter. Why would a Zeleny help a Simek? What would your father say?"

Peter winced.

"Wait Anne, I mean it, those killers think Vaclav passed his secrets to you."

"Then why didn't they call me at Whalebone Junction. They didn't! But you know that. You were my backup. They don't care about me."

She added.

"Besides, I told you before, Vaclav gave me nothing. The only thing I know about those so-called 'secret documents,' is that I don't have them,"

"Look Anne, you're in danger. We have to meet. I'll come anywhere."

Anne was silent for several seconds.

"I'll think about it, Peter."

"But Anne?"

"Goodbye, Peter."

She broke the call.

Peter stared numbly at the bar. He lifted two fingers at the bartender.

He needed another Scotch, a double.

***

At Bordens' bed and breakfast in Wanchese, Anne put her phone in her traveling bag. She took a last look around the room. Satisfied, she tiptoed down the stairs, and out the door.

Anne twinged at deceiving Mrs. Borden, but she had never intended to stay longer, even though she had paid in advance. In spite of the bravado she had shown Peter, she knew that Vaclav's killers were at large. She was not safe here. She must disappear.

Anne's confidence, ill-placed or not, lay in her ignorance of Vaclav's purpose. He had not given her anything. Once the killers confirmed that truth, they would leave her alone.

At her car, she put her traveling bag on the back seat, next to her computer.

She gasped.

An inconspicuous green rectangle protruded from the USB port on the side of her laptop.

It was a small drive, a TUFF-'N'-TINY™ with 4 Gigabytes of memory, barely noticeable.

It was not Anne's. She had never seen it before.

Then she understood. Evidently, Vaclav had been inside the beach house before his assailant arrived. He had inserted the memory into her laptop. His critical papers and files were on the USB drive.

My God, I have the files!

Anne shifted and drove away, fast!

***

At the Red Roof Inn in Rockville, Johan Zeleny answered the door. Peter entered.

"Father, Anne Simek won't tell me where she is. She doesn't want to meet me either."

Johan was silent. Peter added.

"I tell you, she won't listen to me."

Johan's mind raced.

"Never mind, Peter. I'll explain to Gustav. Go back to your hotel."

Peter exhaled in relief, but his father continued.

"Peter, lend me your phone for the afternoon. I have several calls to make and my SIM card isn't working here. I'll give it back to you this evening."

Peter hesitated, but handed the phone to his father.

He left.

Some minutes later, Gustav appeared at the door. Before he could enter, Johan spoke.

95

"The Simek woman won't tell Peter where she is. And she won't meet with him either."

"Your son lacks persistence. He has no understanding. He worries about that woman's feelings."

"True. Peter is not like us. He grew up under the 'Velvet' government. He is naive and soft."

Gustav thought of Ivana. He needed to trade the papers for her safety.

"Tell Peter he must meet her. There is no other way. I must find Simek before Karel's men do. Do not fail me Johan."

Johan swallowed hard. He knew what Gustav was capable of.

"Wait. I have Peter's phone. It has Simek's number. If she doesn't call him back soon, we will call her ourselves."

***

In Prague, Ivana Novotna stared at her desk. She had worked hard all day. Her meeting with Karel was scheduled for five, but something was wrong. Karel's men had not called her. Plus, there had been no message from Gustav. She had nothing to report to her boss on his most important project.

Not good, Ivana. Not good.

She checked her hair in the mirror. Satisfied, she stood up, smoothed her skirt, and straightened her blouse. Then she walked down the corridor to Karel's office.

She knocked lightly on the door and stepped into the spacious high-walled office. When she was ten feet from the massive desk, Karel looked up.

He was pleased. Ivana's reports were a highlight of his day, but not because of their content. He enjoyed their beautiful photogenic author.

"Ivana, dearest. You are radiant tonight."

"Thank you, but I must tell you, I have not heard from your team in North Carolina."

Karel smiled broadly.

"No matter. They have reported to me. And at the moment they are in Maryland, not North Carolina. I expect to hear from them shortly."

He paused. Furrows creased his forehead.

"But why would they not keep you informed? Is there something I should know?"

Ivana's knees wanted to shake, but she controlled them. She was expert at concealing emotions from this man. She answered.

"I have not heard from Gustav either."

Karel's brow smoothed. He smiled.

"That is because Gustav failed, as I told you he would. But that is not your fault. I know that you will learn from his failure, as I told you."

Karel stared. Ivana did not smile. She stood motionless. The plaster angels on the ceiling overhead likewise did not move.

Finally, Karel shifted in his seat.

"Ivana, do not trouble yourself. Smile. You know that I need you."

Absently, he rubbed a spot on the walnut desk to a dark sheen. He admired his handiwork. Then he spoke softly.

"Tonight we shall dine at the Zlaty Andel Restaurant at the Hotel Barceló. Would that please you?"

She dared not say no. She nodded affirmatively.

"Good. Now I have work to do. I will meet you at the restaurant at seven."

He shuffled the papers on his desk.

Ivana left.

***

In Kitty Hawk, North Carolina, Anne Simek trudged upwards along the path to the Wright Brothers' Memorial. As she neared the massive stone monument, she paused, hands on her hips, and caught her breath.

The climb cleared her mind. Vaclav's memory chip changed everything. She swallowed her pride and clicked the number of Peter Zeleny's phone.

The man that answered had a Czech accent stronger than Peter's.

"Who is this? Where is Peter?"

"This is a friend of his. Is this Miss Simek?"

"Yes."

"Peter hoped you would call. He wanted me to find out where he could meet you. He is desperate to see you. Are you in North Carolina?"

"Yes."

"He'll come meet you. He can be in North Carolina tonight."

"Who is this? What is your name?"

Here Gustav made a mistake.

"I am a friend of Peter's and of his father, Johan."

At the name of Peter's father, Anne recoiled. She recalled her father's countless admonitions about Johan Zeleny. Gustav misinterpreted her silence. He added for emphasis.

"They want to help you!"

Anne froze. She thought of her own father. *To není možné! 'That's not possible!'*

"Who are you? Do I know you? Where is Peter?"

Gustav spoke fast.

"Miss Simek, I can protect you. Tell me where you are. I know you have Vaclav's information. And I know the diner in Elizabeth City where you met Peter."

Anne gasped.

The car that followed Peter and me. He's no friend. My God!

She hung up and stood frozen.

Alone, she shivered in the cold updraft that swept the memorial hilltop.

***

******

Chapter 14
Monday, November 22

A dutiful son, Peter Zeleny returned to the Red Roof Inn in the evening. Gustav and his father were talking. Peter waited.

The phone on the end table buzzed. Gustav put it to his ear. The caller was a female, but not Anne Simek.

Gustav handed the instrument to Johan.

"It's for you."

"This is Johan Zeleny."

"Mr. Zeleny, this is Dr. Ryan, of Ryan Associates. You met my associate, Dr. Harris. Can you tell me where Peter is? We would like to see him."

Johan put his finger to his lips and signaled Peter to silence.

"Dr. Ryan, I have not heard from Peter. I assume he is still in North Carolina. Can I help you?"

"No thank you. We need to talk to Peter. We'll call back."

The phone went dead. Jeannine had hung up.

Gustav turned to Peter.

"What do Ryan Associates want?"

"I talked to them about Hus-Kinetika and Xolak."

Gustav smashed his palm with his fist.

"I don't like it. What do these people want from you?"

Gustav took out Peter's borrowed cell phone and clicked it to "Speaker." He handed the instrument to Peter.

"This is yours. Call them back. Find out what they want."

Aileen Harris picked up.

"Ryan Associates."

"Dr. Harris, this is Peter Zeleny. You called?"

"Peter, where are you. We have a package for you. It's good news for you, and bad news for Hus-Kinetika."

"What kind of package? What do you mean?"

"It's from someone named 'Vaclav.' A 'Vaclav Pokorny.'"

"Click!"

In Bethesda, Aileen stared at the dead phone. She shouted.

"Jeannine, you won't believe that jerk, Peter. He's impossible. He hung up on me. Again!"

***

At the Red Roof Inn, Peter stared at Gustav.

"Why did you grab the phone?"

Gustav ignored him and spoke to Johan.

"Vaclav sent Ryan Associates a package. It's here, in Maryland."

He turned back to Peter.

"Where are they? How far?"

"They're in Bethesda, off Bradley Boulevard. It's twenty minutes away by I-270, if there's no traffic."

Gustav wasted no time.

"We'll take your car. You and I must call on Ryan Associates."

He turned to Johan.

"Stay here. Here's Peter's cell phone. If Simek calls, find out where she is."

Gustav pushed Peter through the door.

***

Once again the phone rang at Ryan Associates. Aileen hesitated and then picked up. She waited for the caller to speak.

"Is this Ryan Associates?"

"Yes it is. I'm Dr. Harris. Who is this?"

"This is Deputy Harrigan with the police department in Duck, North Carolina. We think that someone named Vaclav Pokorny sent you a package. Is that correct?"

"Why do you ask?"

"We're investigating a homicide. Vaclav Pokorny is the victim."

"You mean he's dead?"

"I'm afraid so. Do you have the package?"

"Mr. Harrigan, please don't take offense, but how do I know who you are?"

"I assume you have caller ID. I'll hang up. You call the department. Better yet, check the number on our web site."

A few deft taps on her computer and Aileen was satisfied.

"Mr. Harrigan, we did receive a package addressed to Dr. Peter Zeleny from Mr. Pokorny. Dr. Zeleny saw us about a research misconduct case. Do you know him?"

"We know the package was addressed to Dr. Zeleny, but what do you mean by 'Research Misconduct?' What is that?"

Aileen explained about falsification of data in medical research and the Public Health Service's definition of 'Research Misconduct.' In illustration, she added a passing reference to Hus-Kinetika and Xolak. Jim Harrigan broke in.

"Dr. Harris, dangerous individuals know that the package was sent to your office. For your safety I urge you to secure the package immediately, and protect yourselves."

"We'll turn the material over to the FDA, and they will log it in with the Office of Research Integrity. I am sure they will make it available to you."

"I need to see it right away."

"In that case we'll make copies for you now."

"Thanks."

Aileen hung up.

"Jeannine, you heard me. We need to make copies of Vaclav's papers and the Xolak memo?"

Aileen removed a plywood panel that concealed storage space under the remodeled staircase. She looked in. Only one open package of paper was left on the shelf.

"We need paper. There's less than a ream here."

Jeannine gathered up the newspapers.

"No matter. Our copier is small. I'll go to FedEx-Kinko's and make large copies. We have an all-nighter ahead. I want to get a revised report and these papers to the FDA first thing in the morning."

Jeannine left. Aileen called her mother.

"Mom, would you feed Mary Catherine and get her to bed. I may be here all night."

"Aileen, not again!"

"Sorry, Mom. I love you, and thanks!"

Aileen returned to work.

***

Gustav Slavik and Peter Zeleny left the Red Roof Inn in Peter's rental car. Following Peter's directions, Gustav drove steering with one hand and fingering his Makarov with the other.

"Peter, your father tells me you know the Makarov. That you used to shoot with him."

Peter's mouth was dry, he nodded.

"Good, Peter, good."

Gustav had an extra Makarov tucked in his rear belt. The weapon wedged between the seat and his spine causing considerable discomfort. But the second gun was insurance. Karel's men were everywhere.

"Peter, your father and I were barely twenty when Husak took over in 1968. We were young and strong. We served together, correcting weak members and enemies of the Party. Your father is a true comrade. You should be proud of him."

Peter did not respond. Some things about his father he did not want to know.

They turned onto Bradley Boulevard. Jeannine's house was only blocks away.

***

******

Chapter 15
Monday, November 22

At the office of Ryan Associates, Aileen sat alone at her desk. Jeannine had not returned. A sudden gust of wind rattled the window.

Aileen looked out. The sun had set, and the tall trees in the wooded backyard kept what rays that remained from reaching the ground where dark matted leaves reflected no light at all.

She peered into the shadows. The tops of the tulip poplars waved erratically while the swirling wind cracked the stiff limbs and twisted the dry leaves free from their branches. A Gray Squirrel, disturbed by some danger on the ground, chattered and scrambled up the rough bark of a White Oak. On a high perch, a lone Fish Crow cawed an alarm and took flight.

Something or someone was behind the oak tree.

Aileen stepped to the door and threw the deadbolt just as motion-sensitive spot lights lit the yard.

In the sudden glow, she imagined that someone had jumped backwards into the shadows, out of reach of the artificial brightness, but in the dark it was impossible to distinguish among individual trees, much less a human form.

She stepped back from the door. *Aileen, stop imagining! Wind-blown branches must have triggered the lights.*

But she heard a sound from the kitchen above. Footsteps sounded on the floor overhead.

Someone was in the house.

The footsteps reached the head of the stairway. Then the stairs squeaked.

Aileen shuddered and looked about. The door to the outside was dead-bolted. She would lose precious seconds there. Besides, someone was outside, waiting.

She turned to her left. When the office was finished, that part of the basement with the hot-air furnace and water heater had been partitioned off. Through that door there was little shelter and no exit. The only other escape was up the stairs themselves, and that way was blocked by the intruder.

Desperate, her eyes darted about. There, slightly askew, was the plywood panel that fit over the storage area under the staircase. She crouched and squeezed herself in. Her back was wedged tight against the sharp shelf and her head was pressed against the underneath of the steps.

Fortunately, the quarter-inch plywood panel was rendered rigid by a wooden strip affixed to its back. Aileen gripped the strip with her fingers and pulled the panel shut after her. It fit tightly. No light squeezed through the edges.

She was secure. From the outside there was no indication that a human, even one cramped as she was, could fit behind that panel.

Directly above her, the wooden steps creaked under the weight of a man, someone large. She felt the wood sag against her skull.

Whoever had come down stopped.

Aileen held her breath.

***

Gustav stood at the foot of the stairs. Makarov in hand, he surveyed the empty office. Satisfied, he released the dead bolt and opened the door. He called into the woods.

"Come on in. There's no one here."

Peter moved into the light. Gustav lowered his Makarov and beckoned him inside. Gustav pointed to Aileen's desk.

"Help me search. You start there."

Gustav went to the lone file cabinet. He pulled out the top drawer and dumped its contents on the floor. He kicked through the loose papers. The two lower drawers were similarly upended. He snorted in disgust.

"There's nothing of interest here. All these papers are the standard American size, 'eight and a half by eleven.' Vaclav's papers would be narrower and longer, Hus-Kinetika would use A4-size European paper. Did you find anything?"

Peter looked up. He had emptied the drawers of Aileen's desk. All her papers were likewise American-sized. He shook his head, "No."

Gustav spoke again.

"Whose car is that parked in the back."

"It belongs to Dr. Harris. She's an associate here."

Lodged in her cramped space, Aileen gasped. *Was that Peter's voice?*

Moments later Gustav removed any remaining doubt.

"Peter, if that's her car, then where is she?"

Aileen bit her lip. *Damn you Peter Zeleny. What the hell are you doing? Who are you, really?*

Gustav frowned. He took out a cigarette, but did not light it. He motioned Peter to silence and surveyed the office anew. *All right Miss Harris, where are you?*

Gustav waved to Peter to search the furnace room.

In the dark, Aileen waited.

***

Cramped as she was, Aileen's left thigh muscles twisted and contracted. She suppressed a moan, and squeezed the tightened mass, but the pain continued.

Outside she heard a door shut, and new steps sounded in the office. She deduced, correctly, that someone had come into the office from the furnace room.

She heard no voices, but footsteps sounded towards the outside door. These were followed by a loud slam. Then silence.

Aileen waited. She shifted her weight as best she could to alleviate the cramping. To no avail, her thigh muscle quivered in increasing tetanus. She gritted her teeth, held her breath, and listened.

Still only silence.

***

Finally, the pain was intolerable. She counted to ten. Still no noise came from the office.

Aileen decided. She pushed with all her strength against the panel. It sprung loose, and she tumbled head first onto the office floor.

The office was dark.

Aileen stretched her leg and sighed.

Her ordeal was over.

The office lights came on. She heard a harsh voice.

"Dr. Harris, I'm sure. Nice to see you. We need your help."

Aileen looked up. A tall man stood over her. In his hand was a gun.

Behind him stood another man. Him, she knew.

Peter Zeleny!

Aileen stood up gingerly, favoring her sore leg. She tried to sound assertive, but her voice shook.

"You'd better leave now. The police are on the way."

***

Gustav grinned at the woman who limped before him.

"Bravely spoken, Dr. Harris, but we both know that the police are not coming."

His face reddened.

"Do not waste my time. I want the package you received from Vaclav. It is Peter's."

He pointed to Peter Zeleny who stood behind him and continued.

"It is not yours. Give it to me, now!"

Aileen spoke through tight lips.

"I have no package."

"Come now, Dr. Harris. Of course you do!"

"Sorry, but I don't."

"Don't trifle with me. Give it to me."

106

Aileen set her lips. She did not reply. Gustav appeared to turn away. As he did so, he launched a looping back hand that slammed into the side of her face. She stumbled against the desk, but steadied herself. Blood trickled from the side of her mouth.

Gustav shouted.

"I have no time for foolishness. Where is it?"

She did not answer.

Gustav's neck muscles bulged and his chest heaved. His face became scarlet. He hit her with his fist.

Her eyes glazed and she crumbled downwards. He pulled her up by her blouse. It ripped, exposing her bra. He shoved her against the wall and seized her throat. He shouted.

"Do not defy me! Where is it?"

She forced a whisper through cracked lips.

"I ... don't ... know."

Gustav glared. Aileen's eyes rolled up. Her silence further enraged Gustav.

"Tell me where it is."

Another forced whisper.

"No."

Breathing heavily, Gustav reached for his Makarov. He held it to her forehead. He would settle this matter now!

"Where is it?"

Aileen shut her eyes.

Gustav's finger tightened on the trigger.

***

Gustav's mad rage caught Peter Zeleny unprepared. He watched in horror as Gustav pushed the weapon at Aileen's head.

No!

He seized the spare Makarov stuck in the belt at Gustav's rear and swung with all his force at the back of Gustav's head.

"Crunch."

Gustav collapsed straight to the floor.

Peter lifted Aileen to her feet. She shrank back pulling the torn blouse over her exposed breast.

"Who the hell are you, Peter? Get away from me. Leave me alone."

"Aileen, please. We have to go."

He pointed to the fallen Gustav.

"Before he wakes up. Please."

Aileen's vision cleared. She saw the body on the floor. *My God! He was going to kill me!*

The fingers of Gustav's hand moved. They gripped the weapon. A reflex?

"Now Aileen, now! We must go. Come on."

"With you? Never!"

Gustav stirred anew. Peter grabbed Aileen's arm. She was limp. With his free hand he lifted her purse off the desk.

"Aileen, come with me. You can't stay here."

"Go to hell."

But she was too weak to resist further.

Peter dragged her by the arm and she stumbled after him. He propped her in the passenger seat of her car and strapped her in. She slumped forward, her weight on the shoulder belt.

He went to the driver's side and fumbled in her purse for the keys.

The motor started easily. He checked the gas gauge. There was lots of fuel. *Good.*

Something poked his stomach. He looked down. After downing Gustav, he had unconsciously stuffed the extra Makarov in his belt. Blood-stained gray hairs were stuck on the handle. He bent and slid it under the seat.

He drove away.

They were just in time. A groggy Gustav emerged from the office. He shook his fist in the air and opened the door of the only remaining car, Peter's rented Accord.

Peter risked a smile. The Accord's tank was near empty. Even though Gustav still had the keys, he could not follow them.

He glanced at his passenger. Aileen's eyes were closed tight.

He sighed. For the moment they were safe.

***

Parked several houses away, the two men in the gray Ford Excursion watched Peter and Aileen leave in the Accord. The passenger spoke.

"What do we do now? Should I finish off Gustav?"

"Not here and not now. Karel's reinforcements are here in Bethesda too. Call them. They can take care of the old fool. He's still dangerous."

The driver reflected a moment then continued.

"We follow young Zeleny and the Harris woman. Gustav knows nothing that we don't already know, but the Harris woman knows what's in the package. And it was addressed to Zeleny. He will understand the contents."

He was pleased with his logic.

"For sure, Zeleny and Harris are our best bet."

They followed Aileen's car at a distance.

***

****

Chapter 16
Tuesday, November 23

In North Carolina, the morning sun shone over the Currituck Sound to the east of the town of Grandy. Peter Zeleny had driven all night. Weary, he brought Aileen's car to a halt at the red traffic light that hung over the highway. He held his foot on the clutch, stretched his arms, and yawned.

The traffic light switched to green.

Peter jammed the accelerator but released the clutch too quickly. The car thrust forward in rough jerks. He had never driven a stick shift, and even after driving all night, had not mastered the manual transmission.

He glanced to his right. The lurching start had jarred Aileen awake. She did not acknowledge Peter, but stared straight through the windshield.

Peter spoke without looking at her.

"We left Virginia an hour ago. We're almost to the Outer Banks. Are you feeling any better?"

"What do you care. Your friend tried to kill me."

"He's not my friend. He knew my family in the old country. My father wanted me to help him. I didn't know. I had no idea he would ... "

Aileen's lip curled downwards.

"Stop it. *You* trashed my office, *not* your father."

Peter lowered his eyes.

"But I did stop Gustav from shooting you."

Aileen glared.

"OK! Thanks, but *you* brought him to the office."

"But you don't know Gustav. He'll kill me for helping you, and my father will help him."

"Great, some father! Who is he, really? And why ever would you listen to him?"

Peter glanced sideways. Even with her bruised cheek and eye half-closed, he found her desirable.

"Aileen, when my mother left us, I was only a boy. My father was stuck with me. He always kept his 'work' to himself. He never talked about what he did, but I guessed enough that I never wanted to know more."

He took a breath.

"Father was a true believer in the system and an active member of the Party. He worked in the prison on Bartolomejska Street. Gustav, the man who attacked you, worked there too. He would visit our apartment and they would drink together, always too much. Vodka! I kept away when they drank, but I could hear them. They would joke and laugh about the 'pink prison.' It seems the ceiling was painted pink."

Peter swallowed and continued.

"When I asked my father what he did in the prison, his answer was always the same. He helped people see the truth of Communism. He rehabilitated those who needed help. Then he would change the subject to hockey. My father loved the Czechoslovak national team. What did I care about hockey, or politics? I lost myself in my studies."

"Thanks to the Party, I attended good schools. I learned not to ask questions about prisons."

"Then the government changed. It was a shock to my father. It seems the new president, Vaclav Havel, had once been in my father's prison. We moved to Kladno, My father was angry, then he became bitter, morose. He withdrew, but by that time I was out of the house. I had my medical studies in Prague, and my friends just thought of my father as old fashioned. Maybe I wanted to believe that. I don't really know."

Peter finally took a breath.

"Since I came to Chicago, I forgot my father, and Prague. I love my work, my patients. I love your country, our country. I have my green card, I'm going to be a citizen."

112

A pickup truck pulled in front of Peter. He touched the brakes to slow down.

"When my father called me from Rockville a few days ago, I was shocked. It had been more than three years since I had seen him. I thought he was just an old man, harmless. He asked me to help Gustav. I thought he had changed. I was wrong."

He coughed.

"I had no idea. When Gustav tried to kill you, I had to club him."

He turned to her. Aileen shifted in her seat. For the first time since waking, she met his look. Peter pulled the car to the side of the road and turned off the engine. He closed his eyes and sighed. His chin drooped onto his chest.

"My father won't protect us from Gustav. He's always been closer to him than me."

He looked sideways and touched her arm.

She pulled away, and remained silent.

"Aileen, we are in danger, and not just from Gustav and my father. There are others too, assassins like Gustav. They work for Hus-Kinetika. They killed Vaclav Pokorny and they will kill us if they find us."

Aileen's head spun. She sat motionless. Peter reached for her.

"I did not think he would hurt you. Please believe me. I'm sorry for what happened. I only want to help."

She shook his arm from her shoulder and looked away.

"I don't know. My head hurts, my shoulder aches and I can't think."

She spoke as if to herself.

"No one knows where I am. Everyone must be worried. Thank God, Mary Catherine is with my mother."

She took her cell phone from her bag.

"I have to call my mother and Jeannine. Meanwhile, you find us a motel. I hurt and I need to collapse, and you drove all night. No more driving. We have to stop."

113

Her neutrality was the best he could hope for. Peter spotted a motel ahead on the right. He pulled back onto the highway and drove to it.

Both he and Aileen were too weary to notice the Ford Excursion that had stopped on the side of the road some distance behind them.

It too drove back onto the highway and headed after them.

***

The two men in the Ford Excursion watched as Peter helped Aileen into the small roadside motel.

The man in the passenger seat spoke first.

"I don't get it. Why did Zeleny drive all the way to North Carolina? He could have hidden in Maryland."

"I'll tell you why. And it's a lucky break for us."

"What do you mean?"

"I mean he's here to find Anne Simek."

"So we don't grab them now?"

"No way. Zeleny's doing us a favor. Let him find Simek for us. Then we make our move We get all of them at once."

He added.

"There's another motel across on the left. I'm tired. We may as well find a bed too. Zeleny drove all night. He is not going anywhere for a while."

***

Peter Zeleny helped Aileen into the room. She took two Advil from her purse and headed to the bathroom for water. Coming out, she grabbed a pillow from the bed. Peter still stood by the door.

Aileen collapsed into the comfortable chair.

"I'll take this. You can have the bed, since you drove all night, but shut the curtains over the window. The sun's too bright."

Aileen buried her face in the pillow. Peter moved to close the heavy curtains, but stopped to peer through the slats of the blind.

114

Aileen moaned.

"Damn it, pull the curtains shut so I can sleep."

She curled into the chair and buried her head deeper.

Peter did not close the curtains.

"Aileen, there's something wrong here."

She opened her eyes. He went on.

"In Bethesda, when we left your office, a Ford Excursion was parked down the street. Just now a Ford Excursion stopped at the motel across the street. Two men got out and went in."

He continued.

"They must have driven all night, like us. Why else would they pick a motel now?"

Aileen sat upright. Peter continued.

"There's something else. The Excursion I saw in Bethesda was gray and had Virginia plates just like that one over there."

Aileen ran to the blinds and looked through. Parked in the motel lot across the way was the empty Excursion. Evidently, its occupants had taken a room.

She turned to Peter.

"They must have followed us from Maryland. They drove all night too. They know we're tired, but so are they. They think we'll sleep for two hours at least. I say we give them a half hour to fall asleep and then leave."

Peter nodded.

"That's good thinking."

Together they stood by the blinds and studied the Ford Excursion parked in the lot across the street. It was deserted.

A half hour later they slipped out of the motel.

***

Columbia, North Carolina is on the southern shore of the Albemarle Sound. Anne Simek stood alone by a small cottage on an inlet of the sound, some miles from Columbia. She had rented the cottage with cash that she had obtained from an ATM in Nags Head before leaving the Outer Banks. Her cottage was a safe distance from the Banks, but still close.

To the Currituck County Sheriff, she was a "Person of Interest" in the death of Vaclav Pokorny, but to Anne herself she was more. She was not only a "Suspect," but a "Guilty" one. She was responsible for his death.

At Vaclav's insistence, Anne had gone to fetch Peter Zeleny, leaving Vaclav alone at Bordens' bed and breakfast. And Peter Zeleny had been useless. She had wanted to stay with Vaclav. She should have stayed with him! *I shouldn't have left you. I'm sorry. Forgive me?*

But Anne could not forgive herself.

Never had she felt so alone.

She stood shivering by the door. The morning was cold. There was little wind and the waters of the sound were still. Across the inlet stood a tall pine, now dead, at whose top was stacked a mix of branches at odd angles, an Osprey's nest. Would Ospreys be here in winter? Out over the waters soared a lone bird, possibly the nest's owner, but too far away to identify.

She stepped back into her room. She choked. There in the corner, motionless against the baseboard, was a brown six-legged creature. She moved quickly to squash it, but drew back. Somehow she could not kill it. The roach scurried into a crack. Anne returned to the open door.

She thought of her cousin. Mila had been right about the Corolla rental. It had been roach-free. Maybe she should call Mila?

No! Mila, you should have told me it was Vaclav.

Anne decided. She picked up her phone and called Peter Zeleny. It shifted to message.

"Peter, this is Anne. I'm at the Moccasin Rental Cottages, near Columbia, North Carolina. I've thought about what you said. I will meet you. Call me."

Too late, she realized her foolishness. *My God, what have I done?*

Suppose that horrible stranger still had Peter's phone!

***

In the Red Roof Motel in Rockville, Maryland, Johan Zeleny listened to Anne Simek's message.

He put Peter's phone down and turned to Gustav Slavik.

"That was the Simek woman. She left a message for Peter. She told him where she is."

Gustav raised his eyebrows. Johan laughed.

"She's in a cottage near Columbia, North Carolina. She's waiting for Peter to call back."

Gustav did not smile. He studied Johan's expression. Satisfied, he fingered the swelling at the back of his head and grimaced.

"That woman is naive, like your son. Good. We shall go to North Carolina."

He finished cleaning his Makarov and stood up.

***

It was mid-morning on the Carolina Coast, but afternoon in Prague.

The phone buzzed on Ivana's desk. It was Karel's secretary, Fiala. Her tone was tart.

"Karel wants you in his office, immediately."

Ivana looked at her Rolex. It was early, not yet time for her regular meeting. She frowned and picked up her folder. She checked her makeup and hair and stood up.

She walked fast down the hall. Outside Karel's office, she paused to smooth her skirt before opening the door. She stepped in.

The chair behind the massive desk was empty. Karel stood directly in front of her. He seized her arm.

"Ivana, why are my men unwilling to report to you?"

"Karel, you're hurting me. What do you mean?"

He released his grip.

"I mean, where is Gustav? My men say you know where he is."

"That's ridiculous. I have no idea where he is. You told me your men would handle him, remember?"

117

"So you have not heard from him?"

Ivana shifted her stance to present her best profile to him. She bit her tongue.

"No, and I see that your men have not found him, so they blame me! How convenient."

Karel relaxed. Ivana was becoming. He changed gears.

"You are right. They seek to shift their failure onto you. They missed Gustav at the office of that Ryan and his associates."

Ivana knew that "Ryan" was a woman, but she would not let Karel know that she knew anything about the Drs. Ryan and Harris. Thorough as she was, she had done her homework. For now she wished to appear dumb.

"Who is that?"

"All you need to know is that they are enemies. They seek to have Xolak removed from the U. S. Market. We cannot allow them to succeed. Not yet, anyway."

He continued.

"You may go now. I have to contact the teams in America."

"I can give them your instructions."

He hesitated.

"No, it is better if I call them. You do not need to worry about them."

Ivana nodded. She started for the door, her mind racing. *Gustav, where are you?*

Karel seemed to read her thoughts. He spoke as if to himself.

"That traitor Gustav is not dealt with yet. He will die soon."

She turned back towards him, but he spoke first.

"Ivana, we are finished. Go!"

She left.

As Ivana walked down the hall, she realized that Karel had not arranged their evening together. She murmured under her breath.

"He knows. And about Gustav too."

118

Her bravado vanished and her knees shook.

She arrived at the door to her office.

Her hand trembled as she reached for the handle.

***

In Nags Head, Jim Harrigan stopped at the doughnut shop for a mid-morning snack. He sat at the counter and ordered a chocolate-covered glazed.

Jim took his coffee black, with no sweetener. The only added flavor he would tolerate was the chocolate from the doughnut. That combination he enjoyed. He lifted his cup and took a long swallow.

He felt a tap on his shoulder. He looked up. Mila, all smiles and casually dressed in fashionable jeans, tennis shoes, and a loose sweatshirt, stood behind him.

"Mila, how did you know I was here?"

She laughed and pointed to the Duck Police Cruiser parked outside.

"How many Duck policemen get free doughnuts in Nags Head? Aren't you going to buy me a cup of coffee?"

When the coffee arrived, Mila fingered her cup nervously.

"Jim, I still can't reach Anne. I'm really worried. Have the police found out anything."

"I can tell you that Anne, or someone with her card, drew out a sizable amount of cash from an ATM yesterday, not far from here."

"Cash. That means she's running."

"That's what the sheriff thinks."

"Jim, Anne's in real danger. What can we do?"

Jim finished his doughnut and took a long swallow of coffee. He studied Mila's eyes. They were moist.

He stood up and rubbed her shoulders.

"Mila, there's one thing you haven't tried yet."

She looked at him, eyes questioning.

"It's pretty simple really. You told me Anne and her father are close, right."

"She loves her father, but she doesn't always agree with him."

"Mila, call him. She wouldn't want him to worry. I'll bet he knows where she is."

Mila's eyes lit. She clicked Havel Simek's number on her cell phone and placed it to her ear.

***

As Peter and Aileen left Grandy, North Carolina, the sun shone bright on Highway 158. Peter yawned as he drove. Aileen sat upright and talked to keep him awake, but gradually her speech slowed and slurred.

They crossed the bridge towards Kitty Hawk. It was Peter's first daylight crossing of the Sound. In the bright sun, gulls glided slowly over the shining waters of the sound. Not long ago in the darkness, unaware of the wide extent of the waters, he had followed the tail lights of Anne Simek's Focus over this same structure.

Despite the natural beauty of the scene, he continued to yawn.

Aileen's eyes were shut. She was sound asleep. The swelling over her eye had gone down. Her mouth was closed, but the nasal passages were clear and her breathing was regular.

They had just passed Kitty Hawk when the yawns increased.

He needed coffee.

Ahead on the left was a doughnut shop with a police cruiser parked in front. He imagined the aroma of dark roasted Arabica beans.

He turned into the lot and parked, choosing a spot away from the cruiser and not visible through the window.

Aileen's breathing was slow and rhythmic. He let her rest, stepped out, stretched, and clicked the door locks.

He went into the shop.

***

******

120

Chapter 17
Tuesday, November 23

The doughnut shop featured a long counter as well as a row of tables that lined the front windows. A group of roughly-dressed men, talking loudly, sat at the counter. Peter assumed that they were fishermen. A glance out the window proved him correct. A jeep-like vehicle mounted with vertical tubes for surf rods was parked outside. Waders were piled in the open back.

Several of the window tables were occupied. At one was a middle-aged man, youthful in bearing. He sat with an attractive woman. He held himself with authority.

Peter guessed that the man belonged to the police cruiser that was visible through another window. That was confirmed a moment later when he shifted in his seat. He had a weapon at his hip. Idly, Peter noted that it was not a Makarov.

At that thought Peter panicked. Gustav's Makarov was stashed under the seat of Aileen's car. How could he explain to the police his possession of an untraceable Makarov with hair and blood on the grip.

He canceled his plan of resting to sip coffee inside.

He pushed to the counter and ordered a large coffee to go. While waiting, he took one last survey of the tables. The policeman sat silent while the woman spoke on the phone. She appeared to be talking business.

Oddly the policeman's inactivity comforted Peter. He thought of Aileen. Others had their problems too. Peter realized that the woman's long phone conversation while her partner waited was no way to build a relationship.

Peter paid for his coffee. He took one short, too-hot swallow, burned his tongue and headed for the exit.

***

As Peter left, he passed the table with the policeman. The woman there was speaking Czech!

At the sound of his native tongue, Peter forgot about the Makarov and Aileen. He blurted.

"*Prominte.* 'Excuse me.' You are Czech?"

Mila clicked off. She looked up.

"*Ano.* 'Yes.' And you?"

"I am, but I live in Chicago now."

At the word "Chicago" Mila's gaze intensified. Anne Simek and her father Havel lived in Chicago and Mila had just been on the phone with the father seeking Anne's whereabouts. It had been fruitless. Either Havel did not know where Anne was or he was not willing to say.

Mila gathered her thoughts. Association with Jim Harrigan had taught her reticence. She withheld her identity and waved at Jim.

"This is Jim Harrigan. May I ask your name?"

"Dr. Zeleny, I studied at the Motol Teaching Hospital in Prague. Do you know Prague?"

Mila started. *Zeleny, as in Vaclav's package?*

She looked at Jim. Apparently he had not noticed. She turned her answer into a question.

"Of course, but what brings you to the Outer Banks?"

Peter hesitated. He was exhausted, and he needed to trust someone. Mila appeared honest, and she was Czech. He abandoned all caution.

"Actually, I'm looking for a woman. Her name is Anne Simek. Do you know her?"

At those words, Jim Harrigan bolted upright.

Mila merely smiled.

"I should know her. I'm her cousin. I'm Mila Patekova."

It was Peter's turn to relax.

"So you're Mila. I'm Peter. I told her she should call you. I need to see her again. It's very important. Where is she?"

Mila frowned.

"Again? I'm hoping you can tell me. Sit down Peter. When did you last see Anne?"

122

"Last Saturday, at the Comfort Inn just south of here, but I called her from Maryland yesterday. She's in North Carolina somewhere. She wouldn't say where."

Jim Harrigan intervened.

"Look, I'm not comfortable talking here. They're too many people around us. Why not come to Duck with us. We can talk in my apartment."

Peter was not sure.

"I have someone with me. She's asleep in the car. She's badly bruised. If you don't mind two of us, I'll come. We both need rest. We drove all night."

Jim Harrigan spoke.

"What do you mean, 'bruised.' Who is she?"

"Her name is Dr. Harris. She's with a small company 'Ryan Associates' in Bethesda, Maryland. They ... "

"Ryan Associates!"

Jim stared at Mila. Then he added.

"And the bruises?"

Peter opted for honesty.

"She was beaten up, but not by me."

Jim continued.

"All right Dr. Zeleny, I can accept that for the moment, but you must come with us. If she's with Ryan Associates, neither of you is safe here. You can tell us the rest of your story at my apartment. We need to find out all you know."

Peter hesitated. Mila took his arm.

"Peter, it's OK. Jim is with me. He understands us. He's on our side."

Peter nodded and followed Jim and Mila out the shop.

The police cruiser headed towards Duck.

Peter followed. Aileen still slept.

***

It was late afternoon in Prague and the shadows had lengthened. Ivana sat staring at her desk.

She had no message from Gustav since Friday. Where was he? Was he dead? How much did Karel know? He certainly suspected her.

She had reason to worry. At their last meeting, Karel had not been himself.

And not just Karel, but more disturbing, Fiala, the secretary had subtly changed. She no longer looked down when she addressed Ivana, but actively sought eye contact, as an equal, or maybe more?

Ivana glanced at her Rolex. It was not an imitation. No, Karel had bought her the real thing to seal his admiration for her.

The watch was highly accurate. She noted the time. Karel's office hours were over. His plans for the evening were already established. Clearly, Ivana was not part of them.

Warning bells clanged in her mind. She sensed danger.

She heard sounds in the hallway, the clicking steps of a woman in high heels. Curious, Ivana went to the door. She cracked it and looked out.

Down the hall strode Fiala. Her gait was confident, her face radiant. She was evidently dressed for a night on the town. Despite her dislike for the secretary, Ivana had to admit that Fiala was most alluring.

Fiala stopped at Karel's office. The door opened from the inside. In the sudden glow of light, Ivana could see clearly. She sucked in a breath.

Fiala was wearing a red silk scarf, one similar to Karel's favorite for Ivana. But it was something else that upset Ivana.

Shimmering on Fiala's wrist was a brand new Rolex!

***

Ivana returned to her desk. Her shoulders shook as she buried her face in her hands. She knew Karel, and she knew the significance of that Rolex. All doubt disappeared. She *was* in danger.

The phone rang on her desk. She started to answer but drew back. After four rings it stopped.

Ivana had not become Special Assistant to the Director because of lack of intelligence. She had foresight. She had prepared for this day.

She texted her plans to Gustav. She had no idea where he was or whether he would receive it. No matter. She had to act.

She had prepared well. She picked up a satchel from behind her filing cabinet and went to the executive powder room down the hall. It had a full bath and shower. Ivana disappeared inside. A half hour later she emerged.

The woman with well-coiffed long blonde hair was gone. In her place was a brunette whose short-cut jagged black hair revealed a shapely neck. The elegant business suit had been exchanged for jeans, sweatshirt, and backpack, while high-heeled Italian footwear had morphed to comfortable flat Nikes.

She leafed her new passport. The cover was burgundy, the color shared by member states of the European Union, but the words on it were not "Česká Republika" and "Cestovní Pas," but rather were, "Deutschland," and "Reisepass." Fittingly, her name was now Irma Neumann, a German national, at least according to this document.

Deliberately, she walked to the cleaning closet. There she tied a kerchief over her newly short hair, and put on an oversized smock. She emerged, pushing a cleaning cart in front of her.

Back at her office, Ivana's next task was to push papers and memos into her shredder. That done, she entered on the most dangerous phase of her departure. In her office safe were two "key cards." One was her own. The other was her insurance, a duplicate of Karel's.

The phone on her desk rang again. She jumped and stood frozen. Again it sounded four rings, then stopped.

Still, the most important task remained. She stopped at the door to Karel's office and slid his card through the slot. Click, and she was in. She pulled the cart in after her.

She knew exactly where to go. She knew Karel's files, she had arranged most of them!

Breathing heavily, she punched his code in the lock and pulled open the drawer.

There it was. A large brown folder, stuffed with CD's, papers and photos, and even a flash drive. She often had seen Karel frown as he studied the contents of that folder spread over his desk.

She shoved the contents into her backpack, and re-secured the file. She moved towards the door.

Too late! The hallway was filled with running feet.

She stopped. Her heart palpitated.

Heavy footsteps raced in the direction of Ivana's old office.

She retreated and crouched behind Karel's desk. The massive structure was no longer intimidating, it afforded welcome concealment. She exhaled.

A crash down the hallway signaled the destruction of her office door. Shouts and curses echoed in the corridor.

She stayed huddled behind the desk. She did not move.

***

Only when all sounds in the hallway had abated, did Ivana stand up. She peered out Karel's door. There was no movement. All was quiet.

She entered the hallway. The cart with its mops and buckets rolled smoothly in front of her. She looked in her old office as she passed. The door lay flat on the floor. Her desk was upended. Papers and folders were scattered about. Everything was a shambles.

She made her way to the freight elevator.

She pushed the button. She heard the groaning of gears as the lift started upwards from the basement below.

She watched the dial rotate slowly.

S-One, ...One, ...Two, ...

Hurry up. Hurry!

Three, ... Four, *Come on.*

... Five. *At last!*

The dial stopped.

She fronted the cart and lifted the heavy grate.

A voice called from down the hall.

"*Počkat!* 'Wait!'"

She pulled the cart on and pulled downwards. The grate rattled and thumped shut. She hit the "Down" button, hard. The machinery cranked anew.

By the time the guard arrived, only his shoes were visible through the grate as the elevator inched its way down. She saw his heels. He had turned away.

She arrived in the basement without incident.

***

In full view of the guards, Ivana hung up her smock before parking the cart in the storeroom.

She waved her ID casually. They were uninterested. She stepped out onto the loading dock.

Moments later she was free, a young student attired in jeans and sweatshirt, breathing hard as she lugged a heavy backpack.

Ivana walked fast in the direction of the Vltava River. Already the lamps of the Charles Bridge shone through the dusk that settled over the dark waters.

***

In the restaurant at the Hotel Leonardo, Karel's cell phone sounded. He took his hand from Fiala's thigh and answered.

His face reddened.

"What do you mean, she's gone?" That is impossible."

A pause. He spoke again, louder.

"Search again. She has to be in the building."

Karel slammed his phone on the table. The wine in Fiala's glass slipped over the rim and onto the table cloth.

She lifted her glass and dabbed the spot with her napkin.

Karel did not notice. His eyes lowered and narrowed. *Ivana! How dare you?* His jaw muscles contracted. *No one leaves me!* He ground his teeth.

Across the table Fiala's face paled. She took a deep breath.

Karel recovered his aplomb. He smiled and touched her wrist. Color returned to Fiala's cheeks. She smiled back.

The smile decided him.   He would take Fiala to his apartment (formerly Ivana's) where he would have privacy to explore Fiala's charms. Ivana would not dare return there!

And Ivana's Mercedes still was in her space at the office. There was no need to worry. On foot, she could not escape him. By tomorrow, his men would bring the ungrateful bitch to him.

Still, he resolved to change the locks on the apartment.

***

The next two hours were all that Karel could hope for. Fiala was energetic and enthusiastic, a welcome change from the reticence Ivana had shown over the past weeks. Fiala pressed against him anew, but he was exhausted. His head sunk into the pillow and his eyelids closed.

The buzz of the phone jarred him awake. The call was from Vienna. The man spoke English like an American.

"Gustav has gone to the Americans. He'll tell all he knows about you if they will protect the 'Goldfinch.' That's the CIA's code for 'Ivana.' He wants them to give her asylum."

Karel did not speak.   Gustav had no human feelings or emotions, and he hated the Americans. Why was he desperate to protect the girl?

His silence prompted the caller to speak further.

"She texted him her plans. She knows you're watching her car. She's headed for Ruzyne Airport by metro and bus."

Karel wanted to scream, but he did not wish to alienate this informant. He took a deep breath .

"This is most helpful. Thank you. You will be rewarded."

Karel jumped from the bed and made two brief phone calls, one local, one to the United States. Then he stood in thought. *Ivana, what have you done to Gustav? What hold do you have on him?*

The damned "Goldfinch" was now a major problem!

Fiala opened her eyes. She pouted.

"Karel, why are you up? Come back here."

He looked at her, and shrugged. *Why not?* He had done all that could be done for the moment.

Moments later he was on top of her.

***

Ivana left the Metro at "Dejvická." Head lowered, she walked to the waiting bus, 119. It was the end of the line, or rather, the beginning of the return trip to Ruzyne International Airport.

Most of the seats were empty. She chose one by a window, halfway back. She stacked her backpack on the aisle seat to discourage any potential occupant. Then she leaned her head to the side and pretended to sleep.

All the while, she vigilantly observed each new boarder through half-closed lids. One man in particular unsettled her. His shoes were shiny leather and expensive. He did not belong on a bus. He chose a seat between her and the front door.

The last man to board appeared to be American. He stopped and studied her backpack, as if to move it. She held it firmly in place. Her signal was clear. He backed away.

He sat behind and opposite, next to the window. Ivana pushed herself further against hers.

At last, the driver engaged the gears and the bus pulled away.

***

On the bus to the airport, Bill Hamm was in a quandary.

The young woman seated across from him matched the description of "Ivana Novotna," but under that kerchief her hair was short and black. He had expected long blond tresses.

Her behavior was the key. She was clearly on the run. And her destination was Prague's Ruzyne International Airport.

This must be the "Ivana" he sought.

***

Bill Hamm worked for the CIA out of the United States Embassy in Vienna. The day before, he and his coworkers had received an alarming text message from a known assassin and former Communist, Gustav Slavik. He appeared desperate.

A stockpile of deadly "Novichok nerve agents," ostensibly destroyed by the Russians to comply with the Chemical Weapons Convention, had been secretly transported to the United States by former Czech Communists under the aegis of the pharmaceutical giant, Hus-Kinetika. Gustav would share what he knew of the secret stash in exchange for American protection and asylum for a young woman, Ivana Novotna, who also had evidence of the conspiracy.

The scenario stretched all credulity. Nerve agents were incredibly difficult to handle, and many had died doing so. Still, Hus-Kinetika had the means and knowledge to store the material Gustav described. But Gustav was vehemently anti-American. What hold could "Ivana" have on him that he would seek help from his enemies? The team's inclination was to ignore his allegations as some sort of ruse.

Then Bill Hamm's friend, Jeannine Ryan, had called and told him of the problems in Hus-Kinetika's report on Xolak. Two negative references to the giant company in one day tipped the scale. Bill and his partner Tom had flown to Prague to investigate. There, another text from Gustav stated that Ivana was on her way to the airport.

For someone on foot, the logical route from Ivana's office to the airport was by metro to the "Dejvická" stop and thence by bus to the airport. Bill had waited at that stop. When the young woman appeared and boarded the bus, he had done likewise.

***

The bus ground its gears towards Prague's Ruzyne Airport.

Bill watched the man with the expensive shoes shift in his seat and fidget with his phone. His hands moved constantly.

Opposite him sat a mother with her young son. The boy slept on her shoulder. Doubtless, she was a single mother who had worked late. He was sure they were not headed for the airport. They would likely leave the bus soon.

He settled in his seat.

Across from him, a weary Ivana feigned sleep and tightened her grip on her pack.

***

******

130

Chapter 18
Tuesday, November 23

In Prague darkness had fallen. Bill Hamm studied the riders on the bus. The interior lights, though dim, made mirrors of the windows, reflecting the activities of the various passengers.

Hamm's attention was directed to the man seated several rows in front of Ivana. While on his phone, he periodically checked on her image in the window across and behind him.

The bus stopped. The mother hustled her young son out the door. A woman, fashionably dressed with phone in hand, mounted the steps. She paused to survey the seats and chose one directly behind Bill.

The doors of the bus closed, the gears ground, and the bus was underway once more.

Minutes later, the lights of the airport brightened the sky ahead.

Bill sat up, muscles tensed. The reflection of the woman behind him revealed her staring onto the street. She showed no interest in anyone.

The phone in his pocket vibrated. It was Jeannine calling from Bethesda. He pushed "Talk."

"Bill, where are you? Can you hear me?"

"Yes."

"Someone is there? You can't talk now?"

"No."

"But can you listen? This is important."

"I can."

The woman behind him leaned forward towards his seat. Bill turned away towards his window. Jeannine spoke rapidly.

"Last Saturday we got a package from a man named Pokorny ... worked for Hus-Kinetika. ... His memo proved that they faked data for Xolak just like we said. ... And other papers, newspapers, marked up. ... Last night they trashed the office.

.... I had the papers with me to copy. ... Beat up Aileen, barely got away to North Carolina. ... She's safe, but we've talked. ... Hus-Kinetika may have nerve gas called 'Novichok,' ."

Bill's pulse quickened at the word "Novichok," but before he could reply, the bus driver hit the brakes for a red light.

Across the way, Ivana stood up and reached for her backpack.

The woman behind Bill jumped to her feet.

In her hand was a semiautomatic pistol.

***

At her desk in Bethesda, the next few seconds were like minutes to Jeannine. She no longer heard Bill's voice.

The sounds on her phone were like a rasp drawn over the edge of a metal sheet. Amid that static, she heard grunts and heavy breathing followed by a distinct moan and a woman's cry.

Then nothing. The connection was broken.

Bill!

***

Bill Hamm knew no Czech. In accented German he called to the bus driver. The traffic light had not changed.

"*Helfen Sie mir.* 'Help me.' This lady fell. She needs a doctor, now."

He pointed to the fashionable woman crumpled unconscious in her seat. At the same time he seized the backpack from Ivana and took her arm. He whispered.

"*Bitte, Fräulein*, please come with me. That woman tried to kill you. I will help you."

The man wearing fine shoes stayed in his seat and reached for his cell phone. He wanted no part of Bill. He had seen him handle his partner.

Ivana was numb. She, too, had seen Bill subdue her attacker. She did not resist.

Bill pointed to the back door and spoke to the driver again.

"*Öffnen Sie die Tür, bitte.* 'Please, open the door.'"

The driver complied.

132

Bill pushed Ivana off the bus. She stared at his hand. In it was the weapon the woman had intended to use on her. Bill caught her glance and tossed the gun under a hedge.

Through the windows, they saw the driver lean over the groggy woman. The well-dressed man up front spoke on his cell phone.

Ivana stood shivering. Bill spoke.

"*Ivana ist dein Name?*"

"*Ja.*"

"Do you speak English?"

She looked up and nodded.

"Yes."

"Good. My German is so-so and my Czech is non-existent."

Bill pointed to the glow in the sky that indicated the airport not far ahead.

"We can't go to the airport. They're waiting for you, and there will be too many of them. Do you trust me? Will you come with me."

She managed to nod, "Yes." What else could she do?

Bill turned to his phone.

"Tom, you're in the airport parking? I have her. Pick us up. We're a mile away. Hurry. The bad guys know she's here."

The only houses were on their side of the highway. Across the way, gray fields alternated with tracts of leafless hardwoods.

Bill hustled Ivana across. They dashed for the nearest trees and sought shelter behind a large oak. Ivana slumped at the base of the trunk and closed her eyes. She did not speak.

The moonlight accented her high cheek bones. Bill studied her features. Ivana was attractive. *Jeannine!* He bit his lip.

She needed to know that he was all right. He reached for his phone, but his pocket was empty. Apparently it had fallen during their dash across the roadway. He looked up as a car approached from the direction of the airport. A bright beam pierced the shadows and probed the roadside. A spot light.

Tom's car had no such light!

Bill jumped behind the oak.

Just in time.

The beam struck the trunk of the tree and paused. Bill pulled Ivana to the ground. She lay still, her body pressed against him. Through his jacket, he felt warmth. He held her tightly.

The light wavered above them.

The car stopped.

***

In Bethesda, Jeannine had waited for more than an hour. Finally the phone on her desk rang.

"Bill, are you all right?"

"Jeannine? This is Aileen. Why did you think I was Bill?"

Jeannine recounted to her partner the fateful phone call. Aileen hesitated.

"Do you want me to get off the line in case he calls back?"

"We won't talk long, and something tells me he can't. But I need to know more about what happened. Are you all right?"

"I hurt, but I'm managing. At least Peter got me away from that madman Gustav. We're with two people. Jim Harrigan is a cop. He's the one who called us and wanted us to give Pokorny's package to the police. Mila Patekova is a realtor here on the Outer Banks. Her cousin, Anne Simek, is missing."

"Who did you say? What was that name?"

"Simek, Anne Simek, she is ... "

"No, before that. Was Jim's name Harrigan? Bill knew a 'Harrigan' at the CIA. Ask him if he ever worked there."

The phone went silent. Then Aileen came back on the line.

"One and the same. He remembers Bill well."

Jeannine was about to speak further, when her phone clicked.

"Aileen, I have a call. It could be Bill. I'll call you back."

Jeannine checked the calling number. It was Bill Hamm's.

"Bill, what happened? Are you all right?"

But the caller wasn't Bill. She heard what to her was gibberish.

"Prosim, kdo jste? Našel jsem tento mobilní telefon."

She did not recognize the language.

"Please, who is this? Do you speak English?

134

"No English, Czech. Aber, sprechen Sie Deutsch?"

At least she knew that was German.

"Nein. No. I speak English, please. ... English."

The caller was as confused as Jeannine.

"Phone, I find this phone on road. Yours is last call."

"Please, who are you? Where are you?"

The caller tried two languages.

"Jsem v Praze, na letišti Ruzyně, ... auf dem Prager Flughafen Ruzyně, ..."

At Jeannine's silence, the caller struggled with English.

"Prague Airport. Ruzyne Airport, Prague."

"Prague! How did you get this phone. Where is the owner?"

Loudspeakers drowned out the answer. The caller tried again.

"I find in road. My plane leaves. I put phone to Informace desk, ... Auskunft, ... You find there."

The line went dead.

Jeannine's hand shook. She put the phone down.

My God, Bill, Prague? And your phone? What happened?

She sat, elbows on the desk, face in her hands.

***

It was afternoon in Kitty Hawk, North Carolina. Karel's men sat in the Excursion. If "mood" had a color, theirs' was "black."

First, they had been angry when they awoke in Grandy and found their prey gone. Zeleny and the Simek woman had tricked them. Second, they had driven to Kitty Hawk in the hopes of spotting the pair. No luck.

After that, a furious Karel had called from Prague. Gustav now was the number one target, not Simek. He was to be eliminated immediately. Yesterday was not soon enough!

And Karel blamed them for Ivana's flight!

No more excuses.

***

In Jim Harrigan's apartment in Duck, Aileen retreated directly to the kitchen while Jim, Mila and Peter Zeleny sat around the

135

coffee table in the small living area. Their strategy was to hope that Anne would call Mila whose phone lay on the table.

The discussion was loud. The phone was silent.

Aileen sat at the kitchen counter. She rested her head on her arms to avoid pressure on her swollen face. A dull pain in her shoulder provided a constant background to the throbbing behind her eyes. Finally they closed and she dozed.

She awoke to a touch on her arm. Mila stood next to her.

"Dr. Harris, this apartment is too small to sleep. I have a house in Corolla that has more room. Are you up to moving?"

"I guess. Are we leaving now?"

Mila nodded and helped her up. They left for Corolla.

***

At the Moccasin Cottages in Coastal Carolina, the sun was low in the West. Anne Simek, alone and scared, stood on her porch. Far out on the Albemarle Sound, the lights of a single craft shone through the evening mist. Across the inlet a lone Osprey sat on a rubble of sticks atop a dead Pine. The landlady had told Anne that some Ospreys stayed the year round. Anne wondered if that bird felt as alone as she.

And Anne was plagued by the cabin's roaches. She had now seen six. Large, they ran making scuttling noises. Her thoughts turned to Mila. She had been trustworthy about the roach-free rental. But about Vaclav? *Mila, you should have told me?*

She studied the small green chip in her hand. Its files were password-protected. Whatever they contained, someone was willing to kill for it, and that same someone was looking for her!

At that thought, Anne decided. She put Vaclav's chip in her purse, loaded laptop and bags into the Focus, and went to the office to pay the bill. Minutes later she was back in her car.

All right, Mila. You win. I need help and you're it.

She headed for Nags Head and Mila's house.

***

******

136

Chapter 19
Wednesday, November 24

Daylight brightened the countryside near Ruzyne Airport. The sun's rays broke through the bare branches and crossed Bill Hamm's eyes. He awoke on his back, shivering in a layer of leaves and broken twigs that surrounded him.

He turned his head to see Ivana huddled under a nearby bush. She sat trembling, her arms locked about her knees to retain body warmth. She wore only a sweater, her jacket covered Bill's chest. Apparently too, she had pushed leaves and branches around him for insulation and concealment.

He focused upwards. Above him was a horizontal branch, shoulder high. Now Bill remembered. They had fled through the woods from the searchers' lights.

Evidently he had run into the stout limb and been knocked unconscious.

He felt his forehead. His fingers came away tinted with blood, but not much. Whatever gash he had sustained was not deep.

Finally, he lifted himself up.

Ivana rubbed her ankles. She spoke.

"Are you better?"

"I think so. How long have I been down."

She shrugged.

"Maybe an hour, maybe more."

"And you didn't leave?"

She shrugged again.

"I thought about it when they stopped looking for us, but you saved my life. Besides, I have no money and no place to go They found my knapsack."

She added.

"It was by the tree when we ran. I heard them shouting. It had my Euros and the papers I took from Karel."

"Karel?"

"Karel Moravec, my boss. Those men after me were his."

"What 'papers' do you mean?"

"It wasn't just papers. There were official company records plus CD-ROMs, hard copy files and photos. Gustav said it would be my insurance policy against Karel. With them, we could prove Karel is an international criminal, demonstrate his crimes against humanity."

"Gustav? Do you mean Gustav Slavik?"

"Yes, but how would you know him?"

"He's the reason I'm here. He wants us to protect you."

"Me? But you are American. He hates Am ... "

Ivana stopped and frowned.

It was Bill's turn to shrug.

"Evidently he likes you more than he hates us."

Ivana shut her eyes. She owed that old man. *Thank you, Gustav.*

***

Ivana stood while Bill surveyed the bare winter woods. Only a few brown leaves populated the otherwise bare branches of the oaks. A cold breeze whispered through the tree tops. Ivana pressed her arms to her body. Bill returned her jacket to her shoulders.

"Thanks for the loan of your coat, but we have to leave now."

He felt in his pocket for the phone. His hand came out empty. *Damn!* He remembered. He had lost it crossing the road.

He looked about. There, to the north was an opening through the trees, a cultivated field of stubble.

"There is a farm over that way. The house can't be far. We'll say we are hikers who are lost. You can ask to use their phone. We'd better start walking."

Bill picked his way through the brush.

Ivana followed.

***

138

In North Carolina, the sun was still low on the eastern horizon when Gustav Slavik and Johan Zeleny arrived at the Dare County Airport in Manteo.

Gustav stepped down from their charter. Across the tarmac, the Emergency Management Services' Medevac Bk 117 helicopter stood ready for use. Further beyond, the waters of the Croatan Sound rippled under the morning mist.

Johan rubbed his left knee and descended. He limped after his leader.

"I'm not as young as I used to be. Who do we locate first, Simek or Mila."

"We go to Nags Head. I want to see Mila. Simek is scared. She'll stay and hide at the Moccasin Cottages. There is no hurry for her."

"Any news about Ivana?"

Gustav glared. Ivana was a concern he shared with no one. He walked to the rental car.

Johan limped after him in silence.

Gustav knew the way to Mila's house. He drove.

***

In Nag's Head, Karel's men drove past Mila's house. The nearby houses appeared shuttered for the winter and no cars were visible. Only Mila's had clear windows and was in current use. Still, its driveway was empty. Evidently she was not home.

The driver steered the gray Ford Excursion around the corner. The street was deserted. He spoke.

"I'll park past that third house. That way no one can see us from Patekova's windows."

The passenger touched his ear, still sore from the smashed listening device. He spoke.

"What are we doing? Are you sure Gustav will come back here?"

"Karel says Gustav left Maryland for the Outer Banks. Give me a better idea. This is the only place we know Gustav has been. Maybe Simek and Zeleny will show up too."

He stopped and thought. He pointed to the house next to Mila's. Like hers it was lifted on sturdy posts, one floor above the ground. The only structure visible in the open area underneath was a partitioned shower for bathers. It had swinging "saloon" doors supported by two of the load-bearing posts.

"You wait in that shower. Stand inside behind that post. I'll do the same across the street."

The house across the street was likewise mounted on posts. It too had a framed shower in the open space underneath.

"No thanks, it's cold. I'll wait in the car."

The driver looked at his partner. They were in enough trouble with Karel. There was no point in fighting among themselves.

"All right, I'll take the far shower. You stay in the car. But when I signal, get in that other shower, fast."

Both men wore body armor. Each had a modern-variant AK-47, with a classic curved 30-round magazine. Armor and weapon were heavy, but they would be in fixed positions.

The driver slung his weapon over his shoulder and made his way under the house. Once in the shower, behind the swinging doors, he looked over and waved. The passenger waved back through the car window.

This was no fancy plan. This was an ambush, one with overwhelming firepower.

Gustav would die!

***

In Corolla, North Carolina, the night spent in Anne Simek's rental was uneventful. Mila slept in Anne's bedroom off of the great room on the top level. Peter Zeleny, Aileen Harris and Jim Harrigan had separate bedrooms on the mid level below.

Jim was the first to rise. He made his way to the top level where he found coffee. Soon a "wake up" aroma filled the great room and filtered to the bedrooms below. In response, Peter Zeleny smothered his face in his pillow and lay motionless. Likewise, in her bedroom Aileen did not stir.

140

On the top level, Mila smelled the coffee and dressed. In the great room Jim poured her a cup She sipped slowly.

"Jim, what are your plans today?"

"I'm sorry, I'm on duty. I tried to switch assignments, but I couldn't. I'll be back about four this afternoon. Meanwhile, you have to promise to stay away from Nags Head and your house. Stay here with Peter and Aileen. Don't go anywhere alone."

Mila did not like orders, even kind ones. She responded.

"But Jim, I have to pick up some clothes at my house. You don't want me looking like a witch."

"Tell you what, I'll meet you at noon in Nags Head. We can go together to your house to pick up your things."

Mila nodded. *This guy likes me. He's worried about me.*

"Noon will be fine."

He left. Mila watched him go. *I like you too, Jim.*

Downstairs, Peter slept. Likewise, Aileen's door was closed.

Upstairs Mila sat and shut her eyes, but her cell phone vibrated. She looked at the calling number. It was Anne Simek.

"Anne, dear God, where are you? I've tried to reach you."

Anne's reply was punctuated with sobs. The only word that Mila was sure of was "Vaclav."

"I know he's dead, Anne, but you're not to blame. Blame me first. You didn't know. Now tell me where you are."

Anne's words were garbled, but Mila understood.

"Anne, don't go near my house. It's too dangerous. Come to your rental house."

But static overtook the connection, and the phone went dead.

***

Gustav Slavik was a survivor for one reason, he was a thinker. No operation was so simple that it did not merit analysis, including this return to Mila's house. On his prior visit, Gustav had approached Mila's house from Route 158, her Office side.

This time he chose another approach, from the beachside road. He drove past Mila's street. Moments later, he stopped. To his right there were no homes, only low dunes with sea oats that waved erratically towards the beach. Gustav stepped out the car, took a deep breath of the salt air, and rubbed his hands together against the cold. He turned towards his passenger.

"Johan, did you see that car parked back there?"

"Where? What car?"

"Back under that yellow beach house, the gray Excursion."

"I didn't see anything."

"You are as soft as your son. You have aged, Comrade. That Ford Excursion means Karel's men are waiting for us."

"But, how do you know?"

"His men followed me to Ryan Associates in Bethesda. They drove a gray Ford Excursion."

"What are we going to do?"

"*You* are going to do what I say. Take the keys. Give me five minutes, then turn left at the next cross street and go to 158. Turn left again and drive back to Mila's. Stop behind the Realty Office. Do not get out of the car. Leave the rest to me."

Johan Zeleny took the keys.

***

In Corolla, Peter Zeleny was awake and drinking coffee. Mila was at the stove where bacon sizzled in the frying pan. A half-empty carton of eggs sat open on the counter.

Aileen came upstairs. Her eyes were clear. Evidently her headache was gone. Peter spoke.

"Aileen, I ... "

"No Peter. Don't talk to me."

He bit his tongue.

***

Johan Zeleny drove as directed on Route 158. He saw the sign for Patek Realty, and parked behind the office. No one was in sight. He cut the engine and waited.

He heard a knock on the rear passenger-side window.

It was Gustav.

Blood smeared the window where he had rapped.

***

******

Chapter 20
Wednesday, November 24

Johan Zeleny clicked the rear door locks open. Gustav laid two AK-47's on the floor in the rear. His hands were bloody.

Johan spoke.

"Are you hurt? Where did the guns come from?"

Gustav shrugged, and sat in the back on the passenger side.

"It's not my blood. No questions. Drive around the corner and stop by that Ford Excursion."

At the Ford, Gustav transferred the weapons to its backseat. He tossed a blanket over them. Then he spoke to Johan.

"I'll drive our car. You follow me in the Excursion. Stay at the speed limit. You don't want to get stopped by the police. There are two bodies under the tarp in the back."

"Two?"

"Karel's men work in pairs. No more questions."

"But where are we going? Why?"

"The mainland. The map shows a wildlife refuge by the Alligator River. There must be a place there where nobody will find these scum."

Gustav added.

"Karel will have to guess what happened to his men."

***

To Anne Simek it was a homecoming of sorts. The house at Corolla was unchanged. The white siding glistened in the noon sun. Out on the Currituck Sound, a lone fisherman sheltered his head and neck with a wide-brimmed straw hat. A jacket, needed in the early morning cold but superfluous in the warm afternoon sun, was tied about his waist.

Anne parked her Focus near the rear stairs. She clasped her laptop and climbed the steps.

She moved slowly, with trepidation. The police wanted to talk to her about Vaclav Pokorny's death, but Mila had assured Anne that the policeman, Harrigan, was not there.

Anne had a key, but did not use it. As she reached for the knocker, the door opened.

A woman stood in the doorway.

Anne gasped. She was looking in a "mirror." This person could be her twin.

Anne recovered quickly as she registered the differences. The woman had a black eye, was slightly shorter, had lower cheekbones, a more upturned nose and was a bit heavier.

Anne found her voice.

"I'm Anne Simek, I expected to see Mila. Where is she?"

"Hello Anne. I'm Aileen Harris, Mila's upstairs. She ..."

Aileen did not finish. Mila burst down the steps and wrapped Anne in a huge hug.

"Anne, thank God. I've been worried sick."

***

The rest of Anne's reunion with her cousin was personal. She and Mila huddled together at the kitchen table. They spoke in low tones.

Peter Zeleny left for a walk on the beach. Aileen, after stating her desire to return to Maryland, descended to the mid level to shower.

By the time that Aileen, bright and freshly combed, came back up, Anne had retired to a chair on the side deck. Mila sat alone. Aileen joined her.

Mila spoke.

"Aileen, do you think you should go back to Maryland? They know about Ryan Associates. You're no safer there than here."

"My daughter needs me. And I need to see Jeannine. She may know how to access the chip that Vaclav left with Anne. Safe or not, I have to go back."

"What about Peter?"

"I won't have him with me, but if you think Anne would be better with us in Maryland, she's welcome."

Mila thought for a moment.

"She'd better go with you. If she stays here, the Currituck County Sheriff might keep her as a material witness. Jim Harrigan wouldn't be able to stop him. Besides, Jim is a cop. He might not want to stop him. He probably agrees with the sheriff."

"But will Anne come with me?"

"I already talked to her. She wants to follow you in her car. She's better off away from the local police, and she's leery about Jim Harrigan."

"Where is Jim now?"

"He's in Nags Head. I'm meeting him for lunch, then we're going to my house to pick up some of my clothes. Jim has agreed to stay with me here in Corolla. I'll be safe with him around."

"What about when he's at work?"

Mila pointed to a shiny short-barreled .38 Smith & Wesson revolver lying on the table. It had five chambers.

"Jim loaned me this. He's teaching me to shoot."

Mila looked at her watch.

"Aileen, I have to go now. Jim will be waiting for me. I know Anne wants to be gone before Jim and I come back. Thanks for caravaning with her."

"No problem. We'll keep you posted."

One last hug, then Mila left.

***

Peter Zeleny was frustrated. Aileen Harris wanted nothing to do with him.

"Peter, I told you. I'm going back to Maryland. I need to take care of my daughter, and no, you can not come back with me. I need to be alone."

"But Aileen, we are on the same side?"

"So you say, but your father is not. Anne Simek is following me in her car. Maybe she'll let you ride with her."

145

Anne piped up.

"What's this? A Zeleny wants a ride from a Simek?"

"Yes, I need a ride."

"But what would your father say?"

"Please. I am not my father."

Anne turned away. She held out her hand to Aileen.

"Here's Vaclav's chip from my laptop. It's password-protected. Maybe you folks can access the files."

She turned back to Peter.

"Dr. Zeleny, grab your coat. You can ride with me."

***

Scot Henderson was a Special Agent for the Fish and Wildlife Service charged with law enforcement. Today, he drove along Sawyer Lake road in the Alligator River National Wildlife Refuge in North Carolina. He was investigating a report that a Red Wolf had been shot the night before.

The Red Wolf, an endangered species had been introduced into the refuge in 1987.

Scot drove slowly, his eyes on the road's shoulder to his right.

A flash of russet in the roadside weeds caught his eye. He stopped and stepped out of his vehicle. He trudged through the dead plants. The decaying body of a Canid lay at his feet.

It was a Red Wolf.

Scot saw that the animal had been dead for several days. This was not the wolf killed yesterday. Somewhere ahead was another carcass. He resolved to stop the carnage.

***

Gustav led the way along an unpaved road in the wildlife refuge. Johan followed in the Excursion. He drove slowly. With two bodies under a tarp in the back, he did not want to be stopped by the police.

Johan was afraid of Gustav. He hoped that Gustav would forgive his son.

Peter, you never should have struck Gustav.

146

In the midst of these thoughts, flashing red and blue lights appeared in Johan's rear view mirror. A policeman in an SUV was signaling him to stop. Johan looked ahead. Gustav had just rounded a bend in the road. He was out of sight.

Johan pressed the brake.

***

When the Ford Excursion stopped in front of him, Scot Henderson stayed in his car. He had dealt with poachers before. They were always armed. He called park headquarters with his location and the license number of the vehicle that he had stopped.

Only then did he open the door, unsnap the strap on his holster, and step out.

Scot did not like the driver's looks. Could he be the poacher? He was glad to have an excuse to stop this car. He tapped on the window.

"Sir, your right brake light is out. May I see your driver's license"

Johan lowered the window, but before he could speak, Scot had drawn his gun.

Johan stared. A 9 mm Glock was only inches from his nose..

"Sir, keep your hands where I can see them and step out of the car. Now!"

Scot took a step backwards as Johan opened the door.

"Sir put your hands on the car."

Johan obeyed.

Moments later, hands secured behind his back, he spoke for the first time.

"I've done nothing. Why the handcuffs?"

Scot scowled and pointed to the back seat of the Excursion where the barrels of two AK-47's protruded from under a blood-stained blanket.

"Sir, are those yours?"

Johan's mouth went dry.

He could not answer.

***

When Johan failed to appear around the bend in the road, Gustav stopped his car and went back on foot. Standing behind a pine tree, he watched the drama enacted by the policeman and Johan.

If the policeman found the two bodies, Johan would be arrested, unless Gustav intervened.

He fingered his Makarov.

Perhaps?

Gustav hesitated, but then another police vehicle, lights flashing red and blue, arrived at the scene.

The odds were wrong now. Johan would have to take care of himself.

Gustav returned to his car as a beep on his phone signaled the arrival of a text.

He read it. The Americans had retrieved the package. Ivana was safe.

A last glance through the trees as his former partner was led by the police to their vehicle.

Sorry, old comrade.

It was time to return to Europe!

***

Scot Henderson opened the back of the Ford Excursion and lifted the tarp.

He gasped.

"What the hell!"

The bloody remains were not Red Wolves.

They were human!

***

In Chesapeake, Virginia, it was mid afternoon when Aileen Harris, Anne Simek and Peter Zeleny stopped to eat at a Thai restaurant off of Route 168.

The three sat together, but Aileen refused to acknowledge Peter. She concentrated on a bowl of flat rice noodles swimming in a colorful mix of garlic, and assorted vegetables.

"Anne, this is really good. How is yours?"

"Excellent, the curry picks it up. What about yours, Peter?"

"Mine's not bad. Aileen's looks better."

Peter glanced sideways at Aileen to see if she had heard him,

But her eyes were fixed on the large television that dominated the dining area. A red "Breaking News Alert" was on the screen.

Double murder on the Alligator River Wildlife Refuge This just in from our correspondent in Columbia, North Carolina. A man stopped on suspicion of poaching Red Wolves was arrested on Sawyer Lake Road when the bodies of two men were found in the back of his car. No further details have been released by the police, but an anonymous source says that both victims had gunshot wounds to the head.

Aileen pointed.

"That's the gray Ford Excursion that followed us from Bethesda!"

But Peter's eyes were on the man slouched by the vehicle. He was handcuffed and his face was blurred to prevent identification. Still, Peter knew him.

"That's my father! My God, what has he done?"

Peter stood up.

"I have to go back. I have to see him."

Anne looked as Peter's cheeks paled and his lower lip quivered. She rose from the table.

"Peter, I'll take you back to North Carolina."

Aileen stayed seated.

***

Only minutes later, Aileen and Anne Simek said their good byes outside the Thai restaurant.

"Anne, I hope you know what you are doing?"

"Peter has to see his father."

"His father is a horrible old man."

"We Simek's have more reason to hate him than anyone. But times are different now and Peter is not his father. Peter needs to go. He has to get free of him."

"You're a better person that I am."

Anne smiled.

"I doubt it. But I know what bitterness did to my own father. Justified or not, it possesses and destroys whoever has it."

"What about you? The police are waiting to interrogate you."

"It doesn't matter. I have nothing to hide. I'll survive."

"Anne, I hardly know you, but you are getting one big hug."

They embraced.

Moments later Anne headed south on Route 168.

Aileen headed north. She looked in the rear view mirror. The lane to the south already was empty.

Anne's Focus was out of sight.

***

******

Chapter 21
Wednesday, November 24

Aileen was still on the road in Virginia when her cell phone vibrated. She recognized the caller.

"Jeannine, I'm on the way back to Maryland.

"Where are you?"

"I'm on Route 64 between Hampton and Williamsburg."

"Who's with you?"

"Nobody, I'm by myself. Anne Simek and Peter Zeleny went back to Corolla. Peter's father was arrested for a double murder. I don't know the details and I don't want to know. He and that Gustav are monsters."

Jeannine took a moment before she spoke.

"After what you've been through, I'm just glad you are all right.

"Thanks, but why did you call?"

"First to check on you and then to tell you about Xolak and Larry Hodges."

"I'm beat up and exhausted. Forget Hodges, tell me first about Bill Hamm."

"It's scary. I haven't heard from him since you and I last talked."

"Jeannine, I'm sorry, really sorry. All right, tell me about Hodges."

"He's a damned wimp. He left town on official travel. He finally called this morning. He wants the FDA to accept the Hus-Kinetika report."

"What about Vaclav's memo?"

"He hasn't seen it. I think that's why he extended his travel, so he wouldn't see it."

"What can we do?"

"I've done it. I threatened him. He didn't like it, but he agreed to inform the members of the review panel. He'll abide by the majority opinion. I'm satisfied. The members are not political. When they hear our results, they'll tell him to reject the report."

"So It will be the panel's decision, not his."

Jeannine laughed.

"That's what he hopes, but I think his Chief is going to assign him a new office, the broom closet!"

"No sympathy here."

At that point the phone went dead.

Aileen's car was between towers.

***

In the countryside not far from the Prague airport, Bill Hamm and Ivana sat in the warm kitchen of a stone farm house. Ivana sat near an iron stove that was situated in a huge former hearth.

"But I don't understand. Why are the Americans, I mean you, doing favors for Gustav?"

Bill looked out the window.

"Gustav has information for us, and apparently you do too. That's why Karel Moravec wants to kill you both. You know too much about his operation. If Gustav hadn't texted me, you'd be dead on that bus."

Ivana shivered. She looked down.

"You mean if you hadn't stopped that assassin."

"Whatever."

He returned to the window. A car was coming, his partner Tom Fletcher.

"Our ride is here. We have to go. Do you have any ID, or was it in your knapsack?"

Ivana produced a passport from a jacket pocket and tossed it to Bill.

Bill saw "Deutschland" and "Reisepass" on the cover. He looked inside, "Irma Neumann" was a German national.

"All right, 'Irma,' that works."

He put a small sheaf of Euros on the table for the farmer who was in the barn, tending his stock.

Bill took Ivana's hand and led her to the waiting car.

***

Tom drove. Bill Hamm sat in the passenger seat. Ivana was in back.

Bill spoke.

"What's the situation at the airport?"

"They're watching the flights to Vienna. The same guys have been checking the gates. This guy Moravec has high connections."

"What do you suggest?"

Tom turned right onto a main road and then answered.

"We should leave the Czech Republic. I filled up the gas tank. We can cross into Germany at Dolni Poustevna, it's about 150 kilometers, just under 100 miles, from here. From there we can drive to Dresden, under forty miles."

"So we go north because they think we will go south to Austria?"

"That's the idea."

"And it's a good one, but Dolni Poustevna is a small crossing out of the way. We can take the E55 autoroute. It's faster, and if nobody is looking north it will be safe."

"Whatever you say, but after Dresden where do we go?"

"We fly to Brussels. Lots of our people are there."

Tom nodded agreement. He headed towards Route E55.

Bill continued.

"Tom, did you text Gustav that the 'package' is safe."

"I did."

Ivana cringed. She was a "package?" She had lost control of her own destiny.

For the first time since meeting Bill Hamm, she was afraid.

Who are these Americans?

***

In Corolla, North Carolina, the sun hung red and low in the West as Anne Simek steered her Focus into a space under the beach house. She parked next to Mila's white SUV behind which was a Duck Police car with blue stripes.

The presence of Jim's police car reminded her of her own difficulties. She would be questioned by local law enforcement about Vaclav Pokorny's death.

She turned off the engine and glanced sideways. Peter was slumped in the passenger seat, his eyes closed.

"Peter, we're back. Let's go."

She opened her door and stepped into the chilly air. She looked back. Peter had not moved.

"Come on Peter. It's cold out here."

Peter opened his door. He stepped to Anne's side. His voice was low.

"Anne, thank you. I am grateful."

"You're welcome. Now let's go and check in with Mila."

She guided him up the wooden steps to the living level.

***

It was two in the morning in Prague. Fiala slept soundly. Karel Moravec left the bed and went to the window. Across the river, the lit walls of the Castle glowed a warm yellow in marked contrast to the cold dark waters of the Vltava.

He stared at his phone. Its screen was blank.

He had not heard from his first team. And the second team, still in Maryland, knew nothing except that the first team was in North Carolina. There was no good news from either group.

Worse, apparently Gustav was still alive!

Karel ground his teeth. Ivana had slipped through his net. Damn that woman. Still he missed her. It was truly a pity that she had to die. The second night with Fiala had lost the enthusiasm of the first.

Karel would never admit failure, but he was troubled. The stranger who had saved Ivana was an American from Vienna, and certainly with the CIA. What did they know? Had Ivana tipped them?

Fortunately, she did not know everything. He took some relief in that.

154

He turned from the window. It was 8:00 pm in Maryland. The second team was awaiting his instructions. What was the name of that company?

He had it.

Karel punched a message on his phone. It was simple.

"Eliminate Ryan Associates!"

***

A weary Aileen Harris steered her car along Bradley Boulevard in Bethesda, Maryland. Homes were set well back from the roadway and hidden among large trees whose branches obscured the street lights. In the poor lighting the beams of oncoming cars made her squint.

Her house was dark except for a lone light upstairs.

She fumbled with the key and opened the door. The light went on the hallway. Aileen's mother stood by the switch. She pulled her bathrobe about her.

"Aileen?"

"Sorry, Mom. I didn't want to wake you. I drove straight through. Is Mary Catherine asleep?"

A squeal from the top of the stairs answered that question.

"Mommy!"

Moments later, Aileen was smothered by a warm bundle of tangled blonde hair, squeezing arms and the flowing folds of a flannel nightgown.

***

******

Chapter 22
Thursday, November 25

In Bethesda, the early morning sun shone bright. A sleepy Aileen sat at the breakfast table. Mrs. Harris stood by the door.

"Aileen, Mary Catherine will be late for school."

Aileen tightened the collar of Mary Catherine's jacket, and handed her a brown lunch bag.

"Be a good girl and listen to Granny, She'll pick you up after school. Now give me a kiss."

A final hug, and Mary Catherine left with Mrs. Harris.

Aileen poured herself a cup of coffee After everything, it was good to be home. She was sipping coffee, when the phone rang. It was Jeannine

"Aileen, you made it home. Are you feeling better."

"Much. Mary Catherine just left for school. Where are you?"

"I don't want to say. I'm where we met last month about the Israeli contract. Meet me here. Don't go to the office. It's not safe. Did you bring the item?"

On the table in front of Aileen was the chip that Vaclav had left in Anne Simek's computer.

"I'm looking at it right now."

"Bring it as soon as you can. We have work to do."

"I'm on my way."

Aileen put a small bag of Cheetos on the kitchen table and wrote a note.

Mary Catherine, just a little treat for a big girl,
Love, Mommy.

She pocketed the memory chip and left.

***

Gustav Slavik awoke to the noise of the passing traffic on the Delaware Turnpike. His neck was sore, and his back ached. He had slept in the back seat of the car. It was early morning, but the parking lot of the turnpike rest stop was filling rapidly.

Gustav's route from North Carolina was different from Aileen's. From the wildlife refuge, he had taken Highway 64 west to Interstate 95, north. Rush hour traffic on the Beltways around Washington, DC and Baltimore slowed his progress, but still he had reached the rest stop in Delaware before exhaustion forced him to stop and sleep.

He sat up as his cell phone buzzed. A text had arrived.

The message was brief.

"The package is safe."

The Americans had Ivana, but was she really "safe?" Gustav bit his lip. No one with those corrupt capitalists could be safe. Still the CIA had worked fast. By now Ivana was in Belgium.

Gustav needed to free Ivana from the Americans without, in turn, revealing what he knew about Moravec's plan. He could never help the greedy yanks. And he must not wait until Ivana was brought to the U. S. It would be far easier to dupe the Americans in Belgium than in their own country.

Gustav knew Belgium. In the mid Eighty's he had funneled weapons from Czechoslovakia to the Cellules Communistes Combattantes, a group led by a Belgian terrorist who was finally apprehended in Namur.

He would fly to Brussels immediately.

He must hurry to New York and JFK Airport.

The sooner he arrived in Belgium, the better.

***

Aileen drove north to Rockville on I-270. Her destination was the Best Western Hotel at the Route 28 exit. The former Ramada was no stranger to intrigue. In 1985 John A. Walker was arrested there after spying for the Soviet Union for eighteen years.

Jeannine's room was on the sixth floor. She was standing by her door when Aileen got off the elevator.

"Come in, you look better than I thought you would. How's the eye?"

"I'm really tired, but the eye is fine, at least I can see."

"So Peter went back to North Carolina to see his father?"

"Yes, he went back. Anne Simek drove him."

"And Vaclav's chip?"

"Right here. You need a password."

Jeannine took the small green drive.

Aileen frowned.

"Sorry, but my head's spinning. I need to lie down."

Jeannine took her arm.

"Take this chair over here. I'll get you a pillow."

Aileen settled in and shut her eyes.

Jeannine stood a moment. Then she turned and plugged Vaclav's chip into the USB port of her laptop.

The chip was indeed password-protected.

Damn. What now, Jeannine?

She needed that password!

***

Jeannine spread the newspapers from Vaclav's package on the dresser. She muttered to herself.

"Damn it. Vaclav wanted Peter Zeleny to read this drive, he must have hidden clues in these papers. And Peter is no computernik, so the password can't be too hard to find."

She thought again.

Or can it? If it's in Czech I won't have a clue!"

She looked at the Cyrillic newspaper. If there was anything there, she would never know it. She stared blankly.

Come on Jeannine, try!

At least the Prague Post was in English. In it, Vaclav had marked several words and phrases, but only one word was circled rather than underlined, "green."

No words were circled in the Cyrillic paper. She looked at the Czech papers. Among the many words underlined, only two were encircled.

The first circled word, was "Petr." Surely that meant "Peter." Perhaps Vaclav had telegraphed his method.

The phrase was "Svatý Petr," but only "Petr" was circled. Using Google Translate, she saw that "Svatý Petr" meant "Saint Peter."

The other circled word was "svobodný." Where had she heard that word before?

Of course! Peter Zeleny had said that he was "svobodný," that is, "single" or "free."

There remained only the word "green." Jeannine typed it into the translator. The answer was immediate.

"Green" in Czech was "Zelený!"

Both Vaclav and Peter were Czech. Of course the password would be in their language. After some trial and error with Google Translate, she wrote down her most likely candidate, "singlePeterZeleny."

svobodnýPetrZeleny.

She tried the password. The drive remained locked. She added the verb "is," "PeterZeleny**is**single."

PetrZelenyjesvobodný.

Still locked! She grimaced.

Damn. This is the easiest permutation and Vaclav wanted Peter to read these files.

Wait! In America, Peter had dropped the accent from "Zeleny." In Google, Zelený appeared with an accent on the "y." It was a masculine adjective form, like svobodný.

Jeannine tapped the letters again. This time with the accented "ý."

PetrZelenýjesvobodný.

Bingo! She was in.

She chuckled and rubbed her hands together.

In the corner chair, Aileen still slept soundly.

***

In Corolla, North Carolina, Peter Zeleny, stood shivering on the beach. He pulled the hood of his sweatshirt tight about his head.

160

To no avail, the cold wind penetrated the light cotton. He bent against the wind, and trudged away from the beach house.

Thanks to the last week's storm, the beach was narrow. Peter stepped carefully. The tide was coming in. The encroaching waves strove to reach the white dunes, only to fall short and retreat back into the ocean.

Peter was thinking of his father, securely locked in jail when a voice, muted by the wind, called from behind him.

"Peter, what are you doing out here. It's cold. Come back to the house."

He turned and saw Anne Simek, some steps behind. Her hood was pulled tight. The wind pushed her pullover against her body revealing an attractive form.

Peter looked down.

"I had to be alone. I didn't want to talk to anybody."

"But it's miserable out here. And it's starting to rain."

He looked at the sand. Tiny craters appeared where large rain drops splattered the surface.

"Peter, I'm sorry your father refuses to see you."

He looked into her eyes. Those soft moist pupils *were* sorry.

"Anne, I have no illusions about him or his life. It's just that I want closure with my father. I needed to talk to him."

She took his hand. Peter shivered, but not from the wind.

"Peter, you are not your father. I've been hard on you. I'm sorry, but believe me, don't ever think that you are like him. I've only known you a little while, but I know you could never do the things he has done."

"Like what he did to your father?"

"Like what he did to my father. Times are different, we are different. Our lives are ahead of us. The past is the past. Maybe, we can help each other dispel our ghosts."

She lowered her voice.

"And Peter, Hus-Kinetika never paid me. Professor Pokorny did proposition me. I would never lie about that."

He squeezed her hand. He knew she was right. He spoke, but a whistling gust swept his words down the beach. She looked up at him.

"Peter, maybe, just maybe, things can be very different for the two of us."

As she realized what she had said, her gaze fell on the seaweed at her feet.

Peter blushed. His voice failed. He put his arm about her shoulders. She leaned against him. They stood in silence, unaware of the waves that lapped over their shoes.

Finally he spoke.

"Anne, thanks, really, for bringing me back to Corolla. I'm grateful. I like you, a lot. I'm not sure what else to say."

The rain began to fall in earnest. Massive drops pelted their shoulders. Still holding hands, they turned and dashed for the house. By the time they reached the deck, they were soaked.

Neither cared.

***

At the Best Western Hotel in Rockville, Jeannine filled the coffee maker anew and groaned. She had worked for over two hours.

Aileen, eyes shut, was still in the chair. The bruises on her face were less apparent and her breathing was regular.

"Aileen, wake up. I've accessed Vaclav's disk and read his notes. They confirm your worries about nerve gas. It's deadly and there's lots of it!"

Aileen sat up.

"What's this about nerve gas?"

"Vaclav wrote his notes in English for his trip here. You told me about the Novichok Agents developed by the Soviets in the 70's and 80's, but there's more. Vaclav reports that a Czech scientist was instrumental in the development of the deadliest of these nerve gases. He named it 'Novichok-H,' for the Czech hero, Johan Hus."

She continued.

"Vaclav says that before 1990, when the Soviets realized that the USSR would dissolve, they moved all their stockpiles from Uzbekistan to a holding facility, code-named 'NNNK,' in Russia. They could not leave those agents under the control of a soon-to-be independent Republic of Uzbekistan. When Russia, the U. S., and other nations signed the Chemical Weapons Convention in 1993, the Russians agreed to destroy all stockpiles of nerve agents and to allow inspections, but the Novichok agents were not included as 'Schedule 1 Weapons,' like Sarin and Soman whose stocks were to be destroyed."

Aileen jumped erect.

"That's right. Novichok Agents would not be covered by the treaty. Prior nerve agents like Sarin and Soman possess a carbon-phosphorus bond and are banned by the convention, but a number of the Novichok agents don't have a C-P bond and would not be banned."

Jeannine grimaced.

"I'll take your word for the chemistry. Vaclav says that the Russians claimed that Novichok agents were a non-issue for the treaty. They asserted that only experimental quantities of Novichok agents ever existed and that those had been destroyed, so that the CWC did not need to be changed."

Now Aileen was fully engaged.

"OK, but it's impossible to ban all chemical weapons. Many, like Sarin, can be stored as two separate and harmless precursors that must be mixed in proper proportions and at the right temperature to produce the lethal product. Treaties need to identify chemicals that have *no other use* except as steps to a final deadly product, or have *no peaceful use* in large quantities. Novichok agents have particularly innocuous precursors that occur normally in fertilizer production or in the manufacture of pesticides."

She paused and frowned.

"But what is Hus-Kinetika's connection with all this? What's Vaclav's point?"

"The Russians lied when they said they had no stockpiled Novichok-H. They still had 95 metric tons in the form of its two precursors. In 1990, this was shipped to NNNK from Uzbekistan along with thousands of metric tons of Sarin and Soman. Later, when the West found about the 'Newcomer' Agents, the Russians labeled the Novichok-H 'A-255' (Soman) and hid it among the Sarin and Soman stocks at NNNK."

Jeannine took a breath.

"When the CWC treaty was signed. All stockpiles of Sarin and Soman at NNNK were designated for destruction. In 1994 a group of hard-core Czech ex-communists diverted the Novichok-H (labeled as Soman) to a former chemical weapons facility near Brno in the Czech Republic, a facility that now belongs to Hus-Kinetika."

"How did they manage that?"

"They labeled the two precursors as 'Pesticide.' But that's not all. Vaclav says that in 2005, the conspirators moved all 95 tons to a Hus-Kinetika facility in another country. Vaclav thinks it's in the United States."

Aileen paled.

"So they want to use it on us!"

She caught her breath.

"But maybe Vaclav is a pathological liar? Maybe we shouldn't believe him?"

"If he was a liar, he died for his lies."

Aileen fell silent.

***

The coffee maker stopped dribbling. Jeannine poured two cups and handed one to Aileen who drank in silence.

Jeannine paced and sipped before resuming her account.

"Later, when site NNNK transferred its chemical weapons to the Russian Chemical Weapons Destruction Facility designated by the CWC, the transfer was 95 tons short because of the missing 'Soman' (Novichok-H.) Fortunately for the conspirators, 95 metric tons was a piddling amount compared to the total tonnage of all agents shipped for destruction."

"So no one noticed the discrepancy?"

"No one, until 2009. Inspectors for the Organization for the Prohibition of Chemical Weapons, the OPCW, looked through some old Russian files and spotted the shortage of 95 tons."

"What happened then?"

"One member of the OPCW inspection team was from Hus-Kinetika. He told the conspirators that the inspectors had noticed the shortage. The conspirators concocted the story that even though the 95 tons of 'Soman' was not on the list, the error had been corrected immediately, and that records would prove that the stock was in the process of being destroyed. They fabricated destruction records for the missing tonnage and paid the team member from Hus-Kinetika to slip them into the files. The team discovered them and everyone was satisfied."

"Everyone?"

"Everyone at the OPCW. There were other discrepancies to resolve, and the inspectors are overworked."

"If the case was closed, what can we do?"

"Vaclav had the conspirator's destruction records. I constructed this table from his numbers. Look."

Jeannine laid a print-out with numbers on the table.

Conspirators' Destruction Numbers

Year	Initial Number of Metric Tons Declared	Cumulative Number of Metric Tons Destroyed
2000	95	26.81
2001	95	32.06
2002	95	34.28
2003	95	34.75
2004	95	35.68
2005	95	39.32
2006	95	43.99
2007	95	45.36
2008	95	45.36
2009	95	54.02

Aileen studied the numbers while Jeannine continued.

"These are the conspirators' numbers for the Novichok-H (labeled as 'Soman') that they claim is in the process of being destroyed.

"Maybe these numbers are OK?   Maybe Vaclav is all wrong?"

"I wish that was so, but these numbers are fraudulent, just as Vaclav claimed."

***

Aleen stood stunned. Jeannine went on.

"The annual reports for the OPCW are on the Internet. Look at this table of the destruction of stocks of the nerve agent Sarin up to the year 2009."

OPCW Destruction of Sarin Stocks 2000 to 2009*
(All Participating Nations)

Year	Number of Metric Tons Declared	Cumulative Number of Metric Tons Destroyed	Cumulative % of Metric Tons Destroyed
2000	15048219	4246686	28.22
2001	15048219	5078600	33.75
2002	15048177	5429614	36.08
2003	15048177	5504390	36.58
2004	15047039	5652199	37.56
2005	15047045	6228144	41.39
2006	15047039	6967127	46.30
2007	15047039	7184961	47.75
2008	15047039	7184961	47.75
2009	15047039	8556331	56.86

***Organization for the Prohibition of Chemical Warfare. (www.opcw.org) Note various adjusted values for Declared Tons of Sarin. (Values for year 2005 may need correction.)**

"But Jeannine, Sarin's not a Novichok agent.   It's the gas that the Aum cultists used in the attack on the Tokyo subway."

"Right. It just happens that Sarin is listed first in the OPCW tables of Schedule 1 Weapons"

"So you are not saying there's a connection between Novichok-H and Sarin?"

"No."

"Then why Sarin?"

"I wondered how conspirators would fabricate realistic destruction data to satisfy the inspectors. I guessed that the fakers would look at real data for ideas."

Jeannine tossed the hair from her forehead.

"And that's what they did. They looked at the data listed first by the OPCW. That's Sarin. When I saw that no Sarin was destroyed in 2008, so the 2008 numbers were the same as those for 2007, I checked the Novichok-H numbers. They also were the same for 2007 and 2008 so I knew. And here's the proof."

She put another sheet of numbers on the table.

Jeannine's Proof of Fakery
(Last Column is Calculated, not Real)

Year	*Cumulative Sarin Destroyed % Tons.	*Cumulative % Sarin Destroyed, Divided by 100 then Multiplied by 95, (Tons.)	**Cumulative Amounts of Novichok-H Claimed Destroyed, (Tons.)
2000	28.22	26.81	26.81
2001	33.75	32.06	32.06
2002	36.08	34.28	34.28
2003	36.58	34.75	34.75
2004	37.56	35.68	35.68
2005	41.39	39.32	39.32
2006	46.30	43.99	43.99
2007	47.75	45.36	45.36
2008	47.75	45.36	45.36
2009	56.86	54.02	54.02

*OPCW Data   **Faked Numbers

Aileen looked.

"The last two columns of numbers are the same!"

"Exactly, the Novichok-H values were manufactured using the Sarin numbers. The fakers divided the percentages for Sarin by 100, to yield numbers ranging from zero to one. Then they multiplied those numbers by 95, the total tons of Novichok-H. That gives the *fake amounts* destroyed. That's how they generated the Novichok-H Table."

"Is there any chance the Novichok-H numbers are real?"

"None. The Sarin numbers are valid percentages. The Novichok-H numbers are supposed to be amounts in tons. There's no physical reality to link the two sets. Also, the Sarin numbers are for all destruction facilities in all the nations in the Convention, including the USA. The numbers for the Novichok-H Agent are supposed to be for a single destruction facility in Russia."

"Then Vaclav's story is confirmed."

"I'm afraid so."

Aileen sat down, head in her hands.

"That means there are 95 tons of the most deadly nerve agent ever known stashed somewhere, probably here in the U. S."

"And it could be anywhere. Hus-Kinetika is huge. In the states alone they have at least a dozen facilities from coast to coast."

Aileen cringed.

"No matter where it is, they have enough stuff to wipe out New York and Washington both!"

***

******

Chapter 23
Friday, November 26

In Namur, Belgium, Gustav Slavik looked out his window onto the rue de Bruxelles below. He was at home here. Almost twenty years ago, he had met with a Belgian terrorist and communist to discuss the resupply of his group with arms from the Socialist Republic of Czechoslovakia.

Shortly thereafter, the terrorist had been arrested while eating American-style hamburgers at the "Quik," an imitation McDonald's located across from the train station. To Gustav, that circumstance had been ironic to the point of bitterness. American hamburgers! Capitalism had corrosive effects, even on true believers!

In Berlin, the "Wall" had stood strong then.

But later, in that fateful month of November, 1989, Gustav's way of life changed forever. The Berlin Wall was opened on November 9, and the Czechoslovak Communist Party relinquished its exclusive power on November 29, thanks to the Czech "Velvet Revolution." After that Gustav's life was never the same.

And the town of Namur had changed too since he was last here.

Then, the Iran-Iraq war had raged, and the rue de Bruxelles had featured political posters of Iranians, horribly maimed and burned by Saddam Hussein's mustard gas. (Many Iranian victims had come to Belgium whose physicians had access to medical records from the German's use of mustard gas at Ypres in 1917.)

Now World War II was a remote event, much less World War I. November 1989 was but a memory and the Iran-Iraq war was long over, and more recently, Saddam Hussein had been executed. The rue de Bruxelles now featured posters of Lady Gaga.

At the local level, the rue-de-Bruxelles eatery that had served the best "Frites" (deep fried in "blanc de boeuf") was gone. Like others, Gustav had dipped the fries in mayonnaise.

Additionally, the nearby shop that made his favorite sub sandwiches called "Dagoberts," had disappeared. While sometimes light on meat, the fresh-baked baguettes had made them always tasty.

And Gustav had changed too. He no longer had the strength or endurance he had enjoyed then. Now he was old, but he hoped, still strong enough. Perhaps his accumulated experience would trump the loss of physical abilities. His intuition had improved greatly since those earlier days!

One thing was the same. Belgians still smoked. At that happy thought, he reached into his jacket, and drew out a pack of Petra cigarettes. He lit one and inhaled. It was pure delight.

***

After arriving at the Brussels airport, Gustav had bought a new Subscriber Identity Module (SIM card) for his mobile phone. Then he had made two calls. The first was to a former Communist, a contact from years ago. For him he left a message.

The second call had been to the U. S. Embassy in Vienna. They instructed him to go to Namur and wait for Bill Hamm to contact him. The train station was located under the Brussels airport, and the trip by rail south to Namur had been easy and quick.

Now Gustav lay on the bed fully dressed, ready to move out quickly. His left arm hung off the bed, cigarette dangling. His eyes were closed, but his mind raced.

Ivana are you in Namur? I hope so. After twenty years, the town may be different but this is still my turf. And what is this Bill Hamm like? He must have some skill. He got you away from Moravec. How much of a problem will he pose? How will I free you from him?

His fingers felt heat. He rolled towards the end table, and stubbed the Petra into the ashtray. Then he fell back, exhausted.

The jet lag took its toll. Heavy eyelids closed. He slept.

***

In Prague, Karel Moravec sat at his massive desk. Two lights on the phone blinked simultaneously. He picked up the leftmost. The call was from the U. S. A., from Maryland.

"Yes?"

"Gustav Slavik flew to Belgium from Kennedy Airport yesterday."

"So Slavik is back. I'll handle him. What about Ryan Associates?"

"We are watching for them, but they have not been back to the office. They are only two women, Jeannine Ryan and an Aileen Harris. Ryan is a mathematician, a statistician, and Harris is a physiologist."

"No chemists?"

"None, but Harris must know organic chemistry and some molecular biology. Her training is in physiology."

Karel snorted.

"Pinhead female academics!"

"Not exactly, the Israelis credit them with helping the Mossad foil a plot to assassinate their prime minister."

"*Sakra!* 'Hell!' So maybe they are dangerous. The more reason to destroy them and whatever Vaclav gave them."

Karel did not wait for a response. He ground his teeth and switched to the other blinking line.

"What?"

"Josef Hrubec, here. I'm in Brussels. Ivana is in Belgium, we think Namur. She's traveling under a German passport as 'Irma Neumann.' She's with a CIA operative named Hamm. Apparently they knew we were watching Ruzyne Airport, so they drove north to Dresden and flew to Brussels from there."

"Find her and bring her to me, untouched! And watch out for Gustav. He's in Belgium too, and he's cooperating with the CIA."

"Gustav with the Americans? Never! That can't be true."

Karel was silent. Hrubec retreated. He spoke to someone in the background before continuing.

"We just got confirmation on Ivana. We were right. She *is* in Namur."

Karel ground his teeth. *Gustav, Ivana, and now these "Ryan" women. Damn them.*

He hammered the buttons on the phone.

The lit lines went dark.

***

Bill Hamm stood in the train station of Namur, Belgium. He was tired and vexed. The loss of his secure phone in Prague had hampered his communications with Vienna. And he needed to hear Jeannine's voice. He had been unable to reach her. There was no answer at the Bethesda office, and her cell number was on the lost phone.

And Ivana required attention. He had sat next to her on the flight from Dresden to Brussels. She was vulnerable in her current distress. On the plane, he had tried to comfort her, but she had pulled away. She was out of her element, afraid and leery of Americans.

Once in the "gare," surrounded by scattered groups speaking mostly French, but also a mix of Flemish and English, she appeared calmer. Bill studied her demeanor as she stood silent. While she was no longer the self-assured assistant to Karel Moravec, she had regained some composure, and she was still attractive. There was no doubt about that. She turned to Bill with a quizzical smile.

Damn! I can't figure what she's thinking.

Bill cleared his thoughts.

"Ivana, do you speak French?"

"*Oui, un peu.* 'Yes, a little.'"

"Good."

He decided to trust her. He pointed to a kiosk just outside the station entrance. Nearby, several cabs were discharging passengers and luggage.

172

"I'm going outside. You wait here. If anyone speaks to you, answer them in French, not in German, and surely not in Czech, understood?"

Ivana managed a slight smile.

"Not English?"

"No English, only French. Remember, you are just another Belgian waiting for someone. Just wait here. Can I trust you to do that? I'll be right back."

Bill walked away.

I'll be right back. She's afraid of Karel. She won't run.

***

Ivana watched Bill disappear outside the station. She looked about as she smoothed her jeans against her hips. She smiled. She may have lost her high heels and long hair, but she still had her feminine charms.

For the first time in 48 hours, she was alone. Lips pouting, she spoke under her breath in a defiant English.

"No one tells me what to do. I wait for no man."

She was in control of her own destiny once more!

***

At the kiosk outside the station, Bill purchased a prepaid phone. His first call was to Aileen's mother, Mrs. Harris, in Bethesda, Maryland.

"Mrs. Harris, this is Bill Hamm. I'm trying to reach Jeannine. I lost my phone with her cell number, and no one is answering at the office. Do you have Aileen's cell number?"

"Bill, where are you? There's static."

"I can't say. Do you have her number?"

"Just a minute, I'll get it for you."

Bill fidgeted. He shifted his weight from one foot to another. Finally, Mrs. Harris came back on the line. She repeated the numbers slowly.

"Thanks Mrs. Harris, thanks a lot. I appreciate it."

Bill did not wait. He punched Aileen's number right away. When she answered, he sighed with relief.

"Aileen, this is Bill. Do you know where Jeannine is?"

"Bill! Hang on, Jeannine is right next to me."

Jeannine grabbed the phone.

"Bill, thank God you are all right. You are, aren't you?"

"I'm fine, I mean it. I'm sorry I couldn't call you sooner. Are you OK?"

"I am, and Aileen too. There's so much to tell you."

The conversation encompassed important events such as Vaclav Pokorny's death, Anne Simek's discovery of Vaclav's notes, Gustav's wrecking the office of Ryan Associates and his vicious attack on Aileen, and the connection of Novichok-H with Hus-Kinetika.

At the reference to Hus-Kinetika, Bill broke in to recount his experience in delivering the "Goldfinch" from that company's Karel Moravec.

Jeannine listened patiently as Bill told her of his attractive charge and her escape from Moravec's agents.

After that, their conversation turned purely personal.

***

Ivana stood dutifully waiting where Bill Hamm had told her. But some minutes after he disappeared from sight, a crowd of students descended upon the station. Namur was home to a university, the *Facultés Universitaires Notre-Dame de la Paix*, and the boisterous group, freed from the *"Fac"* for the weekend, jammed the concourse filling it with the sounds of youthful exuberance.

Ivana's eyes moistened. Once she had laughed like that. Why not again?

She hesitated, but only for a moment. She turned towards the station's side exit.

Outside on the sidewalk, she edged along the building and peered around the corner.

Bill Hamm, his back turned in her direction, stood near the main entrance, speaking on the phone.

Ivana ducked backwards and collided with a man behind her.

She started to speak in Czech, but remembered to use French.

"*Promiňte, ... Pardonnez-moi.* 'Excuse me.'"

The man was young, casually dressed, and good looking. He was more than willing to excuse this eye-pleasing woman. He spoke first in French before switching to English.

"*Pas de problème, mais vous avez un accent.* 'No problem, but you have an accent.'"

He smiled at her and continued.

"I'm Flemish. I speak French, but my English is better. Can you understand my English?"

She nodded affirmatively. His smile broadened.

"Do you know Belgium?"

She shook her head negatively. He smiled and touched her arm.

"Then let me introduce you to a Belgian treat, one of my favorites, Liège Waffles."

She looked about. The street was crowded. Surely she was safe here with all these people.

She let him guide her down the block to a shiny steel stand. On it, irregularly-shaped hot waffles were arranged in a row. A hand-printed cardboard sign said "*GAUFRES DE LIÈGE.*"

He paid for two and handed one to Ivana.

"These aren't 'Brussels Waffles.' These don't need syrup or fruit toppings. Some put Nutella on them, but they're good by themselves. You can eat them hot, like this."

He took a bite of the warm sticky treat. Ivana did likewise. The "gaufre" was sweet and crunchy.

"This is good, is very good."

She licked her fingers, a definite "no-no" in Prague's Platina Restaurant.

That done, she examined her new "friend." He was dressed like a university student, but was, perhaps, older. He had broad shoulders and an infectious smile.

Ivana took stock of herself. Her jeans clasped a slim figure, and her loose sweater, jacket and sneakers, completed a youthful look.

She relaxed.

"Could I try another waffle?"

Her new friend bought two more and gave her one.

They sat at a sidewalk table to eat. She laughed and licked her fingers.

***

******

Chapter 24
Friday, November 26

Outside the train station in Namur, Bill remembered Ivana. He spoke into the phone.

"Jeannine, I have to go. I've been talking too much. Ivana's waiting."

"You mean she's not with you?"

"She's inside the station. I have to go. I'll have to call you back. Love you."

In Vienna, a CIA analyst had interpreted Gustav Slavik's concern for Ivana, a woman young enough to be his daughter, to mean that he was no longer dangerous, but Jeannine's account of the assault on Aileen proved that the analyst was way off base. Gustav was still the "Old Gustav," and extremely dangerous. And Bill was to meet this man here in Namur, with no backup!

But first things first. He had to take Ivana to a secure location. *At least she's too afraid to run.*

He dashed through the concourse to the counter where he had left her.

No attractive young woman with short black hair was in sight.

Ivana was not there.

She was gone.

***

Outside, Ivana had just finished her gaufre when her new friend spoke.

"Namur is the Capital of the French-speaking region of Belgium. Would you like to see the old Citadel, it overlooks the city and the Meuse?"

Ivana hesitated, but the young man did not wait for an answer. He put on a helmet and mounted a red 250 cc

Kawasaki. Pulling her from the chair, he handed her the extra helmet, and beckoned her to sit behind.

"We'll take my moto. Jump on back."

Ivana was unsure. This man was a stranger. She did not wish to go with him, but he lifted her onto the rear seat and mounted the moto.

Still smiling, he spoke over his shoulder.

Sorry, I hope I didn't hurt you, but you are too pretty to leave alone with all these students around. Then he added.

"Tu vas aimer la Citadelle. 'You'll like the Citadel.'"

He gunned the motor and sped away.

She had no choice. She wrapped her arms around him to hang on.

No way could she jump off!

***

Bill Hamm knew he had screwed up, big-time.

The only comfort he felt after seeing that Ivana was gone, was that no trains had left the station in the last twenty minutes.

A single train, headed to Jemelles and Luxembourg, was about to leave. A few quick questions to porters and conductors indicated that no "Irma Neumann" or anyone answering her description had boarded it.

Bill's inquiries outside the station produced better results.

The proprietor of a nearby Liège-waffles stand recounted to Bill how a young woman had enjoyed one of his waffles, evidently her first. She had left with a young man on his "moto," a red Kawasaki, maybe a 250 cc.

The proprietor wasn't sure of their destination, but he had heard the young man mention "La Citadelle."

Bill thanked him and ran back to the train station.

He took the first cab in line.

"La Citadelle, s'il vous plaît, vite. 'The Citadel, please, quick.'"

The driver recognized Bill's American accent. He looked back.

"Are you sure, Monsieur? Nobody's there. The concessions and information center are closed this time of year. And it's cold and windy up top."

***

Namur's Citadel is spectacular. True, it lacks the architectural splendor of the Prague Castle that shines over the Vltava and dominates the "Old Town," but the Citadel, located at the confluence of the Sambre and the Meuse rivers, dominates Namur with a massive display of impregnable rock, raw cliffs and tall trees.

From a distance, Ivana had been impressed by the sheer size of the former fortress, but now, on the other side of the Sambre, the upper reaches of the Citadel were lost to view. They were too close to the base to see the top.

They were alone on the Boulevard Frère Orban, alongside the Sambre River, when her companion stopped the Kawasaki and cut the motor. Ivana lifted the helmet from her head, and shook her short hair. The stiff wind penetrated her jacket. She shivered.

Her companion put his arm about her and gestured upwards across the river.

"You need a warmer jacket. The wind up there will be freezing. Forget the Citadel. The university social center is near here. Hop back on, we'll go there and warm up."

Ivana was relieved. *I'll be safe, there will be lots of people. Maybe this guy is OK?*

The "guy" flashed that winning smile.

"By the way, my name is 'Hans,' and yours?"

She remembered the new passport.

"Irma, Irma Neumann."

He stared at her.

"Then you're German. You must understand my Dutch."

Ivana did not want to continue this exchange. She rubbed her arms to warm them.

"Can we get out of the cold? And I'm hungry too."

"Sure. The social center is in an old Arsenal built by Vauban, Louis XIV's military engineer. It has several restaurants. We'll go to La Cafet. I'll buy you a 'Croque Monsieur.'"

"A 'what?'"

"A grilled cheese sandwich."

Ivana relaxed. Hans had a winning way about him and besides, soon they would no longer be alone and she would be warm. The Kawasaki turned onto rue Bruno.

***

Bill Hamm sat in the rear seat of the Cab. He was disgusted with himself. His poor judgment in trusting Ivana would likely end his employment with the Agency, and deservedly so. He had thought that he had developed a bond of trust with Ivana. He had been sure that she would not bolt, if for no other reason than her fear of Karel Moravec.

How wrong he had been, and stupid!

He had to find her or his career was over.

He punched the number of a secure line to an office in Brussels. His partner, Tom, answered.

"Bill, when do you see Gustav?"

"I'm to call him in an hour, but there's a problem. I've been really dumb."

He told Tom of Ivana's flight.

"Now I'm in a cab driving around Namur looking for a red Kawasaki with a brunette riding on the rear seat."

He took a breath. What more could he say?

Tom broke the silence.

"Bill, this guy sounds like a student. Drive around the university. If it's as cold there as it is here in Brussels, they will be somewhere indoors. Check the social center, it's called the 'Arsenal.' It's a long shot, but better than nothing."

"Thanks, Tom. You're right about the cold. We went to the Citadel. There was nothing at the summit except a vicious wind and a few parked cars."

Bill touched the cab driver's shoulder.

"Are we near the University? Or the Arsenal?"

"Straight ahead. For the Arsenal, we turn left on rue Joseph Grafé."

"Do it!"

***

Inside the Arsenal, La Cafet was not crowded. Many of the FUNDP students commuted from other towns in Belgium, and Fridays often saw a mass exodus from the "Fac."

Hans chose a table near a window. He watched Ivana eat her grilled cheese sandwich. She displayed none of the reserve required at Prague's elegant La Platina restaurant. A large morsel of the crunchy toast distended her cheek as she munched with enthusiasm.

Hans did not eat. He leaned back and watched her with an ever-present smile. She was too hungry to notice his occasional glances at the street outside.

Ivana gulped and her distended cheek flattened to its normal attractive shape. She reached for a can of Coca-Cola Light and took a long swallow.

She looked up at Hans. He was staring out the window. A dark VW sedan had just stopped at the curb. She spoke.

"Hans, why didn't you order a sandwich too? This is good."

He ignored her. A balding man stepped out of the VW. Hans turned back to Ivana, and put his arm around her as if in affection. But his smile vanished as he whispered in her ear.

"I'm not hungry. Besides, 'Irma,' or should I say 'Ivana,' I have a message for you. Your friend Karel Moravec wants to see you. He insists."

***

Bill Hamm spotted the red Kawasaki motorcycle chained at a stand near the Arsenal. He tapped the driver on the shoulder.

"Stop here."

Bill jumped out. He ran to a student standing by the door.

"You understand English."

"Some."

181

Bill pointed.

"That red Kawasaki. The guy and the girl who came on it. Are they inside?"

"No. They left."

"They didn't take the moto?"

The student shrugged. He waved at the empty curb.

"They left with another guy in a VW, a big one, a Passat. '*La copine*' was not happy."

"*La copine?*"

"The girlfriend. They had to push her into the car."

***

******

Chapter 25
Friday, November 26

In North Carolina, Jim Harrigan and Peter Zeleny waited outside the Currituck County Sheriff's building. Peter looked at his watch.

"Mr. Harrigan, how much longer will it take. It's been over an hour."

"First, I'm not going to call you 'Doctor,' so I'll be 'Jim' and you'll be 'Peter,' OK?"

"Second, Anne Simek is a witness to the assault on Vaclav Pokorny, and possibly even his murder. She's was late coming forward. She's at least a material witness and maybe a suspect. The sheriff has a lot of options here."

"But Mr. Har ..., sorry, Jim, she came here voluntarily."

"Peter, she should have come to the sheriff right away. It's been a week. You can't blame the sheriff for thinking Anne has something to hide. If it weren't for Mila I'd be damned suspicious of her myself. Maybe I'm still am. This could be a long wait."

"Jim, Anne says that Vaclav was shot only once that night. She has medical training. She would have confirmed a single wound when she patched him up at that bed and breakfast in Wanchese."

"Did you see him yourself?"

"No, he was gone when I got there. There was only that note. Someone had taken him away."

"How did you know he was there?"

"He was there all right. There was blood all over the bed, and bloody clothing in the bathroom."

"So what's your point about only one bullet wound?"

"You told me there were at least four bullets in his body when they dragged it from Currituck Sound. That means someone else shot him three times after Anne last saw him. That person is the killer."

"That's probable, but can you say for sure that Anne wasn't there when that happened?"

"Damn it, she was with me. She was trying to save Vaclav!"

Jim thought of Mila's lustrous eyes and her total faith in Anne.

"I know that, and personally I'm sure she was, but my opinion does not count. The sheriff needs proof."

"Then check the ballistics. You said several of the slugs were 7.62 mm rounds, like from an AK-47. The handgun slug would be 9 mm."

"Normally you'd be right. Lots of handguns use 9 mm rounds. Unfortunately, the CZ-52 uses 7.62 mm ammo, like the AK-47."

"Then check the striations. Surely you can tell if more than one slug came from the CZ-52."

"The State lab says that two of the slugs are in bad shape, just fragments. They must have ricocheted off something. They could be from the CZ-52. They're not sure. The other slugs do appear to be from another weapon."

Jim put his hand on the younger man's shoulder.

"Peter, you and I trust Anne. We believe her story. The sheriff can't do that. It's only Anne who says there was just one wound. We found one gun, true, but there could have been another there that night. Everything depends on her story."

Peter fell quiet. Then his eyes lit again.

"What about the slugs from those two bodies found on the wildlife refuge? The men they say my father killed."

"Those slugs are nine mm. They're the wrong caliber."

Jim Harrigan took a breath. *Damn it, the Park Service seized two AK-47's in that arrest. Had the Currituck sheriff asked the state lab to compare them with the slugs in Vaclav's body? If one of these weapons matched the slugs, Peter's father could be in more trouble, but Anne Simek was worth more than 100 Johan Zelenys.*

Jim, the cop, knew that those slugs should be checked.

"Peter, you may have something. Wait here, I'm going inside to talk to a friend in the Sheriff's office."

He went up the steps and disappeared inside.

Peter waited by the car. All he could think of was Anne's smile when she had left him and climbed those same steps.

She's only there because she drove me back here. I've got to help her!

***

At the Best Western in Rockville, Maryland, Jeannine jumped up as Aileen entered with two sandwiches.

"Which, Jeannine? Ham and Swiss on Rye or Ham and Swiss on Whole Wheat?"

"On Rye, thanks."

Aileen handed her the sandwich.

"What is Bill doing overseas?"

"He's protecting someone, a source, for the CIA."

Jeannine did not add that the "source" was a woman named "Ivana." She added.

"Get this, the source worked at Hus-Kinetika."

"Our Hus-Kinetika?"

"Exactly, there's a CEO at Hus-Kinetika named Karel Moravec. He ordered the killing of Vaclav Pokorny, and the man who led the CIA to Bill's source is the assassin who assaulted you at the office. His name is Gustav. He's to meet Bill somewhere over there."

Aileen shuddered. Her voice shook.

"I remember his eyes. He's a killer. Bill has to be careful."

"That's what I told him. He assured me he'd be OK."

"What about Vaclav's files from Hus-Kinetika, and their weapon of mass destruction, Novichok-H?"

"I told Bill that we had proof the stockpile wasn't destroyed. Gustav claims to have information about where it is. He's holding back, to trade with the CIA."

Jeannine frowned. Her voice lowered.

185

"Aileen, this 'Karel' has other goons here in America. Gustav told Bill there was a team of Karel's men watching our office when he went to search it."

Aileen winced. *"Search" as in "Search and Destroy!"*

Jeannine continued.

"Bill thinks we need protection. I asked him how. There wasn't time to talk and he said he'd think about it. Short term, he says to go to North Carolina, to the Outer Banks."

"Why the Banks?"

"Bill's former mentor at the CIA, Jim Harrigan, lives there. You and Peter met him. He retired from the Agency. He's a policeman now. Bill says there's no better person to watch out for us."

"Do you think we should go?"

"I do."

"But I don't have my laptop. It's at the office."

"You can't go there. Karel's men will be watching. Ryan Associates will buy you a new one. Most of the files you need were shared with mine. And here, you keep Vaclav's chip, I've copied it."

"All right, I'll go, but I have to make arrangements for Mary Catherine."

"What about your mother?"

"She's going to visit my aunt in Pennsylvania this afternoon because she didn't go at Thanksgiving. I'll ask her to take Mary Catherine. She'll have to miss some school next week, but she should be safe."

"Then it's done. I'll call Harrigan. You call your mother."

***

Jeannine drove her car. Aileen sat in the front seat, eyes closed.

At the Beltway, Jeannine turned away from the American Legion Bridge, the normal crossing of the Potomac south from Bethesda or Rockville. Instead she turned towards Annapolis. She would follow the Beltway where it dips south towards Clinton, MD.

She planned to cross the Potomac at Route 301, near Dahlgren, Virginia. This route was longer, but prudent. Any watchers waiting for her to travel to the Outer Banks would likely station themselves on the heavily-traveled I-95 to Richmond.

Over an hour later, Aileen rubbed her eyes.

"You must be tired. Where are we?"

"I'm not, and we're about to cross the Potomac into Virginia."

Aileen now was wide awake.

"I'm really puzzled. What connection could there be between Xolak and Novichok-H. Why would Hus-Kinetika fake the Xolak data? Did Bill know about Xolak?"

"He'd never heard of it, but you're the physiologist. Tell me what you think."

"I don't know what to think. I haven't a clue."

She paused.

"But Jeannine, there just has to be a connection!"

***

In Corolla, North Carolina, Jim Harrigan and Peter Zeleny ascended the steps to the beach house. Mila met them at the door.

"Where's Anne?"

Peter looked down. Jim responded.

"The sheriff is holding her overnight as a material witness. He says she's a flight risk."

Mila's eyes flashed. She turned away from Jim.

"Peter, I know this is hard for you. Come get something to eat. I have macaroni and cheese baking in the oven."

She led Peter to the kitchen, but her thoughts were of Jim Harrigan. She muttered under her breath.

"I knew it. Špatné policie, 'Bad police' ... The same everywhere. You can never trust them."

She served Peter. Jim had to wait.

***

Dr. Lawrence Harold Hodges, "Larry," Senior Administrator at the Food and Drug Administration, sat at his desk in the

Parklawn Building in Rockville, Maryland. It was late. It was Friday. The staff was long gone. He yawned.

There. He initialed the memo rejecting Hus-Kinetika's Xolak report.

That done, he frowned.

This will satisfy that stubborn Dr. Ryan. Now maybe she'll have lunch with me?

An image of the shapely redhead flashed before him.

He picked up the brown envelope addressed to his Chief. He was about to seal it when he heard footsteps. He looked up. A man stood before his desk. Larry spoke

"You're a half hour early."

The man shrugged and moved behind the desk. He wore Latex gloves and held an odd-shaped pen. He touched it to the back of Larry's wrist. Larry started.

"What? ... "

The words stopped. His pupils shrank to pin points. *No air, no air.* He gasped and clutched his throat. At least he tried to, but his arms did not respond. He slumped forward. His head struck the desk. In only seconds, he was dead.

The visitor removed Larry's memo from the envelope. He inserted another that was identical except that Hus-Kinetika's report was accepted. Its initials were identical to Larry's. He dropped it into the "Out" box.

Larry's memo he stuffed in his pocket. Then he studied the corpse. There was no lesion where his "pen" had touched the skin, nothing, a simple case of Cardiac Arrest.

He smiled. Even if performed, tests for the usual nerve agents would reveal nothing.

He switched the lights off and left.

***

******

Chapter 26
Friday, November 26

In Namur, Gustav Slavik paced back and forth in his room. He paused and looked out the window. The traffic on the rue de Bruxelles was at a standstill.

He smashed his hands together. The American's call was overdue. *What's his name, "Hamm." Hamm, where the hell are you?*

Something was wrong! *Ivana, what happened?*

***

Not that far from Gustav's room, the rue de Borgnet enters the place Leopold. Rush hour traffic jammed the juncture. The motionless cars would have looked like a parking lot, but for the fact that they were jammed in random directions, rather than in orderly lines.

The VW Passat, caught in the midst of this impasse, was squeezed far to the right of its destination. The driver, Josef Hrubec, cursed and hammered the horn in frustration.

In the back seat, Ivana huddled in fear against the driver-side door. Next to her sat Hans. The smile was gone. His cheek had three red streaks, a memento of her struggle. He pressed a tissue to his face, it came away smeared with blood.

Hans glared. Ivana pushed harder against the door. It did not yield.

Hans' smile became a grimace, truly ugly. He balled his fist and cocked his arm for a smashing blow. Ivana shrank away.

Hrubec intervened.

"Damn it Hans, stop! What the hell are you doing? Are you crazy? Karel said not to touch her. If he finds a bruise on her, he'll kill you. He alone will 'deal' with her."

Hans continued to glare, his fist still balled.

"So?"

"So trust me. Do not cross Karel. You've never met him. When you do, you'll thank me. I just saved your life."

Hans looked away. He lowered his arm and relaxed his fingers.

Hrubec studied Hans in the rear mirror. He spoke over his shoulder.

"That's better! We'll both be rewarded for this. Mr. Moravec is very generous when he gets his way."

He spied an opening and pulled in front of a Mercedes truck. One more lane and he would be on the N91, headed for E411, the main route to Brussels.

Hans withdrew to his side of the car. His retreat was little comfort to Ivana. She sat trembling.

Hrubec understood her fear.

No one quits Karel. He alone must be the one to terminate a relationship.

He drove on.

For this girl, the "termination" would be permanent.

***

Bill Hamm was desperate. He had blown his assignment, but he was not thinking of his own career.

Now he was certain that Karel Moravec had Ivana.

He thought of that old assassin, Gustav Slavik, who was waiting for his call. He had read Slavik's dossier. Years ago Gustav had supplied arms to a communist cell in this very town. Now Bill must ally himself with this man to deal with Moravec and his enforcers.

An alliance with a monster? Hamm, this can't work.

He smiled ruefully.

If it doesn't, I'll be dead soon anyway!

At that cheerful thought, He punched Gustav's number in his phone.

He needed to talk with the monster.

"Brrring, Brrring, Brrring, Brrring, ..."

***

Hrubec drove the VW north on the E411 towards Brussels. The Passat rode smoothly, absorbing the vibrations of the roadway.

The comfortable ride meant nothing to the two riders in the back seat. They sat spaced as far apart as the car's interior permitted. Neither spoke.

Hans sat erect, muscles taut. He glared at Ivana

Ivana slumped sideways, eyes down. She stared at the floor mat under her sneakers. Incongruously she noted that it smelled new. She coughed and her shoulders began to shake.

The cultivated fields on either side of the highway were gray and lifeless, devoid of snow. Far to the right, a long line of trees, branches bare, marked the horizon.

Hrubec slowed the VW and exited the throughway.

Ivana rolled with the turning car. She saw a sign "Chaussée de Charleroi," but there was no town, no house, only dry dead fields awaiting next Spring's planting.

Hrubec laughed and turned to Hans.

"The Americans will think we went to Brussels. They'll never find us. There's a farm ahead. We'll stay there and wait for Karel's instructions."

Hans bristled at Ivana. *Just wait bitch, I'm not done with you yet.*

***

In Namur, Bill Hamm, a camera slung on his shoulder, stood across from the train station. Like any other tourist, an open map was in his hand. In reality, he surveyed the Gaufres-de-Liège stand across the way. Gustav would come there. He would sport a dark blue baseball cap for recognition.

Bill waited. A cab stopped at the entrance to the train station. A man got out. Maybe? No, he was hatless.

Bill felt a tap on his shoulder. He turned to see an older man, beardless but with gray stubble on his cheeks. He wore a dark blue cap. The man spoke.

"Mr. Hamm, when you do surveillance in Belgium, keep your hands out of your pockets. It's so American."

Bill looked down. His left hand *was* in his pocket.

"And don't pose as a tourist. You must have known I would look for an 'American.'"

The last word was pronounced with a sneer. Bill bristled, but Gustav was not finished.

"No wonder you lost Ivana."

At that jibe, Bill's hand slid into his jacket. His hand found the 9 mm M9 in his shoulder holster. Gustav stepped back, hands open in front of him.

"No wait. I'm unarmed. Your American airport security was too much. I had to leave my Makarov in New York."

His hands dropped.

"Besides, you stopped Moravec's assassins from killing the girl. That was not easy. I respect that and I thank you for it."

Bill's hand left his jacket.

"Please Mr. Hamm, I accept your offer. I will do anything to help you find her."

Gustav held out his hand. Bill ignored it and spoke.

"All right. I have descriptions of the two men who took her. One was young, good looking with fair skin, tall, with a Flemish accent. He had a red Kawasaki, a 250 cc. He abandoned it when they took Ivana."

Gustav shook his head negatively.

"This man I do not know. He would be a local hire."

"The other man drove a VW Passat, black."

Gustav showed a faint smile. Bill continued.

"He was short, stocky and slightly bald, with a narrow face and sharp nose. He wore a well-pressed suit. Apparently he was the boss of the two."

Gustav's smile disappeared.

"That one is Josef Hrubec. He likes German cars. He is one of Moravec's top men. He's short and looks mild, you underestimate him and you die. He's very dangerous. Even I avoided him when I was in Prague."

Gustav paused. He looked away and spoke, as if to himself.

"Hrubec! Damn, that is bad news."

***

The house was not far from the little town of Malèves, Belgium. Built of stone, its style was typical of old Belgian farms. Half of the elongate building had been a barn for livestock. The other half had been the living area. The halves were joined together in a single structure to conserve heat during the winter.

At present, the former barn was split into a garage plus a windowless room that extended the living area. Thick oaken doors guarded the only exterior opening to the garage. Looking from the outside, there was no telling what might be hidden behind those closed portals.

From the front of the house, a mile-long lane ran through barren fields to the paved road. To the back, bushes and scattered trees lined a small creek.

Josef Hrubec waited in the Passat while Hans got out and swung the garage doors wide. There was ample room for the car inside. Hrubec signaled Hans not to close the doors, then he spoke to the rear seat.

"*Bitte Fräulein*, open your eyes, we are here."

Hrubec waited. Ivana, stirred and sat up.

"*Bitte Fräulein*, I cannot wait. Get out of the car, now."

She stepped out. From the garage a single door led to the living quarters. Hrubec gripped her arm and led her through it into a room with no windows. The walls were painted a glaring white. There was a lone bed in the corner. Above it, a bare bulb hung from the ceiling. The door opposite opened onto a hallway.

"Fräulein 'Irma,' this is your room. Please do not leave it except to use the 'WC,' the bathroom."

He pointed to the hallway.

"The first door on the left. Now I must leave. Hans will care for you in my absence."

Hrubec went back into the garage, got into the Passat, and drove away fast.

***

Hans watched the Passat disappear down the lane. Then he pulled the garage doors shut and went into Ivana's room. She lay on the bed, her face buried in the pillow.

Hungry, he went to the kitchen. He had not eaten at the Arsenal while Ivana had munched her Croque Monsieur. That did it. He made himself a grilled cheese sandwich.

Hans touched his sore cheek. The girl must pay for that. He would fix her face. Forget this "Karel," whoever he was.

There was plenty of time. Hrubec would not return for several hours.

***

The rented Renault sedan headed from Namur towards highway E411. Bill Hamm drove. Gustav sat in the passenger seat. His eyes were closed. He was either asleep or planning his next move. Bill suspected the latter. He spoke.

"Why don't you think they took her to Brussels."

"There are too many of your people there. Hrubec will avoid Brussels if he can."

"Then why are we taking the E411?"

"The E411 was highway A4 when I was here last. There was no European Union then."

Bill snorted.

"Answer the damn question. What's the plan? Why Route E411?"

"We Czechs had two safe houses near here. I think Moravec kept them after your corrupt friends took over my country. Hrubec used one of them in the old days, me too. We take E411 to the Chausée de Charleroi."

Gustav's forehead furrowed. His shoulders drooped. His voice became a whisper.

"I have no God, Hamm, but if you do, pray for my Ivana. If Karel gets hold of her ..."

***

******

Chapter 27
Friday, November 26

Bill Hamm guided the Renault north on E411. In the passenger seat, Gustav, head slumped, sat silent. He had not spoken since his comment on prayer.

Bill did not relax. His passenger appeared to sleep, but relying on appearances with a dangerous individual like Gustav could be fatal.

They were twenty kilometers from their exit when Gustav sat up. There was no sleep in his eyes or hesitation in his voice.

"Hamm, you cannot deal with Hrubec alone. I need a weapon."

Bill kept his eyes on the road.

"Hamm, listen to me. I know you have a spare. I know your procedures."

Bill smiled. *Procedures? My group is total chaos.* He kept his focus on the traffic ahead. After a moment he spoke.

"Tell me about Josef Hrubec. Why do you fear him?"

"It was in the pink prison on Bartolomejska Street. I assisted him in an interrogation."

"But you were senior to him."

"Only in age, not in Party rank. Anyway, he was in charge. I watched. It was too much, even for me. I found an excuse to leave the room. I went to the toilet and threw up. When I got back, the subject was dead. Useless too. Hrubec did not get the information."

"I don't believe you. I read your file. You ran hundreds of interrogations, and some died."

"This was different. The boy was 18. The body, face were completely mutilated. He begged for death over and over. I almost shot him myself. Hrubec enjoyed it. He did not want answers. He wanted it to last. I don't believe in angels, but Hrubec almost convinced me they are real. In that room, that day, there was pure evil, Satan himself. The air was rank. I couldn't breathe, my arms felt paralyzed."

"Finally, Hrubec put down the power tool, an American brand. I remember that, a 'Milwaukee.' At that moment, I escaped to the toilet."

"When I got back, Hrubec stared at me. His eyes were black. He saw my fear and knew I could never challenge him. He smiled, put his hand on my shoulder, and pointed to the remains on the floor."

"I was whipped. My legs were jelly. I gathered the boy up, blood everywhere, on my hands, clothes, unavoidable. I put him on the cart and pushed him away."

Bill shuddered at the term "gathered." His eyes turned back to the road.

Gustav fell silent again.

***

In the stone farmhouse, Ivana sat up on the bed and surveyed her surroundings. Except for the bed, the room was bare. There was nothing to use as a weapon.

Ivana's fear of Hans was replaced by anger at herself. Her juvenile escapade had been stupid. *Ivana, you know better. What were you thinking?*

She had not succeeded as top assistant to Karel Moravec by sex alone. Rather her success had preceded her seduction. Ivana was intelligent and resourceful, her carefully prepared flight from Karel had proved that.

She scanned the windowless walls once more. Nothing. She turned to the door to the garage. Locked. Her only choice was the corridor with the WC.

Ivana heard the sound of something frying in the kitchen. Hans must be there.

She stepped into the WC and closed the door. It had no lock.

The toilet was against the wall. To the right was the shower. A flimsy semi-circular curtain separated it from the rest of the "closet." It offered little shelter from leering eyes, and no protection from assault.

196

She turned on the fixture. The overhead spout was detachable, fed by a flexible metallic tube that allowed its use as a hand spray.

There was hot water. She turned it on, but drew back her hand quickly. Evidently the thermostat was set high.

Footsteps sounded from the kitchen. Ivana jumped.

Hans had finished eating.

The footsteps approached.

***

Bill Hamm pushed the Renault to its limit, but larger cars, Mercedes and others passed him with ease. A large sign appeared on the right.

Sortie Chausée de Charleroi, 1 km.

Bill glanced sideways. Gustav nodded.

"This is it. This is where we get off."

Bill slowed. They quit the autoroute.

***

At the farmhouse, Hans stood at the door. Ivana was on the bed. She looked up and smiled.

"Hans, forgive me. I should not have scratched you. I was scared of that man, the driver. He frightened me. I'm sorry. You know I like you. The ride on your moto, remember?"

Hans eyebrows lifted. He fingered the scratches on his cheeks. Ivana spoke again.

"No, I mean it. I'm sorry. You're a real man. I can see that."

She stood up and smoothed the jeans on her hips.

"You're a man. I know you like what you see. You can have whatever you want. I promise I won't fight you."

He seized her shoulders, and pushed his lips against hers. After a moment she pulled back. She licked her lips.

"You *are* a man."

She kissed the scratches on his cheek.

"I told you I won't fight, but I'm filthy. These clothes stink. Let me freshen up first. You'll be glad. I like real men."

She smiled and dropped her jeans. Hans stared. He nodded. She went into the WC and shut the door.

Hans stood outside and listened to the water running in the shower.

He licked his lips. After she kept her promise, he would return to "business."

***

Bill drove the Renault on the Chaussée de Charleroi. After a short time, Gustav touched his arm.

"Turn here. We go towards Malèves."

Minutes later, Bill spotted a farm house, far back from the road. He looked at his passenger once more. Gustav nodded.

"That's it. But it's not how I remembered it. It's more modern. Karel has made changes."

Bill slowed to turn onto the lane that led to the house. Gustav touched his arm again.

"No, not that way. It's too open. Keep driving ahead, up to that creek."

He indicated a small bridge. Just past it was room for several cars. A path worn by fishermen led down to the bank.

"We'll park there. The creek runs behind the house. The bushes along the bank will hide our approach."

Bill parked on the other side of the bridge. He looked in the rear mirror. The road had curved. The lane to the farmhouse was not in sight. Anyone driving to the farmhouse could not see the Renault. It was safe here.

Bill got out of the car. Gustav plunged into the brush. Bill followed him.

Soon Gustav was out of sight. Bill kept on, guided by the sounds of shuffling leaves, twisting branches and snapping twigs ahead of him.

***

In the farmhouse, Hans stared at the door to the WC. He had waited long enough. When would this woman finish?

He pounded on the door. There was no answer. The water continued to run in the shower.

He opened the door and looked in. A blast of hot water scalded his eyes. Sightless he grabbed forwards.

He felt bare flesh, but not in time.

The shower head crashed against his face, followed by a second blow to the head. At the third blow, he fell to the floor. All was black.

Hans did not feel the fourth blow that smashed behind his ear.

***

Ivana nudged Hans' body with her bare foot. He was unconscious.

She replaced the shower head in the overhead holder and rubbed her ankle where the hot water had seared it. She stepped over Hans and retrieved her jeans from the bedroom.

Fully clothed, she headed for the kitchen. She looked about for a weapon. She chose a carving knife from a wooden rack.

She opened the door and stepped outside. The wind struck her face. She shivered, her jacket was in the Passat.

She ran towards the creek.

***

Downstream from the farm house, Bill Hamm stopped and listened. There were no sounds ahead. Where was Gustav? Bill clasped his 9 mm with both hands. He pointed and swept the brush ahead with a semi circular motion.

Nothing.

He could not trust Gustav.

Eyes forward, he crept through the brush in the direction where Gustav had disappeared.

***

In the farmhouse, Hans pushed himself up off the floor. His head ached, but his first concern was to see. He stumbled to the basin and fumbled for the spigot.

He lowered his head under the faucet and let the water wash over his tortured face and swollen eyelids.

199

The cold flow soothed him. After a minute he stood erect and opened his eyes. All was blurred. Usually-distinct objects merged seamlessly together with no sharp outlines.

He wrapped a wet towel about his face and stumbled to the kitchen. Empty! The back door was open. The bitch was gone.

Hans left the house, face still wrapped. Ahead of him, the bushes were a gray amorphous mass of branches. He tried to focus, but with little success.

Frustrated, he drew his gun, a Browning Hi-Power 9 mm made in the Fabrique Nationale in Herstal. He held it ready.

Something rustled in the brush to his left. He pointed and fired.

A Hooded Crow flapped skywards, unharmed. Hans cursed and lowered the gun.

He turned to his right. Over thirty meters away, a figure emerged from the brush and ran limping through an adjoining field.

Hans was sure it was Ivana. He raised the Browning to fire.

***

Hans hesitated. The dim light of evening plus his impaired sight caused the fleeing form to waver in and out of focus. He lowered his weapon. Just then the runner stumbled over a low ridge of cleared stones that marked the border of the field and disappeared.

Hans picked his way along the stone border, searching for Ivana. He heard a scraping sound to his left. Stepping carefully he circled that way.

Scarcely visible in the twilight Hans saw a human form crouched motionless behind an overgrown pile of stones. He approached from behind.

It was Ivana.

His balled fist slammed against the side of her head. She fell, stunned, eyes glazed.

Desire for the fallen woman swept over Hans body, but his anger was too great. This bitch had hurt him, twice.

He pointed the weapon at her head.

His trigger finger began the fatal squeeze.

***

A roaring animal crashed through the nearby brush and ran straight for Hans. He turned.

It was a man, arms waving and mouth foaming. Hans did not know Gustav, but he saw the brute expression of that face and the malice in those eyes. He had to stop the mad rush.

Hans fired. His bullet struck home, but not in to time slow the madman. Hans' gun was knocked free and his arms pinned in a bone-crushing embrace. He fell backwards, with his assailant on top of him.

The fall jarred his left arm free. His hand felt a hard object, one of the field stones. He gripped it tightly and swung with all his strength.

"Crunch!"

The deadly grip loosened, the body on top of him went limp.

He pushed himself up from the dead weight and stooped to pick up his 9 mm.

He examined the attacker. The bullet had struck home. The madman's chest was covered in blood, but his breaths, while weak, were regular. Hans looked at his own shirt. It was stained with the brute's blood.

He glanced at Ivana. She had risen, wobbly, to her feet.

He turned back to the fallen madman. He would finish him first.

He pointed the Browning at the prone Gustav.

***

For a second time Hans underestimated Ivana. She launched herself at him, striking with both hands. He pushed her back. She fell to the ground.

He looked down in disbelief. A brown handle protruded from his chest. The bitch had driven the carving knife into him.

Could she be that strong?

He exhaled. Bloody bubbles foamed through his lips.

The bitch got my lung.

Hans raised his gun, but it was struck from his grasp. The madman had recovered. Death shone from his eyes, but Hans was scarcely aware.

He saw the madman's hand that now held the Browning. He stared at the deadly opening of the barrel directed at his face. There was time only for a thought.

My own gun?

That was his last.

"Crack."

The Browning jerked upwards.

Hans fell backwards.

The bubbly breathing ceased.

***

******

Chapter 28
Friday, November 26

Bill Hamm emerged from the creek-side brush to find Ivana kneeling next to the prostrate form of Gustav.

"Bill, help. He is hurt, bad."

Bill stared at the dead body behind her. He raised his eyebrows. Ivana answered.

"That's Hans, the man I rode away with. I'm sorry. I was careless."

"Where's the other one, the one Gustav calls 'Hrubec?'"

"The one with the dark eyes is gone. But we must take care of Gustav. I can clean his wound at the house. It's warm and there's water, and I'm sure we can find antibiotic ointment too. I saw an aid kit on the kitchen shelf."

Bill nodded. Gustav needed immediate help. He took the Browning from Gustav's outstretched hand and stuffed it in his belt. Then he lifted the fallen man placing the left arm over his shoulder.

Together, he and Ivana guided the semiconscious Gustav through the bleak fields towards the farmhouse.

They laid him on the bed. Not the bare mattress cot that furnished Ivana's windowless former prison, but a broad old fashioned poster with a colorful comforter. This room had windows with lace furnishings. Still there was little natural light. The evening sun was low on the horizon.

Bill spoke.

"The bleeding seems to have stopped, but he needs help, now. Cover him with blankets, and get towels from the kitchen to clean him up. If the bleeding starts again, use the towels to stanch the flow and call me. Whatever you do, keep him warm. I'll call Brussels."

He held up a cell phone, but the signal was weak.

"I'm going out backside. Maybe the reception is better there."

On his way he pointed to the closet.

"There may be towels in there too."

Ivana squeezed Gustav's wrist. She laid two blankets over him and leaned close to his ear.

"Keep fighting. Don't quit on me. I need you. I don't trust these Americans."

Gustav opened his eyes and looked at her. His will to live was evident. He set his jaw before he closed his eyes.

Satisfied, she went to find the towels.

***

Ivana returned to find Gustav breathing heavily amid sporadic coughing. He was sweating. She rubbed his forehead with a cool towel.

He shivered in spite of the sweat. She found another blanket and laid it on him. The shaking stopped. She whispered in his ear.

"You saved my life."

He opened his eyes and closed them. His voice, too, was a whisper.

"And you mine. Why did you warn me about Karel?"

"I don't know. Maybe it was memories of you and the house near Kladno when I was little. I felt I should, that's all."

Gustav tried to raise his head.

"Ivana, you never knew your father."

"I know he deserted my mother when I was born. Probably because of me. That's why mother could never talk about him, me either. I don't want to know him."

Gustav's eyes remained closed, but his hand gripped hers. She could not pull away.

"Ivana, you are wrong, truly wrong."

He gasped once and went on.

"Listen to me. Ivan did not desert your mother. He loved her. He never would have hurt her. He was arrested for crimes against the State. They took him away."

He continued.

"I warned him there would be trouble if he married her. She was a Catholic. When they were married, she made him have a religious service too."

"What are you saying?"

"Religious people like your mother were a threat to us. Your mother was popular. That made it worse. People knew her and liked her. They listened to her. She treated everyone the same, everyone, rich or poor. She was publicly religious, but she had important friends and it was a small town. They brought in outsiders, Party members from Kladno, even Prague. Still it was not easy to accuse her. They accused her husband instead."

Gustav rubbed his hand on the sheet as if wiping it clean.

"Ivan was my friend and a good worker. He worked in the mill. He was a true comrade. They said he was a spy."

"Was he?"

"Of course not, but they said he was. That made it true. They arrested him."

"What did you do?"

He looked to the side.

"I wanted to help, but I couldn't stop them. Maybe I didn't want to."

He turned back.

"The truth is I was afraid they would arrest me too."

"What happened to him?"

"He disappeared. I was afraid. They knew he was my friend."

"Are you sure he's dead?"

"Positive. He died somewhere in Slovakia, before you were born. It would have been quick. They weren't gentle with "spies" in those days. Husak had to impress Brezhnev. The Soviets were not patient."

***

Ivana stared at the wall. She held her breath.

"You said *before* I was born?"

Gustav's head fell back, eyes closed. His chest heaved up and down. He gripped her wrist. His breathing slowed and he opened his eyes once more. He stared at the ceiling.

"*Prosim*, 'Please,' Listen. After they arrested Ivan and took him away, your mother changed. She retreated into herself. She would stare out the window towards the East, towards Košice, in eastern Slovakia. She knew. She never smiled. She had lost hope."

His eyes found Ivana's.

"Ivan was my friend. I could not help him so I wanted to help his widow, your mother. I thought she needed me, that she could be herself again."

Ivana stiffened. She detached her wrist from his grip. She sensed where he was headed. She looked away. Gustav took a deep breath.

"I slept with her. Later you came."

Ivana hid her face in her hands. Gustav's voice shook.

"It's true. I'm your father. You are my daughter."

Ivana could not speak. She headed for the door.

***

Gustav's lips bubbled blood. He called to her.

"*Počkejte, prosím*, 'Wait, please.' Please listen."

Ivana stopped, but stayed facing the door.

"I knew your mother did not love me. She named you 'Ivana' after her husband. I stayed after you were born, but she became worse. She prayed a lot more. We would be walking together and she would stop on the street and make the sign of the cross. I hated that. I did not want anyone to think I was superstitious. I was in the Party."

His voice gave out. He paused several seconds and continued.

"Her guilt infected me. It weakened my beliefs, sapped my strength. That was too much. The Party was my life. When you were six, I left her, ... and you."

Ivana's eyes narrowed. She spoke through taut lips.

"My mother suffered. Her grief killed her. I was seven when she died. You did nothing."

"I was in the Party. You don't understand We watched each other for 'weakness.' They watched me to see what I would do. I could not help her, but I did help you. I got you into the best kindergarten, for Party children, and after, into the best group of Pioneers."

"Ah yes, the Pioneers."

Ivana frowned upwards at the ceiling.

"The talks were boring, stupid. At least the parades were fun. I liked the uniform, the badge and the red scarf."

She mimicked the memorized slogan.

"Always be ready to build and defend your socialist country."

She added its reply

"We stand always ready."

She put her right hand to mid forehead, fingers tight together in the Pioneer salute.

Gustav hesitated. Was she mocking him?

"Ivana you were safe, protected. You were part of a collective."

Her eyes filled with moisture.

"But you weren't there, and neither was my mother. You never came to see me. No one did. And my mother was innocent and alone. How could you desert her? She died of a broken heart."

His eyes fell. Sadly, he had no answer. From outside, Bill Hamm's voice sounded.

"We have to go. I see headlights on the lane. It must be Hrubec."

Ivana stood in the doorway. She blocked Bill's entry.

"Gustav is hurt. The bullet hit his lung. You can't move him. You have a gun. *You* stop Hrubec."

She turned to see Gustav, hand on his chest, sitting up on the side of the bed. He spoke.

207

"No Ivana, we cannot fight him. And there will be others with him."

"No! Do not move. I will not leave you. We can surprise Hrubec, an ambush."

Gustav struggled to his feet. He stood before her.

"But I *am* moving. Besides one does not "surprise" Hrubec. He has phoned Hans and gotten no answer. He knows something is wrong. He will not be alone. The devil tells him what to do. Maybe he *is* the devil!"

Gustav shuddered. Ivana sensed his fear and turned to Bill.

"You have Hans' gun plus your own. Give one to me. We will fight this Hrubec."

Gustav stumbled towards her. A splotch of red appeared through his bandage.

"Little Ivanka, you are brave, but trust me. You cannot stay. You will die."

"I will not leave you."

Gustav stood up straight. The red splotch widened.

"But look, I am coming too. We must not stay."

Bill lifted Gustav's arm around his shoulder and held him. He turned to Ivana.

"Gustav's right. We have to go. We can leave through the kitchen and follow the creek to the Renault. Hrubec will stop to assess the situation. He will not rush in blindly. That will give us a little time."

As if at Bill's command, the approaching car halted. Its headlights went dark.

Bill helped Gustav through the back door. Ivana followed.

From the other side of the house, she heard several "thunks" of car doors closing.

Hrubec was not alone. He had reinforcements.

***

With the loss of the sun, the temperature outside quickly fell below freezing.

Bill helped Gustav struggle into the thick brush that lined the stream. There was no path and progress was slow. They pushed through cold stiff branches that sprang back angrily against their arms and faces. Their steps were marked by snapping and cracking as brittle twigs and frosted leaves crunched underfoot. In the still country air, the noise of their passage was amplified.

Behind them the shouts of their pursuers sounded clearly.

"*Par içi, ... Par içi, le ruisseau,* ... 'Over here, ... Over here, the creek.'"

***

Bill stopped. Gustav slumped to the ground. His spasmodic breaths were wheezes.

"Hamm, I can't go on. Give me a gun. I'll hold them back. You take Ivana and go."

"Get up. I could leave you, but Ivana never would. If you stay, she'll stay. If you want to save her, get up. We have to keep moving."

Ivana knelt next to Gustav.

"Please. Try."

The voices of the pursuers were closer now.

"*Par içi, ... Ils sont passés par içi.* 'Over here, ... They went this way.'"

Gustav struggled to his feet, his arm around Ivana's shoulder. Bill turned to Ivana and pointed to a tall willow tree.

"Lead Gustav over there. Cross the stream, it's cold but shallow. There's a field and a thick woods beyond. Get to those woods and rest. When Gustav is ready, follow the woods all the way to the road. Hide there and wait for me."

"But, what about you?"

"I'll hold them off here. They won't know you've crossed."

Ivana hesitated no more. She guided Gustav towards the willow tree.

***

With Ivana gone, Bill positioned himself behind a fallen log. He pulled out his M9 Beretta and chambered a round. He took out Hans' Browning and did likewise. Then he laid the Browning and an extra magazine for the M9 in front of him.

The sounds of the pursuit grew closer.

***

Bill waited. He had picked his stand carefully. Directly in front of him the brush was impenetrable. To his right, the brush alongside the stream thinned, While still dense, the tangled branches allowed human passage. Bill, Gustav and Ivana had come that way. To his left, the brush ended at the edge of the field. A pursuer would certainly avoid the brush, perhaps moving slowly to match the pace of his companion in the thickets.

Bill had heard two distinct voices, both speaking French. From what Gustav had told him about the canny Hrubec, he felt sure the latter would not have revealed his position with shouts. Besides, Hrubec's fluency in French was doubtful. The silent Hrubec was the major unknown in this battle.

***

The beam of a flashlight appeared to Bill's right. Bill poured six rounds from the Beretta at the only opening in the brush on that side. The beam waved wildly and came to rest pointing straight upwards. The bearer of that "lampe de poche" was no longer a threat.

Bill turned to his left. In the open, but diving for cover, was a second pursuer, Though barely discernible in the darkness, Bill had determined his field of fire before hand. Another four rounds from the Beretta covered the target area at ground level. There was a distinct gurgling moan, then silence.

The firefight was over in seconds. Clearly these two pursuers had not expected any resistance.

Bill stood. He released the Beretta's magazine and jammed in a fresh one. There was only one question on his mind. *Where is Hrubec?*

Then Bill heard the sounds of branches snapping. They became faint and disappeared altogether. Hrubec had retreated.

The battle by the creek was over.

***

******

Chapter 29
Saturday, November 27

It was 10 am when Mila Patekova stopped her SUV in front of the Currituck County Detention Center in Maple, North Carolina. Anne Simek was waiting on the steps. She came to the car.

"Mila, thanks for picking me up, but why didn't Peter and Jim Harrigan come?"

"Peter went to find a lawyer for his father. I told Jim you didn't want to see him."

"But why? What made you say that?"

"Because he's a cop. He made you talk to the sheriff, and look how that turned out. You spent the night in jail."

"It wasn't bad. I had my own cell. And it was my mistake. I panicked and didn't go to the sheriff when I should have. It's not Jim's fault."

Mila frowned.

"Maybe not, but the police are the police. I thought I liked Jim Harrigan, but he's just a cop after all."

"That's silly. You still like him, and he likes you."

"That's what you say, but what about you? What about the sheriff? What's the verdict?"

"The 'verdict' is they asked me not to leave the state before they depose me, that's all. I'm just a witness, nothing more. 'Your' Jim Harrigan spoke up for me. You're mad at him for no reason. You should tell him you're sorry."

Mila tightened her grip on the wheel. She was happy she could still be friends with Jim Harrigan, but she damned well was *not* going to apologize.

They drove in silence. Mila glanced at her passenger. Anne looked drawn.

Mila had forgotten Peter Zeleny. *Wake up, Mila. You are really stupid.*

"Anne, I'm sorry. I almost forgot, Peter wants to take you to lunch. He'll be back at the beach house by noon, if you want to go."

Anne smiled to herself and began to hum.

The rest of the drive to Corolla was relaxed.

***

When Mila and Anne arrived at the beach house, the parking area was full. Jim Harrigan's F250 was next to Anne's Focus. A Honda Accord with Maryland plates was parked in the farthest spot.

Mila stopped the SUV behind the F250 pickup, blocking it. *Take that, Mr. Harrigan. You won't leave unless I say so.* She switched off the motor

Mila and Anne were still in the car when Peter Zeleny emerged from the house and came down the steps.

Anne stepped out of the car to meet him.

"Peter, what's wrong?"

Peter tried to answer, but choked on his words. His eyes were reddened and moist.

"Peter, what's wrong? Tell me."

"It's my father, Johan, he's dead."

"Dead, how?"

Peter started to answer, but Anne did not hear him.

Her thoughts drifted to her own father, and the many times he had shared the story of Johan's desertion with her. She had been too young to comprehend the stories of his pain at Johan's treachery, the drawn-out suffering in the prison on Bartolomejska Street.

Now that Johan was dead maybe her father could overcome the bitterness that had destroyed half his life. Maybe he could find peace, maybe?

Peter's voice jerked her back to the present.

"Anne did you hear what I said?"

"I'm sorry Peter. How? I mean what happened."

"Cardiac arrest. Exercise time, right there in the prison yard."

"Peter, I'm sorry. I know you needed to talk to him."

But Peter was staring across the dunes. He seemed lost in thought, as she had been.

She took his arm.

"Come on. Let's go in the house."

They went up the stairs together.

***

The great room of the beach house was bright with light. In a far corner, Anne recognized Aileen Harris deep in conversation with Jim Harrigan and a woman with red hair. *That must be Jeannine Ryan.*

Anne guided Peter to a couch as far-removed from Aileen as possible.

Mila headed for the kitchen, and soon was busy opening and closing cabinets and arranging pots on the stove.

Anne turned to Peter.

"Cardiac arrest? Was this expected in any way?"

Peter shook his head, "No."

Maybe with my father gone, this woman and I can have a future together? At that thought, guilt assailed him. He focused anew.

"It's odd. One of the witnesses in the exercise yard said my father had a seizure, that he was paralyzed and couldn't move. He died within a minute."

Anne held his arm.

"Where was your father when this happened?"

"At a Federal facility near Butner. They moved him upstate yesterday from the Currituck Detention Center in Maple where you spent the night. I didn't get to talk to him."

"That's not your fault. He refused to see you."

Peter hung his head.

"Maybe it's good I didn't see him."

He paused and looked into her eyes.

"You told me we should live in the present. We can't relive our fathers' lives. Our life is ahead of us."

Anne inhaled. She loved the words "our life."

***

In the kitchen, Jim Harrigan informed Aileen about Johan's death. She walked to the couch where Anne and Peter were huddled together.

"Peter, what did they say caused your father's death?"

"They said cardiac arrest."

"And you think?"

"Some of the symptoms were odd, as if he had some sort of seizure. One witness said it was like his chest froze. He couldn't breathe. He couldn't move his limbs."

Aileen's eyebrows rose.

"That sounds like organophosphate poisoning, maybe a nerve agent?"

"Maybe, but they told me there was no vomiting, little sweating. Why do you ask?"

"Because we know that Hus-Kinetika has stocks of a nerve agent more deadly than VX or Sarin, but different. And because the FDA Administrator responsible for the Xolak report was found dead this morning in his office in Rockville. He was healthy, a runner. There were no prior problems with his heart."

Aileen paused.

"They said it was cardiac arrest too."

Peter started to reply, but Anne Simek broke in.

"Come on Peter. You can talk about this later. Mila has food ready in the kitchen."

She pulled Peter away.

Aileen rejoined Jeannine and Jim.

***

It was mid afternoon in Prague. At the knock on his office door Karel Moravec looked up.

It was Fiala. She was as attractive as ever, but Fiala lacked something that Ivana possessed. How would the Americans put it? Fiala lacked the "Spunk," that Ivana had. "Spunk!" He liked the word. It was strong. It propelled itself from his lips.

"What is it Fiala?"

"Mr. Hrubec, called you, Sir. He wants you to call him back."

"Where is he?"

"In Belgium. In the countryside near Brussels."

"Does he have Ivana?"

"He didn't say, Sir."

Karel scowled. Hrubec had failed. He did not have Ivana or he would have said so.

Faced with that scowl, Fiala withdrew. She shut the door carefully to make no noise.

Rather than please him, that accommodation irritated Karel. *Damn it.* Ivana never catered to his moods. Her departures had flair. Once she had slammed the "holy" door to his office. Ivana had "Spunk."

Karel looked at the photo of Bill Hamm lying on his desk. The American was an ignorant bore who doubtless had never heard of Mozart, Dvořák or Beethoven. Karel studied his hand-crafted Italian shoes. In the photo Hamm wore sneakers. Yet he had spirited Ivana out of the country in spite of Karel's best men. He ground his teeth and turned the photo face down.

Karel sat, face between his hands.

Fiala spoke through the intercom.

"Sir, it's North America, on line 1."

Karel looked up. Indeed a button was lit. He punched it and spoke.

"Yes?"

"Johan Zeleny's mouth is closed, permanently."

"Do they suspect how?"

"No, and they won't. They're going to cremate the body tomorrow."

"OK, Zeleny is no longer a problem. What about Hodges, and Xolak?"

"A janitor found his body this morning. They called it a heart attack. And the Xolak report has been fixed. There should be no more problems with the FDA."

"Unless Ryan and Harris protest. Eliminate them! Where are they?"

"We lost them. They never returned to the office. Our best guess is North Carolina."

Karel's face turned red.

"You guess! Find them. Take care of them now!"

Karel slammed the button and broke the connection.

He tried to call Hrubec, but there was no answer, only a whining sound.

***

******

Chapter 30
Saturday, November 27

The beach house in Corolla, North Carolina, was the site of considerable activity. Jeannine had tried to contact Bill Hamm in Belgium, but without success. Thus Jim Harrigan was dependent on her account of Bill's efforts to obtain Gustav's cooperation.

And Jim had a new concern. The house in Corolla was not safe. If not already known to Karel's men, it soon would be. It was a week ago that Jim had smashed the electronic bug at Mila's house. If they knew of her, they would be able to trace her rentals.

Meanwhile, Mila kept herself busy with household chores so as to not think of Jim. Occasionally, she would glance in his direction as he talked with that attractive redhead, Jeannine.

Anne Simek and Peter Zeleny kept to themselves. Anne acted as if Peter needed protection from Aileen more than from Karel Moravec. Aileen found that ironic. She had lost all attraction for Peter after his "friend," Gustav, had destroyed her office and nearly killed her. Though Peter then had saved her, he had brought Gustav to the office in the first place.

Besides, Aileen was busy. Lacking input from Gustav, she was to check which Hus-Kinetika facilities in the United States were equipped to handle nerve agents. Handling such extremely dangerous agents requires buildings with special ventilation systems.

Moreover, the Novichok agents, unlike Sarin and others, had precursors that occur normally in the production of pesticides. Perhaps some Hus-Kinetika facility was near a pesticide plant. There, the presence of critical chemical residues could have an innocent explanation.

Another possibility was for the facility be near a CWDF, a "Chemical Weapons Destruction Facility," mandated by the

JAMES E. MOSIMANN / THE PRAGUE PLOT

CWC, the "Chemical Warfare Convention." In the U. S. these facilities were located at or near former production sites, like Pine Bluff Arsenal in Arkansas, or Edgewood Chemical Biological Center in Maryland. There suspicious chemical residues could be explained easily.

Her search was like that for a needle in a haystack. Doggedly she perused website after website on her laptop.

Additionally she was nagged by the thought of Xolak. It had to be linked to her search.

But how?

***

At Jim Harrigan's approach, Aileen looked up from the laptop.

"Jim, what did your friends at the CIA say when you told them about the 95 tons of Novichok-H."

"They don't believe Gustav, and they're skeptical about Jeannine's analysis, but they'll check on it."

"That's no help."

"No it isn't. They say they will check if the nerve agent could be in the States, but they're skeptical. They think it would be too dangerous to ship without special containers that would have been detectable."

"But Novichok-H is a "binary agent," it's not dangerous until the two precursors are combined. And the evidence is that both precursors occur in normal pesticide production. If we can't keep illegal immigrants out of the country, why would anyone think we can keep 'legal' pesticide chemicals out."

"Aileen, I agree, 100 per cent. The CIA will continue checking, but I think only to cover their butts in case something bad happens. Maybe Bill Hamm has found more."

"But we haven't heard from Bill, so it's up to us, and we have no resources."

"But you have the internet. Use what you have."

Aileen went back to the computer as Jeannine appeared holding a cup of coffee.

"Would either of you like some coffee?"

Jim took the cup as Aileen jumped in her seat.

"Wait. Here's something, Hus-Kinetika has a facility in Maryland, not far from the Aberdeen Proving Ground."

Jim looked over her shoulder.

"Use Google Satellite and take a look."

"Google won't let me focus on the proving ground. It's blurred."

"Right, that's military security. But move away from it to the Hus-Kinetika plant. You can focus in close there."

"What am I looking for?"

"An add-on to the complex. An isolated building, with few or no windows. And special ventilation, fans, pipes, on the roof or along the sides. Like the Aum Cult building in which they made and tested Sarin for their attack on the Tokyo subway."

Aileen Googled in on Hus-Kinetika's plant.

To the north stood a single building with almost no windows but with structures on the roof that looked like ventilators. It was isolated from the southern part of the complex by a high fence. A thick grove of trees shielded it further.

Bingo!

***

Aileen looked up at Jim Harrigan.

"What next?"

"This is a possible site. It's better than nothing, but we need more. Check the arrival of ships at the Port of Baltimore from 2005 to 2006. Particularly search for ships from Hamburg, and its Vltava Port, what the Germans call "Moldauhafen.""

Aileen turned back to the computer to Google "Moldauhafen."

Jeannine spoke.

"But Jim, the conspirators have had years to perfect a plan. They could be ready to strike any time."

"True, but there are two things in our favor. The handling of nerve agents is difficult and dangerous, and you need special facilities, like that isolated building with super ventilation, as well as trained lab people."

He added.

"And delivery systems are damned complicated. They take years to perfect. It's not easy to impact the target without killing the deliverer. Novichok-H needs to have its two precursors mixed in specific proportions and at the right temperature just prior to delivery. The development of the M687 binary Sarin artillery shell at Pine Bluff was a slow difficult process, for years. And the conspirators don't have the resources of the military. They may not be ready yet."

Before she could frame a reply, Mila called from the kitchen.

"Jim, come and give me a hand with these sacks of garbage. Tomorrow is pickup day."

He left.

Jeannine shook her head and went to Aileen's side.

***

Aileen was not the only individual on the Outer Banks using the Internet for research.

In Nags Head, a man hunched over his computer and adeptly clicked keys to craft searches. He did not need much skill to find what he wanted. The Patek Realty website listed its rentals.

He completed his task and signaled his partners.

"There are six possible rentals where Patekova could be hiding people. Three of them are in Nags Head, two in Kitty Hawk and one up north in Corolla."

Hugo, a short stocky individual with the look of an "enforcer" answered.

"What do we do?"

The third individual, Hermann, was tall and had a well-groomed beard. He closed his eyes as if reflecting.

"We'll check Nags Head and Kitty Hawk because they're closer and on the way, but they'll be in Corolla. They want to be as far from Patek Realty as they can get."

He opened his eyes.

"We must go. Karel needs results, not excuses."

***

At the beach house in Corolla, Mila sent Jim Harrigan to wheel the large garbage can to the roadside. Jeannine followed. She wanted a moment alone with him

"Jim, I don't think that these former communists will gain enough by destroying our cities."

Jim recalled his cold war service with the Agency. He had no doubts about the ruthlessness of those guys, whether Czechs or Soviets.

She read his mind.

"I know they could wipe us out with a clear conscience, but I don't think revenge is enough of a reward for them. In the present clime, they are more thugs than communist ideologues."

"Get to the point, Jeannine. What are you saying?"

"They want money. Lots of money. What if jihadists, who lack the knowledge and means to mount a massive nerve gas attack, are willing to pay them multi millions of dollars to cripple the 'Great Satan.'"

Jim frowned.

"Jihadist Petrodollars for cold-war weaponry?"

"Right. The loss of lives and the damage to the U.S. economy would be much worse than after 9/11. That could be the communists' revenge for the destruction of Communism. Plus, millions of Euros for each of them would satisfy their thuggish appetites. And the jihadists would further their goal of establishing the Caliphate."

Jeannine made sense. Jim's brow furrowed as he spoke.

"So what holds the conspirators back is not the means of delivery, but negotiations to maximize their payoff. They want to extract as much as they can from the radical Islamists. When people are willing to die, the delivery system can be simpler. Those who deliver the agent will die, but they want to."

A cloud passed before the sun. The air chilled. Jeannine shivered and pressed her arms about her body while climbing the steps to the house. At the top, she looked back.

To the West behind them, the sun shone blood-red on the horizon. Was it an omen, a portent of what lay ahead?

221

The terrorists would strike, but when and where?

But there was no time to reflect.

Jim Harrigan knew that the conspirators could easily locate the beach house. And his truck and the other cars parked outside proved that it was occupied.

It was only a matter of time before Karel's men found them.

They all needed to leave, now.

In thirty minutes, everyone was packed!

*****

******

Chapter 31
Saturday, November 27

William M. Jones was born thirty years ago in Fairfax, Virginia. He was baptized a Christian for cultural reasons, but religion was not a factor in his upbringing. The agnostic tendencies of his mother and father failed to stimulate any reaction, much less belief, in their son.

William was a natural athlete, but in High School, he disappointed his father by disdaining organized sports. He eschewed discipline unless imposed by himself on himself.

He was no nerd. He kept physically fit by pumping iron and running. With his friends Barry Wilson and Monica Barrett, he partied, slept late, and mostly ignored his studies. He did not do drugs, he valued his trim muscular form.

At his high school graduation, the name on his diploma was William Morris Jones, "Morris," after his maternal grandfather.

Then, during his third year at university, William's political science professor encouraged him to examine the tenets of Islam. William eagerly immersed himself in the abundant internet offerings of radical Muslims.

Faced with the emptiness of his life, William realized that his eternal destiny was to serve Allah. He became William "Masoud" Jones, joined the Muslim Student Association, and a year later, as a senior, headed a study group on "Militant Islam." He abandoned alcohol and studied long hours. He could not make up completely for his lazy years, but he managed to graduate with a degree in civil engineering.

Masoud attended a local mosque. Filled with fervor, he vowed to serve Allah, and only Him. He impressed his spiritual advisors who told him to avoid public displays of his religion, and that he must no longer frequent the Mosque. He would be a warrior but only in Allah's time.

When he received a wedding invitation from his former friends, Monica Barrett and Barry Wilson, he sent a present, but did not attend the Christian ceremony.

He himself did not marry, but moved to a small town in Virginia where he joined the Volunteer Fire Department. He became a local hero when he carried the daughter of a prominent farmer to safety moments before the ceiling of her bedroom collapsed.

Masoud enjoyed the fame, but he felt rejected. He should be a warrior for Allah. Surely that was his destiny! And he was tired of keeping the name "Jones," no matter how important his mentors thought the deception was needed

But William Masoud Jones, domestic terrorist, was obedient. He waited.

***

And Masoud's patience had been rewarded this past September, when he received several electronic communications.

First, there was the money. A new account established in his name contained more money than he could ever have thought existed.

Then there were the instructions. He was to move immediately to Dethorens, Virginia, to form a Volunteer Fire Department. An anonymous benefactor had given a large amount of money to the town specifically for that purpose.

The benefactor's only stipulation to the authorities was that Masoud be appointed Fire Chief. They voted on the gift in a special session, and William "M." Jones the "hero of Marshall" was unanimously approved.

Already the benefactor had started the erection of a steel frame building in the town's sole commercial area. The target for completion was early October, at which time the latest in fire equipment, a modern tanker-pumper, an ambulance, and yes, special Hazmat equipment, was to arrive.

Masoud also received a list of "volunteers" to interview. From it he was to choose three shifts for the volunteer fire department, but he must accept everyone on the list whether or *not they were assigned to a shift. He was to house everyone in a multi-million dollar mansion located on over sixty acres that the benefactor had rented.*

And he was to train everyone in Hazmat procedures endorsed by the Occupational Safety and Health Administration (OSHA) as well as in the use of his own special equipment.

Head down on his prayer mat, William Masoud Jones had thanked Allah.

The waiting was over.

***

In Belgium, Josef Hrubec had postponed making this call for 24 hours. He could wait no longer. He was not afraid of Karel, far from it, but Hrubec was proud. He hated failure. This call would confirm the failure at Malèves to himself, as well as to that pompous ass, Karel.

He picked up his phone, paused, and punched the number. The voice that answered was familiar.

"Fiala, let me speak to the Chief."

"*On není tady.* 'He's not here.'"

Hrubec started to hang up, but Fiala continued.

"He told me to ask you two things. 'Where is the package? and Where is Gustav?'"

Josef Hrubec swallowed. To have to answer to this blond idiot was a major punishment. Evidently, the delay had proved to Karel that the news was bad.

He contained his distaste for the secretary, took a deep breath, and recounted to Fiala the 'mishaps' of the Belgian operation.

Then he provided her with the latest from his informants.

The Americans had placed Gustav Slavik on a military flight to the U. S. He was to be treated at a hospital in the DC area, probably Naval Medical in Bethesda, Maryland.

A CIA hack named Hamm, stationed in Vienna, had flown with Ivana to the U. S. in a private charter. The two of them were likely at a safe house somewhere in Virginia.

Hrubec was deliberately brief in his account. He omitted all details of how Bill Hamm and Gustav had thwarted his abduction of Ivana, particularly the casualties his group had sustained.

By the time he hung up, Hrubec was smoldering. He would not forget Karel's snub. He was sure that Karel had listened to his entire conversation with Fiala.

He was right.

Almost instantly, his cell phone buzzed. It was Fiala again.

"Karel wants you to fly to America immediately. Your flight is arranged. Pick up the tickets in Brussels. A member of the Maryland team will meet you at Baltimore-Washington Airport when you arrive. He will have instructions for you."

"Click."

Hrubec ground his teeth. Another demotion. Instructions from one of the Maryland lackeys?

Karel, be careful, I too have limits.

***

In Maryland, in a Hus-Kinetika laboratory not far from Aberdeen, Michal Pacak retrieved a remote printout with the High Performance Liquid Chromatography (HPLC) results. The high performance chromatograph, and the samples it measured, were located in a specially sealed and isolated area where robotic arms and other devices performed their programmed tasks under the watchful eyes of a multitude of television cameras.

Michal was a Czech chemist, a graduate of the Technical University of Brno. He was young, his entire education was after the Velvet Revolution. All he knew of Communism, was the bitter old men who sat at street-side cafes to share stories while they soaked in beer or stronger spirits. Their archaic notions bored him.

Michal was no ideologue, but he was gifted. At the Technical University his professor of chemistry had recognized Michal's intelligence and abstract lack of moral sense. The

226

combination made him a natural recruit for Hus-Kinetika's "special project."

Michal's professor had been a protégé of a well-known Czech Colonel who conducted research on nerve agents at an institute in Brno. With the dissolution of the Czechoslovak Socialist Republic, the records and equipment of the institute had been purchased by Hus-Kinetika. At the university nearby, Michal's professor had introduced him to the world of organophosphate and carbamate pesticides.

After an internship with Hus-Kinetika and the subsequent completion of his studies, Michal, seduced by an absurdly high salary with multiple benefits, was sent to the laboratory in Maryland, in the United States of America.

Now he had a key role in the conspirators' plans.

***

Michal Pacak hunched over his lab bench to study the output. There were no windows on this floor, and his eyes strained under the fluttering fluorescent lights that flooded the work area. To his right, an array of over twenty TV's served as monitors of various robotic activities taking place in a "sealed" laboratory area.

Michal focused on the latest print-out from the Varian chromatograph. The peaks were clearly defined and occurred precisely above the correct points on the axis. This was the signature of Novichok-H.

Meanwhile, "peaks" from both precursors all were nearly flat, at most two per cent of those chemicals remained. At this temperature and mix, the reaction had yielded the lethal product with an efficiency of 98 per cent.

Michal thrust his fist in the air with a silent cheer. This was the last of the containers to be tested, After years of shipment and storage, the chemical precursors had not deteriorated. Tons of Novichok-H were available for whatever plan his superiors had in mind.

Whatever the plan was, it required a large volume delivery. Michal's next requirement was to scale up the reaction volume to a 320 liter tank. This had problems beyond those for the small volumes already tested. He would need a "stirring" device inside the tank to ensure rapid mixing and reactivity of the precursors.

A footstep sounded behind him.

Michal turned and recognized a coworker, Elena Krkova. Like Michal, she was in her mid-twenties. She was clad in a long rubber apron and her hair was concealed in a protective wrap which she loosened to let long brown tresses tumble free.

She tapped her finger on a pack of American cigarettes.

"Michal, come take a break with me. I need a smoke."

Elena was a new arrival from the Czech Republic. The dire warnings of the United States Surgeon General had not yet intimidated her.

Michal stood quickly. Elena was a "Dish."

"Why not, I just found good news. There's no deterioration in that shipment of pesticides."

He said no more. He did not know what Elena knew about his real work. She may have been assigned to watch him, or maybe she was simply friendly. In either case she was attractive. He would enjoy her company

They took an elevator to the ground floor. This was the United States. She had to leave the building to smoke.

***

The air outside was cold and the wind was brisk. Elena stood in the open while Michal stayed in the shelter of the doorway. It was not possible to wander. A high fence topped with razor wire barred access into the nearby tulip poplars, now bare except for small dry cuplike clusters of seeds, that dominated the surrounding woods.

Elena lit up and inhaled. Only then did she hold out the pack to Michal.

"Would you like one?"

"No thanks."

Elena was relieved. At today's taxes, each cigarette was precious.

"What pesticide are you working on, Michal?"

Michal replied with a question of his own.

"Where are you from, Elena? And where did you attend university?"

"From Kladno, near Prague, and Charles University, of course."

Michal was not sure if her reply was a put-down. Graduates of Charles University often acknowledged no other institution but theirs, but Michal was not offended. The Technical University of Brno was world-class. He continued.

"Why did you come to Maryland? Why the States?"

Elena inhaled and lit a second cigarette from the first. She smiled. She too could be evasive.

"This is my first time in the States and I need to see some sights. Maybe you could take me to Baltimore tonight. We could eat at the harbor."

She turned in his direction. She possessed an ample chest under the drab rubber apron. Michal could not say no. He didn't.

"That would be great. You're off at six, yes? I'll meet you at the main gate. We'll take my car. It's a brown Audi."

Elena noted with satisfaction that he knew her schedule. *So he is interested.* She not only knew the make and color of his car, its license plate was committed to her memory, along with his cell number and address. She had her assignment and she would complete it. *But what a nerd!*

"Thanks, Michal."

She stubbed out her cigarette.

They returned to the third floor.

***

Once on the third floor, Michal went directly to his lab bench.

Elena re-wrapped her hair and resumed her task of monitoring the robotic manipulation of lab vessels on closed circuit TV.

Next to the battery of TV's, a large panel exhibited rows of green lights. Elena checked them periodically, a blinking red light would signal a leak from one of the sealed hoods. If that occurred, the cubicle (itself sealed) that contained the leaking hood would have to be flushed and decontaminated.

A third layer of protection was indicated by a row of large lights, likewise green. Each light represented a major "Zone" that contained multiple modules. The zones were graded by degree of risk. Zone A contained the hoods where the most toxic reagents were handled.

Elena sighed. This was boring work, but it placed her near to her assigned "target."

***

Michal sat back and shut his eyes. Images of stacks of Euros flashed before him. He would soon be rich and not just Elena, but women of all sorts, would seek his company.

The thought of the shapely Elena in a bikini-top, sunning on the white sands of a Caribbean island delighted him.

But the Baltimore Harbor in the evening, with lights shimmering over the waters and its excellent restaurants was a romantic setting too. And afterwards, if he obtained a room high over the waterfront, perhaps Elena would reward his attentions.

***

The fieldstone house was located at the end of a long wooded lane in the Virginia countryside near Middleburg. The small house had a central kitchen and living area with a bedroom on either side. The kitchen was ultra modern, and the open living area sported a large High Definition TV on the wall.

Ivana sat and faced the big screen. In Prague, Karel (for whatever reason) had forbidden her to watch the HBO series, "The Sopranos." Here she was free. She clicked the remote relentlessly. After several minutes of fruitless search, she settled for the Food Channel and Bobby Flay grilling burgers "southwest" style. She imagined the delectable aroma of cooked meat.

But the aroma was real. Ivana looked over her shoulder. Bill Hamm stood over the kitchen stove. He held a spatula ready to flip two hamburger patties that sizzled in the pan.

Ivana smiled. She was beginning to like American ways.

"Bill, I want my burger 'Over easily.'"

Bill laughed.

"That's 'Over easy,' and that's for eggs. You mean you want some pink in your burger, maybe like 'Medium Rare.'"

She left the TV to stand by him. He skillfully slipped the meat patties onto their buns, and added toppings along with browned onions.

Ivana did not wait. She took a major bite, smacked her lips and smiled.

"Bill that's really good. I like it."

Ivana's burger was half gone when Bill picked up his own plate and waved her to the kitchen table.

"I'm glad you like it. Let's sit to eat."

Ivana finished fast. Her last bite was in her mouth when Bill leaned back and spoke.

His first question did not surprise her.

"Ivana, what do you know about Hus-Kinetika's plant in Maryland."

But the second startled her.

"And what was your relationship with Michal Pacak, the chemist?"

***

Bill Hamm waited for an answer.

Ivana stared. *Is this question professional or personal?* She rubbed her hands as she answered.

"Bill, you saved my life, twice. And Gustav's too. You know I like you and you know I'm grateful. Why do you want to know about Michal?"

Bill softened his tone, but tried to stay on topic.

"When did you first meet him, Ivana. Was it in Brno?"

She nodded.

"I was in the Fakulta of Fine Arts at the Technical University. He was in the Fakulta chemická. He was quiet, but intelligent, and he knew people."

"What kind of people?"

"People. He became an intern in one of Hus-Kinetika's labs. They worked on pesticides."

"How well did you know him?"

Ivana's face reddened.

"We dated, of course. But I didn't sleep with him, if that's what you want to know!"

Bill tried to appear objective.

"When is the last time you heard from him?"

"He's at the Hus-Kinetika plant in Maryland. I sent him a postcard in January. I never heard back from him, I know about him because his Chief reports to Karel."

She continued.

"So I can tell you that, 'Yes,' Michal is now an expert on the Novichok agents, and 'No' just because he works on them in Maryland, does not mean that the main stock of 95 tons is there. And 'No,' Gustav knows nothing I don't. Even Karel doesn't know how much I learned. I wasn't dumb, and I kept my eyes open."

She looked into his eyes.

"But tell me. Why do I think you already knew the answers to these questions, except that I didn't sleep with Michal?"

Bill flushed. Ivana studied his face and went on.

"Your next question will be about Karel Moravec? Of course I slept with him. You already know that. Why do you want to make me say it?"

Her shoulders drooped. She trembled and her voice shook.

"It's something I regret, but I can't change. I was alone. I wanted to be away from Prague, far from Kladno. I went to Brno where I met Michal. He was smart and he had connections. When I graduated, he introduced me to Hus-Kinetika. They respected me. They offered me a promotion to move to Prague. I went. A year later, I was promoted again."

"Then Karel noticed me. At first he kept his distance. I learned how to run his office. I was good at that. He leased a Mercedes for me to use on 'business.' I was flattered. A few months later, he leased an apartment for me, an expensive one. Of course I slept with him. What else could I do? You don't tell Karel, 'No.' He didn't love me, but I fooled myself that he did. He gave me gifts to 'die' for. Something inside me did die."

"For over a year I was *his* property, a trophy to *display* in public and to *use* in private."

"One morning recently, I woke up, I felt dirty. I took showers. Nothing helped. I was soiled inside, unclean, worthless."

"I thought of my mother. I didn't want to. I tried not to, but the thoughts would not go away. My mother was Catholic and she suffered for it. In spite of everything she endured, she never lost faith. She kept her dignity. She died clean. I imagined her praying, wanting me to be clean, wanting me to be worth something."

"I felt sick, rotten. I knew I had to get away from Karel."

"Then Karel told me he was going to kill Gustav, a former friend of my mother. I warned him and Karel found out. I had planned my escape well, but not well enough."

She looked into Bill's eyes and began to tremble.

"You saved me on that bus, and in Belgium. Even after I had deserted you, you found me and saved me again. And Gustav too. Bill, you risked your own life for me. You could have been killed."

She looked down.

"My God, I still must be worth something for you to do that!"

Her words became sobs. She shook uncontrollably.

He moved next to her and took her hand.

***

******

Chapter 32
Monday, November 29

In Maryland, Michal Pacak was back at his lab bench, but his thoughts were not of work.

His Saturday date with the beautiful Elena had started well. For over two hours, they had gulped beer and cracked crabs at a Baltimore harbor restaurant. Michal had been particularly pleased at Elena's interest in, and admiration of, his work.

Afterwards, while sleek crafts cut back and forth through the harbor, they had walked along the docks. There, sundry boats tied to the sea wall were hosting onboard parties that featured splashing cocktails, loud music, and suggestively-clad bodies gyrating and bouncing to the beat.

Michal had admired one boat in particular, a Chris Craft Corsair whose owner informed him that for $160,000 plus a sizable tax, Michal too could captain his own Corsair. In the past, a jealous Michal would have been offended by the ostentatious man, but not this evening.

He knew that as soon as the Middle-Eastern buyers stopped dickering over the price, he would have enough Euros to buy a Corsair 28 or any other "toy" he might desire.

When the owner asked Michal and Elena to join the party, Michal's foot was already on the ladder when Elena demurred.

That was his first disappointment of the evening. They had continued their stroll along the docks.

An hour later, Elena had complained of a headache. She asked to be driven home and he had complied. At the apartment, she had fled the car in haste, before Michal could open the driver-side door. By the time he stepped out of the car, she had disappeared into her apartment.

What had started as a fine evening had ended in utter frustration!

Afterwards, to counter his disappointment, Michal had consoled himself with the thought of his near riches. He would "buy" lots of Elena's, all of them "hotter" than the original.

Now the weekend was over and he was back at work. There was Elena, not far away. She was scanning her TV monitors.

He had to admit that she was "hot." Maybe he still could ... ?

***

Michal's thoughts returned to Novichok-H. Thus far he had mixed the two precursors of the nerve agent in a two-liter volume, the size of a large soda bottle.

Now his orders were to combine the two precursors in a volume suitable for a Mark 82 dumb bomb. With an average cross section of about 91 square inches and a conservative container length of 66 inches, he needed to mix the precursors in a volume of 6000 cubic inches (320 liters), a 160-fold increase in volume. This larger volume posed serious engineering problems.

Michal diagramed his solutions and ideas onto a yellow pad. He had filled two sheets with scribbling when the phone on his desk blinked. It was the boss.

"Michal, come down to my office."

"Can it wait? I'm working on the Mark 82 problem."

"No it can't. The negotiations with our Muslim friends are moving forward, and we're scrapping the dumb bomb delivery. We'll try a more personal route. You'll only need to scale half that size."

Michal looked at his latest notes in dismay. Were they now worthless?

The boss continued.

"That's not why I'm calling. Get down here, now."

Michal left his desk. On the way to the elevator, he passed Elena. She turned from the monitor to smile at him. He nodded.

The "Down" arrow lit up and the doors slid apart.

Michal stepped into the elevator.

***

The lab secretary was not at her desk and Michal went straight through the inner door to the office. This was no staff meeting. There were only two people in the room. The Chief stood in front of his desk. Next to him was a stranger. He was dressed in a gray suit that sported a vest. Slightly bald, his hair was streaked with gray that bore no evidence of artificial coloring.

The man was several inches shorter than Michal, but he was not smaller. Michal realized that in any physical confrontation, he would be vanquished, and quickly.

It was the stranger's eyes that affected him the most. They were deep, dark and perceptive. Michal knew, somehow, that those eyes would "see" his thoughts before he could speak them.

Michal stood silent, waiting for someone to speak.

No one did. The stranger waved his hand at the door and Michal's Chief left the office. He closed the door after him.

***

The stranger sat behind the Chief's desk. He motioned Michal to sit and spoke.

"My name is Josef Hrubec. I have just arrived from the home office to supervise security here. You are Michal Pacak?"

Michal could only nod.

"And you have two degrees from the Technical University of Brno?"

Michal found his voice.

"I do. I specialized in organic chemistry, in pesticides and the synthesis of organophosphate and carbamate compounds. I also interned at Hus-Kinetika while I took supplemental courses in chemical engineering and design."

Hrubec appeared bored.

"Yes, Yes, and you know about our special task force. Do you know Elena Krkova?"

"She works at a station near mine. The third floor."

"How long have you known her?"

"She's new, from the old country. She just arrived."

Hrubec frowned.

"Do you know if she is aware of the task force? Does she know about Novichok-H?"

Michal drew back. He shook his head.

"No."

Hrubec opened the jacket of his suit. exposing a shoulder holster with a weapon. He spoke.

"I tell you frankly that Elena Krkova is *not* an associate of the task force. She should *not* know anything about our project or the nerve agents. Think carefully, Michal, before you answer. At any time have you told Elena, or implied to her, that your work went beyond pesticides? And have you ever indicated to her that you knew about Novichok Agents?"

Hrubec drew a 9 mm Browning from the holster and placed it on the desk.

Michal looked into Hrubec's eyes. It did not seem possible, but those eyes had blackened further. Dissimulation was impossible. He stammered.

"We dated Saturday. I had too much beer, I wanted to impress her. I implied that I knew about Sarin and Soman. I did mention Novichok Agents. I assumed she was one of us."

Hrubec replaced the Browning in its holster.

"Michal, because you told the truth, you just saved your life. You are an asset to us, but do not be indiscrete again. Your expertise will not save you twice."

Michal swallowed as Hrubec continued.

"Did you know that Elena Krkova studied one summer in Vienna, that she met many Americans there?"

Michal shook his head. Hrubec continued.

"All right. Tell me about Bill Hamm. How did you meet him?"

"I never heard of him. I don't know him."

"And 'Gustav Slavik,' surely you heard of him?"

"No, never."

"Do you know the address 16 Boltzmanngasse, Wien?"

"No."

"Think. You've never been to the U. S. Embassy in Vienna?"

"Never."

"All right Michal. We are almost done. A few more questions. You and Ivana Novotna were students together. Have you heard from her, or spoken to her since Brno."

"I had a post card from her in January. I've heard nothing since."

"Did you answer her, write or call?"

"No."

Hrubec appeared satisfied. He rubbed his hands together. Then he waved Michal to the door.

Michal gulped and looked back.

"Sir, what about Elena? Am I allowed to speak with her, about ordinary things in the lab I mean?"

"Of course. Talk to her about anything. She will not survive to tell."

Shaken, Michal turned to leave.

Behind him Hrubec spoke into the phone.

"Get her now. Bring her to me at once. Her name is Elena Krkova. She's on the third floor."

Michal heard, but dared not look. Head down, he hurried to the elevator.

***

A pensive Michal pushed the button for the third floor. Had he tried to deceive Hrubec, he would be dead now, a bloody mess on the office floor. He shuddered. Hrubec was evil.

For the first time Michal thought about the consequences of his research.

They told me that the Novichok Agent would be used in Africa, in local wars, and only as a deterrent to stop the other side from using their WMD's. And my binary delivery system would be used for pesticides in the third world, to improve agriculture and health.

He had accepted these explanations. His boss was a scientist. He wanted to believe him.

The promise of a million Euros had dazzled him. He had locked his conscience behind a wall of abstract science. But Hrubec was the true soul of the task force.

Michal you are a fool. They won't pay you in Euros, only in bullets. Their plan cannot be peaceful. My God!

Michal looked up. The red "3" above the door was lit.

The elevator had arrived on his floor.

***

Michal Pacak stepped out of the elevator and turned. Elena Krkova blocked his path.

"Michal, I'm sorry for Saturday night. I shouldn't have left you like that."

Michal shrugged. Elena went on.

"No, I mean it. I can't explain now, but I like you. That's why I had to leave. It was fun being with you. It's just that I, ... I'm not 'free' to have a relationship right now."

Michal looked into her eyes. She truly was upset.

He looked back at the elevator. It had started downwards. He watched in silence as the light blinked "3," then "2," and then "1." There it remained. He turned back to Elena.

"Elena, who are you, really? Why do they want to kill you?"

She paled, stricken silent.

Michal looked back at the elevator. It was on the way up. The "1" was no longer lit.

"My God, Elena, they're coming for you. They're on their way!"

Now the "2" was lit. Michal hesitated. *Michal, forget the money. They were never going to pay you. Hrubec is a murderer. Help her!*

He took her hand.

"Elena, you must trust me. Come with me. Now!"

Moments later the "3" above the elevator door shone red as the doors opened. Two muscular security guards stepped out.

Each had his weapon drawn.

***

******

Chapter 33
Monday, November 29

In the "safe house" near Middleburg, Virginia, Bill Hamm was on the phone with Jim Harrigan. Jim's phone was not secure and the conversation was elliptic.

"Jim, the package, is here with me. It's in good shape."

Bill glanced at Ivana. Her eyes were shut, but she truly was in good shape as she lay on the couch with a cushion under her head and bare feet stretched over the arm rest."

He continued.

"I want to thank you and Jeannine and Aileen, for identifying that suspicious 'facility.' That confirms our worries. We already have someone in place there. I'll get back to you."

The "facility" was the Hus-Kinetika plant in Maryland. Some months before, a civilian scientist at the Edgewood Chemical Biological Center had raised suspicions about the plant. The army had passed on the suspicions to the FBI, who had contacted the CIA in Vienna, Austria, since Hus-Kinetika was based in Prague. When Gustav had offered information about that company and Novichok-H, Bill's unit had taken action and assigned a young Czech, Elena Krkova, to work at the plant.

Yesterday Elena had reported to Bill her concerns about Michal Pacak. Although whether Michal was simply a braggart, or had real information was not yet determined.

Elena was to call Bill at 7:00 pm. He looked at his watch. Three hours to go. He would not risk calling her.

On the couch, Ivana stirred. Bill looked at his phone. He had a secure message from his partner, Tom.

Josef Hrubec passed immigration at Baltimore-Washington Airport at 3:00 pm yesterday.
The name on his passport was Joseph Herrmann.
Whereabouts not known at present.

Bill turned off the stove. He left the kitchen, collapsed in a soft chair, and took a deep breath.

Not again!

***

At the Hus-Kinetika plant in Maryland, Josef Hrubec sat at the desk he had appropriated. His coat was folded on a chair behind him. His Browning lay on the desk, pointed at the empty chair that faced him.

Hrubec was confident. It would not be long before Hamm's protégé, this "Elena Krkova," told him everything she knew.

Hamm had defeated him in Belgium, and caused him to lose face in the eyes of Karel Moravec. Hrubec would take additional pleasure in this interrogation. First, Elena would suffer more than necessary, then she would die.

He rolled up his sleeves. He leaned back in his chair and shut his eyes.

This would be Hamm's first payment, but not his last.

***

Hrubec opened his eyes to a repeated screeching and clanging.

Brang-Wheep-up, Brang-Wheep-up, Brang-Wheep-up.

Michal's supervisor crashed into the office. He ignored Hrubec and went to a panel on the wall. Among rows of green lights, several blinked orange.

Brang-Wheep-up, Brang-Wheep-up, Brang-Wheep-up.

The Chief clicked rapidly on a console, but the blinking orange lights turned a permanent red. The alarm changed to a different more shrill rhythm.

Wheep-up-Wheep, Wheep-up-Wheep, Wheep-Wheep-up.

The Chief cursed.

"There's a fire in hood number 17 on the third floor. The ventilator fan is jammed and there's leakage into Zones A and B. We had a Novichok precursor in Hood 15. Its fan is working, but Hood 15 is in Zone A. I can't take a chance. I have to seal off the third floor and evacuate the building. Come with me."

Hrubec arose. They left the room for the main corridor.

In the corridor, Hrubec watched a technician in a Hazmat suit help a coughing, face-blackened, Michal Pacak, off the elevator.

They were followed by two stumbling security men. Both coughed soot-flecked mucous.

Hrubec glared at them. They were empty-handed.

He barked orders into his cell phone.

***

The scene outside Hus-Kinetika's Maryland plant was one of confusion. The plant had not conducted emergency drills for a year, and the exodus from the plant was not orderly. Workers of all sorts mingled together in a confused mass, awaiting instructions from the authorities. Those who knew of the dangerous chemicals on the third floor, positioned themselves far from the building, ready to flee. Others stared upwards to the third floor, hoping to see a cause for the alarm, but the windowless wall gave no indication of what was inside.

In contrast, Hrubec had organized his security teams. They checked everyone departing the building. Only those with self-contained breathing systems, Hazmat and local Firemen, were allowed to enter. They in turn hustled occupants to the exits.

Hrubec took his stand at the main door. Elena would be forced to leave. She could not escape.

***

Besides the security teams, one other group stood out from the chaos.

Three fire trucks from two local stations, were parked at the ready, hoses primed as they waited instructions. Behind them, several ambulances, motors running, awaited victims for transport. A cadre of EMT's administered oxygen to a dozen prone victims of smoke inhalation.

One ambulance was parked slightly apart from the others. It was to this vehicle that his Hazmat rescuer led Michal. With the help of the driver, Michal, coughing dark mucous, was strapped to a gurney and loaded through the rear doors. Lights flashing, the driver left, as an arriving ambulance took his space.

***

The last straggler was out the building. The fireman signaled "All Clear."

No one had seen Elena.

Hrubec gnashed his teeth and threw himself at the entrance. His own man held him back from the firemen who blocked the doorway.

Snarling, Hrubec stepped back. He motioned his men to search the crowd.

***

Once on the John F. Kennedy Memorial Highway, Highway 95, Tom Fletcher, the driver of the ambulance, switched off his flashers, and headed at a normal pace towards Baltimore.

He turned to Michal's rescuer. Elena Krkova disconnected her breathing apparatus and removed her hood. She unwrapped her hair from its binding.

"Tom, thank God you got my signal. I hoped I would never need extrication. But how did you know to bring the ambulance?"

"Police radio. A major alarm. It's a chemical plant. The ambulance seemed a good cover. But what about you? Where did that Hazmat outfit come from?"

Elena pointed back to the gurney. Michal Pacak was sitting up, holding an oxygen mask to his face.

"It was Michal's idea. Hrubec's goons were after me. He told me to put the full-body suit on. Then he went to the chemical fume hood, jammed the exhaust vent, and lit fire in it. Smoke filled our lab area. Michal inhaled a lot of it himself. He saved me."

She turned to Michal who still held the oxygen mask over his nose and mouth. His eyes were still glazed.

"You saved my life. Are you all right?"

Michal lowered the mask and coughed.

"Not sure. Think so."

Elena turned to Tom.

"He should see a doctor."

"We'll stop in Bethesda. I'll take him to Navy Med. They'll take care of him. Later he may want to cooperate with us."

"Tom, from my point of view, he already has. But I should report to Bill Hamm. Where is he?"

"At a safe house. You'll see him soon enough. He's not far. I already signaled him that you're OK."

In the back, Michal breathed normally. He recognized the name "Hamm" from Hrubec's interrogation.

His eyes shifted from the rear of Tom's head to Elena's and back.

Who the hell are these people?

Michal blew his nose. The Kleenex filled with dark mucous.

He put the oxygen mask back on his face. He never could go back to his job.

Now what?

***

In Virginia, Jim Harrigan drove north along route 15 towards Leesburg. He was alone in his red F250 pickup truck. Blasting from the radio were the classic clangs of Bruce Springsteen and the E Street Band, "Born to Run." Jim's free hand pounded the wheel with the stirring rhythm.

Finally Jim spotted the odd structure on his right, a brick and cinderblock "castle" constructed by some rural "Virginia Knight" to house his family. Jim smiled, if his memory was accurate, the turn off was not far ahead.

He was right. He left the highway for a narrow road that wound alternately through fields and wood lots. As the fields became scarce and the woods more dense he knew he was near his goal. He turned off the music. Somehow stealth and silence were appropriate here.

He saw the iron gate that blocked the passage to a narrow lane. Jim stopped his pickup by the entrance. He looked around but saw no one.

Then he spotted it. Its position had not changed since his last visit, some years ago. Nestled high up on a branch of a large white oak was the camera. His every move was being recorded. Jim pulled out his phone.

"I'm here at the gate. Let me in."

Jim Harrigan stared at the camera so that Bill Hamm could 'ID' his face in the monitor.

Moments later the gate opened.

He hopped back in the cab of his pickup and drove down the narrow lane.

Behind him, the gate closed.

***

Jim parked the pickup under a large tulip poplar. Bill Hamm waited at the door.

"Jim, good to see you. It's been a long time. Thanks for coming."

"It *has* been a long time. I'm glad I could find the house."

Once inside, Jim threw up his hands.

"Whoa! What have you guys done to the place? That's a new kitchen. And the furniture?"

He turned to examine the new furnishings and spotted Ivana on the sofa.

"And you must be Ivana. You've been through a lot, young lady."

Bill spoke.

"Ivana, this is Jim Harrigan. He was my mentor at the agency. He taught me everything I know, well, almost everything."

Ivana nodded to Jim, and turned to Bill with an impish expression.

"Why didn't Jim bring your friend, Jeannine Ryan, to see you?"

Jim raised his eyebrows. Bill ignored her and kept on.

"Jim, I'm glad you can spend the night. Tom Fletcher is on the way here with Elena Krkova, our agent at the Maryland plant. With Elena and Ivana together, maybe we can piece together this puzzle."

He added.

"There's someone else, a Michal Pacak who worked at the Maryland plant. They're treating him for smoke inhalation at Navy Med. Tom's questioning him now. He may have information for us. We'll know tomorrow."

He pointed to a door,

"Meanwhile, get some sleep. We'll all talk then."

***

In Prague, Karel Moravec had slept the night in his own flat. He needed a break from Fiala. She bored him.

He rolled over and opened his eyes. The display on his clock said 5:00 am. He thought of Ivana and sighed. In spite (or because?) of his anger, he wanted her. The woman was a challenge, unlike Fiala.

Karel had convinced himself that he welcomed disagreements and challenges to his authority. In truth, the only appealing aspect of such confrontations was the superiority he enjoyed in crushing the challenger.

He had chosen to forget his anger at Ivana's sharpness. Instead he decided to recall his generosity and tolerance towards her.

In the midst of these comforting thoughts, his phone sounded. It was his team in North Carolina.

Karel checked his clock again. It was 11:15 pm of the previous day on the Carolina coast.

"Yes?"

"Anne Simek and Peter Zeleny are driving back to Chicago together. Should we go after them?"

"Forget them. Simek knows nothing, and Zeleny's only worry is Xolak. Where are Ryan and Harris? And Harrigan, and that woman, Patekova?"

The speaker hesitated. He fingered his well-groomed beard.

"We lost them."

Karel stayed silent. The speaker coughed and continued.

"We think Ryan and Harris went back to Maryland. Harrigan is probably still in North Carolina."

Still silence. The speaker continued.

"We don't know where they are. What do you want us to do?"

Karel spoke slowly.

"You are incompetent. What I want you to do is beyond your capability. Now listen carefully. I am sending you to Erik Holub. He will be in charge of our facility in Warrenton, Virginia. Do you know where that is?"

"Yes Sir."

"You and your men will work in security under Josef Hrubec."

"Yes Sir."

"You will obey Hrubec, understood?"

"Yes Sir."

"For your sake, I hope you perform better for him than me. He is not as tolerant as I."

The phone clicked off.

***

Peter Zeleny left the Pennsylvania Turnpike. At the entrance to the Ohio Turnpike, he hit the button for his ticket. His passenger, Anne Simek, was asleep. Her face was worry-free. The Currituck County Sheriff had approved her leaving North Carolina.

The road sign indicated a rest stop, one mile ahead.

They still had to cross Ohio and Indiana to reach Chicago, and he needed a cup of coffee. He could not risk falling asleep and crashing with this wonderful woman next to him.

Peter was smitten. He loved Anne. One obstacle remained.

Anne's father, Havel, lived with her in their home in Chicago. What would he think?

***

******

Chapter 34
Tuesday, November 30

The morning was unseasonably warm in northern Virginia. Michal Pacak had agreed to share what he knew with the CIA. Thus Bill Hamm had chosen a secure location away from the safe house so that Michal could attend. Bill, Tom Fletcher, and the former agent Jim Harrigan, sat on one side of the table across from Ivana, Michal and Elena.

Elena Krkova leaned slightly in front of Michal, as if to protect him should the questions become harsh.

Bill spoke.

"Ivana, Michal, this is an informal debriefing, and I stress the 'informal,' to see if the two of you can 'brainstorm' together to give us some answers concerning the task force's plans for Novichok-H, in the U. S. or anywhere. Michal why don't you start. What were you told to do?"

Michal leaned forward. Elena put her hand on his arm.

"My orders were two-fold. I was to test the condition of the two Novichok-H precursors to see if there had been deterioration due to storage, contamination from the containers, etc. I should say right away that there was almost no deterioration in the chemicals, and no detectable changes or contamination from the containers. The supply is intact and potent."

Michal added.

"And I had samples from every lot of the main stash."

Jim Harrigan broke in.

"What were the sizes of your samples? And how did you test them?"

"I had a liter of each precursor from about fifty lots, over time about 100 liters in total. I tested each lot separately. I devised a container with two one liter compartments. An external lever had two positions. At the first stop, the interior partition collapsed and the precursors mixed to produce the Novichok Agent. Depressing the lever further, opened a pressure valve that, fully charged, could release a jet spray, for maybe thirty yards."

Tom Fletcher erupted.

"How the hell could you work on something like this?"

Elena jumped in.

"Let him finish."

Michal looked down at the table. His voice was low.

"They told me it was for a war in Africa. It would only be used to deter the other side from using theirs."

After a moment, he continued.

"Anyway, the two-stage lever was not really needed. The precursors mixed and combined rapidly so that the nerve agent formed as the pressure valve opened. You could triple the size and still have adequate mixing without stirrers."

Jim Harrigan spoke.

"How heavy was your unit?"

"Even triple the size, a teen ager could handle it, but it would be easier for an adult."

"What else?"

"I also worked on a container suitable for a 500 pound bomb, like the Mark 82. There the mixing was slower. I devised a system with internal magnetic stirrers. It would have worked too, but I was told to stop. And then that guy Hrubec arrived. You know the rest."

Michal looked sideways at Elena. Bill Hamm took over.

"Two more questions. Is the main stock stored at or near your Maryland plant, and would your two-liter system work for a homicide-bomber."

"A suicide attacker could use it with the right concealment, and no, the stock was not at the plant. For safety, the precursors were stored in two separate locations. Sometimes the samples took several days to arrive, but I think both locations are here on the East Coast."

Jim and Bill looked at each other. Their thoughts were the same.

It's here. God, help us!

***

Throughout Michal's questioning, Ivana had maintained her silence, only nodding to herself to affirm statements that she knew to be true. Now she broke her silence.

"Michal's correct. The main stock was never at the Maryland plant. I know that it was never stored there."

Bill turned towards her.

"How are you sure?"

"From Karel's records. They were in my backpack. The one they took near the airport."

"If not at the Maryland plant, then where is the main stock?"

"I know that the precursors are at two different locations. I can confirm what Michal said, that they are in the U. S. and if I had to guess, I'd say Virginia. All I am sure of is that Karel always referred to the locations as 'Area 1' and 'Area 2,' and that the U. S. is the target. If the agent is in Virginia, I would guess the target is on the East Coast. But that's still a guess."

Bill frowned.

"That's not too much to go on. Ivana, you heard Michal. What do you know about delivery systems?"

"Michal's Maryland plant was more of a research plant. Their work was primarily to verify that the chemicals had not deteriorated in storage. Michal just confirmed that they had not. He did that with a two-liter container. Apparently he went beyond that and devised a corresponding delivery system. That was a neat feat of engineering, but it's not the whole story."

"Why not?"

"Because the main task of the Maryland plant was always the chemistry and small units. Most of the engineering was done in Brno. My understanding from Karel's records is that delivery systems larger than any 500-pound bomb are developed and ready."

Michal interrupted.

251

"Larger than the Mark 82? More than 320 liters?"

"Yes. Karel had specs for much larger tanks. They are already tested. There were special nozzles and internal magnets for stirring to speed up the mixing reaction."

Bill Hamm took over.

"Ivana, no aircraft is going to get near the Capitol or the White House to drop any 500-pound or larger bomb on them."

Ivana frowned.

"I didn't say it was a bomb. The specs were for a large stationary tank fitted with special nozzles. That's all I know. I'm not sure how they could distribute the gas from it."

"Like on the back of truck, sprayed from a truck?"

"Maybe the tank could be pressurized, so there could be a spray. I don't know. I did see that there was no explosive included."

Bill's thoughts were far from pleasant.

First, a legion of suicide attackers with spray tanks, and now large tanks under pressure but no explosives. They want to kill thousands, but how? And where?

But damn it, there's no time. The delivery systems are ready!

Around the room everyone was silent.

***

******

Chapter 35
Tuesday, November 30

Jeannine Ryan and Aileen Harris were once again at their temporary office and refuge, the Best Western Hotel in Rockville Maryland.

Jeannine looked up from her laptop.

"Aileen, I'm going nuts. I can't stand inactivity. I have to search through Vaclav's files again. What am I missing."

"Maybe it's a 'Who' you miss. Why hasn't Bill come to see you?"

"You know he's guarding that informant for the CIA."

"Informant? You mean Ivana. Isn't Donald Trump's ex named 'Ivana'? Wasn't she a model?"

Aileen raised her eyebrows and continued.

"'Ivana,' such a mysterious exotic name, 'Ivana!'"

Jeannine frowned.

"That's enough, Aileen. Yes, I want to see Bill, but you know we aren't married. We don't have a real commitment to each other."

"You could fool me. I think you do. And if Bill ... Oh well it's your life."

Jeannine looked away. She tapped furiously on her keyboard.

Aileen stared out the window at the parking area below. Her face brightened to see a familiar car drive into the lot.

"My mother's here with Mary Catherine. I'm going for a ride with my daughter. See you in a while."

Jeannine heard the door slam behind her.

***

Karel Moravec stared out the window of Fiala's (formerly Ivana's) apartment. Fragile white flakes floated by the window only to melt and disappear on the lamp-lit street below.

He was in a reflective mood. The news from North America irritated him, but overall the plan was moving forward. He had no complaints there.

Hamm, Ryan, Zeleny and Simek, and even Ivana were disgusting gnats who got into his eyes and buzzed his ears. His men had swatted them but the creatures had evaded the blows. They were major irritants!

But soon it would be too late for them to affect the project. Nonetheless, their luck in evading his blows astounded him.

The phone in the pocket of his robe vibrated. Karel answered.

"What is it, Erik?"

"Chief, we have finished half the big tanks."

This was not one of Karel's enforcers, but a trained engineer and a skilled manager. Erik Holub was older than Michal Pacak, but like him, was a graduate of the Technical University of Brno. Erik ran a small company that produced fire-control systems.

"Good, Good. Is there any sign of Hamm or Harrigan?"

"No. No one knows us in Warrenton. Virginia is not on their radar."

"Keep it that way. I told Hrubec to manage your security. Is he there yet?"

"Tomorrow. He was busy sanitizing the Maryland plant. It's clean. There's nothing to find there now. Maybe some pesticide by-products. Nothing else."

Karel hung up.

Outside, white flakes began to stick to the streets of the old city.

His eyes drifted to Fiala's sleeping form. He climbed back into bed.

***

Jeannine's eyes ached. She had been staring at her screen for hours.

Aileen had not returned. Jeannine was alone. She stood and stretched her arms, and gazed out. To the west, the sky shone violet as a red sun flirted with the horizon.

She sighed. The phone on the stand buzzed. Jeannine picked up.

"Ms. Ryan, this is the front desk. A Mr. Harrigan is asking for you. May I give him your room number?"

"Please do, and send him up."

Jeannine drew back the chain and waited by the open door. Jim approached from down the long hallway.

"Jim, where is Bill?"

"He's at a safe house with his informant. He's not free to leave. You know that."

"And you?"

"I'm no longer active with the Agency. I can go where I please."

"So why are you here?

"Bill told me to fill you in on the latest findings. Can I come in?"

"Oh, sorry. Of course. Looks like you've had a long day. Would you like a beer?"

She did not wait for an answer but went to a small fridge and popped two bottles. She handed one to him. He took a swallow and sat. He told her about Michal Pacak and Elena and that the stock of nerve agent was as potent as ever. He added their thoughts about the delivery of Novichok-H using small tanks for suicide attackers, as well as with large tanks by means as yet unknown. He did not mention Ivana.

After a while Jim's speech slowed. He was exhausted. Jeannine pointed to a well-stuffed chair.

"Jim, why don't you sit there and shut your eyes. A nap would do you good. Afterwards I could make coffee."

"Thanks, maybe I will grab some sleep before I go back to the safe house. I'll skip the coffee."

He fell into the chair. His eyes shut, but reopened immediately.

"Wake me up in an hour.

"I will and when you get back to the safe house, tell Bill we need to talk."

"Will do. He misses you."

Jeannine frowned. *Sure!*

Jim's eyes closed. In minutes he was fast asleep.

She went to her laptop.

Vaclav, I know you hid more information on this drive. Where is it?"

She flipped the hair off her forehead while her fingers rapidly drummed the keyboard.

***

Jim Harrigan was long gone when Aileen returned to the Best Western.

Jeannine was asleep, slumped at her computer. At the sound of the door closing, she looked up.

"Aileen, where have you been. It must be the middle of the night."

"I put Mary Catherine to bed, but I fell asleep next to her. She needs a mother. But what about you. Why are you still up?"

"Jim Harrigan was here. The CIA knew about Hus-Kinetika's Maryland facility, the one that you Googled. They had an agent, Elena Krkova, planted there. Hus-Kinetika security found out, and she barely escaped with the help of a chemist, Michal Pacak. It was a close call. Elena's at the safe house now, with Bill and that Czech woman."

Aileen bit her tongue at the reference to "Ivana." Jeannine continued.

"It looks like the main stock of Novichok-H is somewhere in Virginia, and Jim thinks there are two plans for distributing the gas. One is by suicide attackers with converted twin breathing tanks, one for each precursor. Without a mask, the sprayer has a minute or two to aim the spray before dying, but the nozzle will lock open. With a mask, he could continue to spray until the tanks are empty."

Jeannine paused to take a breath.

"The other way is more puzzling. Large tanks that might fit in the back of a pickup truck. Trouble is, best info is that the tank is without explosives. The tanks might be pressurized for delivery."

"That's interesting, but I know you, Jeannine. You've found something beyond what Jim said. Tell me."

"You're right. I did find something."

"Well?"

"I think I know how the plotters will use the large tanks."

"Jeannine, stop teasing. Tell me."

"OK, Hus-Kinetika's home office in Prague required delivery invoices for a certain kind of shipment to list a contact phone number in the U. S. Vaclav made a list of phone numbers from those deliveries for the last two years."

"Why would he do that?"

"That was my question too. Why the last two years? I made a graph of the activity by area code, comparing the previous year with the current one. Look."

Jeannine handed a print-out to Aileen. On it was a bar graph.

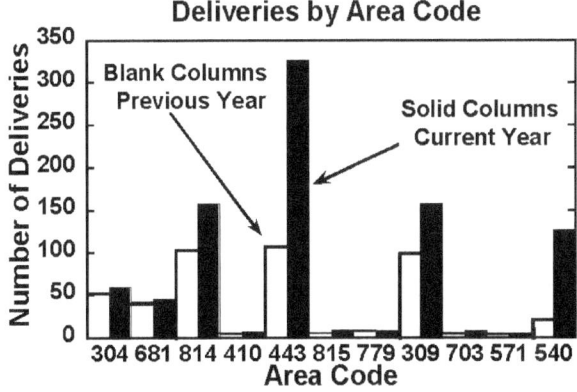

Deliveries by Area Code

"Look, at this. For this year, four area codes have more than 100 deliveries of this type of materiel from Prague, including Area code 443. I checked the phone numbers with that area code. The numbers are for that Maryland plant you found on the internet, the one where Michal Pacak worked. It has a 200% increase in deliveries over the previous year. And we know the conspirators were using that plant."

Jeannine kept on.

"Next I wanted to know what facilities Hus-Kinetika had in these four area codes, so I went on the internet. I found this."

She handed Aileen a second paper. It had a table printed on it. Aileen looked quickly and spoke.

"So the two largest percentage increases for the current year are for Aberdeen, Maryland, Michal's plant, and for Warrenton Virginia."

Area Codes with over 100 Current-Year Deliveries

Code	Predominant Phone Number	Hus-Kinetika Facility	Increase
814	Johnstown, Pennsylvania	Biologics Research Center	53 %
443	Near Aberdeen, Maryland	Pesticide Testing Plant	206 %
309	Peoria, Illinois	Product Distribution Center	60 %
540	Warrenton, Virginia	Unknown Function	477 %

"Right, but the Warrenton code is not associated with a Hus-Kinetika facility, yet it has a huge increase, almost 500%, in deliveries. So I did reverse searches on the numbers. The Warrenton phone numbers are for a small manufacturer and supplier of fire prevention equipment. They produce and distribute SCBA's, self-contained breathing apparatus', as well as fire extinguishers."

Aileen gasped.

"Such as could be modified for suicidal fanatics with nerve gas!"

"Yes, and that's not all, the company makes and installs fire prevention sprinkler systems. And in some cases where the water pressure is less, they install large backup tanks to maintain the pressure in case the supply lines fail."

"So that's their plan. Start a fire and then spray nerve gas from the large tanks through the ceiling sprinklers."

"I think so, but Aileen, do you think the nerve agent would be soluble in water, if it's water pressure that drives it through the pipes?"

"That's hard to say. Organophosphates are all over the map when it comes to solubility in water, as well as fat-solubility. The fat-soluble ones have a delayed toxic effect because the agent is first absorbed in human fat and then released slowly."

Aileen paused.

"The real question is how well does Novichok-H *mix* with water. Let me use your laptop."

Aileen Googled several key words. She looked up from the screen.

"Here's an organophosphate pesticide, *Phosphamidon* that is completely miscible with water at 20 degrees Celsius, that's 78 degrees Fahrenheit. If Novichok-H mixes nearly that well, there should be no problem getting it through the water pipes."

"Then this could be their way of distributing the nerve gas."

"Jeannine, you have to call Bill, now!"

Jeannine looked through the window blinds. The sky to the east was light. Sun rise was near.

She reached for her cell phone.

***

The large warehouse, located some miles off of Lee Highway near Warrenton, Virginia, was filled with activity. At the loading dock, Erik Holub watched his men load the 18-wheeler under the spot lights.

Erik pulled his jacket tight around him. The lights were bright but the air was cold. Still he was pleased.

The destination of this shipment was well-concealed. It had a falsified paper trail. And after this only one more shipment of mixing tanks needed to be "fixed."

Erik sighed. This task was almost completed.

***

The village of Dethorens, Virginia is a "populated place" designated as Code U6 by the U. S. Census Bureau. Some distance away, the similarly designated village of Delaplane is located. Both entities are known for expensive estates and fox hunting.

It was near Dethorens that William Masoud Jones's benefactor had rented a three million dollar mansion located on over one hundred rolling acres of woods and meadows.

A thick growth of white oaks, hickory, black gum, tulip poplars and other hardwoods screened the house from the road and provided needed privacy. On this date, the branches were mostly bare, except for the oaks whose dry twisted leaves refused to fall. No matter, winter or summer the extensive woods blocked all view of the house and its spacious front lawn.

To the sides and rear of the mansion, expansive acres of woodland and alternating meadows stretched to posted boundaries marked either by old fashioned rail fences of locust and cedar, or by overgrown low lines of piled stones. In those fields, Masoud had completed the training of his "volunteer firemen."

Masoud occupied a second-floor bedroom located to the rear. He looked out the window and smiled. Since his arrival in October, no nosy neighbors had visited.

His domain was intact, the training activities had gone undetected. The "volunteer firemen" were ready. All that remained was the final command to complete the mission.

Allahu akbar!

***

******

Chapter 36
Wednesday, December 1

At a booth in the IHOP in Warrenton Virginia, Josef Hrubec and Erik Holub faced each other. Erik sipped his coffee and scrutinized the face of his new Chief of security. Erik had never encountered eyes as dark as these. Perhaps it was the contrast with those pale cheeks?

Hrubec's harsh voice broke into his consciousness.

"Are you through looking? Talk to me."

"Excuse me, I was thinking. What did you want to know?"

"I was asking how many men I have for security?"

"Right now, only two of my welders. When they're not busy, they double as guards."

"From now on, they have no other work than mine. Understood?"

Erik frowned.

"Of course, Karel told me to help as much as I can. But the work cannot wait. We need to modify these tanks. The 'buyers' are impatient."

Hrubec spoke.

"What did you mean when you said 'Right now.'"

"Karel is sending you the North Carolina team. They'll be here this afternoon. Three men."

Hrubec grimaced. *Always Karel, the generous Karel. One day I'll ...*

Erik added.

"When they get here will you still need my welders?"

"First, tell me why your security is so weak?"

"We've never had any of the nerve agent here. The modifications of the SCBA's and those of the large tanks are innocent enough. And we can't be traced to Hus-Kinetika."

Hrubec stared at the engineer. *You idiot! The Americans beat me, twice. They'll wipe the floorboards with you.* He held his tongue a moment, then he spoke.

"Karel is too cocksure of himself. The people investigating Hus-Kinetika are not stupid. Trust me, they will find you."

He changed gears.

"Do you know Ivana Novotna?"

"Karel's mistress? I met her once in Prague."

"She betrayed him. The CIA has her. They got her away from Karel, and when I caught her in Belgium, they got her away from me. In fact, she's somewhere here in Virginia."

This got Erik's attention. Hrubec added.

"They *will* find you. It's only a matter of time. That's why you must speed up your time table. You *will* fix and deliver this last batch of tanks in two days. Your men *will* work all night. When my men get here from North Carolina, you can have your two welders. You will need every worker."

Hrubec was not done.

"Here's a photo of Bill Hamm. He's CIA. Show it around to any men you can trust. Notify me the moment anyone sees him."

He added.

"It's not a question of if he'll show, only when."

For the first time Hrubec lifted his coffee cup. He swallowed and spoke.

"I'm going to finish my coffee. You go back to the shop. You need to schedule double shifts for your men."

***

The car left Route 66 at the Gainesville, Virginia, Interchange and headed south on Route 29, Lee Highway. Bill Hamm drove at the speed limit. On the seat beside him sat Jeannine Ryan. She wore jeans and a sweatshirt. The casual clothes could not hide her feminine appeal.

Outside the wind was chill.

It was the end of the morning rush hour, and on the other side of the highway, the northbound traffic was still "stop and go." In their direction, southbound, cars were few.

Jeannine pushed auburn hairs off her forehead and directed her eyes straight ahead as she spoke.

"Where's your package? I'm surprised you could leave her."

"First, the package is named 'Ivana.' Second, I have to stay with her. It's my job. Either I or Tom Fletcher, my partner, has to be with her. He's there now. That's why I'm here."

"Thanks. It's clear you're not here to see me. You're here to check out this suspicious Warrenton plant."

"That's true, I am working, but it gave me an excuse to see you."

His eyes left the traffic and turned towards her.

"Aren't you glad I'm back in the States?"

She smiled.

"Of course I am, but you'd better keep your eyes on the road."

He had drifted over the line. He guided the car back into his lane and lowered his voice.

"Look, I wanted to see you. It's been a long time."

She smiled and waited. Bill kept on.

"We need time together. Forget the fire-equipment plant. There's an IHOP in Warrenton. We can catch a quick breakfast there before I check out the plant. How about it?"

Jeannine smiled and touched his arm.

"That sounds great. I'd like that. Don't worry. I'll eat fast."

Bill pressed down on the accelerator.

***

Erik Holub, who ran the Warrenton plant, had seen to it, that none of his workers knew the purpose of the tanks they were modifying. All the fixes and alterations were easily explainable as improved devices for fire control systems. Their job was primarily to machine parts and assemble them, mostly by welding.

263

As a manager, Erik knew people. He had seen instantly that Josef Hrubec, in spite of his short stature, was danger itself. And their superior, Karel, was far away across the ocean. There was no time to launch an appeal to him. Besides, evidently, Hrubec was not afraid of Karel.

Erik made his decision. He had to convince the workers that the increased workload was essential to achieve a deadline that he could not adequately explain. He calculated that double shifts (16 hours on, 8 off) were needed for all workers for the two days to convert the sprinkler tanks on time. He drew up the new schedule and called everyone together.

The meeting started badly with angry shouts and gestures.

But Erik understood his men.

He explained to the workers that their hourly rate would be *doubled*, which would result in *quadrupled* earnings because there would be 16, not 8, hours each day. And afterwards there would be no layoffs. After completion, their normal hours and pay would resume.

The assembly quieted. Many nodded their heads in assent. while others appeared thoughtful, adding up their earnings.

Erik climbed onto a stack of wooden loading pallets. From this height he spoke to their higher nature.

"Guys, I have had many different projects."

He scanned the group. engaging each man's eyes in turn.

"And worked with different groups, but you guys are the only ones I would ask to make this sacrifice!"

He paused. Positive murmurs rose above the whir of the ventilator fans. Erik's voice rose in turn to surmount the noise.

"Anyone else would quit, saying that what I ask is impossible, but not you. For you, the 'impossible' is a challenge, difficult, but nothing more."

The murmur of affirmation became widespread. Erik drew strength from it.

"You inspire me. You give me confidence. Together we *will* succeed."

A pause.

"*You* will succeed!

Another pause, then a shout.

"Now let's get to work!"

***

Erik watched the workers quit the assembly. The exit was orderly.

He discerned no hostility in anyone's manner. Some, in small groups, talked with excited gestures. Others smiled at their neighbors with assurance.

He stepped down from the pallets. His knees buckled and he staggered.

His hand shook. The quivering would not stop.

Back in the corner office in the warehouse, he swallowed and gulped short breaths.

He thought of his meeting at the IHOP. Fear and relief mixed to flow through him.

Thank God for my workers. They saved my butt.

He wiped the perspiration from his brow onto his sleeve and let out a deep sigh.

That Hrubec would have killed me.

***

Josef Hrubec sat in the booth at the IHOP in Warrenton, Virginia. He lifted his cup to his lips. *Damned weak American coffee. Just like the flabby Americans themselves.*

He thought of the "masses," he had "rehabilitated" at Bartolomejska Street. They had seen (after some persuasion) the truth that they had been duped en masse by greedy Capitalist overlords who sucked all life out of a society.

But the ignorant American masses wallowed in their system. They were bought and paid for by television sets or large cars, at the cost of losing all ability to think!

In the midst of these thoughts a young family - a mother, father, two girls, and a boy - took the table near his booth.

Hrubec studied their faces. The children appeared happy, and their eyes reflected (he had to admit) intelligence and curiosity.

The youngest was handed a kid's menu. She applied herself immediately to some sort of puzzle for which her father offered advice and comments. The mother was engaged in a serious conversation with the older girl.

The boy, a teenager, was trim and physically fit, obviously into sports. When his order arrived, he attacked his eggs and pancakes with gusto. He only looked up when another teenager, a girl, passed near his table.

Hrubec snorted. Even the U. S. society, bad as it was, could admit a few exceptions. He ignored the family and returned to his coffee.

A waitress refilled his carafe and went on her way.

So the damned coffee is weak, at least I can have all I want. Immediately, Hrubec pushed that sentimental thought out and repeated, *It's too damned weak!* Any affirmation of this culture was a sign of decay in his thinking.

In the midst of his socialist reverie, a woman with red hair entered the restaurant. She was dressed in jeans and a loose sweatshirt. The hostess guided her to a booth in a another section.

Hrubec liked her bearing. She definitely was what the Americans would call "Sexy." He returned to his coffee, but something about the woman's face disturbed him.

What?

All came clear moments later when her partner came and sat across from her.

Of course, Hrubec knew the woman from the photo in his wallet. The redhead was "Dr. Ryan."

As for the man, he was the last person Hrubec wanted to see anywhere near Warrenton.

His enemy, Bill Hamm!

✳✳✳

✳✳✳✳✳✳

Chapter 37
Wednesday, December 1

Back at his clinic in Chicago, Dr. Peter Zeleny, doubled his normal office hours. His absence had taken a toll on his practice. His colleagues had covered well for him, but Peter felt personally responsible for his patients.

Peter worked hard through the morning. Now it was lunch hour. He sat at his desk and studied the chart of his next patient while chewing on a ham sandwich. His phone buzzed.

"Dr. Zeleny, a Miss Simek is on line two."

Peter punched the button, and spoke.

"Anne, are we still on for tonight?"

"Of course, but we might have a problem with my father."

"Have you told him about me? ... About us?"

"Not really, I mean he doesn't know about you, but I told him about your father dying."

"What did he say?"

"Nothing. I mean he said 'Jan' several times. Then he sat in his Lazy Boy and stared. Not a word, just sat and rocked back and forth. He didn't seem to know I was there. And I worry about his heart."

"Anne, you must tell him about us. He loves you. He'll understand."

Anne recalled her father's bulging eyes and ash-purple face when she had shown him Peter's picture in the Chicago newspaper. She was not sure that her father *would* understand.

"I'll talk to him, tomorrow."

The possible rejection by Anne's father darkened Peter's mood. He did not want to lose her to the past or her father. Moreover, the longer they waited to tell him, the more likely that any rift between Peter and Havel would devastate her.

"No Anne. We shouldn't wait. We can tell him tonight. I'll pick you up at the house. I'll talk to him and we'll go out to eat afterwards. Will you agree to that?"

"I guess so. If you think that's right."

"It is and I love you."

Anne's voice was a whisper.

"And I love you Peter. I do."

"Good. I'll see you up at the house."

Anne put down the phone. She was not sure about this.

***

At the IHOP in Warrenton, Virginia, Josef Hrubec sat in his booth. A copy of the Washington Post afforded him ample cover from behind which he watched Bill Hamm and his attractive partner.

They had finished their pancakes and eggs. Now the two were engaged in animated conversation, one filled with smiles and punctuated by laughter from both sides.

Hrubec knew that Hamm had just arrived from Europe. He surmised that the couple had been apart for some time. He saw the joy that arose in each of them, as anxieties and imagined fears were replaced by confirmed affection, and yes, even Hrubec could admit it, love.

Hrubec was pleased. He would use the woman to strike Hamm a lethal blow!

And his reinforcements from North Carolina were less than an hour away.

When Hamm's back was fully turned, Hrubec rose from his booth and slipped out of the restaurant. He muttered.

"All right Hamm, so you know about the fire equipment plant. This time I'm ready."

***

Back at the plant, Hrubec entered the warehouse and strode to Erik Holub's corner office. Hrubec studied the revised schedule and tossed it on the desk. He frowned.

"Hamm is in Warrenton. He must suspect you and this plant."

Erik blanched.

"Then there's no time to finish the containers. I'll tell the men to stop and move another project on the floor. We'll delay the shipment."

Hrubec gripped Erik's arm.

"You will not. You must finish. Hamm cannot act yet. All he has is suspicions. If he had proof, the FBI would be here now. First, Hamm will check you out, sometime today. He'll need probable cause for a search and then he'll have to notify the FBI, so that they can organize it. And they'll have to get a warrant. The Americans are slow about such things."

He released Erik's arm.

"Control yourself. You have, maybe, two days. Push your men harder. Leave the rest to me."

Erik stared in disbelief. Hrubec continued.

"Hamm won't live to tell the FBI what he finds."

The office phone rang. Erik listened and turned to Hrubec.

"Your security men are here from North Carolina. There's a construction trailer to the right as you leave the loading dock. They're waiting for you there."

"Good."

Hrubec had one last instruction.

"Hamm's driving a blue Accord. This is the license plate. This is a photo of the woman with him. Her name is Ryan. Don't be fooled by her looks. She's sharp. Stay alert."

He went on.

"They won't get by me, but if they get by one of my men, you know how to signal me. Just push the button."

Hrubec held out a small device that featured a single red button. His dark eyes read the fear in Erik's.

"Stand up. Be a man. Now go make sure everyone is busy."

Erik turned and left Hrubec in the office.

The farther away he was from Hrubec, the better.

***

At the Warrenton IHOP, Bill Hamm was filled with coffee, pancakes and joy. This time with Jeannine had revived him.

269

He and Jeannine were back on track.

He stood to leave, but Jeannine's face grew serious. Bill paused. *What did I do now?*

"Sit down a minute, Bill."

He sat.

"Do you see that booth over there?

Bill turned to look. It was in the far corner of the restaurant.

"There was a man there. He was watching you from behind his newspaper."

Bill smiled.

"Maybe he was watching you? Guys like to look at you."

"Get serious, Bill. This guy waited until he knew you were occupied. Then he left."

She smiled and touched his hand.

"Maybe you didn't notice him because you were looking at me, thanks. But he left in a hurry by that aisle furthest from us. He did not want you to spot him. When he was outside, he looked at our car. I think he memorized the license plate."

"Are you sure you're not imagining things?"

"I snapped a picture of him through the window."

Jeannine handed him her cell phone.

Bill studied the image, but the face was obscured. He reached into his wallet and put a clean photo on the table.

"Is this the man you saw, short but stocky?"

Jeannine nodded.

"That's him. Where did you get that picture?

"From the files in the Vienna office. Damn. I should have spotted him. His name is Josef Hrubec. He's bad news. Now that he knows I'm here he'll be waiting for me. This confirms your suspicions about this fire equipment plant."

He frowned.

"We have to leave now, but you need to be safe. You need to go back to Maryland while I check out the plant."

He helped her out the booth.

They left.

***

The W&C Fire Equipment Company of Warrenton, Virginia, was accessible by two roads.

The first was a paved two-lane road that left Lee Highway and dead-ended at a gated entrance to the plant and warehouse area. A high wire fence, topped with coils of razor wire, surrounded all buildings of the complex. Eighteen wheelers and smaller trucks used this road to carry supplies and remove finished goods.

The second had not been used recently. It was an unpaved overgrown and rutted "ATV trail" that wound south through abandoned farmland to a narrow road off of Highway 17.

Along that trail, old fields with dense clusters of junipers alternated with wooded tracts of thin Virginia Pines surrounded by vigorous hardwoods that crowded out the dying evergreens.

***

It was late afternoon when Jeannine Ryan and Bill Hamm drove south on Highway 17 past Warrenton. An old billboard marked their turn. A short distance away a red F250 pickup had parked. Its tailgate was down and heavy planks provided a ramp to the ground. At the foot of the makeshift ramp, Jim Harrigan stood next to a mud-splattered All Terrain Vehicle.

Bill got out of the Accord. Jeannine turned the car about, waved to Jim, and drove off.

Bill spoke.

"Jim, you got the ATV, good."

"Here it is. It's full of gas, and there's an extra tank strapped to the side. The rental guys wanted to hose it down, but I said not to worry. Where is Jeannine going?"

"She's going to Hertz in Gainesville. Josef Hrubec has the Accord's license number. She'll swap it for another rental, and head back to Maryland."

"Will she be safe?"

"She should be OK in Rockville at the Best Western with Aileen. No one has found them there yet."

"Why not send her to the safe house?"

"The damned CIA won't let me. No clearance."

271

"What's next, Bill. You said Hrubec is expecting you, I'd better come with you."

"No, but thanks. Hrubec will never see me. I don't need to get inside the plant. I have night-vision glasses. Besides, you're my exit strategy. There's a shack one mile down the road. Park your truck there. Wait for me there, ready to load this thing."

He patted the fender of the ATV and continued.

"Coming back it will be dark. I'll leave the trail and cut through the old fields to that shack. The ATV can weave through the junipers. Anyone chasing me, even with 4-wheel drive, won't make it through them. We'll load her up and go."

"But you still need backup."

"You're it, Jim. Don't worry."

Without further words, Bill mounted the ATV and drove onto the overgrown trail towards the plant. A moment later, he was lost in the twilight.

Jim loaded the planks into the pickup and drove to the old shack.

***

Jeannine knew that Hrubec had the license plate of the Accord, so she returned it to a Hertz office in Gainesville, Virginia. There she picked up a blue Ford Fiesta.

But she did not head for Maryland. She would spend the night in Gainesville, closer to Bill. The nearby Hampton Inn was inviting.

She took a comfortable room and settled in to await a call from Bill.

***

******

272

Chapter 38
Wednesday, December 1

At the Simek home in Chicago, the sound of the TV echoed through the hallway. Anne peered into the den. Her father, Havel, eyes shut, mouth open, dozed in his comfortable chair. The large-screen television blared from the opposite wall.

She slipped into the room and turned the sound lower. Havel did not move. His breathing remained deep and regular.

She was concerned. Her father had eaten little that evening and he needed rest. But there was nothing she could do. He was determined to watch the basketball game. The game would start in about an hour.

Tonight's contest was important. His team, the Chicago Bulls were to play their division rivals, the Detroit Pistons. How he had become a fan of American basketball, she did not know, but he never missed a game. He spent his evenings in that chair.

Anne did not wake him.

Tonight she had reason to leave him be. Peter would arrive shortly, and she could protest to him that her father not be disturbed. The meeting she dreaded would be delayed until they returned from the restaurant.

She looked at her watch. It was time to freshen up before Peter came.

***

Peter waited in the hall while Anne put on her coat. She took his arm. They shut the door after them.

Havel slept in front of the television. The sound of the front door closing entered his subconscious.

The dream always started the same way. A door that opened and shut. A room with a garish pink ceiling under which ran exposed pipes. Lights that blinded and a voice, it had to be his own, that repeated over and over.

"*Nevim, Nevim, Nevim nic.* 'I don't know, I don't know, I don't know anything.'"

And then the blows, many to the kidneys, to the shoulders, the repeated shrieks of pain, his shrieks, always followed by a welcome blackness that undulated to nothing, to an empty nothingness. Nothing at all.

At this point in the dream, half awake, Havel always wiped a wet forehead and loosened his sweat-drenched collar before drifting into darkness through which a voice cursed and pleaded. It was the voice of Johan Zeleny, his "friend," Jan.

"Tell him, Havel! Tell him. For God's sake, tell him."

But what? Tell who what?

More blows to the back, pain, pain, pain, followed by darkness.

Then that final voice. Rasping tones that Havel did not recognize, barely human and surely evil. The voice of the unknown man who was the source of all Havel's suffering.

At this point, as always, he would awake, arms clasped, body shaking.

Tonight was no exception. He stared blankly at his ceiling. It was white.

The television blared as the announcer introduced the Bulls.

The home crowd roared.

Havel shook himself awake. He forced his eyes wide as the game started.

The Bulls won the tipoff.

***

Near Warrenton, a thick growth of juniper branches entwined with thorny Smilax vines blocked the trail. Bill Hamm stopped and dismounted the ATV. He unsheathed his machete and hacked at the tangle. The overgrown vegetation was an irritant, but also a comfort. The trail had not been cleared this past summer. Bill's approach route would not be guarded.

Bill shoved the machete in its sheath and remounted his machine. It was growing dark fast and he was still several miles from the plant.

The ATV rumbled and bumped along. A doe leapt across his path and disappeared between two junipers.

Bill shivered. With the sun gone, the air was cold.

Ahead and some distance to the north, a shotgun blast broke the silence of the mixed pine woods. Startled, Bill stopped the ATV and listened. Had he heard what he thought?

Yes. Moments later a second blast echoed from the distant woods.

Bill started forward, but proceeded slowly.

He thought of the deer he had spooked. It was dark now. If the shots were from some random individual, then a poacher was at work in the woods. On the other hand, if the shots were from one of Hrubec's guards, Bill's route was under surveillance.

Bill had no desire to encounter a trigger-happy poacher in the dark. He had even less desire to shoot his way through an alerted guard.

Bill thought for a moment before setting his jaw. He needed to scout this plant.

He weaved the ATV forward through the brush-invaded trail.

***

Hrubec had studied the layout of the W&C Fire Equipment Company of Warrenton, Virginia. He had hidden video cameras in the trees along the main entrance road. He knew the layout of the grounds.

He expected Hamm to approach along the main route.

But Hrubec was aware of the overgrown trail from the south. There the gate in the high fence had rusted hinges, was thoroughly chained, and overgrown with ivy. The entrance had not been used for years.

But he had underestimated Hamm once, he would not repeat that mistake. Hrubec decided to guard the gate.

For the task, he chose William Johnson. "Willy" was the least-capable (in Hrubec's estimation) member of the North Carolina team. However "least" was relative. Willy not only was good with computers, but highly skilled with an AK-47.

And he knew this area. The year before, he had hunted deer on the unfenced wooded tracts that belonged to the company.

***

Hrubec sat before the TV monitors in his makeshift office in the construction trailer. Where was Hamm? He should have appeared by now.

He leaned back and rubbed his eyes. He was tired. Much had happened in the few days since his arrival in the U. S.

His cell phone vibrated. It was Willy Johnson.

"Sir, someone fired a shotgun not far from here. Two shots. Could be a hunter, but maybe it's your guy 'Hamm.'"

"If it's him, it might be a diversion. Hamm is smart."

Willy waited. Hrubec decided.

"All right. When Hugo gets back I'll send him to you. Hermann will stay here with me. Stay alert. Any more shots let me know right away."

Hrubec scanned the monitors. An eighteen wheeler had stopped at the gate. He watched as Hermann checked the driver and verified that the van was empty.

Immediately after, the van backed to the dock and the loading began. The complex was bright with lights. Forklifts moved red tanks from the warehouse to the dock in rapid succession.

On the warehouse floor, scattered white lights blazed as numerous welders worked hard on tomorrow's shipment.

Hrubec smiled.

All right, Erik, so you made these guys work! But you know too much. One more load tomorrow night and we won't need you anymore.

Hrubec returned to the monitors.

***

Willy Johnson was nervous.

He was on the safe side of an overgrown gate rusted shut and not opened for years, and he had his AK-47 with a 50 round magazine ready to fire, along with two 30 round magazines in

276

his pack. Moreover he had heard no more shotguns, probably just a good old boy sneaking some extra venison for the freezer.

But still he shook and shuffled his feet. He wished Hugo were here with him.

Where was Hugo? Hrubec had said that he would send Hugo to Willy when he came back. Why would Hrubec weaken his security by sending Hugo away? Even with Hugo they were short-handed.

It was dark now and his post was too well illuminated.

He was a sitting duck for an intruder who could eliminate him with a single well-placed shot.

Willy looked about. Not far from the lit perimeter was a tall oak, its trunk thick enough to shelter a man. In the shadows behind it he could watch the gate and be safely out of sight.

Willy lifted his pack by the straps and went to the tree. He took up his position next to the oak.

***

In Chicago, Peter Zeleny and Anne Simek returned to the Simek household. From within, the sounds of a basketball game echoed through the hallway to the outside door. It was late, but the game was in overtime.

They embraced.

"Anne, can I come in? Maybe we could talk to your father now?"

"Peter, the game is still on. He won't like being interrupted. Besides it's best if we give him more time."

"Anne, I don't want to wait. He has to know about us sometime. And my father is dead. What can be the problem?"

"I'm worried, that's all. Please, for me, wait until tomorrow."

Peter seized her and kissed her full force. A voice came from inside the house.

"Anna, shut the door. Is Chicago, not Carolina. The draft is freezing me. I'm watching the game."

Anne looked up at Peter. The tone of her father's voice confirmed that this was not the time to talk.

Peter smiled and kissed her forehead.

"Good night, *Anne*."

He left.

***

At the Hampton Inn in Gainesville, Jeannine lay fully clothed on the bed. Her cell was at her side, ready for Bill's call. She tried to stay awake, but she was tired from the lack of sleep the night before.

Her eyes closed and she dozed.

***

At the southern gate, an unhappy Willy Johnson stood in the shadows of the white oak tree. He was still alone. His reinforcement, Hugo, had not arrived.

Hurry up, Hugo. It's spooky here.

A twig snapped behind him.

Willy wheeled about and peered into the darkness where the perimeter lights were ineffective. He pointed his weapon in the direction of the sound.

He strained to distinguish individual forms in the blackness.

Nothing moved.

***

Josef Hrubec surveyed the bank of monitors. The eighteen wheeler was loaded and on its way. His cameras followed the truck's progress towards Lee Highway. He was relieved. Hamm had not stopped the shipment, and tomorrow night would see the last delivery from this plant.

His phone vibrated. It was Hugo, not Willy.

"Sir, you were right. Hamm's Accord was a Hertz rental. I waited at their Gainesville office like you said. The woman who turned it in rented a Fiesta instead. I followed her to the Hampton Inn in Gainesville. She's there for the night."

"Her face matches my photo?"

"It does. And she has a great shape."

"Her name is Ryan. This is what I want you to do."

***

Jeannine's sleep was interrupted by the buzzing of the phone on the end table. She picked up. It was the night clerk.

"Ms. Ryan, I'm sorry to bother you, but the Hertz rental office just called. There's a problem with the insurance form for your rental. They forgot to give it to you to sign."

"It's late. Isn't the office closed? And how did they know I was here?"

"It is closed and we're the fourth hotel in the area they called. But it was their mistake and they want you covered and don't want any problems with their insurance company. One of their agents is here with the form. May I give him your room number. He'll bring it up for you to sign."

"No. Don't do that. I'll come down."

She slid off the bed, and slipped into her sneakers. The elevator was only two rooms down the hall. She punched the down button and waited. The doors opened and she stepped in.

Out of the side of her eye she saw the form of a man. She tried to back out, but too late. An arm wrapped around her neck. She smelled the strong odor of chloroform.

The elevator doors closed as she slumped to her knees.

Then all was black.

***

Josef Hrubec was still watching the TV monitors, when his cell phone vibrated anew.

"Sir, I have Ryan. I chloroformed her. She's in the van."

"Did anyone see you?"

"I had to talk to the night clerk, but he never saw Ryan, or us together. I trapped her in the elevator."

"Good work, Hugo. That woman is my answer to Hamm. Get her here as fast as you can."

Hrubec sat and rubbed his hands together, but his satisfaction ended quickly.

Automatic weapons' fire resounded from the direction of Willy's gate.

***

At his station by the rusted gate, Willy Johnson fired a second burst into the darkness behind the oak tree.

Again, nothing. No sounds, no rustling leaves. No cries, animal or otherwise, from the deep shadows. Nothing.

He moved towards the fence. The lit area stopped at the rusted gate. Beyond that the fence stretched back towards the warehouse complex.

Willy stepped carefully, to avoid cracking the dry branches that littered the "fire-break" alongside the fence.

All was quiet.

He hefted his weapon. The extra magazines were in his pack at the oak tree, but he was not worried. He had discharged maybe 20 rounds, but it was a 50 round magazine. Still plenty of firepower.

The clouds above him broke and a partial moon lit the fence in a faint glow.

Willy looked up. There, intact but shredded in spots, a thick tarp lay draped over the sharp wire that topped the fence.

Someone had crossed the barrier and was inside!

He was no longer alone.

***

Willy Johnson had to notify Hrubec. He reached for his cell phone.

Damn. It's in my pack.

He spun about. In the dim moonlight, the path along the fence was clear as far as the gate. He retraced his steps, AK-47 ready.

Willy reached the white oak. His pack lay at the base of the trunk.

He stooped to reach for it.

Damn it. Where's my phone?

A sound came from behind him. He looked back. Too late.

The butt end of a 9 mm Beretta smashed his head. Willy fell unconscious.

***

Bill Hamm secured the hands and ankles of the prostrate form at his feet. The ID was a Virginia License issued to a "William Johnson." Bill texted Tom Fletcher at the safe house.

"Check on William Johnson, age 26, Chantilly, Virginia. If he's dirty, call Bill Weaver at the FBI in Manassas to get a warrant to search the W&C Fire Equipment Company of Warrenton, Virginia for him. I'll make sure they find him. I have him tied up."

Bill dragged Johnson's unconscious form deep into the shadows.

During the next half hour, Bill watched the activity at the loading dock. Forklifts had placed a number of large red tanks there, waiting for the arrival of the next truck.

Bill jumped as he heard a whisper from near the gate.

"Willy where are you. This is Hugo. I'm back. Hrubec sent me to help you."

Bill fingered his Beretta. Minutes passed. Apparently Hugo was talking on his phone.

The next words he heard were Hugo's, directed into the nearby trees.

"Hamm! We know you're here. We know you have Willy, but Hrubec has your girl. I tracked her from the Hertz rental in Gainesville. She's dead if you don't come out now."

A pause.

"You hear me, Hamm. Give up. If you want to see your precious redhead again, come out. Now!"

"You have three seconds."

"One, ..., Two, ..., "

***

******

Chapter 39
Thursday, December 2

Jeannine Ryan's head ached and she wanted to throw up.

What? Where am I? The hotel?

She opened her eyes. She was on a dusty tile floor. She struggled to rise, but her ankles were taped together and dizziness overcame her. She lay back against an empty shelf and tried to recoup her thoughts. The desk clerk at the Hampton Inn had talked about insurance forms.

I went to the elevator. There was a man. Ouch, my head!

A bare bulb hung from the ceiling overhead. There were no windows. On either side of her were rows of shelves lined with cartons and small crates.

A storeroom or a large closet? How?

She shook her head to remember.

The elevator! Someone had gripped her neck and thrust a rag over her face. A sickening smell, then nothing.

Her wrists were bound. She tried to twist free, but the duct tape held. She was going nowhere.

She was a prisoner.

***

Erik Holub stood in front of his desk at the W&C Fire Equipment Company. He waited for Hrubec to speak. The latter sat comfortably in Erik's chair.

Finally, Hrubec broke the silence.

"Erik, last night went well, very well. The last shipment is today. Will it be ready?"

Erik looked out over the shop floor. Bright flashes of white light punctuated the work area. Each welding station had twin Oxygen and Acetylene tanks mounted on a rolling cart. All were in use. By each cart, a welder and assistant were hard at work. The whole area was alive with activity.

Erik was satisfied. The men were busy in spite of little rest. He turned back to Hrubec and nodded.

"We'll be ready."

"All right. You can leave now, I need to think about security."

Erik exhaled in relief. As he left, he heard Hrubec's voice behind him.

"Get in here Hugo. We need to talk."

***

Josef Hrubec rose from the chair and paced behind the desk. Hugo stood and waited. A few more paces, and Hrubec turned and spoke.

"All right, tell me again, slowly, you did not find Willy?"

"No. And I went back again in the daylight. There's no sign of him, except his backpack. He's disappeared."

"His phone?"

"Not in the backpack. Willy's gone. There's an old tarp or blanket on top of the fence. He must have climbed over."

Hrubec frowned.

"You said Hamm was there. What made you think that?"

"You told us Hamm would come. When I saw Willy was gone, I assumed Hamm had him. I phoned you first. When you told me to call into the bushes, I did it. I told him to come out, or you would kill the girl. He didn't show."

"But you never saw him, or heard anything?"

"Nothing."

"So you only guessed Hamm was there?"

"Right, I guessed somebody had Willy. I thought it must be Hamm."

"And when no one came out when you counted the seconds, you concluded Hamm was not there?"

"Yes, Sir."

Hrubec stopped pacing. He sat behind the desk and rubbed his eyes. *I need men to work for me, not idiots.* Then he stared at Hugo.

"So you think Willy deserted us, that he ran away."

"Yes."

"Did you ask yourself why Willy would do that?

Hugo stood silent.

"All right, Hugo, there's a cot in the corner. Catch a nap. I'll wake you when I need you."

Hrubec frowned and resumed pacing.

Very clever, Hamm. I know you were there. And you knew this idiot had not seen you. But I have Ryan. You still have to come to me!

***

Hrubec was thorough. He had not survived by being careless. If Hamm were on the grounds, the FBI would soon follow.

He called a certain individual at the Northern Virginia Resident Agency of the FBI in Manassas, Virginia.

That individual had at times performed "innocuous" favors for Hus-Kinetika staff. Today his answer to Hrubec's innocuous question was brief and to the point.

"Yes, they are getting a search warrant for the W&C now. Judge Henley will be back about two this afternoon. He should sign it then."

Hrubec hung up. Rather than being upset, he was pleased. His gut feelings were still sound. The Americans are too slow.

Nice try, Hamm. Too bad the FBI won't be here in time to help you or Ryan.

***

Hrubec picked up his cell to call Erik Holub, but the phone vibrated before he could punch the number. It was Fiala in Prague. She gave no greeting.

"Please hold for Mr. Moravec."

Hrubec gritted his teeth. *You little snit.* He waited.

"Josef, what can you tell me?"

"I have Ryan, and with her as bait, I'll soon have Hamm."

"Good. Now what about W&C Fire Equipment?"

"I moved up the schedule. Half the tanks went out to the first charging area last night. The rest will ship today."

"Excellent. I'll inform our buyer. Anything else?"

"Yes, Holub is a weakling. I'll have to silence him once the tanks are ready."

"No, we need him to supervise the charging of the tanks."

"But last night's tanks are already at Area One. They're being charged now."

"Correct. But they are being charged only with Precursor A. There's no danger until the tanks are moved to Area Two to be charged with Precursor B."

Karel continued.

"If shipping or charging the tanks causes any leaks in the partition, A and B will combine to form Novichok-H. Our men will die instantly. Holub knows that. Go with him to Area Two to supervise the charging with Precursor B. Believe me, he will make sure the partitions have no leaks. He doesn't want to die."

Another breath.

"We need him to install the tanks at the objective. Do not think of killing him before that."

The conversation was over, but Karel did not slam the phone down as usual. He spoke instead.

"Well done, Josef. You are essential to our success. Thank you, comrade."

Karel hung up.

✳✳✳

Hrubec punched Erik Holub's number. He had already lost precious minutes talking to Karel.

"It's eleven am. Start loading the finished tanks for shipment. The Feds are looking for a judge to sign a search warrant. Hamm will have the FBI here this afternoon. We must ship right away. What's your status?"

"The welding is finished, but only half the tanks are checked for leaks in the partitions. That will take hours, and I can't skip these checks!"

"You need to load all the tanks now. You can finish the tests for leaks at Area 1 when they arrive."

Hrubec continued.

"Listen carefully, Erik, I know Hamm is watching us. Pull the eighteen wheeler to the main dock, and have it look ready for loading. Keep some men and forklifts moving around looking busy. Hell, load any junk you want on it."

Hrubec breathed heavily.

"Hamm will watch the main dock. You use the fleet of step vans. Bring them to the side dock. Load them one at a time. Send each off as soon as its ready. Send them in different directions. Tell the drivers you'll call them with final directions to Area One. Just get them on the road now!"

Hrubec's tone admitted no debate.

"Go"

Erik pocketed his phone and went to the side dock.

***

Bill stood behind a large tulip poplar in the woods to the east of the plant. He studied the eighteen wheeler that was being prepped for loading at the main dock. Moments later he saw a step van drive from the other side of the building and leave down the main road. He checked his watch. It was noon.

Bill was torn, tortured. If he had not judged Hrubec correctly, Jeannine could well be dead.

No. I know that man. She is still alive. He would not give up his advantage. He will use her to force my hand!

He called Jim Harrigan who had slept in his truck, a few miles away.

"Jim, did you find the ATV?"

"No problem, and Willy too. You tied him up good."

"How is he?"

"His head is sore. He's tied up in the back of the truck, next to the ATV. It's secured. It won't roll on him."

"Jim, what's the news on the warrant?"

"The judge will be back at two. He'll sign it then."

"Good. They are loading the 18 wheeler now, but the earliest they can finish is four or five."

Bill felt a reprieve. For once the damned red tape worked in his favor. The warrant would not be signed until two. He had at

287

least two hours to locate and free Jeannine before the shooting started.

He studied the eighteen wheeler at the main dock. The activity there had increased.

He thought of Jeannine. He had to get inside the warehouse.

As he planned his next move, another step van drove from behind the warehouse and left. It disappeared down the main road.

***

******

Chapter 40
Thursday, December 2

In Chicago, Anne returned home from the university to fix lunch for her father. The fare was strictly American, hamburger patties, green beans from the freezer and instant potatoes with chives.

She called up the stairs.

"Father, lunch is ready. Come on down."

Her father appeared at the head of the stairs. His eyes were red, his step unsteady.

"Father, what's the matter? What's wrong."

"I didn't sleep good."

"That's because you watched the game. It went into overtime, it was too late for you father."

She reached for his arm and helped him down the last steps.

"It wasn't the game. The Bulls won. I had bad dreams."

"Father, not Bartolomejska Street and the pink ceiling?"

"That too, but it was the last dream that scared me most."

"What?"

"Anna, I was alone. I called you. You weren't there. My little girl was gone. I called and called, but you were gone."

Anne looked away to hide her tears. She took him to the kitchen table and sat him before his plate.

He squeezed her hand.

"Anna, my Anna, what would I do without you?"

***

That morning, Dr. Peter Zeleny had paid the price for his absence from the clinic. Four extra patients had been squeezed into an already full schedule.

Now, collapsed at his desk, his only thought was to be with Anne. They could lunch together.

He called the graduate student office at the university. Another student answered.

"Sorry, Anne is not here. She left some time ago. I think she went home to fix lunch for her father."

Peter hung up. His life with his dysfunctional father, Johan, and his youthful "socialization" in the Pioneers, had not prepared him for personal attachments. He loved Anne, and he struggled to understand her commitment to her father, but he could not relate to such ties. Havel was old, maybe irrelevant. His life was behind him. Surely Peter and Anne were entitled to happiness unencumbered by memories of the past.

He got up from his desk and took the elevator to the lobby.

In the lobby cafe he ordered ham on rye and a coke.

He ate alone.

***

In Warrenton Virginia, Bill Hamm studied the confused scene at the loading dock. All the men were workers wearing jeans and sweatshirts. There was no evidence of security.

Bill, was dressed similarly, in jeans and a sweatshirt. He could not wait. He had to take chances for Jeannine's sake. He edged through the trees to a point closest to the building. Then he lit a cigarette taken from Willie's pack and ambled towards the loading dock.

A voice challenged him immediately.

"You! What the hell are you doing? There's no time for a smoke. Get your lazy butt over here. Who do you think you are? Get to work."

Bill had prepared his answer. He pointed to the eighteen wheeler.

"I'm the backup driver for the rig you're loading. I'll work as soon as you have it ready to go."

"Lazy ass."

The man turned away. Bill climbed onto the dock. The other workers ignored him.

He dodged several "speeding" forklifts and stepped into the warehouse proper.

He was in.

***

Bill looked about the building. Most of the welding stations, identifiable by their twin oxygen-acetylene tanks were abandoned. Only a few were still active as evidenced by flashes of intense blue-white. Numerous small groups of workers were strapping tanks with protective wraps for shipment. The men he saw were ordinary workers, nothing more.

Then Bill spied a tall man with a mustache in a distant corner. He guarded a door to what appeared to be a storeroom. He definitely was not one of the workers. That man belonged to Hrubec.

Bill pulled his cap down to shield his face. He leaned back and felt the reassuring pressure of his Beretta against his spine.

He merged with a small group of men and helped load a tank onto a pallet while the driver of a forklift waited. He stayed with the group as they moved to load another tank nearby.

These workers were ordinary Americans, apparently unaware of the deadly nature of their tasks. He gained little comfort from that observation.

Even less comforting was Bill's observation a few minutes later. Most of the activity in the building was directed away from the main loading dock where he had entered. None of the loaded forklifts headed towards the main dock. They went to another side of the warehouse.

What does that mean? What's going on?

He stayed with his group as they hefted another tank onto a pallet. The forklift speared the wood frame. Its driver, too, headed away from the main dock.

Bill stared after him.

What the ... ?

***

Josef Hrubec stood by the door to the office he had commandeered. He watched the activity in the main area. He was pleased to see that more than half of the tanks were no longer in view. He smiled. *Too bad, Hamm, your stupid FBI and slow legal system do not deserve to survive.*

He studied the workers. Hamm would soon be here, if not already.

He called into the office.

"Hugo, wake up. Get out here now."

A disheveled Hugo appeared at the door.

"Listen. Hamm may be here already. Go look for him on the floor. If you see him, call me, but do nothing. No disturbance. The work can't be interrupted. In one more hour the last step van will be loaded."

Hugo left. Hrubec picked up his phone.

"Hermann, anything suspicious? Any sign of Hamm?"

"Nothing. The girl is secure, and Hamm has not shown his face. What makes you think he will come."

"He'll come, and soon. Stay alert. I'm on my way now."

Hrubec locked the office door and headed onto the floor.

***

Erik Holub was a hands-on manager. He stood on the side dock, and filled out the manifest for the current driver. He waved him on his way and looked to his left. A string of step vans waited to be loaded.

Damn. The forms pad was empty. Too many vans, too many triplicate sheets.

Last night, with a single eighteen wheeler his task had been easier, only one form, albeit long, had been needed.

Erik headed into the building. The room where the forms were stored was near the side dock.

A tall man with a mustache blocked his way.

"You can't go in there."

Erik was nonplussed.

"Who the hell are you? Get out of my way."

The man stood firm.

"Mr. Hrubec says no one gets in."

Erik picked up his phone. He was angry. Momentarily, he lost his fear of Hrubec.

"You want these tanks shipped, tell your goon to let me into my storeroom. I'm out of shipping forms."

Hrubec was too concerned with the shortness of time to take offense.

"His name is Hermann. Tell me what you need. He'll get them for you."

"There's over fifty boxes in there, how'll he find it?"

"All right, hand him your phone."

Erik could not hear what Hrubec told Hermann, but the latter opened the door partway and beckoned. Erik stepped in with Hermann close behind. The door clicked shut.

The windowless room was dark. Erik spoke.

"Light! Damn it, turn on the light, I need to find my forms."

A single bulb came on. Its glare cast shadows on the shelves.

Erik grabbed the box with his forms and turned to leave.

What the hell?

There, on the floor between the shelves lay a woman. There was duct tape over her mouth and around her wrists and ankles. Her eyes sought his.

My God! Erik looked away.

Stolid Hermann stood motionless by the door. At Erik's shocked glance, Hermann shook his head sideways and pointed to the door.

"You leave. Now!"

Outside, Erik took a deep breath. He gestured for his phone. Hermann ignored him and put it in his pocket.

"Mr. Hrubec says if you want to call him, come see me for the phone."

Erik gripped the box of forms and fled to the side dock.

The next step van was waiting to load.

***

When the light went on, and the stranger had appeared in her prison, Jeannine had felt a ray of hope. She had seen immediately that he was not like her captors.

But her hopes were dashed. The man had left without a word and the room was dark once more.

Jeannine was on her own. The chloroform headache was gone. At least now she could think.

The first order of business was to free her mouth of the tight tape. There were two strips, overlapping. She rubbed her face against a metal shelf. After minutes, the edges had rolled back on one side. Pushing her face against the shelf, she rubbed and rolled the loose ends away from her mouth. Moments later the tapes fell away.

She gasped and gulped for air.

It was a small victory, but she could breathe.

***

******

Chapter 41
Thursday, December 2

Josef Hrubec moved among the workers on the plant floor. *Hamm is here, I can smell him.* He spoke into his phone.

"Hugo, where are you?"

"I'm near the main dock. There's no sign of Hamm."

"Get over to the store room. Keep Hermann in sight. Hamm may try something there."

He returned the phone to his pocket. Some distance away, four men lifted a tank onto a pallet. A forklift speared the load and started towards the side dock. The group of men headed to load another tank.

The small group of workers wasted no time. They were already pushing another tank onto a pallet. Hrubec was impressed. Erik Holub knew his men. Erik was weak, but he had succeeded at finishing the work. When the FBI arrived they would find nothing.

Hrubec turned back to see the tank slip off its pallet and pin the foot of one of the workers. A second worker jumped in to restrain the tank and relieve the pressure on his partner. As he did so his helmet fell off his head exposing his face to the light.

Hrubec started. He reached in his coat and gripped his Browning

The rescuer was Bill Hamm.

***

Bill Hamm pushed his shoulder against the tank with all his strength. The worker's foot pulled free. At that, Bill let go and jumped backwards. The tank crashed off the pallet.

The worker balanced on one foot. He looked at Bill.

"Hey, thanks man."

Bill inhaled deeply.

"No problem. Is it broke?"

The man stopped hopping and put his weight on the foot. The result was favorable.

"It feels all right. It's OK."

He grinned and held out his hand.

"They call me Jack."

Bill's hand was lost in the big man's grip. Jack was strong.

"I'm Bill. Let's get this tank back on board."

Two more workers joined Bill and Jack as they wrestled the tank up onto the pallet.

They waited for an oncoming forklift.

***

Hrubec scanned the floor. Most of the tanks had been moved to the side dock for loading, but there was still a number on the floor awaiting pallets. He estimated that in thirty minutes all would be stacked on the side dock, and in another thirty, loaded in the step vans, well before the FBI could be expected.

There would be nothing for the Feds to find!

Hrubec was torn. To apprehend Hamm was to risk disrupting the work in progress. A fracas could cause a delay that would jeopardize finishing before the arrival of the SWAT team.

But the hated Hamm was within his reach. Hrubec had to act.

He slipped quietly through the teams of workers.

At last, he had Hamm in his sights.

He licked his lips.

***

Hrubec lacked neither confidence or ability.

He approached Bill Hamm from the rear and shoved his browning into the small of Bill's back. Simultaneously his free hand felt under Bill's sweat shirt, removed the Beretta and pocketed it.

"Hamm, I've waited for this moment. You're a dead man. Come with me."

Bill did not move, nor did the other workers. Hrubec glared at them.

296

Good. Weak Americans. They freeze.

But Hrubec had no understanding of American workers, or of their friendship, even one of only minutes' duration. Jack faced him.

"Mister, who the hell are you?"

He turned to Bill.

"Who is this guy"

Hrubec spoke first.

"Police. This man is wanted for murder."

Jack was not deterred.

"If you're a cop, show me a badge. You don't talk like an American. Who in hell are you? And get that damn gun out of my face."

Josef Hrubec was short in height, but his frame was solid. Still the man addressing him was built as solidly and on a taller frame. And Hrubec did not want a disturbance in the work schedule.

Bill twisted to answer Jack.

"He's no cop, and he's no American. He's a ... ."

That was enough for Hrubec. He slammed the Browning on the side of Bill's head. Bill crumpled to the ground. Then Hrubec turned to face Jack.

Jack was quicker. He grabbed Hrubec's wrist and twisted leaving the Browning dangling from useless paralyzed fingers. Not done, he seized Hrubec by the neck, and slammed him on the floor.

The Czech's eyes glazed over. Bill's Beretta fell loose and clattered on the tiles. Jack stuffed it in his jeans, and lifted Bill up.

"Come on buddy. I don't care if this guy is a cop. He's messed with the wrong crew."

Jack glanced at Hrubec. He was out cold.

With Bill's arm about his shoulder Jack walked him towards the main dock. He yelled over his shoulder to the other workers.

"If that 'cop' comes to, tap him on the head again. Take him to Mr. Holub. He's on the side dock. He'll know what to do. I got to get my friend out of here."

Had he been conscious, Hrubec's sole consolation would have been that, aside from Jack's crew, the mass of workers continued their tasks without interruption.

***

The SWAT members assembled behind the massive five-story FBI building outside of Manassas, Virginia. Black Kevlar vests and automatic weapons were the rule as they awaited word that Judge Henley had signed the warrant.

A Hazmat team waited also, along with Tom Fletcher, Bill's partner, who stood nearby with Michal Pacak.

Tom had left Elena Krkova to guard Ivana at the safe house. Michal was here to provide expert assistance with bipartite canisters and tanks.

Tom prayed that none of the containers contained "live" mixed precursors. He shifted his feet. It was nearly 2 pm.

Damn. How long could judge Henley take for lunch?

The SWAT commander put his phone to his ear. He held his thumb up and nodded to Tom.

"The warrant is signed."

Moments later a caravan of vehicles turned onto the 234 By Pass that skirts Manassas and headed towards Gainesville and Route 29 to Warrenton.

The W&C Fire Equipment Company was forty five minutes away.

***

Jack put a dazed Bill Hamm into the passenger seat of his F150 pickup, and strapped him in.

"It's OK buddy. We're out of here. My place is not far. You'll be all right there."

Bill tried to speak.

"Jeannine, ... Jeannine."

Jack smiled.

"Whoever she is, we'll call her. Don't worry. You'll have a headache, but you're going to be all right."

A car pulled in front of Jack. He braked and felt the pressure of Bill's Beretta against his stomach.

"I've got your gun for you. But who are you? Don't worry, I owe you. You can tell me later."

Bill mouthed 'Jeannine,' but his lips refused to part. The effort was too much. He drifted into darkness.

Jack drove on.

***

Hrubec opened his eyes. His head pounded.

His vision cleared. He was on a cot in the warehouse near the side dock. Just outside stood Erik Holub, clipboard in hand. Erik was busy writing something. *Of course, the step vans.*

Hrubec sat up, or tried to. A sharp pain shot across his forehead, behind his eyes. He slumped back. He pushed himself up again. Success. He called towards Erik.

"Where the devil am I? What happened."

Erik continued to write, his eyes fixed on his work.

"The men brought you here. You fell against one of the tanks as it was loading."

"They assaulted me and you know it."

Erik turned and stared.

"You were on the work floor, without a helmet. My men know what they are doing. You don't. I believe them."

Hrubec grimaced. *You simpleton, I will kill you, as soon as Karel permits, maybe sooner.*

He struggled to take in his surroundings. Only one step van remained in line behind the one loading at the dock. He focused on his watch. It was time to leave, but first he needed information. He spoke.

"The men who brought me here, who were they?"

"They were part of Jack Cannon's crew. One of my best."

"Jack Cannon?"

"A big guy. Huge, you can't miss him. But he wasn't with them."

Hrubec stood from the cot. He balanced himself and took a step towards Erik.

"Where's this 'big guy' live?"

"Haymarket, up on Bull Run Mountain somewhere."

Hrubec was amazed at Holub's naiveté. *You idiot. You just signed Cannon's death warrant.*

Hrubec was not done. He still had to deal with Jeannine!

"Where are my men?"

"Your two goons? They're guarding the store room." They've been there the whole time."

Hrubec turned in that direction, but his legs refused. He fell back onto the cot. Erik's face spun in circles before him. *Not now. I must ...* His eyes closed.

Erik frowned. Most of the workers had been sent home. The plant was nearly empty. Hrubec would have to take care of himself.

Erik signaled the last van to approach the dock.

***

******

Chapter 42
Thursday, December 2

The FBI SWAT team arrived to an empty building. Throughout the main floor, abandoned work stations with twin tanks of oxygen and acetylene gave testimony to the intense activity of the morning.

An initial inspection by the Hazmat team revealed no evidence of dangerous substances. Chemically, the plant was clean.

While the FBI searched the plant, two elderly watchmen arrived for duty. They were totally bemused at the empty installation. Neither could offer information concerning the vacant plant. They knew nothing of activities prior to their arrival.

Their only information of interest was that their services had not been needed the two previous nights.

Jim Harrigan had joined Tom Fletcher and the FBI upon their arrival. He had handed Willy Johnson over immediately. Willy was wanted on two additional warrants, beyond the initial ones. He would be in jail for some time.

But Jim was deeply disturbed. Tom too.
Where was Bill? And Jeannine?
Were they alive?

***

The brown van headed north on Lee Highway, Route 29. Hermann drove. Josef Hrubec sat in the passenger seat. The vibration from the road accentuated his headache, but his main suffering was from frustration and failure.

He groaned silently.
Damn you Hamm.
From the back seat, Hugo leaned forward.
"Why don't we kill the woman now? Why are we keeping her?"

Hrubec turned and gave him a baleful stare.

"Shut up. You want to lead this party?"

Hugo froze. Hrubec continued.

"Check on her ankles and wrists."

Hugo looked on the floor behind his seat. Jeannine was securely bound. He turned back to his Chief.

"She's not going anywhere."

Hrubec turned to the driver.

"Hermann, turn left ahead, onto Old Carolina Road. We're going to Haymarket and Bull Run Mountain."

"But you said you wanted to go to Area One to check on Holub."

Hrubec licked his lips. This was personal. Jack Cannon would die, and Hamm would see his girl tortured before he himself came under Hrubec's knife. He spoke.

"Later. First, I have something I need to do."

Hermann swung the van onto Old Carolina Road.

***

In Prague, the sun had disappeared leaving an eerie twilight that cloaked the streets of the old town in hazy shadows. Karel Moravec stood and watched the smooth waters of the Vltava ripple their way under the Charles Bridge. To his German mother, the river was the "Moldau," but his mother had been a gentle woman and pliable. His Czech father had not allowed Karel to use that name.

Karel's phone vibrated. He shook the thoughts of his mother out of his head and punched "Talk."

"Yes?"

Erik Holub spoke.

"The last tanks are on their way to Area One. I'll check the partitions on them tomorrow. We had to ship early because the FBI was coming. After I check, I'll supervise the loading with the first precursor, and then move them to Area Two for the final loading."

"When do you think you'll be done at Area Two?"

"Hard to say. We don't want to die. It will be slow."

"How slow"

"Two days, at least."

"Erik, you're doing well. Finish fast, but do not take unnecessary risks. The sooner we hand over the Novichok-H to the crazy jihadists the better. Let them kill themselves if that's what they want. We need to get our money and get the hell away."

On the other end of the line, Erik agreed with that assessment!

On the Charles Bridge, the lamps came on. Prague at night, what splendor! Karel watched a moment in appreciation as he evaluated the situation in Virginia.

Josef Hrubec called Erik Holub a weak link. Yet Erik had achieved the nearly impossible task of finishing the tanks and shipping them in only days.

Karel needed Erik.

"Erik, Hrubec hasn't called me. Where is he? He's supposed to be with you. He needs to secure Area One."

Erik hesitated, swallowed and spoke.

"He left me. He took Hermann and Hugo. They're going to the house of one of my workers. It's on a ridge called Bull Run Mountain. The other direction."

"What?"

"He's crazy. He wants revenge because a worker beat him up. He has forgotten the mission. He thinks someone named 'Hamm' will be there too. And he's kidnapped Hamm's woman. It's all personal with him."

Karel frowned. *So Hamm is still alive. Josef, leave him alone. The mission comes first. You know that. Damn it, Hrubec! We're almost done with our part. Don't screw up now.*

He spoke.

"Erik, you go to Area One. They need you there. I'll call you later."

He hung up.

303

Across the river the Prague Castle glowed, but now its beauty was lost on Karel. He muttered.

"Hell, Hrubec, what *are* you doing?"

***

Erik Holub drove north on Route 17, away from Warrenton, Virginia. He had planted a seed in Karel's mind about Hrubec, but how long would it take to ripen?

Erik was fearful. Hrubec was ruthless. As soon as Eric's usefulness ended, Hrubec would get rid of him.

Karel needed both him and Hrubec, but once the tanks were finally loaded, he would have to choose between them. Whatever choice Karel made would be based only on logic and necessity. Besides, Karel was far way!

Erik shivered. If he were to survive he needed to act. There was one way to deal with Hrubec.

He put a handkerchief over his mouth and called the Prince William County Police in Manassas.

"I want to report a kidnapping. A woman, maybe 28 years, red hair. Three men forced her in the back of a brown van with Maryland plates. I trailed them to Bull Run Mountain, some house on Mill Creek Road.

Erik guessed that Hrubec was headed to Jack Cannon's house. He continued.

"These men are armed. They're dangerous. You have to act fast."

"Sir, who are you? What is your name?"

"It's not important."

"Click."

Take that Hrubec!

***

Jack Cannon stood by the rear door of his house on Bull Run Mountain. He had put Bill Hamm on the bed in the spare room, now he had a moment to rest. At the rear of his lot, the thick dry woods, mostly oak and hickory, were dark in the twilight. Nothing moved.

Jack lived in the same house that his father had built in the late forties, after the war. Some said that Jack Senior had operated the last still on Bull Run mountain and that his whiskey had been the most popular of any local's.

Jack could not verify that, but before his father's death (Jack was twelve) he often had heard his father complain about the Feds and their "new" helicopters.

"All they do is fly around till they see smoke curling up through the trees where nobody's supposed to live. Then they come back later and wreck the still and spill the liquor. It's a waste and it ain't fair. A little 'White Lightning' never hurt nobody?"

His father was long gone, but Jack kept his independent spirit. The concern now was not for Treasury agents, but the local game warden. The woods in the back of Jack's house were full of pampered and protected deer, and Jack liked venison.

To keep his freezer supplied, Jack had hidden a salt lick not far from his back door. Thanks to this "lick," and a pump-action 12-gauge (loaded with buckshot) his freezer was never empty.

The only problem posed by this "hunting" was the secret disposal of the hides and bones, but this he accomplished in an ingenious way thanks to plastic contractor sacks and the Prince William County landfill.

Jack's lack of respect for the law's technicalities had served Bill Hamm well earlier this day. That man (Hrubec) had identified himself as the police, but Jack had struck hard and fast. It did not matter whether Bill's assailant was telling the truth. Cop or not, he had hurt Jack's friend. That was enough.

Jack left the back door and went to the spare room. He looked in.

On the bed, Bill Hamm slept. A thin line of blood marked where Hrubec's Browning had made first impact.

Jack wandered back to the rear door and stood looking out. In the twilight, a graceful doe slipped out of the woods and delicately approached the salt lick.

Jack laughed.

That doe was lucky. His freezer was full.

***

In the back of the van, Jeannine was sore all over. Every pothole and bump on the road up Bull Run Mountain had transferred its energy directly to her cramped limbs and weary torso.

And she had difficulty breathing. When Hugo had moved her to the van, he had noted that her mouth was free. Now it was taped again.

Her body jerked forward and then rolled backwards as the van came to a stop. She froze. The voice she heard was Hrubec's.

"Hermann, that's the big guy's house we just passed. You work your way through the woods and go around back. Cover the back door. I'll walk back down the road. There's a tree in the front yard. I can cover the front door and the large window from there."

A pause.

"When you're ready in back, whistle. We'll move in at the same time."

She heard the driver's door shut, steps leave, and once more, Hrubec's voice.

"Hugo, you stay here with the bitch. I'll call you when we have Hamm."

Bill's alive!

"I want him to see his woman die before I finish him."

But for how long?

Jeannine struggled against her bonds. They did not yield.

Despair and fear filled her.

***

The rear door of his house was Jack Cannon's favorite spot to appreciate "nature," meaning that from there he could spot a target when the freezer was low. But this evening he was not "hunting." The quiet doe at his "lick" proved that.

As Jack studied the peaceful woods, another form appeared in the shadows.

From the dark foliage, a young buck stepped gingerly into the clearing. A six-pointer, it froze, and checked sideways before taking another step. This was no trusting doe, but a skittish male well aware of the dangers about him.

The buck froze again, looked to either side, and then stepped forward to the salt lick. The doe backed off to wait her turn.

Once more the buck looked to either side. Only then did it lower its head.

Instinctively, Jack reached for his shotgun, full freezer or not.

The buck's tongue never reached the salt. He lifted his head and froze, wide ears focused toward some sound not audible to Jack. The pose lasted but a millisecond.

"Crack, snap. Crash!"

Branches broke as the buck sprang backwards and bounded, white tail flapping, into the brush. The doe hesitated a split second, then followed.

Jack's grip tightened on the shotgun.

Peace had departed the back yard. Something, or someone, had spooked that buck.

He pumped a shell into the chamber.

***

Josef Hrubec stood by the tall Pin Oak in Jack Cannon's front yard and waited for Hermann to whistle that he was in position. That signal never came.

"Brroom."

The dull blast of a shotgun broke the evening stillness, followed immediately by an agonizing scream. The next sound was that of Herman's assault weapon.

"Brup, ..., Br, Br, Brup."

But that burst was brief.

"Brroom."

The shotgun again, then silence.

Hrubec stood motionless in the protection of the oak. The light in Jack's front room went dark. Whoever was inside was scanning the front yard.

Hrubec did not move. He waited a moment and then retreated into the roadside brush.

Hermann was gone. That was clear. Hrubec was on his own.

With surprise and Hermann on his side, he had liked the odds, but his Browning against a shotgun? *No thanks.*

Sticking to the shadowy shoulder, he headed back to the van. The Ryan woman must die. Now!

As Hrubec rounded the bend in the road, not only his van came into sight, but also two police cars with red and blue lights that flashed crazily.

He saw Hugo, face on the hood of one car being handcuffed from behind, while other police, guns drawn, addressed the van front and rear. *Hapless Hugo!*

Moments later, a limp Jeannine, her legs and arms free, was helped from the van.

Hrubec turned as an ambulance, siren wailing, raced in his direction. A third police car followed.

Hrubec ducked into the brush.

On the map he saw that a nature preserve was nearby. It was his only chance. He could get lost there.

Hrubec holstered his Browning and pushed blindly through the scratching branches.

***

******

Chapter 43
Saturday, December 4

The Prince William Hospital in Manassas Virginia is a medical complex of several buildings. The main entrance from Sudley Road offers only valet parking, but drivers are allowed to wait for short periods to pick up or discharge patients.

Jim Harrigan, his freshly washed F250 clean after its Warrenton exploits, waited, motor running, for Bill Hamm to appear.

Behind him, its path blocked by Jim's pickup, another truck also waited. Jim did not recognize the driver, but the truck was a member of the "Ford" fraternity. The silver pickup was an F150 with an extended cab.

When the aide pushed Bill Hamm's wheelchair out the doorway, Jim was surprised to see a man jump from the F150 and give Bill a warm hug.

Jim stepped down from his truck and broke in.

"How are you Bill? And who's this?"

Bill stood up straight from the chair.

"I'm fine, the damn wheelchair is a formality, something about hospital liability. They kept me for observation. Nothing's wrong. And Jim, this is Jack Cannon. He saved my bacon twice, once at the plant and again back at his home on the mountain. He decked Hrubec at the plant, and when Hrubec and his thug followed us to Bull Run Mountain, Jack shot the thug, the tall one with a mustache."

Bill paused.

"That guy's enjoying a "dirt nap" thanks to Jack."

He added.

"Otherwise I wouldn't be here today."

Jim Harrigan studied Jack's eyes. He smiled and put forth his hand. Jack seized it and spoke.

"It was what any friend would do. If it weren't for Bill I'd be lame and on crutches."

Jim Harrigan was about to reply when another aide pushed a second wheelchair through the automatic doors of the hospital.

A liberated Jeannine jumped to her feet. After hours of observation she was free.

There were smiles and hugs all around, but her last and longest was for Bill. He did not let go.

Jack Cannon turned to Jim Harrigan.

"Bill's a lucky guy. It looks like that redhead will take good care of him."

"They're good together."

Jim changed the subject.

"Jack, you can't go back to the Fire Equipment Company after the way you handled Hrubec and that thug Hermann. You'd better look for another job. Why not law enforcement?"

Jack's insides jumped. *Me, a cop, is this guy for real?*

He studied Jim's eyes. *Damn, he means it. But give up my salt lick? My venison?* He switched the subject back to Jeannine.

"I'm told the redhead, Ryan, is a 'brain.' Is that true?"

"No doubt about it. Both she and her partner, Aileen Harris, have Ph. D.'s. They work in stats and biology."

"What's Aileen look like?"

"She's pretty, a blonde."

"Why isn't she here? I'd like to see for myself if she's like her partner."

"She took her daughter to her aunt in Pennsylvania."

"Daughter?"

"No worry. She's divorced. Maybe you'll meet her someday."

At this point, Jeannine came towards them. She gave Jack a big smile and a warm two-hand shake.

"I want to thank you for saving Bill. He's told me all about you."

She grinned.

"Also, I love venison. I grew up in West Virginia. My dad kept his freezer full too."

Jim Harrigan laughed.

"It's good you and Bill are both OK. I have to go back to North Carolina now. Mila's waiting. You guys be careful."

He hopped into his truck, waved, and left the patient discharge area.

Jeannine turned back to Bill and Jack Cannon.

"I'd better call Mila and let her know Jim will be back on the Banks in time for supper tonight. But I'm famished. Let's eat lunch. I'll pick Jack's brain about Warrenton and the W&C Fire Equipment Company. We can take my car, the blue Fiesta over there by the street."

Jack laughed.

"I don't ride in dinky death traps. We'll take my truck. It has an extended cab. Bill, you get in back. Jeannine, sit in front and we'll talk."

Jeannine smiled and hopped into the front seat next to Jack.

Bill sat in the rear.

Jeannine stopped smiling.

"Now, Jack, tell me about the different sorts of tanks you worked on at Warrenton. And all you know about where they were shipped."

***

In Prague, Karel Moravec was irritated. His forehead was damp, and his armpits were like twin saunas under his elegant personalized shirt. Worse yet, his unease was visible to Fiala who stood before him. Even the massive desk did not hide his discomfort.

He shouted into the phone.

"Holub, where are you? Where is Josef? "Why isn't he with you?"

311

"We're done at Area 1. I'm on my way to Area 2, but Hrubec is on the run. The police are looking for him. Hermann is dead and they arrested Hugo."

"What happened?"

After calling the police on Josef Hrubec, Erik was not about to defend him.

"Hrubec forgot the mission. He had a personal vendetta against Hamm and his woman. What more do you want me to say?"

"All right. Where are Ryan and Hamm now?"

"Our source says they're at Prince William County Hospital. They will be released today."

Karel calmed himself. He must regain control. Fiala had not taken her eyes from him.

"All right, Erik, forget Hamm and Ryan. Where are you?"

"I'm close to Area Two now. Yesterday, I finished the loading of the first precursor at Area One. Everything arrived except one step van that broke down."

Erik swerved to avoid a truck that had drifted into his lane. He resumed.

"When I get to Area Two, I'll check for leaks before we load the second precursor. Any mistake and we're dead."

"Erik, calm yourself. Don't forget you have the Xolak. You are almost done. Our part of the mission will be complete, and you and I will drink *pivo* together in Prague. I promise you a good time."

Karel winked at Fiala. He was in control once more and Erik was on schedule.

"Click."

Erik sighed. If the police would find Hrubec, then he could relax.

He thought again. *Relax?*

He would be loading the damned binary tanks with nerve gas!

His hands shook on the wheel.

***

From behind his desk, Karel frowned. He would confirm his superiority. Fiala needed training if she was to replace Ivana.

"Fiala, I have a task for you. It concerns Vaclav Pokorny, and Xolak."

"But Vaclav is dead."

"Precisely. The task is simple. Search my files and find out what Vaclav discovered about changes in Xolak, and how he attempted to use that information to betray me."

He sensed her insecurity. *Good.*

"You will give me an oral report tomorrow. And do not speak of this to anyone."

Any sense of weakness that Fiala had perceived in Karel evaporated. She knew he detested failure.

Nervous, she went to his files and withdrew some papers.

She left quietly.

***

On the outskirts of Johnstown, Pennsylvania, Aileen Harris sat in Aunt Agatha's kitchen. The past week had been hectic, but today the house was peaceful. Aileen's mother and her aunt had taken Mary Catherine to eat at McDonald's, one with a play area.

Aileen relished the quiet.

She opened her laptop to study Vaclav's files. Jeannine had copied Vaclav's drive onto the company computer, but Aileen still had his TUFF-'N'-TINY™ drive. She inserted it into the port and typed the password.

PetrZelenýjesvobodný.

She was in.

Although cold outside, the sun shone into the bright kitchen, and the screen reflected Aileen's image back at her. She shifted the computer to eliminate the glare.

Vaclav had worked in the pharmaceutical division of Hus-Kinetika. He had sent Peter Zeleny the critical memo that confirmed Peter's observations (and Jeannine's analyses of fake data) for the FDA. And Vaclav had used the crumpled newspaper packing to tell Zeleny the password for the chip with the fabricated data that the conspirators had submitted to the OPCW to prove that the Novichok-H had been destroyed.

But something was missing.

What connection existed between Xolak and the agent Novichok-H?

Why had Hus-Kinetika persisted in pushing Xolak on the American market?

Why risk fabricating Xolak data? Why not withdraw the drug, and avoid investigations that could lead to Novichok-H?

***

Aileen rubbed her eyes. She scanned Vaclav's folders. She was intrigued by one with the name "Plants." Perhaps it referred to production facilities? She opened it.

But the "Plants" were not facilities at all, but weeds.

In one file, Vaclav had listed scholarly articles on members of the "Potato family," the *Solanaceae*. One of these, *Atropa belladonna*, the "Deadly Nightshade," was widespread in Europe and introduced as a weed in parts of North America. This plant was notorious. The poison that killed Emperor Claudius was thought to be an extract of it

Vaclav also had listed another member of the Potato family, Jimson Weed or *Datura stramonium*. This North American plant had parts and seeds that could be used as hallucinogens.

Hallucinations? Surely Vaclav was not interested in hallucinations?

Wait! She paced and murmured to herself.

"Deadly Nightshade is a source of the drug Atropine and the leaves and stems of Jimson Weed also contain Atropine. But injection with Atropine is used to treat organophosphate poisoning where surplus Acetylcholine binds to receptors on the nerve's sodium channel so that the nerve cannot fire. Atropine counteracts the Acetylcholine at those receptors so that the nerve can fire."

She kept pacing and muttering.

"And the injected antidote often includes something else, namely a pyridinium oxime, like Obidoxime or Pralidoxime to restore the enzyme cholinesterase by freeing its active site from the poison compound, so that enzyme once again can break down acetylcholine."

Bingo!

Sometime around 2002, Hus-Kinetika must have altered the composition of Xolak by increasing the level of Atropine and adding a pyridinium oxide, thereby changing Xolak into a treatment for nerve gas poisoning.

The conspirators wanted to protect themselves and their workers from the nerve gas.

But the altered Xolak had bad side effects and Peter Zeleny had seen them in his patients."

Aileen rushed to the phone in the hallway.

Peter knows Xolak. If it includes these compounds, that confirms that Xolak is an antidote for Novichok-H.

Hurry up, Peter, answer the damned phone!

***

But Aileen's call to the clinic in Chicago, was a bust. Dr. Zeleny was not expected. He was at home.

At first the receptionist refused to give Peter's number to Aileen, but she identified herself as "Dr." Harris and stated the urgency of the matter. Finally the receptionist relented.

When she called Peter's home number, a woman answered. Aileen spoke.

"May I talk to Dr. Zeleny?"

"He's not on duty today. Call the office and speak to his associate."

Aileen recognized her voice.

"Anne, Anne Simek is that you? It's Aileen Harris, I need to talk to Peter."

315

There was no response. Aileen thought they had been disconnected, but then heard Anne's voice in the background.

"It's Aileen Harris. She wants to talk to you."

Peter came on the line.

"Aileen. What's this about?"

"Peter, it's Xolak. Tell me what you know about its active ingredients? I think I know why Hus-Kinetika wants it available. It's an antidote for their nerve gas."

Moments later, Peter had confirmed her suspicions. Aileen hung up.

She needed to call Jeannine.

***

As soon as Peter Zeleny put down the phone, Anne spoke.

"What did Aileen Harris want?"

"She thinks Hus-Kinetika has modified Xolak to be an antidote for their nerve gas. I think she's right."

"But this number is unlisted. Why did you give it to her?"

"She must have gotten it from the clinic."

Anne dropped her eyes. Peter took her arm.

"Anne, will you forget Aileen? I only care about you. I *love* you. You have to know that. Trust me, and trust me tonight too. I promise to be careful when I talk to your father. Are you OK?"

"I think so. Please be careful, and I do trust you. It's all arranged. Father's expecting you."

Anne forgot Aileen. A more important concern was Peter's visit to her house.

How would Havel Simek react to the son of his betrayer?
***

Jeannine was enjoying burgers and fries with Bill and Jack Cannon in a diner not far from the hospital, when her phone vibrated.

It was Aileen in Pennsylvania.

316

"Jeannine, I know why Hus-Kinetika cheats to keep Xolak on the U. S. market. Xolak contains Atropine as well as two distinct pyridinium oximes."

Jeannine swallowed and cleared her throat.

"Aileen, please make sense."

"Injection with these compounds treats cholinesterase inhibitors."

"So?"

"Don't you see. Hus-Kinetika can use Xolak to treat Novichok-H poisoning! They're planning something big with their weapon. They want their people protected. That's why they kept Xolak on the U. S. market. They need it to ensure that their own crooks feel protected while they work on that damned nerve agent."

***

******

Chapter 44
Saturday, December 4

At Area Two, a large farm on Remount Road, south of Front Royal, Virginia, Erik Holub, stood in a field, removed his Hazmat helmet, and surveyed the rows of shiny red tanks before him.

There were two types, small and large.

The small tanks were joined in groups of three with straps, evidently intended for the backs of individual "firemen." One of the three was intended for oxygen, while the other two, connected by a complex valve, were, respectively, for the two precursors of Novichok-H. The first precursor had been loaded at Area One.

The large tanks posed a separate problem. These bipartite tanks also had been loaded with the first precursor at Area One, but their interior partitions were largely inaccessible, and some had possibly defective welds that needed to be checked for leaks before the second precursor could be loaded.

Any leak would be lethal.

***

After several hours, Erik, and his technicians, finished their checks for leakage from the first compartment into the second. Only two tanks had defective welds. These were immediately discarded.

Erik sighed. The moment he dreaded had arrived. He could no longer delay the loading of the second precursor into the remaining empty partitions. Any mistake and the precursors would react to form Novichok-H and death would result.

He and the technicians donned their Hazmat suits, sealed the helmets, and started to work. Each man had a syringe filled with Xolak nearby. They were ready.

With great care they checked the special valves on the tanks. All were OK.

Erik signaled to his men and the loading began.

The first tank was filled without mishap. It sat silent and innocent on its pallet. It would not be moved to the van until the remaining tanks were loaded.

Erik exhaled in relief. *Maybe this will work after all.* He thought of the money that awaited him in Prague. *It has to work!*

He and his men moved to the next tank, and the following one.

When the large tanks were loaded with the second precursor, Erik and the technicians turned to the small tanks. Their loading was relatively safe, because the tanks for the two precursors were physically separate. Still, as always, a mistake would be deadly.

Several step vans drove onto the field and the loading of the small tanks began.

However the unmarked eighteen-wheel truck remained on the road. It was too heavy for the loose soil of the old field where the large tanks waited, strapped to their pallets.

Near the van, several forklifts waited. Erik signaled the drivers to begin loading.

A cold wind swept the dry field while the pallets were speared, lifted, and driven to the van, deposited on rollers inside, and pushed to a stable resting place.

The wind in the open field was cold, but drops of perspiration beaded Erik's forehead. He wiped his brow. *So far so good!*

That thought was premature.

At that moment, one spear of a fork lift missed its slot. The driver did not notice. As he elevated the tank, it tilted, rolled off and crashed to the ground, valve first.

The valve opened and emitted a dark mist.

Either in a last selfless act, or in a vain effort to conceal his mistake, the driver of the fork lift jumped off and squeezed the valve closed.

Then he fell writhing to the ground as saliva foamed about his lips. Fluid drained from his eyes across purple cheeks. What appeared to be urine stained his jeans, and his chest froze. A series of awful wheezes failed to expand his paralyzed diaphragm. Starved of oxygen, his brain lost all function. His head fell back, with eyes rolled upwards. After some tetanus, all motion ceased.

A technician in a Hazmat suit rushed to the stricken man, a Xolak syringe ready, but Erik waved him away. The man was dead. There was nothing to do.

The final loading continued in a somber mood.

***

In Dethorens, Virginia, Masoud was not proud, nor over-confident, but grateful. In his bedroom, an arrow on the floor pointed towards the location of the Kaaba in Mecca. He placed his prayer mat on the floor and oriented it in that direction. His prayers were personal Duas.

He prayed from the Quran (2:250) for endurance and for help against those who reject faith.

Surely, the enemy had rejected the true faith!

He prayed that he not be tested beyond his strength (Dua 2:286), and asked for forgiveness, mercy, protection, as well as for assistance in dealing with deniers of the truth.

They must yield to the truth of Islam!

With the help of Allah, he and his warriors would strike a mighty blow against the infidels.

Allahu akbar!

***

In her kitchen in Chicago, Anne Simek wiped her brow. The heat from the stove was intense, but that was not the cause of the perspiration. Peter Zeleny was on his way to eat dinner with her father. He was due in ten minutes.

In anticipation of the dreaded event, Anne had prepared her father's favorite meal. The simmering pot of *kuřecím masem a knedlíky,* "chicken and dumplings" filled the kitchen with a delicious aroma that Anne had known and loved since childhood.

She lowered the heat on the burner, and turned to the blender. She would hand Peter a frozen Daiquiri at the door to mellow him.

Havel already held a bottle of his usual beer, Plzeňský Prazdroj, better known to Americans by its German name, Pilsner Urquell. And a second bottle of the golden-hued beverage stood ready on the counter.

For herself, Anne wanted no alcohol this evening. She needed all her wits to head off any confrontation. The two favorite men in her life had no reason (other than Anne) to like each other.

She lowered the heat on the burner as the doorbell sounded. She stopped in the powder room and straightened her blouse. She fluffed her hair.

Satisfied, Daiquiri in hand, she approached the door.

***

Peter Zeleny stood at the entrance to the Simek home. Anne kissed his cheek and invited him in. He removed the coat from his six foot plus frame, and hung the garment on the hall rack. Trim as ever, he sported a loose gray sweater and fitted jeans. He looked dashing and respectable.

Surely father will approve of this man. He has to.

Anne threw her arms around his neck and kissed him. Her lips pressed against his and lingered, moist and tingling.

The voice of her father dispelled that tender moment.

"Anna, is that your boy friend? Bring him in here. I must meet him."

Anne let go and shrugged. Peter winked.

He took a long sip of the Daiquiri, and followed into the father's den.

Havel Simek sat in his adjustable chair. He levered the position to upright, but remained seated with his eyes focused on Anne. She responded.

"Father, this is the friend I told you about. We're very close. He wants to meet you."

Peter held out his hand and came straight to the point.

"Sir, I'm Peter Zeleny. I love your daughter, and I would like your permission to date her. My intentions are serious, and I promise to respect her and your wishes."

Havel's eyes glazed momentarily.

"That is good. You must be from the old country. No American would ask an old man for permission to court his daughter. Where are you from?"

Before Peter could answer, Havel looked up at the ceiling.

"I once had a friend named 'Zelený,' but he betrayed me."

At that thought, Havel shuddered and began to cough. His left leg twitched. Anne intervened.

"Father, sip your beer. Your throat is dry."

Havel sipped his beer and cleared his throat. His eyes were moist. He tried to speak, but he did not finish.

He slumped back in the chair, eyes closed.

The ceiling was painted pink. He was no longer in Chicago. He shivered but not from the cold. He was afraid. It seemed that a door opened and shut. Lights blinded him and all he could hear was a voice, his own. He repeated over and over.

"Nevim, Nevim, Nevim nic. 'I don't know, I don't know, I don't know anything.'"

And then the blows, the pain!

"Bože, pomoz mi! 'God help me!'"

As a medical doctor, Peter instinctively reached for the slumped Havel, but Anne restrained him.

"No wait, Peter. This will pass."

She was right. After a few moments, Havel opened his eyes and sat up.

"Excuse me, Mr. Zeleny, what was your father's name."

Peter had to be honest. Anne saw his look and grabbed him. To no avail.

"Sir, my father's name was Johan. He once was your friend, but he changed horribly. I cannot make up for your suffering, and I do not ask you to forgive *him*, but please forgive *me* for what he did to you, and to others. He is dead. Let him hurt you no more."

He paused and put his arm about Anne's shoulders.

"I love your daughter, and will do all in my power to make her happy. I promise to honor you, her father, and I will never keep her from you."

Havel stared. Peter awaited a response, but a burnt odor emanated from the kitchen. Anne gasped.

"My *knedlíky,* 'the dumplings!'"

She dashed out of the room.

The supper that evening was a complete failure. Most of the dumplings were fine, but they had a residual taste of carbon from the bottom layer in the burnt pot. Peter and Havel exchanged opinions on the weather in Prague versus Chicago, but neither spoke about Peter's request to court Anne.

Havel finished eating and returned to his basketball game where the Bulls were up by 16.

Peter helped Anne with the dishes. Then he left. Havel, engrossed in his game, did not look up.

Anne fled to her room. In minutes, her pillow was soaked in tears.

***

******

Chapter 45
Monday, December 6

In his elegant office in Prague, Karel Moravec sat and read the Sunday Edition of a Washington newspaper. He concentrated on an article in the "Style" section.

CONGRESS TO CLOSE EARLY FOR NATIONAL UNITY CELEBRATION

On Pearl Harbor Day, Tuesday, December 7, the Congress of the United States will close a day early so that members may participate in Wednesday's National Unity Day celebration at the newly completed Pavilion of National Unity in Front Royal Virginia. An estimated half of the members of the House, over forty Senators, and more than half of the nation's 50 governors will be present. Guests include, industry notables, Hollywood entertainers, union leaders and media personalities.

The President will address the assembly on the landmark bipartisan Comprehensive Debt Control Act, a bill hailed by both parties as restoring fiscal sanity to Washington. He will declare December 8 as the "National Day of Unity."

As a symbolic gesture, the joint session will be held "Outside the Beltway" at the Pavilion of National Unity in Front Royal Virginia. The pavilion along with a future museum is a gift to the University of Virginia from contributors to both political parties. The location will become a satellite campus for the university.

Reaction to the celebration is mixed. "The days of the big-time spenders inside the Beltway are done, finished." said Tim Higgins of Baltimore, Maryland, "Our representatives are speaking for us, the people, again." ... But perhaps reflecting the opinion of most Americans is Ashley Rivers, of nearby Dethorens, Virginia. "It's about politicians promoting themselves. No one cares. ..."

Moravec smiled. The Americans were on schedule and the plan was on track.

He was interrupted by the buzz of his phone. He picked up. "What is it Fiala?"

A gentleman called you. He spoke English with an odd accent. He said that you were awaiting his call, and that you would know where to reach him. I asked him his name, but he hung up."

"It's all right Fiala, I know who it is. And Fiala, it's noon. You can go to lunch now."

Karel arose from his desk and went to a nearby wall where a somber painting by Caravaggio stood guard. Karel shifted it to the side, tapped in the electronic combo to the safe, and took out a cell phone.

It was his personal instrument, and very secure. He punched a number.

"Mr. Rahman, you called?"

"Mr. Moravec, what is the status?"

"In less than an hour my men will be at the pavilion to install the remotely-operated fire-control tanks. This is our last task. Our part of the operation will be complete."

Mr. Rahman did not reply. Karel added.

"There's nothing more for us to do. Your men received the small tanks, fully charged, yesterday, but of course you already knew that."

Karel felt Mr. Rahman nod at the other end of the line and added.

"The installation will be finished today. That will complete all our deliveries. Is the money ready to transfer? Have you the account numbers?"

Karel had provided Abdul Rahman account numbers for three different Swiss banks. Fully one half the total would go into Karel's personal account at the first bank.

Mr. Rahman frowned. Thousands would die, and this *kufar* was only concerned with himself and money. The decadence of the godless West! He spoke.

"Of course, Mr. Moravec, we are not stupid. But how will I know when my final delivery is complete?"

"I will call this number and speak one word, 'Geronimo.'"

Karel liked this choice. Somehow, he felt the Apache Chief would be pleased. He spoke again.

"Mr. Rahman do not hesitate to deliver the money. We have our own wireless control of the remote that triggers the release of the agent. We can jam the remote and your men would fail."

Mr. Rahman hung up.

***

An early morning mist hung over the work site near Front Royal, Virginia, where Harold Watts, the superintendent of construction of the huge new Pavilion of National Unity, surveyed the work in progress.

Watts had been in charge since the ground breaking last February. The task had been routine until July, when the president and congressional leaders had decided to hold a signing event in the new pavilion on December 8. The mostly ceremonial session was to honor national unity, hence the building's name.

From August on, Watts' ulcers had bedeviled him. The close deadline and the added burden of security had caused him many sleepless nights, at home and on site. But now success was near. Barring an accident, the work would be finished in time. He looked forward to evenings with his family once more.

This morning found him near a gate in the tall wire fence, topped with razor wire, that enclosed the newly finished structure. Outside the fence, as demanded by Homeland Security, his bulldozers had placed large blocks of stone to block vehicular access to the perimeter. No van loaded with explosives could be driven sufficiently close to the pavilion to pose a serious danger.

Apart from a small "presidential" entrance gate, the only access to the complex was through the lone well-guarded gate where he stood. Any truck of size could only enter here.

He sighed. Only 48 hours remained before the president and members of congress would assemble for their signing ceremony.

Damn it Watts, you have it ready or I'll have your head!
Those words of his boss still echoed through his brain, but no longer disturbed him. He was done, almost.

The interior of the pavilion was finished. Several crews were busy patching flaws in the drywall, while painters stood by waiting for the "mud" to dry. The laying of carpet in some "dressing" rooms was underway, and the seats for the auditorium had finally arrived yesterday evening. Watts's most experienced men had worked all night. Already, half the seats were bolted to the floor.

Wherever possible, cleaning crews were busy sweeping and finishing up.

Now Watts worried about the landscaping. From the gate, through the fog that hung over the site, he surveyed the work in progress. A fleet of Bobcats was pushing imported topsoil over the construction-exposed clay that was everywhere. Two flatbed trucks, piled high with rolls of green sod stood ready, waiting for the Bobcats to complete their task. Next to the building, numerous large evergreens were freshly set in mulched beds. To the untrained observer, they appeared to have grown there, *in situ*, for several years.

There was no time to pour concrete paths and driveways, but gravel substituted well, a reminder that the pavilion was indeed new.

For the first time in months, Watts relaxed. *Damn it, We're going to make it!*

***

The sound of a motor disturbed the peace. Harold Watts turned to see an eighteen-wheel semi approach the gate. It was followed by a flatbed truck.

The guards waved them to a stop.

Watts watched as a man stepped out and came towards him. The man handed him a sheaf of papers. Watts spoke.

"What the hell is this?"

"That's a work order to replace the fire prevention tanks."

328

"What do you mean? What's wrong with the damn tanks? Can't you see that we're working on the landscaping. Everything has to be ready in 48 hours."

The man, Erik Holub, was not dissuaded.

"Hey, don't blame me. Read the reports yourself. County inspectors found most of the tanks in your fire suppression system are defective. The welds have extensive lack of weld fusion and porosity. They're dangerous."

"So what. There's no time."

"There's time. The solution is new tanks. We have them. My crew can replace the defective tanks in twelve hours. The pipes and valves are already in place. All we need is to hook them up and cart away the defective hardware."

The superintendent pulled out his phone.

"I need to check with Homeland Security. This work order needs their approval?"

"Go ahead, but we already have their authorization."

Erik handed the superintendent another document. It was signed by an official from Homeland Security. (The official had received a nice stipend from Hus-Kinetika. No terrorist, he had been assured that fixing a defective fire prevention system was necessary.)

Watts grimaced.

"All right, what do you need."

"We have the diagrams from the county inspectors. We need a place to set up that won't upset your landscaping."

"There's a loading dock at the rear of the Pavilion. You can unload your rigs there."

Watts pointed to the gravel roadway.

"Try not to tear up my roads. The gravel may not support your load."

Erik nodded. He exhaled and mounted the passenger side of his van.

He was in!

***

329

Before the trucks could proceed, two men blocked the path. Both wore blazers and ties. Neither smiled.

The man closest to Erik flashed a badge and spoke.

"Secret Service. Step out the truck, Sir. May I please see your ID?"

Erik's hand shook as he handed his license to the man. The man examined his photo and returned it.

"Sir, this is a restricted area. What are you doing here and where are you going?"

Watts came running.

"They're here to fix the fire prevention system. The county inspectors found bad welds in the tanks. They'll swap the old tanks out with new replacements."

The Secret Service Agents stood their ground. An advance team for the president, they could not afford mistakes. They examined the report of the county inspector.

While they read, Watts handed over the rest of the documents.

"They have the approval of Homeland Security."

Instantly, one of the agents was on the phone to speak with the official who had signed the approval. After what seemed a lifetime to Erik, the agent hung up and frowned.

Erik's knees shook. He wanted to throw up.

Finally the agent spoke.

"Have your men step out of the truck, with their photo ID's please."

The agent checked each man against the list from Homeland Security, while his partner entered the van. After some minutes he called out.

"Looks OK back here, a load of red tanks for the fire system, and several forklifts. Matches the invoice."

The first agent turned back to Erik.

"All right Mr. Holub. You can proceed. But don't let your men outside the work area. You have to finish fast. In twenty four hours this area must be secure."

Erik nodded and exhaled.

He stumbled as he mounted the cab, but no one appeared to notice.

Wordless, he signaled the driver to roll forwards. The wheels dug into the gravel.

He was in.

But all he wanted was to get the hell out!

***

Although the tasks were performed with great care, Erik Holub and his men finished in seven hours, not twelve.

All the bipartite tanks with the Novichok-H precursors were installed, and the old "defective" tanks removed and loaded for disposal.

Erik had been truthful that the replacement was straightforward, that the valves and pipes were already in place and only the tanks needed to be swapped.

But that was not the whole truth.

The fire prevention system was a unified whole with sensors reporting constantly to a central computer that controlled alarms and valves remotely. To his tanks Erik had attached new valves with remotes no longer subject to central control, but only to his own remote controller.

With the new remote, tanks could be opened and closed, and corresponding alarms activated or deactivated. The central fire prevention system no longer had a role.

The conspirators and their jihadist clients could open and close the tanks at will.

The stage was set.

***

Erik and his men mounted the trucks and pulled up to the gate.

Watts, the construction boss, was pleased. The fire-prevention system was ready on time. One more task checked off.

Uniformed guards approached to check the trucks.

Everything, and everyone, matched the paper work. The guards appeared satisfied.

331

Erik stayed in the truck and waited for clearance to leave. His role was finished.

He thought of the tickets in his pocket. Tomorrow, a flight to Europe for his payday, followed by a flight to Rio de Janeiro the week after.

He would be gone from the U. S. when the fireworks erupted!

For a brief moment he thought of warning Hus-Kinetika's man at Homeland Security to flee. He thought better of it.

That compliant bureaucrat would discover that greed has real consequences!

The guards waved Erik through.

He was done!

***

At 4 pm in Virginia, 10 pm in Prague, the Hradčany Castle glowed in the spot lights. In the cold air, lovers embraced next to a lamp on the Charles Bridge under which the dark waters of the Vltava River rippled in an incessant flow. The scene reminded Karel Moravec of his own mortality. How many before him had experienced the same sentiment?

Despite the late hour, Karel was still in his office, awaiting a special call.

The secure phone on his desk sounded.

Karel turned from the window and picked up.

As expected, it was Erik Holub. In his relief and excitement he spoke in his native Czech.

"Dokončil jsem to. I have finished it."

Karel could only smile.

"To je dobře, velmi dobře. 'That is good, very good.'"

Karel hung up and punched Rahman's number on the secure phone. He grinned, and spoke a single word.

"Geronimo!"

***

At Masoud's mansion near Dethorens, Virginia, Quanit Ibn Husayn was deep in prayer.

332

He bowed and touched his head to the reddish tablet of Karbala clay that lay on his mat. Quanit was a Shiite. His father had been named for Husayn Ibn Ali, the martyr of Karbala, and the third of the twelve Imams.

As he prayed, Quanit asked that all twelve Imams be honored. They, were his "Imams, Masters and Intercessors before Allah." He would love all of them, and shun their enemies in this life and the next.

He added a prayer for blessings upon the Prophet Muhammad and his family, that he was the best prophet, and that Ali Ibn Abu Talib, and his descendants, were the best Imams.

Quanit was a "Twelver." He knew that the twelfth Imam, Muhammad al-Mahdi, "The Rightly-Guided One," now hidden in a state of occultation, would reappear at a moment determined by Allah and spread justice throughout the world.

When Quanit was a teenager, his father, Husayn, had been discharged from his job by his Sunni employer. Husayn never overcame the disgrace. Quanit, young and devout, vowed to honor him. He asked his father's namesake, Husayn, the Third Imam and "The Lord of the Martyrs" to intercede that he might give his life to Allah.

Now Quanit knew the answer to his prayer. He would give *his* life for Allah the Merciful.

More, Quanit hoped that his own martyrdom, and the terror it would bring to the satanic Americans, would hasten the return of the Twelfth Imam.

At last his training was complete. His back was accustomed to the weight of the triple tanks strapped over his shoulders, and breathing inside the Hazmat helmet now was second nature.

Initially, Quanit had not trusted Masoud, the leader. He did not like Masoud's fair Caucasian features or blond hair. Besides, Masoud was a convert to Sunna Islam, and he was ignorant of history. He knew nothing of the beheading of Husayn Ibn Ali at the battle of Karbala.

But now Quanit respected his leader. He knew that Masoud liked him. Besides, Masoud was a warrior. And in only days, maybe hours, thanks to him they would strike the *kufari*, the "infidels" a blow from which they could never recover.

Allahu Akbar!

***

Also in the mansion in Dethorens, William Masoud Jones was excited. It was time to act!

The phone call from the "benefactor," Abdul Rahman, the Iranian business man, was the last. There would be no more talks between them, at least not in this life.

Masoud knocked on Quanit's door.

The door opened. Quanit appeared flustered. On the floor Masoud saw the mat and a circular clay tablet. He had disturbed Quanit at prayer.

"Forgive me, Quanit, but I have great news. It is settled. The Dethorens Volunteer Fire Department will be on watch at the Unity Pavilion for the celebration of National Unity Day. No one can stop us now."

Quanit hugged his superior and kissed his cheek.

"*Allahu akbar*, Allah has answered our prayers."

"Truly. And it will please you to know that our financial support is from Shia Islam, from the Mullahs of Iran."

"Thank you for sharing that. I also thank you for your tolerance when you knew my belief that Ali is the first Caliph. Many scorn the Shiites."

"But not here. Most of our group share your belief, but all of us want to defeat the Great Satan."

Masoud put his hand on Quanit's shoulder.

"Quanit, you will command the attack on the rearmost entrance that will be used by the president's party. You will be the sword of Allah. If that evil leader attempts to leave, you will strike him dead."

Quanit was overwhelmed, but he found his voice.

"What exits of the pavilion will you guard to keep the *kufari* from fleeing? Surely you should guard the president's."

"No, you will do that. Your task is important. You will need good men to assist you. You may choose any six you wish."

Quanit's eyes moistened. He hugged his leader.

Masoud freed himself.

"Quanit. together you and I serve Allah, the Merciful. In two days, we shall both die for him."

He pointed to Quanit's prayer mat.

"Now together we will pray that in all things, Allah may be praised!"

***

While Masoud and Quanit prayed, unknown to either of them, the "benefactor," Abdul Rahman, made one more call to Dethorens, Virginia.

Hassan Ibn Ali saw Rahman's number. He punched "Talk" and listened.

"Hassan, will Masoud be strong when the time comes? I am concerned. He has blond hair, like many *kufari*. I find it difficult to trust him.."

Abdul Rahman knew his fate if the mission failed. Hassan replied.

"It is because of Masoud's blond hair that no one suspects us. There are no problems so far. He is strong, a warrior for Allah. True, he knows not that Ali is the first Caliph, but he is American. He cares little for our history."

"I trust you, Hassan, but at the first sign of weakness, you will take over. Do not fail us. We rely on you."

"Click."

***

******

Chapter 46
Monday, December 6

Life in the CIA's safe house near Middleburg, Virginia was far from glamorous and this afternoon Ivana Novotna was frustrated.

She had enjoyed Elena Krkova's company. Elena spoke Czech and she had kept Ivana informed of Gustav's condition at Naval Medical. (He was no longer critical.) But now Elena was gone on assignment elsewhere.

And Tom Fletcher, her guardian, was remote, he answered her requests as best he could, but he was all business.

Ivana missed her *Zlata Praha*, her "Golden Prague," and she missed Bill Hamm. It was he that had saved her from Hrubec and Karel. And Bill talked to her, unlike the sober Tom.

She had never seen Bill's redheaded companion, Jeannine. Apparently she was not CIA and therefore not privy to the location of the safe house.

Ivana could care less. She was bored beyond belief.

***

It was Elena Krkova that called Tom Fletcher at the safe house.

"Tom, there's a new development. Gustav Slavik is gone. He slipped his handcuffs and walked out of his room at Bethesda Naval. No one saw him leave."

"Damn. When?"

"This morning, just after breakfast. Lots of people were moving about."

"Where was the guard?"

"He says he never left the door, but there's a nurse the guard likes. It seems she's attractive and distracts him. Likely he was down the hall at the coffee shop with her."

"What does she say?"

"She won't talk, but it doesn't matter. The point is Gustav is on the loose. This is a guy trained to disappear. He's gone."

Tom thought of Hrubec. *Great, now two ex-commie killers are running loose.*

Elena continued.

"Tom, you should tell Bill right away. I think Ivana's holding back on us. Gustav is her father. She might have kept a 'bargaining chip' she could exchange for leniency for him. Now that he's 'free' she might be willing to give up what she knows for Bill's help."

"She surely won't give it up to me. She barely talks to me."

"But she will to Bill. I'm sure of that. Tell him to tell her that Gustav escaped."

Tom heard a sound. He turned to see Ivana standing behind him.

Damn, what did she hear? The reception had been loud and clear.

He turned back to the phone, but Elena had hung up.

***

Yesterday, Bill Hamm and Jeannine Ryan had spent all day in the blue Fiesta bouncing along roads in the Virginia countryside. They had scanned old fields looking for the W&C red tanks, Holub's step vans, or any traces of either.

The search area included parts of Routes 17, 15 and 29 in a triangle formed by Warrenton, Marshall and Manassas. To no avail. They found nothing. Today, they had searched the same triangle with no success. Now it was five in the afternoon and Jeannine was tired.

"Bill, this is useless. Why do you think that they would load the tanks in the open air where we could see them. Why would they do that?"

"The arrangements in the warehouse at the Fire Equipment Company were makeshift. They make do with what they have. Charging the tanks is extremely dangerous. They won't have a lab near the target. My bet is they'll charge them in the open somewhere near it. Only a fool would haul loaded tanks any distance."

"Damn it Bill, we're close to Washington. It must be the target."

"I don't think so. I don't think they can deliver the gas widely. Any plane would be shot down before it reached the Capitol or the White House. The big tanks I saw in Warrenton were not mobile. Delivery is a major problem for these guys, no matter how suicidal they are."

He added.

"When the Aum cult attacked the court judges in Japan, they failed because the wind shifted. And their attack on the subway was on a soft, though large, target. These guys have scaled down to a soft target. Hell, they couldn't get those tanks near the Pentagon, or the Capitol."

Jeannine thought for the moment. There were plenty of soft targets, the subway, hotels, a long list.

"But Bill, Jack Cannon said he also saw small portable fire tanks fitted with mixing valves."

"Exactly, and that indicates a personally distributed nerve gas."

"You still haven't explained why we're looking in open fields."

"Isolated open fields are my best guess because it's damned dangerous when both precursors are loaded. Any leak, any mistake would be lethal. Seems to me Holub would do the final charging of the tanks in the open air, to minimize the risk.

Bill frowned.

"One thing sure, they don't give a damn about the environment or local farmers and their stock."

***

Bill and Jeannine were hungry, but the terrain was desolate, and there was no sign of a place to eat. Ahead of them, the only building was an old gray barn. No house was visible.

Jeannine spoke.

"This is like looking for a needle in a haystack. How many old fields have we passed. We must have seen hundreds of ..."

She stopped and pointed.

In the field on the left, a farmer was driving a green tractor and pulling a dead cow behind him.

Bill stopped the Fiesta on the shoulder. He waved.

"What happened?"

"Damned if I know, I found her dead in the north pasture this morning. There was a dead raccoon too, and several crows. Never saw such a thing."

"Sir, don't touch that cow. It may be contaminated. Stay on your tractor. I'll call someone to check on it and you."

The farmer sat staring in disbelief. Bill continued.

"Sir, just wait, please. Your cow is contaminated. Please trust me. I'll have a helicopter here to help you. It won't take long."

***

The chopper from Langley arrived in thirty minutes. The farmer remained on the John Deere while two CIA technicians in Hazmat gear did quick tests on his cow.

One of them lifted his helmet and approached Bill.

"It looks like organophosphate poisoning. That cow has a low active cholinesterase level, the lowest I've seen. The poison is more potent than any pesticide. I'll know more when I get the samples to the lab and do more precise tests."

The tech looked at the farmer, still seated on the John Deere.

"That old gentleman appears to be OK, but he should check himself into a hospital. Maybe you could drive him. I doubt there's any danger to you or your wife."

Bill liked the reference to Jeannine.

"No. When I'm done, you guys take him in the helicopter. I'll authorize it."

The tech refastened his helmet and went back to the cow. Bill turned to the farmer and pointed to a distant border of bushes.

"Is the north pasture beyond that hedgerow?"

The old man nodded.

Bill motioned to the helicopter pilot. He opened the door and Bill hopped in. He yelled to Jeannine as the rotors began to turn.

"Hon, you stay here with the techs, I'm going to check that pasture from the air."

Jeannine ducked away from the whirling dust as the helicopter lifted off.

***

Bill and the pilot were back in fifteen minutes.

"That pasture is where they loaded the tanks. There's another dead cow and some crows too. And there are two red tanks hidden near the woods. They piled them with branches so we didn't see them from the road."

Bill turned to the Techs.

"This is not pesticide poisoning. It's a Novichok nerve agent, more deadly than Sarin or VX. Have the lab do their tests as quick as possible. And keep me posted."

He turned to the pilot.

"Get a Hazmat team here to decontaminate that field. And study those abandoned tanks. Take the farmer with you and have our medics check him and his clothes."

The pilot started the rotors. Bill ducked and raced away as whirling leaves, dust and chaff whipped his clothing. Jeannine shut her eyes. The chaff irritated her nostrils and her eyes teared.

The helicopter rose, turned, and headed in the direction of Langley.

Bill turned to her.

"Holub's workers loaded the tanks in that field. An accident must have released some of the gas. The dead animals prove the Novichok agent was there, and that means that the tanks are loaded with both precursors. We're out of time."

Jeannine managed to whisper.

"But where are they? Where will they strike?"

***

An hour later, Bill Hamm's phone vibrated. He punched "Talk" and listened for several minutes. He clicked off and turned to Jeannine.

"That was one of the tech guys. They analyzed the abandoned tanks from the field. They weren't dangerous, only one partition was loaded, the other partition was empty. It hadn't been loaded."

"Is that all?"

"No, there was a valve unit mounted on the tanks that blew their minds. Real advanced. It's a bulbous chamber with valves at either end. The first valve opens both partitions so that the precursors mix in the chamber. An internal magnetic stirrer, activated by a miniature lithium battery, ensures rapid mixing. The battery also powers a temperature-control device, to maintain the optimal temperature for the reaction."

He added.

"Then in seconds the chamber's external valve opens and releases the killer product into whatever device or tube is attached."

He paused for a breath.

"This system is damned sophisticated. Our M687 binary artillery shell for Sarin only had a thin partition between containers of the two precursors. The partition would burst in flight and Sarin would be formed before the shell struck."

Jeannine interposed.

"But the big tanks aren't projectiles."

"Right, so weight is not a major problem. For them, the partition between the two precursors is metal, and on each side there's an external port for loading. Mixing can occur only at the outlet valve for each side.

He paused again.

"On the plus side, if we ever find the loaded tanks, we can discharge one of the precursors through its external port in relative safety and render the tank harmless."

Jeannine interrupted.

"But this means that the rogue Czechs have fulfilled their half of this project. The jihadists have all the expertise they need. The FBI will have to revise their thinking. The terrorists are ready."

She swerved to the left to pass a slow-moving truck loaded with wired bales of hay. Bill spoke again.

"I haven't told you the worst. The mixing chamber has a remote-activated switch to operate the valves."

"No! What's the range of the remote"

"They're not sure, at least a football field."

Bill continued.

"There is one good thing, Novichok-H is relatively heavy. It's not very volatile. It settles rapidly from the air. It looks gray and greasy. That cow had received a sizable dose to die as it did, yet there was little Novichok in the airways. It acted through the skin and the exterior of the nostrils.

Jeannine grew thoughtful.

"Great. So if I touch it I'll die?"

"Exactly. Don't touch any surface you think it's on."

"What about its half-life?"

"Short we hope. As a weapon, that would mean you could attack and then overrun the gassed position without waiting for decontamination."

He frowned.

"But the fact is we don't know anything about the half life."

***

In Chicago, Anne Simek's thoughts were far from terrorists. She called her cousin Mila in Nags Head.

"Mila, my father's spending a few days with the neighbors. Is the house in Corolla available? I have to get away from here."

"It is. What about Peter? Will he be with you?"

Anne swallowed.

"The FBI lab in Quantico is testing Xolak for Peter. He's meeting Aileen Harris in Manassas at the FBI's Northern

Virginia Resident Agency. They're going to Quantico together."

She muttered.

"She's probably already in Manassas waiting for him."

Mila asked no further.

"When will you get here?"

"I'm flying to Norfolk International. I'll rent a car and be in Corolla tonight."

"Good. But I'm not letting you spend the night there alone. I'll be at the beach house to welcome you."

Anne managed to smile. *Good old Mila, I'm trusting you again.*

Anne hoped that the sounds of rhythmic waves crashing on the beach, coupled with the contented waters of the Currituck Sound rippling under a red sunset, would soothe and heal her.

***

******

Chapter 47
Tuesday, December 7

In Virginia, at the Dethorens Volunteer Fire Department, six members of Masoud's squad were in a foul mood.

"This is women's work. Why do we have to wash the Fire Truck."

Masoud admonished them.

"Do not question me. The Americans think they have given us a great honor, to stand by the pavilion while the president is there. To not have this truck sparkle would be a sign of dishonor to him, and would raise suspicions. We cannot afford that."

He added.

"The other two fire companies will have their equipment shine. We must do the same."

Masoud turned to a man standing behind him.

"Hassan, the other two trucks will be parked near us. You must neutralize their crews quickly. Do not give them time to don protective suits. Understood?"

Hassan nodded.

"As rehearsed, we are ready. We shall not fail.

Masoud liked Hassan's confidence.

But Hassan was not done.

"But why do you not pack the truck with explosives? We could blow the *kufari* to small pieces at one stroke?"

"Hassan, this has been discussed. The Americans trust us and our inspection will be minimal. But their dogs know nothing of that. They would sniff the explosives. We would be revealed."

"But we would be at the gate. The explosion would destroy this Unity pavilion."

"You would destroy an empty building. The president and others will arrive long after the truck. No! We have the means to wipe out their leaders, and we shall."

Hassan was satisfied.

Masoud nodded reflectively.

He had done all he could to prepare his men. He was proud of them.

They were ready.

Tomorrow they would strike!

***

In Nags Head, North Carolina, Jim Harrigan arrived at the beach house in Corolla to find Anne Simek weeping on the sofa. Mila motioned Jim to silence and led him into the kitchen.

"What's the matter with Anne?"

"She's all mixed up. She's torn between her father and Peter Zeleny. Peter's father betrayed her father, Havel, to the Communist State Police, the *Státní bezpečnost*. Havel still suffers from their beatings. He needs her, and Peter doesn't understand.

What's more she's afraid that Peter likes Aileen Harris. I know that's baseless, but she worries. Peter and Aileen are going to the FBI lab in Quantico to work on Xolak. Aileen is meeting him at the FBI office in Manassas."

"Did you reassure her about Aileen?"

"Yes, but the real reason she's worried is her father. She's here to sort things out."

"From the looks of her, it's not going well."

"Because she just got a call from her father. He missed her in Chicago so he's flying to Norfolk International to see her. He's too old to drive and he wants Anne to meet him there. His flight arrives in two hours."

Mila's eyes had a familiar glint. Jim knew he was in trouble. "So?"

"So, I was hoping you could drive Anne to Norfolk to meet him. I don't want her going alone and I'm seeing several clients

346

today. With the real estate market the way it is, I can't afford to cancel."

Mila smiled and pointed to the stove.

"And when you get back I'll serve you a mess of shrimp and grits."

"Damn it Mila, that's not fair. I can't say no to both you and shrimp and grits."

Mila laughed and called into the living room.

"Come on Anne. Jim will ride with you to Norfolk to meet your Dad. You have to leave now to be on time."

Jim waited at the door.

***

The hour was late. Alone at the Dethorens Volunteer Fire Department, William Masoud Jones examined the interior of the tanker-truck one last time.

The supposed tank and hose capacity of the vehicle had become a hidden storage area for twenty men in Hazmat suits, along with their weapons, AK-47's and grenade launchers, the latter carefully sealed in plastic to eliminate any tell-tale odor for the sniffing dogs.

Masoud no longer needed the antidote that the Czechs had developed. The Xolak had been for use in case of accidents when training and outfitting his men. But that had been accomplished without incident.

Now their mission was one of death. None of his men would return. Still the presence of Xolak might enable a contaminated warrior to recover momentarily and deal death to more *kufari*. Masoud decided to keep the cartons of Xolak in the hidden storage.

He thought of the movie "Troy." Masoud was no fan of Greek classics, but he knew that thanks to the "Trojan Horse," and the men concealed inside, Troy had fallen.

The authorities would open the gates of the Unity Pavilion to his fire truck. His men would be concealed inside. They would strike from within.

Masoud laughed.

Tomorrow, like Troy, all the key movers and shakers of the United States, the 'Great Satan,' would perish, wiped out.

The rulers of this decadent country would be sent to hell, leaving only chaos behind them!

***

Exhausted, Bill Hamm and Jeannine Ryan decided to spend the night in Marshall, Virginia. A tired Jeannine went to her room. As Bill headed to his, the phone vibrated. It was Tom Fletcher at the safe house.

"Bill, Ivana Novotna wants to speak with you. I know it's late, but it's about Gustav."

"Put her on."

Ivana was choked and hoarse.

"Bill, my father escaped. You must help him."

"Ivana, there's nothing I can do. It's the FBI that is looking for him."

"Yes, but you can speak for him. Tell them how he aided you in Belgium. You know I like you. You saved my life. You must help him. And I can help you. I know the names of some of the terrorists. I saw them in Karel's files."

"Ivana, I can't promise anything, but if you know something, tell me now. Damn it, you should have told me before."

"I was afraid you wouldn't help me. One of the leaders is 'Quanit Ibn Husayn,' he is a Shiite, and probably in your files. Another one is 'Hassan Ibn Ali,' you probably have files on him too. But the main leader is an American, his last name is 'Jones.' His men call him 'Masoud.' No one knows about him. He's a sleeper."

"'Jones' is a common name. Do you know anything about him?"

"Only that he's in Northern Virginia, and he's not allowed to pray in public."

Ivana added.

"That's everything I know. The jihadists did not share much with Karel. His files were sketchy. Now, do not forget my father."

She hung up.

***

In her motel room, Jeannine was stiff from spending the day cramped in the Fiesta. She stretched out on the bed, shook her shoes off and exercised her toes. As she rolled over she saw the local newspaper on the end table.

She unfolded it and stared at the headline.

Nation's Leaders to Meet at Front Royal

Tomorrow, December 8, prominent leaders of the nation will meet in Front Royal, Virginia, to celebrate what will be, hopefully, a new era of national unity. Congressional leaders, governors, prominent executives, union leaders, along with media personalities and many popular entertainers will celebrate the President's signing of the Comprehensive Debt-Control Act, an historic agreement to balance the budget within three years, on this National Day of Unity.

Workers are rushing to finish the Pavilion of National Unity, which features a convention hall, stage, and banquet spaces along with other amenities. The pavilion is located five miles from the city on the grounds of a future satellite campus of the University of Virginia. After the pavilion, next-planned is a building to house the Museum of National Unity, whose exhibits will include panoramas of significant instances of political "compromise" in the nation's history. Ground breaking for the museum is scheduled for summer of next year. A local architect, Margaret Delsol, of Dethorens, Virginia has been selected to design the new museum.

Jeannine knew the town of Front Royal as the site of the northern entrance to "Skyline Drive." She did not know the town of "Dethorens," but the name sounded familiar. She had seen it recently. But where?

Then she remembered. The town was in one of Vaclav's files.

She found the file on her laptop. It contained a list of recent shipments of Xolak, and their destinations.

The last shipment on Vaclav's list had been made on October 10 of this year. It was by far the largest and had been sent to a Dethorens address.

Surely a village like Dethorens had no need for such a large amount of Xolak, no medical need whatsoever. Unless, as Aileen Harris suspected, the terrorists planned to use Xolak to treat their own men if they fell to Novichok-H.

The only explanation was that the terrorists were training at Dethorens!

And Dethorens, Virginia was not far from the new pavilion where the Unity Day celebration was to be held.

High definition images of destruction and chaos flashed before Jeannine's eyes as she understood the implication of her reasoning.

The terrorists were going to strike at the Unity pavilion. They were going to wipe out most of the country's leaders, as well as the president, at Front Royal.

And the attack would be launched from Dethorens.

Tomorrow!

Barefoot, she banged on the door to Bill's room.

***

Anne Simek and Jim Harrigan arrived at the Norfolk International Airport in time to greet her father at his arrival. Anne introduced Jim.

"Father, this is Mr. Harrigan. Jim is a friend of a friend. He drove me up from Nags Head to meet you. He's a policeman."

Havel drew back, but Anne corrected him.

"No, Father, he's a *good* policeman. He's American. He'll help us."

Jim Harrigan reached for Havel's Carry-On.

"Is this the only bag you have, Sir? Let me take it for you."

Havel nodded and turned to Anne.

"When you left, I was alone. You were gone. I was afraid, empty."

"I'm sorry, Father. I have a house at the beach in North Carolina. It's peaceful. We can rest there. Mr. Harrigan will drive us."

They left the airport.

***

At Jeannine's news, Bill Hamm sprang to the phone. Her discovery that Dethorens was the terrorists' base, along with Ivana's identification of terrorists that *were* in Northern Virginia, plus the prior discovery of the "fire" tanks and the dead contaminated cow, provided ample evidence for action.

Jeannine waited while Bill made several calls. Finally, after an hour of talking, he put down the phone. She spoke.

"Was that the CIA, I mean was it your boss?"

"That was him. He informed the FBI, Homeland Security and the Secret Service's presidential detail of the threat to the Unity Pavilion."

"And?"

"Homeland Security won't raise the threat level to Red."

"You're kidding me?"

"No. They're a bunch of wimps. They don't believe in the 'War on Terror.' It's politics to them, or least to their bosses. Besides, they don't trust the CIA. To them we're part of the problem. And the president wants this show tomorrow for political reasons."

"All right, how about the FBI and Justice?"

"They're not fond of the CIA either, but they listened. The regional office in Manassas is alerted, and they're adding extra agents for screening at the Unity Pavilion, but they say they've done a good advance job on the surrounding counties."

Bill paused.

"Mainly, they don't believe the jihadists have enough expertise to launch a nerve gas attack. They say all they will do is kill themselves."

"Expertise? What about the Czechs? And the dead cow? What about that Czech Colonel who researched nerve agents during the Cold War. His lab was in Brno. Hus-Kinetika took it over after the Velvet Revolution."

Bill shrugged.

"I told them that rogue ex-communists were using Hus-Kinetika's facilities to supply the jihadists. They doubted that the Czechs would follow through. Their thought is that once the terrorists paid the Czechs, they would disappear without handing over the nerve agent, or showing them how to use it. They said they get dozens of tips like this. Most never pan out."

"This is more than a tip. And even the Aum Cult had enough expertise to make Sarin and attack the Tokyo subway"

"They admit that, but they reiterated that the experts say that nerve gases are not weapons suitable for terrorists. The bottom line is that the FBI is cooperating with Zeleny for chemical tests, but they are not going to help us defeat a 'threat' that to them is not real."

"All right, that leaves the Secret Service. Did they listen?"

"The Secret Service is part of Homeland Security, but they listened. They've tripled the presidential detail at the Pavilion, and sent more advance teams out. And they found a squad of marines who were training nearby. They will man the perimeter and gates. They've recruited more local cops, and two National Guard units are on standby."

He added.

"Also, the airspace around Front Royal is closed to unauthorized traffic. Secret Service advance teams already had searched nearby sites that could be used to launch a missile, and anti-missile units have been established in a ring from West Virginia, and Pennsylvania to North Carolina."

Jeannine was far from satisfied.

"Bill, we have to go to Dethorens now, tonight."

***

******

Chapter 48
Wednesday, December 8

The Pavilion of National Unity stood complete and shining in the Virginia countryside. Outside, the landscaping was freshly finished; sod, shrubbery and trees were in place. The parking lots and paths were of gravel as planned. The driveways were supposed to be concrete, but cold weather had postponed the pouring of the cement, and they too were of gravel, although temporarily.

Today the weather was mild. No hands were jammed into jacket pockets as the spectators lined the path to the left-front entrance of the pavilion. Tickets and photo ID's were held in the open, ready for scrutiny.

The mood was festive, although the line was long and the wait substantial.

The line at the VIP entrance at the front right of the pavilion was short. This was not due to a paucity of people (the VIP's had abundant invitees) but rather to the speed with which they were processed once inside. The prior background checks of the legislators, governors, judges, entertainers, wall street executives, and rich and famous guests had been easy. Thus, the screening at the entrance was limited to passage through metal detectors, an inconvenience which though minor, a number of prominent individuals pointedly tried to ignore. But such efforts were vain as the guards were on high alert.

In contrast, the spectators in the long line at the left-front entrance were an incongruous lot. Many had won their seats through state lotteries, and their background checks had been tedious, expensive and often incomplete because of the time element. Consequently, before entering, all were screened intensely by metal detectors as well as by other means. Further, many individuals were selected at random (as forewarned on their tickets) for body searches. In spite of the inconvenient, and occasionally aggressive, inspections, once inside the pavilion, the mood of the spectators was one of boisterous anticipation.

Among the spectators, one particular couple was especially joyful. Masoud's former close friends from high school, Barry Wilson and Monica Barrett (now Mrs. Wilson) had won their seats two weeks ago. Even the long wait to enter the pavilion had not discouraged them. Once seated, they joined the other spectators in scanning the seats on the main floor for favorite celebrities.

***

Inside the pavilion, the Secret Service had made special provisions for the seating at this grand political spectacle.

At the right side of the huge auditorium was a vertical wall that rose straight to the ceiling. Midway up the wall was a row of large glass windows that framed box seats reserved mostly for the press.

On the floor, extending from the right wall, were rows of seats that were accessible only by the right-front entrance. The seats closest to the presidential stage were for the VIP invitees, including congressional leaders, governors etc. Behind them, the Secret Service had erected a high thick glass barrier that separated the invitees' guests (aides, friends, celebrities, entertainers and special constituents) from their sponsors.

As the invitees and their guests arrived, they took their assigned seats quickly and quietly.

The Secret Service had arranged that no invitee or guest could be approached by a spectator. Thus the spectators' left-front entrance had access only to the three tiers of balconies that lined the left wall of the auditorium. No spectator could reach the floor seats, because a twenty-foot drop from the lowest balcony discouraged jumping. And even if a landing were successful, an eight-foot-high grid of glass and metal isolated the balcony side from the rest of the auditorium.

No matter, the spectators were in a joyous mood, and they were heard by all. Shouts of recognition and applause as some "celebrity" guest took her or his seat resounded from the balconies, and these sounds easily overwhelmed the loud happy hum that arose from the favored seats on the floor.

The celebration began as the band on the stage responded to the crowd's enthusiasm with rock music that drowned out all conversation.

At that, the spectators clapped and cheered in earnest.

***

At five am this morning, Bill Hamm and Jeannine had driven to Dethorens, Virginia where they had learned that the Fire Chief was named "Jones" and that Dethorens Fire Department's equipment was doubtless already at the pavilion.

At that discovery, Bill and Jeannine had departed immediately.

They were bumping along an unpaved road, a short cut to the pavilion, when Jeannine's phone vibrated.

It was Aileen.

Jeannine was driving. Bill took the phone and narrated.

"Aileen got a flight from Murtha Airport in Johnstown to Dulles. She met Peter Zeleny at the FBI's Northern Virginia Resident Agency in Manassas. They're on the way to the FBI lab at Quantico. They ran tests on Xolak for Peter. They confirm that it's a possible antidote for nerve gas."

He continued.

"Peter has a supply of Xolak from his clinic and others in the Chicago area. He says that if the terrorists attack, we'll need all the Xolak we can find to treat the victims. They'll bring the Xolak to Front Royal."

"Fine but tell them to come straight to the pavilion, and to hurry. We need the Xolak."

"They're on the way, but we'll get there first."

"Bill, you should wait for the Xolak."

"We're out of time. I have to take my chances."

They continued their rush to Front Royal.

***

After several calls, Bill Hamm was connected with a Mr. Roger Dixon, the head of the Secret Service's presidential detail.

"Mr. Hamm, thanks for your heads up last night. What do you have new?"

"I'm on the way from Dethorens. The fire chief's name is "Jones." We are sure that he's a terrorist. His truck and equipment weren't in Dethorens. If they're at the pavilion, then the terrorists are already inside your perimeter. They will have Hazmat suits, nerve gas and maybe automatic weapons. Where is the president?"

"He's already inside the pavilion. in a room behind the stage, waiting for his cue. In addition to my team and lots of local police, a squad of marines is here. Two fire teams are at the main gate, and the third, a weapons team, is guarding the president's entrance."

Dixon continued.

"I'll have the marines check the fire truck, but are you sure this nerve gas isn't just a gimmick. I mean the president is counting on this political show. And he does not give in to threats."

"Roger, the gas is deadly. You don't have to breath it to die. If it just touches the skin you're dead. I'm sure the terrorists have rigged the fire prevention system to spread it. It can be triggered remotely. Get the president out of there, and evacuate the damned building."

"Hamm, after you called last night, I checked with the fire prevention people. They have complete control from the Pavilion's fire center. They can close all valves remotely. I told them to lock down all sprinklers and shut the other valves. Not to worry."

"But?"

"No, Hamm, say no more. You've been a big help, but we have enough manpower to stop some rag-tag religious fanatics. I'll talk to the president and try to convince him to leave, but I know he won't."

Dixon paused and added.

"The marines will take care of the fire truck. Don't worry. We can handle this."

The conversation ended. Bill Hamm felt sick. He turned to Jeannine.

"Damn it, Dixon is too confident. Speed up. We have to get to the Pavilion, now."

He pounded the dash.

"If only we had found about Dethorens earlier."

"Don't beat yourself up. This Jones character hid his tracks well. At least you have his photo from the Fire Department. We know what he looks like."

"We'll need it. I'm sure Mr. terrorist 'Jones' can override any "locked" valves with the Czech's remote activator. I have to stop him before he releases the gas."

"You'll get yourself killed."

"Maybe so, but drive faster!"

***

Parked next to the Pavilion of National Unity, the Dethorens Fire Truck shone bright and resplendent in the noon sun.

William Masoud Jones sat in the cab of the engine. He had pushed the seat to the rear to accommodate the tanks strapped on his back.

Earlier this morning, the Secret Service had sealed the entrance on the left side of the pavilion for reasons of security. This left only three usable entrances, the left-front (for spectators only,) the right-front (for VIP's and their guests,) and the right-side (exclusively for the president and his party.)

The security inside the pavilion was of little concern to Masoud. His main weapon, the fire prevention system, was already in place. Still, he was grateful for the closing of the left-side entrance. That gave him one less exit to block.

Masoud watched the last of the line of spectators disappear into the pavilion. As soon as their screening was finished, the left-front doors would be closed.

Some fifteen minutes earlier, the last of the VIP invitees and their guests had entered the right front doors. These were now shut. Latecomers, as forewarned, would be refused admittance.

Masoud held his breath. The time for action was near. All inside the pavilion would die.

***

From his seat in the Fire engine, Masoud watched as a group of U. S. Marines arrived at the main gate. There were eight of them, two "fire teams" in combat gear. And if, as Masoud guessed, a full squad had arrived at the pavilion, then a third team, maybe a "weapons team" had been deployed at the right-side gate to protect the president.

Masoud was disturbed.

Even with only three entrances to block, he knew he was woefully undermanned. And he had not planned for combat-ready marines!

Next to Masoud, on the passenger seat, sat Hassan Ibn Ali.

Hassan's team had two important functions. The first was to neutralize the men from the other fire departments, so that only Masoud's group would be equipped with Hazmat suits. That initial thrust was to be with the AK-47's and RPG's in the compartments on the side of the truck facing away from the main gate.

After the firemen with Hazmat suits were cut down, any others would be gassed with nerve agent. Then Hassan was to block the right-front entrance of the pavilion to seal in any VIP's who attempted to flee.

In concert with Hassan's attack, Masoud's men were to lead the assault against the gatehouse and guards, first with conventional weapons, and then with nerve gas to eliminate the survivors. After that, his men were to "float" to support others wherever needed.

Simultaneously, Quanit Ibn Husayn was to attack and seal the right-side entrance to prevent the president from escaping.

During all these actions, Masoud would wait for the proper moment to trigger the remote. At the touch of that button,

Novichok-H would fill the pavilion and Allah would triumph over the 'Great Satan.'

True, Masoud and his men would surely die.

But Allah, the Merciful, would welcome them to their reward!

However, none of Masoud's plans had allowed for the marines.

He was scared of them. He knew of their training and skills. At the university, his political science professor had scornfully dubbed the marines as "killers." *Exactly correct. That's why they scare me!*

For the first time in months, Masoud felt the doubt that generates fear.

***

Of course Masoud, like the good commander he was, kept his apprehensions from Hassan. Together they sat in the cab and waited.

The Dethorens Fire Truck continued to shine bright and red under the sun. The reflections from its polished chrome glanced off the shiny new steel of the pavilion. Both front entrances were closed now. The last spectator had handed his ticket to the guard and been searched minutes before.

Masoud watched the small TV in the cab of the fire truck. The VIP invitees and guests were in place, and most of the spectators had been seated. In moments, Masoud would launch the attack.

Masoud's eyes were focused on the TV screen, when he felt a nudge at his elbow.

It was Hassan who pointed to a commotion at the main gate.

The marines at the gatehouse were moving. Their leader, a sergeant, pointed at the fire truck.

Immediately a team of four marines broke away, and headed towards the Dethorens truck and Masoud.

Their boots crunched on the temporary gravel path as they ran. Each held an M16 at the ready.

***

359

Masoud fastened his headgear and signaled Hassan Ibn Ali to descend from the cab.

Hassan dropped to the side of the truck, his movements concealed from the marines. Four men followed him. They fastened the helmets of their Hazmat suits and took up their AK-47's and RPG's.

Masoud needed to gain time for Hassan and his men. He stepped down from the cab and exposed himself, waving to the marines as if in greeting.

The foremost two marines hesitated. The third looked back to his sergeant as if expecting new orders. A fourth leveled his M16 at Masoud.

Masoud pressed the lever of his tank and a jet spray of dark oily material flew twenty feet towards the oncoming marines, enveloping them in a gray mist.

The battle of the Unity Pavilion was engaged.

***

Masoud peered through the shield of his helmet. The scene before him was unreal.

The first three marines were down. They presented a grizzly sight, legs extended, stretching and quivering in final tetanus awaiting death.

But the fourth marine, bubbling blood, had struggled to his knees.

Somehow, he lifted his M16 towards Masoud and squeezed off a series of rounds.

"Br, Br, Br, Brup, ..., Brup, ..., Br, Br, Brup, ..., Br, Br, Brup."

Time slowed. Masoud watched in terror as the 5.56 mm slugs scattered stones from the gravel path in a line that approached his feet. He voiced a final prayer.

"*Allahu ...* "

But the stricken marine collapsed and the M16 slumped downward. Just in time, the last flying stone bounced short of Masoud's toes.

He was untouched.

***

Then Hassan and his men rounded the corner of the fire truck.

Two rocket propelled grenades smoked a path towards the clapboard gatehouse where the remaining marines were clustered. The rattle of automatic weapons fire filled the air.

Masoud ducked to the ground.

When he looked up, the gate house was gone, its foundation smoldering and clouded with thick dust. More importantly, the marines and guards were on the ground, dead or dying.

Masoud watched Hassan's men launch two more RPG's at the other fire trucks. Two explosions were followed by thick black smoke rolling skywards. Near the burning vehicles, firemen lay sprawled, dead or incapacitated. There had been no time to don protective Hazmat suits. The assault had been too sudden.

As Hassan and his men took up positions to block the VIP entrance, several policemen, guns drawn, rounded the right end of the burning vehicles. Immediately they disappeared in a gray mist of sprayed gas. Moments later, they lay motionless, twisted and contorted on the gravel path before the large doors.

Hassan turned and waved to Masoud. His mission was accomplished, the right front entrance was blocked.

At that moment music blared over the pavilion's speaker system. Distracted, Masoud looked up. The tune was "Hail to the Chief." The president's cue. He was in the pavilion. It was time to seal him inside.

Masoud waved Quanit into action. Quanit and his men disappeared around the corner of the pavilion headed for the president's entrance. They would "lock" the president inside. The pavilion would be his tomb.

After the president's exit was blocked, Masoud could trigger the release of the gas.

Masoud felt for the remote. *No!* In his haste to buy time for Hassan when the marines had approached the fire engine, he had left the remote in the cab.

He dashed back to the truck.

***

The actions of the marines at the front gate had forced Masoud to initiate the assault prematurely The battle had started before he was ready.

The president's entrance at the right side of the pavilion was guarded by a "weapons" team of four marines. They had set up their bipod "SAW," an M249 Light Machine Gun with a 200-round belt. Moments before, as explosions and gun fire echoed from the front of the pavilion, they had lost communication with their comrades. They guessed, correctly, that they were on their own.

These men were not to be surprised. At the sight of firemen in Hazmat suits rushing towards them they did not hesitate. The belt of cartridges rattled rapidly as the gun fired.

"Pum, Pum, Pum, Pum, Pum, Pum, Pum, ..., Pum, Pum, Pum, Pum, Pum, Pum, Pum, ..., Pum, Pum, Pum, Pum, Pum."

The rain of 5.56 mm slugs cut through the first three members of Quanit's squad in a bloody swath. The fourth "fireman" fell more discretely, likely a victim of a well-placed shot from an M16.

"Pum, Pum, Pum, Pum, Pum, Pum, Pum, ..., Pum, Pum, Pum, Pum, Pum, Pum, Pum."

The last two of Quanit's men were cut to pieces by this burst. They disintegrated in a red-stained bloody cloud.

Quanit was alone. The charge had been futile.

He was not to conquer by brute force alone.

Quanit threw his hands high in surrender.

***

But Quanit's confidence in Allah was not shaken.

He lowered his arms slightly and stood motionless as two marines rushed towards him, their M16's ready. The others kept the M249 machine gun pointed at Quanit.

He lowered his hands more, as if tired.

For a split second the two oncoming marines crossed the line of fire of the M249.

Allahu akbar. Quanit had dared to hope for that event.

He dropped his right hand and squeezed the lever of his tank. An oily aerosol engulfed the onrushing marines. Stricken, they dropped to the ground gagging and retching, their limbs shaking.

The writhing marines lay between Quanit and the machine gun. For a fatal instant, the gunners failed to fire for fear of hitting their buddies.

Quanit did not hesitate.

He squeezed his lever again, launching a spray twenty yards that surrounded the gunners with a gray mist. They collapsed.

Quanit rushed to the exit. He would coat the passage with the deadly nerve agent. No one, least of all the president, would pass safely.

Success was in his grasp.

***

******

Chapter 49
Wednesday, December 8

Masoud climbed back into the fire truck and grabbed the precious remote. He would not press it until Quanit signaled that the president's exit was blocked. He was sure that the Secret Service would not risk the president in flight. He would be barricaded in an interior room. The president would be inside.

Unknown to Masoud, luck had intervened on his behalf. After the brief episode of "Hail to the Chief," the heavy rock music had resumed. No sound of the explosions outside the pavilion had penetrated the extreme decibels emanating from the stage. The celebration inside the pavilion continued, undisturbed and unabated.

Masoud was worried. The "Pum, Pum, Pum," of the machine gun had ceased. Either the marines, or Quanit's men, were dead.

Hassan's men were needed at the VIP exit, while several of Masoud's team had to guard the main gate.

Masoud had only one man, available. He sent him for news of Quanit. *Was the president's exit sealed?*

A nervous Masoud fingered the remote and waited.

***

Roger Dixon, the head of the presidential detail, was a "meat and potatoes" kind of guy. Practical and realistic, he liked things he could see and touch. The unknown unsettled him, and Bill Hamm had done just that. Roger had no experience with "nerve agents," or "nerve gases," or whatever this "Novichok" thing might be. He had read about Sarin at the time of the Tokyo Subway attack, nothing more.

When Quanit had charged the president's entrance, The president had not yet entered the auditorium with its deafening music. At the sounds of the marine's machine gun resounding through the corridor, Roger had directed the president back to his waiting room. There, he and the agents surrounding the president had barricaded themselves in.

Roger was true Secret Service. No president was going to be lost on his watch, he would sooner die. With the president secure, he slipped out the room and crept down the corridor towards the pavilion entrance. Roger carried an odd-looking machine gun, an FN P90 with a 50 round magazine. Looks or not, he liked this gun. It packed a punch.

Roger's optimism waned. These battle-ready marines were good. They should have prevailed, but their machine gun was silent, and he had not heard from them. Where the hell were they?

Roger turned into a wider corridor that led directly to the exit. Ahead of him in the dimly lit tunnel, a rectangle of light marked the exit itself. He exhaled. That light meant that the exit was open wide. The steel doors that had been shut after the president's entrance now were ajar. Any assassin had free entry.

And there was no sign of the marines. And if there were assassins about, why weren't they inside?

He crept forward.

***

Quanit had just finished spraying the president's exit with jets of the Novichok agent when he heard a sound behind him.

It was a man in a Hazmat suit. Quanit did not remember his name, but he recognized him as a member of Masoud's team.

The man spoke. Inside his helmet, Quanit heard only static. He signaled the man that his receiver was broken. Then Quanit pointed to the door and held up two fingers in triumph.

The message was clear. The president's exit was sealed.

Masoud could press the remote and release the gas!

***

366

From just inside the president's entrance, Roger Dixon spotted the two strangers in Hazmat suits. Next to them, near the doorway, was a fallen marine.

Roger did not hesitate.

He stood erect, pressed the FN P90 against his shoulder and fired. Bursts of the 5.7 mm rounds tore through the visors of the helmeted men. Quanit and his companion fell backward, dead, with no time to mouth a prayer.

Roger stepped over the bodies and surveyed the outside. The bodies of marines and "firemen" were strewed about.

But there was no sign of live hostiles. It should be safe to evacuate the president. Roger turned back to the entrance.

But his hand brushed the wall. It felt greasy. He wiped his fingers.

That was his last voluntary act.

His voice failed. Fluid seeped from his eyes, and he could not breathe. Phlegm oozed from his mouth as he fell. He was already dead when his leg twitched one last time.

***

Inside the Unity pavilion, the crowd awaited the president's arrival. They were unaware of the desperate and deadly battles that had taken place in the last several minutes.

The rock band with its massive sound system continued to crank out mega-decibels. No sound wave from the exterior could possibly penetrate those emanating from the amped-up speakers.

At this time all the prominent invitees were seated. From the boxes above, TV cameras scanned the auditorium as the band switched once more to a booming rendition of "Hail to the Chief." However as the minutes passed and the president did not appear, the crowd grew restless.

The first to express their discontent were the boisterous spectators in the balcony. Someone started a chant that was soon picked up by the others.

"Where is the president? We want the president!"

"Where is the president? We want the president!"

The rockers on stage joined in with chords for the chanted refrain. The resultant din was excruciatingly painful to sensitive ears.

Legislators and business men alike held their ears and stared cryptically at each other. Many studied their watches. They wanted to hear the president. But the president was nowhere to be seen.

A new chant started.

"Mr. President, where are you?"

Monica and Barry Wilson joined in gleefully.

"Mr. President, where are you?"

***

All the while, amid the hubbub, the crowds, whether in the floor seats or the balcony were unaware that the doors of the auditorium were locked tight. In the foyer, at the first explosions of Hassan's RPG's, the Secret Service and the local police had converted the lobby into a defensive bulwark.

Both the left- and right-front doors had been closed and barricaded, and the interior doors to the auditorium shut.

No attacker would be allowed to penetrate their perimeter. Anyone attempting to breach either entrance would receive devastating fire

VIP's and spectators alike, though unaware of the tumult, were safe.

And communications revealed that the president, too, was safe inside a barricaded room, and that although the left pavilion entrance was open, no one could make it down that entrance corridor without receiving intense fire.

All that was needed now was to await the arrival of the National Guard helicopters, and to hope that the rock music inside would keep the waiting crowds from panic.

***

From his post in the fire truck, Masoud smiled. The plan was working. No one was attempting to leave the front of the building. Clearly, the Secret Service, as predicted, was content to wait for reinforcements.

The only uncertainty was at the presidential entrance. *Why, Quanit, did you not call me? And what happened to my messenger. Is the president still inside?*

Ever cautious and thorough, Masoud signaled Hassan. Two of Hassan's men left their post to go check the president's entrance.

With no activity at the main front entrances, Masoud waited for their report.

He held the remote ready.

***

Not far away, Jeannine drove while Bill Hamm sat in silence. Ahead of them to the west, a mountain ridge ran north for several miles. Its top was capped by a "field" of sharp unweathered rocks among which were dispersed scrubby Virginia Pines. To minimize the climb over this natural barrier, the road turned sharply north along the side of the ridge. There it turned west to follow a "cut" up the mountainside.

As Jeannine topped the ridge, the Pavilion of National Unity came into view in the valley below. Jeannine pressed the accelerator, but Bill touched her arm.

"Wait. Stop the car. It's started."

He pointed downwards to a cloud of smoke and dust that hung over the entrance to the pavilion's grounds. He lifted his binoculars and studied the scene.

"There's no more gate house. It's gone, blown up. That's why the smoke. There's the Dethorens Fire Truck. Looks like someone's in the cab. I can't tell from this distance. But there's a group of firemen in Hazmat suits surrounding the door to the pavilion. They must be Jones' men."

"Are there any police or guards left?"

"I see bodies along the fence, but the doors to the pavilion are shut. Our guys must be inside waiting for reinforcements."

"But they're trapped. If the terrorists release the gas through the fire prevention sprinklers, they'll all die."

"Our guys don't know that. Over to the right there's a road that leads to the right side of the pavilion. It avoids the main gate. Go that way."

They descended the ridge. At the base, a rutted road wound through the trees.

"ATV's must use that. It goes to the north side. Go there."

Branches scraped the car on both sides as they approached the pavilion. Bill reached for a pump action shotgun on the rear seat.

"Stop here. Look through the trees. That's the north entrance gate. It's open, I'm going in."

"But the nerve gas"

"Can't be helped. You wait here. I've got this poncho. It'll stop skin contact at least."

"This is crazy."

But Bill was gone, disappeared into the woods.

***

******

Chapter 50
Wednesday, December 8

At first Hakim and Abdul Malik, the two men sent by Hassan to check the presidential entrance, crept together along the right side of the pavilion. Then an impatient Hakim left his older partner and raced ahead.

Arrived at the entrance, Hakim saw the greasy film on the walls and noted the distorted limbs of the fallen marines. Beyond them he counted two Hazmat-clad bodies.

The closer one was Quanit Ibn Husayn, his face mangled and barely recognizable. Roger Dixon's weapon had delivered three rounds through the Hazmat helmet of that warrior. Hakim said a quick prayer.

The helmet of the man in the second Hazmat suit also had been shredded by Dixon's fire. This man Hakim did not know by name. He mouthed another prayer.

Hakim turned. Three black limousines stood alone and unoccupied. Alongside one of them was the body of a man, limbs stretched in death, his face twisted in agony. A gray film coated the doors and hoods of all three vehicles.

Quanit had succeeded. The president had not escaped.

Hakim looked back.

Abdul Malik, had stopped not far from the front of the pavilion.

Hakim signaled him to tell Masoud that the entrance was sealed and the president was inside.

Abdul Malik disappeared around the corner of the pavilion.

Hakim raised both arms above his head in triumph and shouted.

"Allahu akbar!"

Those were his last words.

"Brroom, Brroom, ... Brroom."

From the woods, Bill Hamm worked his Benelli pump action shotgun with deadly efficiency. The first two slugs cut into Hakim's thin waist while the third smashed into his falling upper torso. He dropped, Hazmat suit and body torn and twisted together.

From the front of the pavilion, Abdul-Malik heard the triple reports of the shotgun.

He ran to Masoud as fast as the clumsy Hazmat gear allowed.

***

Like Hakim before him, but with greater urgency, Bill Hamm surveyed the scene of death at the president's entrance. The abandoned cars of the motorcade, with their deadly gray coating, the prostrate marines, the two collapsed bodies in Hazmat gear, these images passed before him quickly. Then he spotted the body of a man who was clearly a victim of the Novichok gas. The man wore a suit and tie, an ear piece dangled from his neck.

Instantly Bill dialed the number that Roger had given him earlier. A voice answered.

"Who is this?"

"This is Bill Hamm, CIA. Roger Dixon gave me this number. There's a dead man here, nerve gas. Was Roger wearing a gray suit, maroon tie?

"Yes. Who did you say you are?"

"Roger is dead. I'm CIA, but there's no time. The terrorists are going to release nerve gas into the fire suppression devices and sprinklers. You and everyone in the building are in a death trap. You have to evacuate the president, now. Roger said you had sealed the south side entrance. Open it and get the president out."

"What about the entrance we came in?

"I'm there now, but I can't chance getting close. It's bad. You can't come this way. The entrance tunnel is contaminated with nerve agent, and your cars are covered with it. Roger's body is just in the tunnel."

"Then how come you're alive?"

"I'm using binoculars. The nerve agent must be heavy. It's not very volatile It's projected in a jet as an aerosol. The agent is heavier than air and settles quickly. You can tell it's there. It's gray with a bubbly oil or greasy look."

The man broke off. Bill heard him directing others to open the south side entrance and check for hostiles and to prepare to move the president. He spoke to Bill once more.

"All right, Bill, my name is 'Harry Thomas.' We're scouting the south side. What's the situation on the north? How many hostiles?"

"Three dead, all with Hazmat gear. There's more behind me, but all dead. No live hostiles in sight. Earlier I counted over a dozen, all in Hazmat gear at the right-front entrance. It looks like that is the only one they're guarding."

"That figures, that's where the big wigs are."

"Look Harry, these terrorists know they can't whip you guys as long as you stay out of range of their jet sprays. They're all waiting to die for Allah. They're ready to release the gas. Get the "big wigs" out of there."

Bill continued.

"Your men could lead a counter attack front-left through the spectators' door now. It's unguarded. Tell them to stay at least 200 feet from the Hazmat guys and their spray. Cut them down if they charge. And tell them that the guy in the camouflage poncho is a 'friendly,' that's me. One of these crazies must be the trigger man. He'll have a remote. I'll see if I can stop him."

"Roger that. Good luck, Bill."

Bill turned and started towards the front of the pavilion.

***

William Masoud Jones sat in the fire truck. Next to him outside the passenger door was Abdul Malik breathing hard. He stammered.

"They're coming. Hakim is dead, shot, I barely escaped."

Masoud looked at him in disgust.

"What did Hakim say. Is the president inside?"

Malik nodded.

"He is."

At that moment gunfire echoed from the left-front entrance as men in plain clothes and police in uniform dashed outside. They rained fire on Hassan's men from a distance.

The stutter and rattle of bursts from AK-47's answered back, but not before four of Hassan's men had fallen.

Hassan raced back to the fire truck. He beckoned Malik to take his place at the VIP entrance while he climbed into the seat next to Masoud.

"Is the president inside?"

Masoud nodded affirmatively.

Hassan spoke again.

"Then kill them all. Push the button!"

Masoud lifted the remote. On it an LED shone green, but it was the button that held his attention. He tried to push it, but the Hazmat glove was too clumsy.

He put down the remote and fumbled to remove the glove.

***

Bill Hamm rounded the corner of the building just as the Chinook helicopter came into view. He waved and pointed the pilot to the south of the building. Hopefully, the president and his entourage were already there.

The low flying Chinook drew fire from the remainder of Hassan's men, but with no effect. It disappeared around the building just as a second Chinook appeared above the trees.

Bill ran towards the Dethorens fire truck. Two men sat in the cab. He recognized the man in the driver's seat from his photograph, *William M. Jones!*

Masoud saw the raised shotgun. At the sight of that ominous barrel, he ducked.

Hassan misinterpreted that movement and held out his hand.

"Masoud, why do you hesitate? Give me the remote "You cannot push the button. You are weak. You are not a true follower of Allah. Abdul Rahman warned me about you, ...

Those were Hassan's last words.

"Brroom."

The blast from Bill's Benelli shotgun shattered the passenger window. The slug tore through Hassan's face and skull and blew the helmet from his shoulders.

The once-human remains fell against Masoud, knocking the remote from his hands.

Desperate, Masoud pushed the body away and fumbled for the remote, but the barrel of a shotgun appeared in the cab, only inches away from him. Bill Hamm spoke.

"It's over, Jones or whatever you call yourself. Put your hands on the wheel and keep them there."

Masoud complied. His knuckles whitened as he gripped the steering wheel with both hands.

***

Bill Hamm looked up.

A contingent of National Guardsmen had rounded the southern corner of the pavilion, but they were not needed. The Secret Service and local police had decimated the terrorists. Only one Hazmat-clad individual remained standing, his hands held high not in praise, but surrender.

Still no one approached the fallen terrorists. All were aware that at the squeeze of a lever, a dying jihadist could release a deadly spray and take others with him.

The battle of Unity Pavilion was over.

***

Masoud studied the scene in front of him. His men, whom he had trained and with whom he had prayed daily, were dead or dying except for that coward Abdul-Malik.

Masoud was no coward. The remote was on the floor, next to his left foot, and the man with the shotgun had shifted his gaze to the scene of surrender.

Deftly, Masoud scooped up the remote with his left hand and pressed the button. He cried out.

"Allahu akb ..."

"Brroom!"

Masoud, face gone, was no longer recognizable. But Bill Hamm was not looking at the twisted remains. The LED on the remote was no longer green, but pulsing red.

Bill gasped. The valves on the tanks were open.

Novichok-H flowed through the pavilion's pipes.

***

******

Chapter 51
Wednesday, December 8

The President already was outside the pavilion and boarding a marine helicopter when Bill called Harry Thomas.

"Get everybody out. Now! The nerve gas release is triggered. Don't go under any sprinklers wherever they are."

Harry wasted no time. He jumped onto the auditorium's stage. His voice resonated through the loudspeaker.

"Ladies and Gentlemen. We must evacuate the building immediately. Listen carefully. If you are in the balconies, exit by rows and walk to the entrance through which you came. Once outside you will be directed to a safe location."

He took a brief breath.

"Those of you still seated in the floor area, must proceed towards the stage, towards me, and then turn left. Follow the line that has already formed to leave by the south exit."

He raised the volume.

"Those of you on the floor level, do not attempt to leave by the exit behind you, the way you came in. Instead, walk towards the stage, towards me. Do not rush. Do not push. Walk, do not run."

Harry looked up to the balconies. The highest balcony had half emptied. The hitherto boisterous spectators were filing in orderly lines down the rows.

For a brief moment, Harry was relieved, but then he looked down to the floor.

The celebrities and guests in the rearmost seats had ignored the order to walk to the front. Instead, many were shoving their way to the rear exit, where they had entered.

Harry could only guess at their thoughts as they scrambled and massed at the doorway through which they had come.

"Get out of my way. I'm too important to die, I must live for the sake of my fans. I cannot disappoint them!"

"Move, damn it move, let me by. The government needs my expertise. Let me by!"

Whatever the personal rationalization, the crush at the doors grew worse, as bodies, smothered and trampled, piled up. Finally the doors gave way and individuals clambered and scrambled over the fallen mass to reach the lobby.

There they dashed to safety through the open entrance.

The first ones through the outside doors were horrified to find themselves on a corpse-littered battlefield.

Still, they pushed forward. They barely noticed the gray lotion-like substance that coated the bodies, bushes and pathways and adhered to their own ankles, hands and arms.

Not that there was time to notice.

The vanguard, the foremost of the panicked crowd, fell gasping and retching as the deadly agent took effect.

Moments later the second wave fell. The remainder of the crowd dropped in waves that swept backwards towards the entrance to the pavilion.

In only minutes, the congressional doors were blocked by the stricken throng.

***

In the hall, those congressional guests who had obeyed Harry Thomas' directions to proceed towards the stage were faring well.

Prior to Harry's emergency announcement, most of the invitees already had left through the open left-side doors to safety. There they waited under the protection of the newly-arrived National Guardsmen.

Thus, when at Harry Thomas' command, the Secret Service opened the temporary glass barrier to the guests, the trip to the left-front exit and safety took only a short time.

As for the balconies, only the lowest one still had occupants, but even there, most seats had emptied.

Consequently, most of the spectators were safe outside at the front and left of the pavilion. They were guarded by the first of the National Guard units to arrive. No one was allowed to stray. Too many areas were contaminated.

***

As Harry Thomas watched the line remaining in the last balcony, fire alarms sounded and red lights flashed above and to his left. He looked up at the Press boxes. Their windows were obscured in a gray mist, the nerve agent. Fortunately those boxes had been evacuated.

But not all. A lone shadow pounded on the glass of the Press box before falling out of sight.

Harry turned to the right as now the alarms sounded from the balconies. He watched a gray mist descend from the respective ceilings. He stared helpless at the lowest balcony where dozens of stricken individuals fell out of sight behind the rail.

Now Harry looked above the stage. The ceiling was low and sprinklers were in clear view but still dry. He looked high up at the ceiling over the main floor. It was a long way down to the floor level. *Would there be sprinklers that far up?*

Harry Thomas was no engineer. *Is the main hall next?*

Fortunately, he did not have to answer that question. Three National Guardsmen, in Level-A protective gear with oxygen tanks came to his side.

"Sir, you should leave now. You aren't protected. We'll take over. Your men are outside. They need you."

As a grateful Harry started to leave, one of the men tapped on his helmet. It was no guardsman. Bill Hamm shouted through the visor.

"Harry, Bill Hamm. These guys and I are going to the fire control room. Thank God you got most of the people out."

"But not everyone. I wish that ..."

But Bill had moved on. He was headed to the north side of the building

A grateful Harry Thomas left through the south side exit.

Just in time. Red lights flashed above and the pressurized mixture of water and Novichok-H rained down upon the stage.

In seconds, the shining floor was splotched a deadly motley gray.

***

The Press boxes on the right side of the pavilion were at a fourth-floor level. The two floors immediately below were occupied with offices. On the ground floor, a narrow elongate kitchen area served several large banquet halls.

The fire control room was located on the second floor, directly above the main kitchen.

One of the National Guardsmen, Ted, was a fireman in real life. He spoke to Bill through his communicator.

"The offices have low ceilings and water sprinklers. Water pressure is driving the flow of nerve agent to the sprinklers. What comes out is an emulsion of water and agent. By now, all of the offices are contaminated   But the kitchen probably has local tanks set for low level suppression by carbon dioxide. There the pressure is from the tanks themselves and hopefully their valves aren't open yet."

Ted opened the kitchen door, and pointed.

"We'll go through here and climb the stairs to the control room.   It has no sprinklers or suppression tanks.   The most danger will be from the sprinklers in the stairwell."

Bill nodded.

They passed through the kitchen. There was no gray coating on the stoves or counters. The valves had not opened. They reached the stairwell in safety.

They were in luck. The sprinkler heads in the stairwell were not functioning yet.

They climbed the stairs to the fire system control room.

***

In the confusion of the guest's fatal attempt to flee through the VIP exit, and subsequent mass of bodies there, Abdul-Malik had slipped unnoticed to the north side of the pavilion.

He had watched that *kufar* (Bill Hamm) dispatch both Hassan and Masoud. Malik wanted away from that killer.

And he wanted nothing more to do with this damned pavilion.

He picked his way carefully to the president's gate. Once outside, he shed his Hazmat suit. No longer of use, it now served only to identify him as the enemy. But he clung to his AK-47, he was not yet in the clear.

He pushed through the thickets and brush of a dense woodland. At every sound of scraping branches or rustling leaves, he turned, shaking, and pointed his weapon towards the disturbance, only to see nothing. After a short time traversing the woods, he was about to despair when through the trees he spotted a means of salvation.

Ahead in a clearing was a lone car.

***

At first, Jeannine Ryan had waited patiently for Bill Hamm. But at the booming shotgun blasts and the more distant rattle of small arms fire, she had left the car to walk towards the action.

Approaching the president's gate, she heeded Bill's warning and stayed well back to evaluate the scene from a distance.

She surmised, correctly, that the gray material coating the motorcade vehicles was the dreaded nerve agent. She recoiled at the bodies of the stricken marines, twisted in death, and noted with satisfaction that at least four jihadists, identified by bloodied and riddled protective suits were dead.

But most important, there was no sign of Bill, or his body!

My God Bill, are you all right? And the president?

Her thoughts were in turmoil, but she steadied herself. She must go no further. Backing well away from the perimeter fence, she retreated into the trees as the roaring whir of a National Guard helicopter passed over her position and out of sight.

You're right Bill. Friendly fire, I'll go back.

All sounds of gunfire ceased and she started through the woods towards the car.

She spotted a movement to her left. It was the shadowy form of a man, creeping through the brush, but it was the weapon at the man's side that most disturbed her.

The silhouetted magazine was long with a markedly forward curvature. The gun was an AK-47. The weapons by the dead Marines at the gate were M16's with short lower-capacity clips.

Jeannine had grown up in West Virginia where her father had been an avid hunter. She was used to shotguns, and there was one on the back seat of the car. Unlike Bill's Benelli police defense weapon, it was an older Marlin 12 gauge, but it had a pump action. And on the back seat, too, were cartridges loaded with buckshot.

But the shadowy skulker was between her and the car!

***

Bill Hamm and the two guardsmen entered the control room. Immediately, Ted, the fireman, dashed for the main control unit. He flipped the main switch.

Nothing. Needles still registered flow in all systems. The nerve agent continued to flow unimpeded.

But Ted was not only a fireman, he once had been an engineer with NoFlame Devices, the company that had installed the Unity Pavilion's system, before Erik Holub had tampered with it.

Ted beckoned Bill Hamm to follow him as he raced down the stairs to the ground floor and entered a small room off the kitchen. There, a large red wheel protruded from an exterior wall.

It took both men to twist the wheel clockwise. Ted called through his communicator to the guardsman upstairs.

"What's the pressure?"

The message came back.

"The sprinklers have stopped. The water pressure is falling fast."

Ted turned to Bill.

"If you know any prayers say them now. We're not done. We have to shut down the carbon dioxide suppression tanks in

382

the kitchen. When we passed them, I saw they were not ours. The terrorists must have replaced them with their own tanks. They're pressurized. They don't connect to the water pipes. I have to shut them down before they get us."

Ted ran. Bill followed.

***

Ted moved quickly down a long narrow storage area that was lined with red fire-suppression tanks that vented through a partition to the kitchen proper.

"Damn it, Bill. I don't recognize this new valve contraption. Let's get out of here before the gas is released. Run!"

But Bill did not move.

"No! I saw these tanks at the W&C plant at Warrenton. There's an override switch just left of where the remote switch assembly is welded to the tank."

"I see it. The red handle is vertical."

"It's open. Shove it to horizontal. That closes it and overrides the remote. I'll get the next one."

Together they raced down the row, shutting down alternate tanks in turn.

Only two tanks remained when Bill heard the ominous whirring sound.

"Quick, Ted. That's the magnetic stirrer, the inner valves have opened. The precursors are mixing."

He moved forward, but Ted was faster. He literally leapt over the last tank pushing the handle down as he slid to the floor.

Bill collapsed next to him. Gasps of relief and teary laughter sounded through the communicators of their helmets.

The threat was over.

***

North of the pavilion, Abdul-Malik licked his lips. The car would be his salvation.

He approached, but the door was locked and there were no keys in the ignition.

383

He looked back to see a woman next to a tree at the edge of the clearing.

So this is her car and she has the keys.

Malik reacted. He pointed and fired.

"Br, Br, Br, Brup."

But the woman disappeared into a cluster of scrubby pines. He ran to the spot, but she was gone.

Malik was not mechanically-oriented, and had no idea how to hot-wire a car. He needed those keys.

He stood for a moment and listened. Faint sounds of rubbing branches and snapping twigs marked the woman's path. He rushed into the woods to follow.

A few yards inside the woods he stopped. The sounds had ceased.

***

Jeannine's hands were shaking as she gasped for breath. The bullets had splintered the tree near her, and one fragment had raked her arm. She stopped to listen. The sounds of pursuit were near. Evidently her pursuer was tenacious.

She looked to her left. A large white oak had fallen over the edge of a small ravine and formed a slim crawl space. She squeezed under it and lay still as the man approached.

She held her breath. The stalker passed and the sound of shuffling dry leaves grew faint. This was her chance. She climbed out from under the log and took off running as fast as she could towards the car.

Behind her, she heard heavy sounds of pursuit.

Key in hand and ready, she broke into the clearing and dashed to the car. She fumbled to open the door.

***

Malik stepped into the clearing. He saw the woman by the car. He had a clear shot, but did not wish to damage the vehicle. Only a defenseless woman stood between him and freedom.

He saw her open the door. Still he did not shoot, but held the AK-47 ready to fire at the first sound of a motor starting. But there was no such sound.

He reached the car and pointed his weapon inside. The woman was not there. The rear passenger door on the other side was open. She had crawled out on his blind side.

No matter, she could not escape   There were no hiding places in the clearing.

But a sound from behind made him turn.

There stood the woman, next to the rear fender. She held a weapon.

Abduk-Malik swallowed.

A mere woman!

"Brroom."

He flew backwards as the full-choke clump of buck shot rammed his chest. His finger tightened and squeezed off a burst.

"Br, Br, Br, Brup."

But the AK-47 discharged harmlessly into the ground as he fell.

Jeannine pumped a second shell into the chamber.

"Brroom."

It was only insurance. Abdul-Malik was already dead.

She dropped her gun. She trembled all over and started to retch.

My God I've killed him.

She did not know it, but the last of the jihadists lay at her feet.

***

Aileen Harris and Peter Zeleny watched as their marine helicopter landed outside the pavilion grounds. The National Guard had cut an opening in the south fence, away from the heavily contaminated main gate and right-front entrance. Aileen and Peter, clad in white Level-A Hazmat suits marked with U.S. Flags, approached the impromptu gate. They were followed by two assistants carrying cartons of syringes each pre-loaded with a single dose of Xolak.

Inside the gate, a National Guardsman, clad in similar gear but of drab color, greeted them.

"We've been waiting. We have victims still alive over here."

He pointed to the left-front entrance where a number of gassed spectators lay stretched on blankets.

"These folks were gassed through the sprinkler system. They didn't die right away like the others. We guess that the water mixture weakened the Novichok-H somehow."

The guardsman pointed further to a row of bodies, uniformed police and Secret Service.

"They weren't so lucky. They were gassed by the jihadist's 'fire-equipment' spray. Death was instantaneous"

But Peter was already leaning over a survivor. He spoke over the woman's gasps and moans.

"I'm Dr. Zeleny. I'm here to help you. There is no time. I'm going to inject you with antidote."

Aileen exposed the woman's shoulder to the needle. Peter emptied the syringe and discarded it into Aileen's tote.

Almost immediately the woman's diaphragm relaxed and her breaths came easier. But Peter had already gone to the next patient.

"I'm Dr. Zeleny. I'm here to help you. There is no time. I'm going to inject you with antidote."

As quickly as possible they moved down the line. Behind them, the treated individuals lay, diaphragms moving up and down, their breathing difficult, but improved.

The Xolak was working.

***

Across from Peter, two National Guard Corpsmen administered Xolak to a second line of fallen spectators, with equally salutary effects.

Peter came to the last of the first row of victims. She was a young attractive blonde. A new wedding band shone from the third finger of her left hand. A Virginia Tech ring adorned the corresponding finger on her right hand.

Peter knelt next to her. The injection of Xolak acted immediately.

The young woman spoke through forced breaths.

"I'm Monica Wilson. My husband, Barry, was with me. Is he all right?"

Peter looked about. Not far away was the body of a young man with shaggy light hair. On his right hand was a Virginia Tech ring, like Monica's. He was obviously her "Barry."

Peter looked at Aileen. She nodded in silent agreement.

Peter turned back to the woman. He spoke slowly and clearly.

"Mrs. Wilson, you just relax and breathe. We haven't listed the survivors yet. Get your strength. We'll know more later."

Nearby, two medics stood next to an ambulance. Peter waved them over and pointed.

"She needs immediate attention. Put her at the head of the list for Front Royal."

They strapped Monica to the gurney and wheeled her away.

Peter looked at Barry's body. He shook his head. Sometimes being a doctor was the pits.

Aileen nodded and looked down.

***

The moment he was out of the pavilion, Bill called Jeannine. She recognized his number and spoke.

"Bill, where are you. Are you all right? Were you poisoned?"

"I'm fine. I'm in a Hazmat suit from the National Guard. We stopped the release of Novichok-H, thanks to a fireman-engineer named 'Ted.' But you? Are you OK."

Jeannine shivered.

"Not really. My arm is scratched and I just killed a man."

"What! How? Who?"

"A terrorist with an AK-47. I used the Marlin 12 gauge."

"My God, I should have told you to leave. Did he hurt you?"

"He got off one burst. It kicked dirt on my new Adidas."

"Are you sure you're all right?"

"I think so. My God, I never killed anyone before."

"You have to leave right away. Go back the way you came, don't come closer to the pavilion. Go to Front Royal and get a room. I'll meet you there."

"And the dead man?"

"I'll send the National Guard for him."

"Maybe I should pick you up."

"You can't. They're setting up portable showers. I'm waiting to be decontaminated."

Jeannine got in the car and wound along the woodland road towards Front Royal.

***

Harry Thomas, the Secret Service Agent, found Bill Hamm waiting near the decontamination tents. He spoke in a low voice.

"They found Roger Dixon. The body was where you said. It's heavily contaminated."

He paused.

"Bill, I want to thank you. Without your warning, the president would be dead. I'll think better of you CIA spooks from now on. Thank you."

"Harry, the country and the President owe you big time, whether they know it or not."

"It's my job."

"I know that, but they still owe you, and Roger Dixon. He gave his life for the president."

Harry started away, but Bill called him back.

"Wait, one more thing. If you're handing out medals, look up that National Guardsman. His first name is 'Ted.' Without that guy we would be in trouble. He's a fireman and engineer in real life. Used to work for a company called 'NoFlame.'"

Bill continued.

"He knew where to shut down the sprinkler system, and then he knew where the fire suppression tanks for the kitchen were located. Those tanks are charged with nerve gas that's not mixed with water. They would have been deadly."

"I don't know about any medals, but I'll make damned sure he gets the credit."

"Thanks Harry."

***

Bill Hamm waited in line on the south side of the pavilion. The showers were almost set up. He called Jeannine.

"How's your arm? Are you in Front Royal yet?"

"It's fine, and almost. When can I come back and pick you up?"

Bill studied the waiting line. The first individuals were in the showers."

"It's hard to say. Maybe two hours, maybe more."

"What should I bring to eat."

"A burger and fries will do. We can eat something else later."

Jeannine signed off. Bill looked ahead.

The line had slowed to a halt.

Bill sat and leaned against the thin trunk of a Crepe Myrtle. His chin dropped onto his chest.

Moments later he was asleep, sitting up.

***

****

Chapter 52
Thursday, December 9

At the safe house near Middleburg, Virginia, Tom Fletcher picked up the phone. It was his Chief who wasted no time.

"Where is Hamm?"

"He's in Front Royal. He was getting checked at the hospital there."

"Tell him he's booked on a United flight from Dulles to Amsterdam this afternoon. He'll connect there to Vienna. I have seats for that 'Goldfinch' and Elena Krkova too. Get them out of the country, now."

Before Tom could reply, the Chief continued.

"The FBI is seriously pissed at the director. They want to know who authorized the CIA to conduct a domestic investigation in the States. It's better if Bill and Elena are back in Vienna with me."

"But it was the FBI that ran the raid on the W&C Fire Equipment Company in Warrenton!"

"I know that. It's a turf war. Bill did a hell of a job, but they don't want him to have the credit. Even so, my director is preparing an award for him. Meanwhile it's better for him to be back here. The director wants to avoid any suggestion that our operation was a domestic one."

Tom turned to Ivana who was on the couch, reading.

"Ivana, you'd better pack. You're going back to Europe this afternoon."

Then he called Elena Krkova and gave her the same message.

***

At a table in a small restaurant in Front Royal, Virginia, Bill Hamm and Jeannine Ryan sat across from Aileen Harris and Peter Zeleny. In front of them were freshly prepared hamburgers accompanied by frozen custard shakes, a house specialty.

Jeannine took a bite of her burger. Delicious. She looked at Aileen.

"What are your plans for today?"

"I'm flying to Pennsylvania, Johnstown, from Dulles this afternoon to pick up Mary Catherine. We'll drive back to Bethesda this weekend. I'll be at the office Monday."

Jeannine answered.

"I probably won't be there. Bill and I are spending the weekend on the Outer Banks. I called Mila. Anne Simek has a room for us in the house at Corolla."

Jeannine glanced at Peter Zeleny. He did not react to the mention of Anne.

"What about you Peter? What are your plans?"

He shrugged.

"I don't know. Probably go back to Chicago."

All had experienced enough action the past two weeks. Each turned to his or her burger and shake in silence. The lull was welcome.

Bill Hamm's phone vibrated. He rose from the table and stood in a corner. When he came back his face was grim. He looked at Jeannine and shrugged his shoulders in dismay.

"I have to fly to Vienna this afternoon. I have to leave now. I can't go to the Banks. I'm sorry."

Jeannine was speechless, not so Aileen.

"Is that blond woman going with you?"

Bill nodded. He hesitated before continuing.

"Orders. I have to escort her back."

"Damn it Bill, what about Jeannine?"

Bill fell silent. Jeannine swallowed and spoke.

"You do what you have to do, but I don't know about this. Your job is too damned demanding."

A car horn sounded outside.

His brow furrowed, Bill spoke to the table in general.

"I'm sorry. That's Tom Fletcher, my ride is here."

He handed the keys of the rental to Jeannine.

"They have an imprint of my credit card. Put all the charges on it."

She rose from her seat and they briefly embraced.

Bill left.

Jeannine slumped into her seat. She took a bite of her burger, but it had lost its flavor.

They ate without talking.

***

Jeannine finished her meal and broke the awkward silence.

"Damn it, I'm sticking with my plans. I'm going to Corolla. I need a place to think. What about you, Peter."

"I need some place to think too, but I doubt I'm welcome at Anne's. I'll probably rent a car and drive back, to Chicago, real slow."

He muttered under his breath.

"*To je život a život je pes.*"

Both Aileen and Jeannine exclaimed.

"What?"

He answered.

"'That's life, and life is a Dog!' In other words, 'Life is the pits.'"

Jeannine reached over and hugged Peter. She kissed him on the cheek.

"This day has been horrific for all of us. We all need to recoup. Aileen's car is at the Manassas Regional Airport. I'm dropping her there before I head south to North Carolina. Why not change your mind and come to Carolina too."

He shook his head. She added.

"Anyway, maybe we'll see you in Chicago some day."

Aileen arose and likewise hugged Peter.

"Peter, thanks for everything. You saved many lives yesterday. And without you and poor Vaclav Pokorny, we would not have known about the Prague plot."

Peter looked up.

"Thanks, but it was really you and Jeannine."

He hesitated and added.

"And Anne Simek too."

Peter slumped in his seat.

Jeannine and Aileen left.

***

Ivana Novotna had never been to the town of Front Royal, Virginia, and she knew none of its restaurants. She was unaware of the glum mood around a certain table in one of them. Had she known, however, she would not have cared.

Ivana was happy.

She was returning to Europe. She was sick of Virginia.

And Bill Hamm was her escort, not that dull Tom Fletcher. She liked Bill and was grateful to him. Surely he would take care of her.

She needed to escape this prison that the CIA called a "safe house." And she would no longer be a "package." Once in Europe, on her own turf, she hoped to restore herself. She would prove to Bill that she was still desirable.

She hummed as she packed her things.

***

Alone in his office, a Homeland Security Official fed the shredder from a stack of memos and documents that implicated him as a "friend" to the Czech pharmaceutical giant, Hus-Kinetika. Thanks to the generosity of that company, his retirement was well provided for.

But it was only a matter of days, maybe hours, before his role in approving the work order for Erik Holub at the Pavilion of National Unity became known to his superiors.

His days as a bureaucrat in the United States Government were over.

These were his last hours at the office. His plane ticket and passport were in his pocket, and his bank account was emptied and shifted to a bank in the Turks and Caicos Islands. He fed the last of the stack into the shredder.

He knew that investigators would locate copies of what he destroyed, but at least, he would not facilitate their search.

Behind him, the special FAX machine beeped. He looked at the originating number in surprise. He had cautioned his contacts that he would be unavailable for a "few" days. (They would learn of his departure soon enough.)

He punched a code and the message came through. It was a single sheet. He decided to provide one last service to his Czech sponsors.

He dialed the safe house in Virginia Beach, Virginia and faxed the message under his code name, "Smetana."

Then he fed the sheet into the shredder and left.

A Gulfstream aircraft was waiting to fly him to the Caribbean.

***

It was noon in Corolla, North Carolina. Anne Simek sat at the kitchen table and looked to the west. She hunched over her laptop and tried to concentrate on her thesis, but thoughts of Peter, and worse, Aileen Harris, refused to leave her.

In the other half of the "great room," Anne's father was engrossed in the large-screen TV.

Anne looked up.

A talking head commented.

This was the scene yesterday when our own Norma Hunt spoke with the 'Man of the Hour,' Dr. Peter Zeleny, after the Unity Pavilion Tragedy. Dr. Zeleny and his Assistant, Dr. Aileen Harris, administered the nerve-gas antidote to those stricken. Here's Norma's exclusive interview.

The camera panned over some two hundred individuals collapsed on rows of army blankets, evidently awaiting evacuation. It came to rest on a man and a woman standing with the reporter.

Anne gasped. *Peter! Aileen!*

"Dr. Zeleny, these people owe their lives to you. How did you come to discover the antidote? I understand it is a common prescription drug for treating neurological disorders."

The camera zoomed in on Peter.

"I first discovered difficulties with the drug when some of my patients exhibited allergic reactions to it. Then Dr. Harris suspected that the drug had been modified to treat the deadly nerve agent used here. She approached me, we analyzed its components, and verified her hypothesis. We were at the FBI lab in Quantico when the terrorists attacked. The marines flew us here with the antidote. That's about it."

The camera switched back to the newsman behind his desk.

Thanks Norma, those are the words of a humble man. And the good news is that almost all of the patients he and Dr. Harris treated yesterday are in satisfactory condition today.

The camera switched to a commercial.

Havel Simek jumped up before Anne could say a word.

"Anne, did you see that? Was that your young man with that woman doctor?"

Anne could not speak. She nodded.

"You should go to him."

"No father, he's busy. I'll call him later."

"Make sure you do."

Anne swallowed and stared at the TV.

***

Monica Wilson sat upright in her hospital bed. The doctor had just told her about her husband, Barry. She was a widow at twenty six. She wanted to cry, but no tears came.

She clicked on the TV.

This just in.

The leader of the devastating attack on the President and luminaries at the Unity Pavilion in Front Royal, Virginia, has been identified as 'William Masoud Jones,' a homegrown terrorist, and native of Fairfax County, Virginia. He attended the University of Virginia for one year before transferring to the University of ...

A picture of a bearded Masoud flashed on the screen. Monica gaped. Beard or not, she knew that man.

"Billy! My God, it's you. You killed Barry! How could you?"

This time the tears flowed freely. She buried her face in the pillow and sobbed.

***

It was evening in Prague when Karel Moravec's phone buzzed. He frowned at the calling number. It was the long overdue Josef Hrubec.

"Josef, where are you? What happened?"

"You've talked to Erik Holub. You know damned well what happened."

"I know you failed. You got Hermann killed and Hugo and William Johnson arrested. Holub completed the mission without you. Why do you call me? What do you want?"

Josef bit his lip.

"I need help. I need money and a passport. Do not forget the years I served you."

Silence.

Hrubec could not wait.

"I ask you to help me."

Hrubec begging? Karel felt a surge of power. He would be magnanimous!

"All right, Josef, where are you?"

"Manassas, Virginia."

"The company has a safe house in Virginia Beach, Virginia. The code is '768904,' you know how to look it up. You'll find a passport there for you, and money. There are passports there for Hermann and Hugo too. Destroy them."

Josef Hrubec did not push his luck. He hung up and headed for Virginia Beach.

***

Several hours later he arrived at the safe house in Virginia Beach where he found the fake passports Karel had described. Hermann's he destroyed but Hugo's he kept. He and Hugo

397

were of similar looks. A careless immigration officer might accept Hugo's photograph as Hrubec's.

He pocketed all the money, his own as well as Hermann's and Hugo's. They had no need of those funds now.

Then he found a metal case with a Belgian-made Browning. His luck was changing. This was his favorite weapon.

Hrubec knew he had to leave the U. S., but not right away. He had a vendetta to settle first.

Bill Hamm!

He was sipping a Pilsner Urquell when he noticed the FAX in the tray.

He read the bureaucrat's final message.

Hamm is not going to North Carolina today. He is flying with Ivana Novotna to Amsterdam and Vienna leaving Dulles (DIA) this afternoon. It is possible Miss Ryan will go to Corolla without him.
Smetana

He looked at his watch. It was just after five. *Damn!* Hamm already had boarded the flight for Amsterdam. The prey had escaped him once more.

But all was not lost He would hurt Hamm through his woman. Ryan was stubborn, and independent. She would not change her plans because of Hamm's departure. Surely she would head to North Carolina.

Hrubec left the safe house. He would drive to the Outer Banks tonight. He would strike at his enemy through the redhead.

Ryan would die, and in pain!

***

*****

Chapter 53
Thursday, December 9

It was evening when Jeannine drove through the rutted sand to Anne Simek's beach rental. Over the Currituck Sound to the west, the sun's red rim hesitated on the horizon. The wind had a December chill, but it was warmer than Front Royal.

She parked next to Anne's rental car. As she reached in the back seat for her satchel, her fingers brushed the Marlin shotgun. *Why not?* She picked up the gun along with her satchel and climbed the steps to the mid-level entrance.

Anne answered the door.

"Where's Bill?"

"Somewhere over the Atlantic, on his way to Europe."

Anne did not enquire further. She knew about separations.

Then she saw Jeannine's shotgun.

"What's that for?"

Jeannine shivered at the memory of Abdul-Malik's mangled body.

"I'll tell you later. Thank God I don't need it anymore. Where's Mila?"

"She and Jim went to her house in Nags Head. My father and I are alone. Jeannine, I know you're tired, but come upstairs first. I want you to meet him."

She led Jeannine up to the great room. Jeannine leaned the shotgun against the kitchen counter and turned towards the sofa where a man sat. Anne leaned over him.

"Father, this is my friend Jeannine Ryan. Jeannine, this is my father, Havel."

Havel rose without speaking and took Jeannine's hand. She smiled. Anne waited a moment before intervening.

"Father, I know you're tired. Jeannine is too. Your bedrooms are down on the mid level. I'll show you."

Anne picked up Jeannine's satchel and started down the steps. Jeannine, exhausted from the long drive, was happy to retire. Havel went straight to his room.

Anne returned up the stairs to the great room. There, disappointed that Peter had not come with Jeannine, she sat alone and listened to the surf crashing on the beach out of sight behind the dunes.

After some minutes, she stepped into her bedroom. The moon shone brightly, lighting the scattered clouds over the Currituck Sound and casting soft shadows on Anne's wall.

Soon she was deep asleep.

***

A door opened and shut.

Anne Simek sat up, eyes wide. *How long did I sleep?* She looked to the west where the moon, now high and distant, lit the clouds a shimmering white against the dark sky. The waters of the sound rippled and glistened in the pale light.

She shook her head clear, stood up, and reached for the light switch. A nearby movement stopped her.

A man stood at the foot of the bed, his face and form vague in the shadows.

She froze. The man spoke.

"Miss Simek, do not scream. It would only bring your father and Miss Ryan, and then I would have to kill you and him too. That would be an unnecessary waste."

Anne's eyes roved the room, wildly searching for hope, for some means of escape, but found none.

"No, Miss Simek, there is no way out, except that you follow my instructions. Bad or good, I am your only hope now. Do not fight me."

At that moment beams of moonlight pierced a high cloud and glanced across the man's face. Anne saw that his eyes were dark, almost black.

"What do you want?"

But the man did not answer. He moved suddenly to the side and stamped downwards. Anne heard a scratchy squish. *He killed a roach!*

But the brown things with six spiky legs no longer mattered to her. She had bigger trouble. She spoke again.

"What do you want?"

"I know Miss Ryan has a shotgun with her. I want you to call her up here to see the moonlight on the clouds. She will come in unarmed and I will subdue her while you sit over there. Then you will watch as I cause her great pain, violate her and terminate her. You will remember every detail, her shrieks, her writhing, and you will tell Mr. Bill Hamm everything, every detail. That is why you will live. I will spare you to hurt him."

"My God!"

"There is no God."

"But there is, and He will punish you!"

"As you wish. Will you call Miss Ryan."

"You are a monster."

"What is your answer?"

"If I say no?"

"I will kill you and your father. And then torture Miss Ryan. You and he will die needlessly, and I will write Mr. Hamm with all the details of Miss Ryan's death myself."

***

Havel Simek's bedroom was directly under his daughter's on the Currituck Sound side of the house. Heating vents in the two rooms shared a common duct, so that when these were open, neither room was soundproof.

The fresh air of the Outer Banks induced slumber. Havel slept.

He heard a door open and close.

The dream!

He was in the room with the pink ceiling and exposed pipes. Bright lights blinded his eyes, as he repeated an all too familiar refrain.

"Nevim, Nevim, Nevim nic. 'I don't know, I don't know, I don't know anything.'"

And then the blows, many to his kidneys, to his shoulders, his shrieks of pain, always followed by a welcome blackness that undulated to nothing.

Awaking, Havel felt his forehead. It was wet with sweat. He drifted off again.

More blows to the back, pain, pain, pain, followed by darkness.

Then he heard that voice. The rasping tones of that unknown man who had led the torture, broken his body, his spirit.

He awoke, but the voice was still there.

The voice was real.

Muted, it came through the duct from his daughter's room.

Barefoot, Havel crept up the stairs to Anne's level.

The moon was bright. Havel could see clearly. No sound arose from Jeannine's bedroom downstairs. Evidently, she had heard nothing.

Havel went to the kitchen. *Perhaps a knife?*

Then he saw it. Jeannine's shotgun lay against the counter next to a stool.

He picked it up and turned towards his daughter's room.

***

The door to Anne's bedroom opened. A man stood in the dark shadows of the doorway. Havel froze.

The man held a Browning, pointed at him.

Behind the man, Havel recognized his daughter.

The man spoke.

"Good Evening, Mr. Simek."

The voice was rasping, harsh. Havel knew those sounds.

"You!"

It was the voice of evil in his nightmare!

Havel pointed the shotgun at the ugly specter.

Josef Hrubec laughed.

"So it's you! The one I called the 'Roach.' I thought I squashed you for good. No matter. You have changed, but you will still obey me. Put down the weapon. Now!"

At the confident strength of that voice, Havel's eyes glazed. Still, he kept the shotgun pointed towards the doorway.

Hrubec continued.

"I know you remember the pink ceiling. We all were younger then you, Johan and I, but you have aged the worst."

A momentary pause, then Hrubec still pointing the Browning at Havel, reached out his free hand.

"You old fool, give me the gun. You won't pull that trigger."

Anne screamed.

"Father! It's not the dream. He's real!"

At the sound of his daughter's voice, Havel's eyes opened wide. He tilted the shotgun upwards.

At point blank range, he could not miss.

Havel pulled the trigger.

***

But there was no explosion.

"Click."

Hrubec's eyes opened wide. Then he laughed.

Jeannine's shotgun was not loaded. Her father had drilled her never to keep a loaded shotgun in car or house.

Hrubec did not wait. He slammed his Browning against the side of Havel's head crumpling him to the floor.

Then he picked up the shotgun and turned to Anne.

"Your father has done us a favor. Now we have Miss Ryan's gun. She is unarmed. Call her up here."

Anne shrank backwards against the wall. She shook her head "No."

Hrubec shrugged and stepped towards the stairs. He passed the expansive windows at the front of the great room and glanced out.

The drapes were pulled back. All appeared normal. In the moonlight the dunes shone white amid the twisting blue shadows of waving Sea Oats.

Then, all at once, the sea breeze disappeared. The fruited heads of the Sea Oats drooped earthwards, still and motionless in the moonlight. There was no wind.

Hrubec was unsettled by the sudden stillness. An omen?

But it was the slight sounds heard after the wind stopped that truly unnerved him.

Footsteps scraped along the deck at the side of the house.

***

Jeannine appeared at the head of the stairs.

"Anne, what's all the noise about."

Distracted, Hrubec turned towards her.

In the dim light Jeannine recognized his dark eyes, her former captor. She drew back.

"No!"

But Hrubec swung the Browning in a circular motion. She saw the blow coming and raised her arm to block it. Though partially deflected, the blow knocked her senseless.

She fell to the floor

***

Before Hrubec could assess Jeannine's condition, a loud banging sounded from the deck.

"Anne, it's Peter. Open up. What's wrong? Who's in there with you?

Hrubec responded. Several rounds from the Browning shattered the safety glass of the doors.

Anne jumped to the side and cried out.

"Peter, watch out. He has a gun!

Hrubec turned and fired at her. Unharmed, she dropped behind the sofa.

Hrubec turned back to the shattered doors, but now, Peter stood before him.

Hrubec had thought Peter unarmed. In dismay he saw that Peter held a gun, a Makarov. It jerked upwards, twice.

Hrubec realized that a shot had been fired. He felt a thrust in his chest as the initial 9 mm round moved him backwards and sideways. Then the second round struck his head and all awareness ceased.

Hrubec was dead before his body hit the floor.

***

Fortunately for Jeannine, Hrubec's blow had glanced to the side and not caused its intended damage. She shook her head and struggled to her feet.

In the center of the room, Anne and Peter Zeleny were locked in a fierce embrace. Nearby, Anne's father sat up with a dazed expression on his face.

Anne looked away from Peter.

"Jeannine, are you all right?"

Jeannine nodded.

"I'm fine. But your father?"

Havel stood up. Anne smiled.

"He's fine."

Anne wasted no time. She took Peter by the arm and dragged him in front of Havel.

"Father, Peter and I want to be married and we need your blessing."

For several moments, Havel stared at the still body on the floor. When he looked up his eyes were clear. He addressed Peter, not Anne.

"My daughter is all I have in this world. Promise me you will take care of her always, and I will give her to you."

Peter swallowed.

"I will."

Havel smiled.

"Then, my son, it is done."

***

Anne covered Josef Hrubec's body with a bed sheet while Jeannine stood by.

They left the body untouched, but no one wanted to stay near it. Cloaked with blankets Peter, Anne, Havel and Jeannine sat on the deck to Anne's bedroom to wait for Jim Harrigan and deputies from the Currituck County Sheriff's office.

It was only after the arrival of the police that Jeannine's analytic mind returned to action.

"Peter, thank God you had a gun, but you don't carry one. Where did you get it?"

"There's an old tin box under the house, like for old milk bottles. It was in that box."

"But how?"

"After I drove Aileen here from Maryland, I put it there. I was afraid of what Jim Harrigan might think so I hid the gun there. It's the one I took from Gustav."

"Afraid of Jim Harrigan?"

"He's police. There was a time when we Czechs could not trust the police. I know it was stupid, but ..."

Jeannine smiled.

"Your 'stupidity' saved us. Thanks."

Anne stepped to Peter and looked into his eyes.

"Let me repeat that. Thanks."

***

******

Chapter 54
Friday, December 10

Early morning in Prague. Alone in his office, Karel Moravec finished packing his satchel. As promised, Abdul Rahman had deposited the many millions of Euros in the three Swiss accounts. And now, thanks to a clever mnemonic device, the numbers of those three accounts were committed to Karel's memory.

And no one could withdraw funds but Karel. That knowledge was insurance. It guaranteed his survival.

The satchel held several passports. The tickets to Brazil were in his suit pocket. Of course that country was not his final destination. He was headed for a remote area east of the Andes in Argentina near Bolivia and Paraguay.

Not that he planned to be a hermit rancher. No, isolation was not for him. He needed luxuries and a night life. He would arrange to spend long "vacations" in a civilization with high culture, in Montevideo, Uruguay. He had already rented a small office there in the shadow of the World Trade Center building. Karel had major investment plans.

He zipped his satchel shut, and turned to the laptop on his massive desk. Erik Holub would arrive soon, and Karel would see to a generous transfer to Erik's account.

His work was done. He leaned back and relaxed. He shut his eyes.

***

Karel opened his eyes to a gentle knock on the door.

"Erik, come on in. That was a great job you did in Virginia."

The door opened, but it was not Erik. Rather the man who entered was disheveled, as if he had traveled all night.

Karel gaped in amazement.

Gustav Slavik stood before him.

And Gustav held a gun, a CZ-52, pointed directly at Karel's chest.

Karel froze.

He forced a smile.

"Welcome back Gustav. Our goods are delivered. Our part of the project has succeeded. We have received our payment, so I can pay you now."

He paused to add.

"But put away the gun. There's no need. I have a magnificent share for you. It's ready."

Gustav did not move. Neither did the gun.

Karel tried to avoid looking at the aperture of that lethal barrel. Somehow he continued to smile.

"What would you like? More money?"

Gustav did not answer. He seemed in a dream.

Karel carefully slid his desk draw open. Gustav appeared not to notice.

Karel's armpits were sweaty. He steadied himself.

"Gustav my old friend. If it's money, I can make you rich beyond your dreams."

At last Gustav broke his silence.

"I am too old for money."

Karel felt hope. He knew that he could out-talk Gustav.

"But not too old for a woman. Beautiful and young! Would that please you? I can arrange it. Along with all the money you need to keep her happy."

"You mean like Ivana Novotna?"

"No, no. Not like her. Ivana is a whore. Trust me. You can do better."

"Yet you lived with her."

"Yes, but only because she begged me. She's a bitch. Besides she may be dead by now. A good thing too."

Gustav's brow furrowed.

"Dead?"

"Yes, I saw she was interfering with the mission, with ours, with yours. She was a threat to both of us."

Gustav's face turned red.

"Karel, you bastard. Ivana is my daughter."

Karel stared. *His daughter?*

Gustav continued.

"You tried to kill my daughter. And you would have succeeded if it were not for the Americans, their damned CIA and that 'Bill Hamm.'"

He added.

"Capitalists! You put me in debt to greedy money-grubbing Americans."

Karel interposed.

"Gustav, I'm sorry, I had no ... "

Gustav did not notice. He scratched his chin with his free hand.

"I could excuse you for the Americans, but for my Ivana? No. Never!"

His eyes focused on Karel's.

"You used my daughter for your pleasure. Then you discarded her."

"No, Gustav. She left me, remember?"

"She told me about that. She only left after you tried to have me killed, and after you chose Fiala over her, not before."

"Not true."

But his voice was weak. His lies could not convince Gustav.

Karel's eyes fell on the open desk drawer. In it his P226 Sig Sauer lay chambered and ready.

Gustav, saw that glance. His voice was dull and monotonal.

"Yes, Karel, reach for the weapon. I have no conscience, but my little Ivana does. It will help her to know that I killed you in self defense, not in cold blood."

Karel did not wait.

He grabbed the Sig Sauer and got off the first shot.

Then he squeezed again. Because of the mechanism, the second round required less finger pressure than the first, but it never left the chamber. The second squeeze had been a weak reflex.

Karel hit the floor, a hole in his forehead.

***

Gustav stuffed the CZ-52 in his belt, at back. He felt his left shoulder. His suit was torn and damp where Karel's slug had grazed him. It was not a problem.

With his right hand he fumbled in his shirt pocket and drew out a king-sized Petra cigarette.

He inhaled deeply, and looked about the spacious office.

The massive desk, symbol of Karel's authority, was unstained. It hid the body from view.

But not from the plaster angels on the ceiling above. They looked down, silent and uncaring.

Gustav left.

Behind the desk a dark pool of blood formed under Karel's head.

***

In Prague, Erik Holub arrived at the main administrative building of the chemical and pharmaceutical giant Hus-Kinetika. He was relaxed for the first time in months. After a restful day in Paris to alleviate his jetlag, he had flown to Prague for his big payday.

In the hallway to Karel's office, he was stopped by uniformed *policie* who blocked the corridor.

Their unsmiling questions left him confused.

"Who are you?" What is your business with Mr. Moravec?"

They noticed the suitcase in his hand.

"When did you arrive in Prague? From what city? Where were you earlier today?"

In vain, Erik peered over their shoulders to see what was happening.

"Sir, you need to come to the station with us. We will drive. Here, give me your bag."

One of the policemen picked up the suitcase and motioned Erik to follow. As he did, a gurney topped by a black plastic body bag appeared in the hallway. Erik found his voice.

"Is that Mr. Moravec?"

With a barely perceptible nod, the policeman pushed Erik towards the exit.

"*Prosim*, 'Please,' come with us, Sir."

A bewildered Erik complied.

***

It was evening in Vienna, Austria, when Ivana Novotna, accompanied by Bill Hamm, arrived at her hotel.

That afternoon, the news of Karel Moravec's untimely death had convinced Bill's superiors that the "Goldfinch" no longer needed protection. Ivana could shift from a safe house to a hotel of her choosing."

Ivana agreed. She was no longer a "package" to be moved about at the whim of others. Further, the Americans had presented her with a good sum of Euros for her cooperation. But to date, of all the Americans she had met, only Bill Hamm appealed to her.

Happily he had been chosen to escort her to her new room.

Ivana was bubbly. Her hair was blond again. It was short, but shaped well to enhance the pleasant curve of her neck. She wore fitted jeans, topped by a quilted lavender jacket that hugged her waist. And she was pleased to see that Bill approved of her outfit!

Bill stopped at the gilded entrance of the hotel.

"Ivana, I have to go. I guess this is goodbye."

Ivana tossed her head. A cold breeze brightened her cheeks as she shivered.

"No, it's too cold. I cannot say goodbye properly here."

She pulled him into the lobby. It was crowded, a convention, but she heard no English, only German. For a moment she feared that he was uncomfortable. No, Bill was at ease in that language.

Good, she wanted him relaxed.

"Bill, there are too many people here. Can you escort me up to my room?"

They rode the elevator up in silence.

***

411

At the door to her room, Ivana paused.

"Bill, thank you for everything. Won't you? ..."

She did not wait for a response. She threw her arms around his neck, pressed her body against his, and kissed him. At the shock of those moist lips, and the softness of her chest, he held tight and kissed back.

After a moment she drew free.

"Bill, come inside, I ... "

He looked into her warm blue eyes. She was most desirable. He took a deep breath.

"Ivana, you are beautiful, but I cannot. Don't make this more difficult for me."

She frowned in disbelief.

"You mean that person, Jeannine?"

He nodded.

Ivana frowned. She turned into her room.

Somehow she managed to slam the heavy door.

***

Inside, the smell of a cigarette assailed Ivana. Instantly, Bill was forgotten. She looked about in terror.

Who?

Gustav stepped from the shadows.

Ivana exhaled. Color returned to her cheeks. She found her voice.

"Father, then it was you that killed ... "

He nodded.

"Daughter, that beast will never bother you again."

***

The hour was late when Bill Hamm returned to the Vienna office. No matter, a smiling Chief was there to greet him.

"Congratulations, Bill, you're a damned hero. The press has been all over my butt for interviews, and Sky Channel wants to do a video piece on you."

Bill started to answer, but the Chief continued.

"Unfortunately, I think you know that with this publicity, your covert days will be over."

The Chief's smile disappeared.

"Also, Bill, a storm is brewing. Some higher ups at the FBI and Homeland Security are desperate to blame anyone for their screw up at the Unity Pavilion. They want to know why you and Elena Krkova were running a domestic operation. They say the CIA had no business running an 'OP' in the States."

"But the Czech side of the 'OP' *was* our business. Everything flowed from that."

"Exactly. You know that and I know that, and we both know they are trying to cover their butts. I'm giving you a heads up, that's all. The Director is on our side. Hell, those guys in Homeland Security can't even use the term 'War on Terror.' Everything is some damned 'incident.'"

"And I kept everybody, you, the FBI and Secret Service, informed at all times. The raid at Warrenton was run by the FBI."

"Of course. But if you have any memos or notes so I can build a paper trail, it would help me."

"You know I don't work that way, memos and all."

The Chief answered with a shrug.

"Right. Look, this is your hour. Enjoy the limelight."

He paused.

"But you should clear your interviews with me."

Bill waited a moment, then spoke.

"If I can't work covert ops, I'm not sure I'll stay with the Agency. I have somebody waiting for me Stateside. She won't wait forever."

The Chief looked down at his desk.

"That might be a good idea for all of us."

Bill left in silence, his lips parted in a grim smile.

***

******

Chapter 55
Epilogue

Both Homeland Security and the FBI invoked the purported domestic operation by the CIA to blame that agency for the disaster at Front Royal, Virginia. Bill Hamm's reassignment by the Agency took the pressure off of his immediate superior, but only confirmed to a compliant media that the accusations were well-founded.

The Secretary of Homeland Security dubbed the events at Front Royal the "Unity Pavilion Incident." Tragically, almost three hundred Americans died in that "incident," including an entire squad of battle-ready marines, numerous police and a number of Secret Service agents. Among the dead were a dozen Hollywood celebrities, numerous "guests," several members of congress, a governor, and well over one hundred "spectators."

In contrast, in their war on the Great Satan, the jihadists lost twenty men.

The disaster would have been many times more deadly if the untested Novichok-H had been more volatile, had a longer half-life, and not been weakened by the alkaline water with a high iron content from the newly-drilled well that supplied the pavilion. Also, without Xolak and the intervention of Peter Zeleny and Aileen Harris, the deaths among the spectators would have more than doubled.

Roger Dixon died in the best tradition of the Secret Service. He gave his life to protect his president, and not in vain. By killing Quanit Ibn Husayn, he gained precious minutes for the president's evacuation to safety. Roger (posthumously) and Harry Thomas, who took charge of the evacuation, were honored in a brief ceremony at the White House. Harry Thomas is now head of the presidential detail.

Neither Quanit Ibn Husayn, killed by Roger Dixon, or Hassan Ibn Ali, killed by Bill Hamm, had time to voice his final praise, *Allahu akbar*, at death. Each perished before the thought could be formed.

Ryan Associates was awarded several contracts by the CIA, but Jeannine Ryan elected to keep the company small. Aileen Harris remains with her as a minority owner. She and Mary Catherine still reside in Bethesda with Aileen's mother.

Bill Hamm occupies a desk at Langley. He still hopes to obtain an assignment overseas. He and Jeannine remain close, but because of professional commitments their future together remains uncertain.

Anne Simek successfully defended her doctoral thesis in philosophy, "Dietrich von Hildebrand, Catholics and the Nazi Persecution," in Chicago. Afterwards, Anne adopted the religion of her deceased mother. She was baptized Catholic at the Shrine of the Immaculate Conception in Washington, DC. There she and Peter Zeleny were wed in the Czech chapel under the image of Our Lady of Hostyn inscribed, ZŮSTAŇ MATKOU LIDU SVÉMU, "Remain a mother to your people."

Jim Harrigan left the Duck Police Department, took a short course in Real Estate, and joined Mila at Patek reality. Mila received her United States Citizenship. They married shortly after. Jim is grateful that his wife does not call herself "Harriganova." Mila pretends to like doughnuts.

In an example of justice trumping truth, Gustav Slavik, who tried to kill Vaclav Pokorny but failed, was convicted of his murder. He pled out and received life with possibility of parole. He is incarcerated in a close security facility in Greene County, North Carolina.

Ivana Novotna moved to the United States to be near her father. She enjoys a peaceful life in Goldsboro, North Carolina. She visits Gustav regularly. Each time she takes him a supply of Petra cigarettes.

Scot Henderson stayed with the Fish and Wildlife Service in North Carolina. He continues to monitor the deaths, accidental or otherwise, of Red Wolves on the Alligator River National Wildlife Refuge.

The death of Larry Hodges at the FDA was ascribed to natural causes. Ultimately, after negotiations with Hus-Kinetika, the composition of Xolak was changed back to its pre-2002 form. The FDA has approved it for the American market.

Jack Cannon joined the Prince William County Police Department. His freezer is still filled with venison.

Monica Wilson remarried. She has a hard time accepting that Bill Jones was Masoud.

Tom Fletcher and Elena Krkova remained with the CIA. They work out of Vienna, Austria.

Michal Pacak returned to Brno. He and Elena Krkova correspond occasionally.

The numbered bank accounts died with Karel Moravec. Erik Holub never received his final payment. After extradition to the U. S. he received a life sentence in a Federal prison.

Shortly after the tragedy at Front Royal, Abdul Rahman was summoned to Tehran. He has not been seen or heard from since.

***

******

Envoi
One year later

They were fortunate to find a parking space among the compact cars parked diagonally on the narrow street of the staré město, Prague's "Old Town." From the front seat, the young man and his wife watched anxiously as the gray-haired elder squeezed out the rear door without, somehow, marring the adjacent Fiat.

The old man motioned the couple to remain seated.

His was a journey to be made alone.

The street was one-way, and there was no traffic. That was fortunate, for he started across without looking in either direction. Slightly stooped, he stumbled once on the uneven stones, but caught himself and successfully reached the narrow sidewalk opposite.

He stood for a moment and looked at the stark unadorned wall of the old church in front of him. Two small windows were topped by a large semicircular one. The latter reminded him of the window under the angled attic walls of his parents' house.

For a moment, he seemed to lose his purpose, and his eyes roved about, as if fearing the approach of an enemy. Then he focused again, and walked quickly down the street.

He entered a double doorway.

No this cannot be it! He stared about, bewildered at the bright foyer.

A kind hotel concierge understood his confusion and came to his aid.

"Sir, there have been renovations. This is a hotel now. Come with me, I know where you wish to go. I'll take you there."

Numb, he followed his guide to the basement. They were in a narrow corridor.

At once, he knew the way.

Eyes closed, he counted the steps and stopped. He was in front of a door.

He looked in. It was his cell, but it was not the same. The half-window, now curtained, let light in from the street above. Double-decker clean cots occupied the wall to his left.

It was peaceful. There were no strident voices.

And the ceiling was no longer Pink!

He stood a moment in silent wonder.

A voice broke into his thoughts.

"Sir, would you like to see the prison cell where our president Vaclav Havel was held, 'P6.' It is this way."

He shook his head, "No." He added.

"Thank you, but this is sufficient. I do not wish to see more."

The concierge nodded and led him back up to the entrance.

He stepped out onto Bartolomejska Street. The sun was shining.

He lowered his head. For the first time in many years, Havel Simek voiced a silent prayer.

"*Děkuji Bohu, že jsem svobodný.* 'Thank you God, that I am free.'"

He stepped briskly to the car and nodded to his son in law, the driver.

"We can go now. It is finished."

From the passenger side, Anne Simek Zeleny smiled.

Peter put the car in gear, backed out, and pulled away.

***

******

About the Author

James E. Mosimann is a retired biostatistician who spent many years at the Computer Division of the National Institutes of Health. He has a Ph. D. in Zoology from the University of Michigan, and a Masters in Biostatistics from the Johns Hopkins University. After NIH, he joined the Office of Research Integrity of the Public Health Service, where he was a scientist-investigator for cases of research misconduct. He has numerous publications and one text. This is his third novel.

He and his wife, Barbara Jean, live in Virginia. They have eight children, all adult.

Author's Note

This is the third book in a series that follows the activities of Jeannine Ryan, a specialist in numerical forensics. Like the first, it was a family project. Thanks again to my wife for her support and to my adult children for their assistance. As before, Tom's many hours of careful reading and editing significantly improved the manuscript, as did comments by Joseph, John, Theresa, Michelle, Mary and Madeleine. Finally Kateri, in addition to her comments, provided the cover graphics and design.

The village of Dethorens is imaginary, as also are Hus-Kinetika and its product, Xolak. While the OPCW data is from their website, Novichok-H and its Czech originator are fictional and invented for this tale. Likewise, Gustav's association with the Cellules Communistes Combattantes is imaginary,

Jeannine Ryan's exploits in the first three novels (*Misconduct's Deadly Denial, The Assassin Chip* and *The Prague Plot*) will continue in the title below:

The Carolina Coup.